Man Enough For Me

Also by Rhonda Bowen

One Way or Another

Man Enough For Me

RHONDA BOWEN

Kensington Publishing Corp.
http://www.kensingtonbooks.com

DAFINA BOOKS are published by

Kensington Publishing Corp.
119 West 40th Street
New York, NY 10018

Copyright © 2011 by Rhonda Bowen

All rights reserved. No part of this book may be reproduced
in any form or by any means without the prior written consent of the Publisher, excepting brief quotes used in reviews.

If you purchased this book without a cover, you should be
aware that this book is stolen property. It was reported as
"unsold and destroyed" to the Publisher and neither the Au-
thor nor the Publisher has received any payment for this
"stripped book."

All Kensington Titles, Imprints, and Distributed Lines are
available at special quantity discounts for bulk purchases for
sales promotions, premiums, fund-raising, educational, or
institutional use. Special book excerpts or customized print-
ings can also be created to fit specific needs. For details,
write or phone the office of the Kensington special sales
manager: Kensington Publishing Corp., 119 West 40th Street,
New York, NY 10018, attn: Special Sales Department. Phone:
1-800-221-2647.

Dafina and the Dafina logo Reg. U.S. Pat. & TM Off.

First trade paperback printing: March 2011
First mass market printing: March 2013

ISBN-13: 978-0-7582-5957-8
ISBN-10: 0-7582-5957-3

10 9 8 7 6 5 4 3 2 1

Printed in the United States of America

*In loving memory of Garfield Gray (1981–2006),
who always made everything look "Easy."
His friendship and kindness cannot be replaced
and will not be forgotten. May he rest in peace
until that great and soon coming day.*

Acknowledgments

Is this real? I still ask myself that question every now and then. I never really imagined I would be here writing the acknowledgments to my first novel. But God has blessed me with this gift and this opportunity to write, and I thank Him first and foremost for everything I am and everything He is doing in me. I never really know what path He will take me on next, but I trust Him completely to lead me to the place I need to be.

I can't go any further without thanking my mother, Vonnie, for starting this whole mess in the first place. If she hadn't taught me to read before I even set foot in school we wouldn't be here now. Her love and support are irreplaceable, and I am so eternally grateful.

Thank you to my daddy, Clive, for always letting me be his little girl, even when I didn't want to be, and for always supporting and encouraging me in my faith and in life.

To my brother, Kevin, thank you for helping me learn to laugh at myself. I love you more than you know.

To two of my closest friends in this world, Shanice Carter and Latoya Kerr, thank you for supporting my dream to "write a book" even when none of us knew what it was about. We knew that life was too funny to laugh at by ourselves—the jokes needed to be shared with the world. You ladies will always be in my heart no matter where we go.

To Simone Erskine, who let me co-write with her on

our very first novel back in third form at Campion when we were barely thirteen years old: I wish I still had that notebook—you know that story was good. Thank you for getting me started. Girl, you know you need to be in print too! Don't let that gift go to waste.

To my editor, Mercedes, thanks a million! You are such a blessing and full of encouragement. Thank you for helping shape this book into what it needed to be, for believing in me and my manuscript, and for loving Jules and Germaine as much as I do.

Thank you to Elaine P. English for being patient with me and helping me wade through the legalese.

Thanks to writer friend Cecelia Dowdy, who answered my questions, encouraged me, and cheered me on as I entered this publishing journey. I am so grateful for your kindness. Thank you also to Tiffany Warren, Tia McCollors, Rhonda McKnight, and all the other talented women of the African American fiction community who have been a support and an inspiration to me. May God continue to bless your ministries.

To all the extended family and church family at Agape in Pickering, Ontario, and Hope in Kingston, Jamaica—there are too many of you for me to start naming names, but I am thankful to all of you for your love and encouragement over the years.

And to all the readers who will read this—thank you! May the path you walk on lead you to His destiny for you.

Be blessed!

Chapter 1

"Miss, another drink for you."

She should have known better than to stand by the bar. But it was the only spot in the house where she had a full view of the floor and all the entrances. That was especially important tonight when it was very possible that media might show up. It would be just like them to slip through a side entrance, and try to sneak an interview with Truuth without checking with her. Those journalists—she couldn't live with them, but didn't have a career without them.

"You know the drill, Owen," Jules said to the bartender. He smirked and sent back the drink to a dark guy lounging at the other end of the bar. Although it was just 10:30 p.m., Owen had already returned three unsolicited beverages for Jules, so they were now on a first name basis.

Jules sighed heavily. What was it with these brothers? Couldn't a girl stand alone at a bar in peace? She was used to the attention that her curvy, size eight figure, smooth, caramel-colored skin, and dark, wide eyes usually attracted. But that didn't make it any less annoying. She pushed a lock of her wild, curly, shoulder-length hair behind her ear, and wished for a moment that her five-foot, six-inch frame could be invisible just long enough for her to get her job done.

It was bad enough that these brothers kept shooting her greasy smiles, but if they were going to send her drinks, couldn't they at least find out what she was drinking and send that? Maybe then she could think about entertaining a conversation with one of them.

Then again, maybe not. She knew exactly how their weak game would go, because she had heard it a million times before. She couldn't help but grimace. What she wouldn't give for something new.

She glanced at her watch impatiently, wondering why the MC was taking so long to put Truuth on stage. From what she'd heard, new music night at the Sound Lounge usually wrapped up around midnight. That only gave them an hour to get Truuth up to do his set.

Scanning the room again, she noted that the reviewers from the free entertainment tabloid *EYE Weekly* and the city's monthly culture magazine *Toronto Life* hadn't left yet. In fact they looked pretty at ease as they sipped their drinks and chatted with a couple other patrons. While she was watching them, she saw Baron Levy and his girlfriend slip in through the side entrance.

Baron was a music reporter for *Urbanology,* one of Toronto's popular urban music magazines. When Jules had called him earlier in the week to pitch the event, she hadn't been certain he would show up. *Urbanology* had a habit of ignoring artists who weren't halfway to a Juno or Grammy award. But for some reason, he had turned out to see Truuth, who was still just the opening act for most opening acts. Maybe they were finally beginning to see in him what she had seen all along.

Maybe this was a sign of things to come. A small shiver ran up her spine, and she downed the rest of her cranberry juice.

"Can I have another one of these?" Jules asked, shaking her empty glass at Owen.

Owen held up one finger, motioning for Jules to wait, as he finished talking to someone on the phone behind the bar. A few moments later he turned back to Jules and gave her an apologetic look.

"Sorry, Jules, I gotta cut you off," he said, taking her empty glass and placing it under the counter.

Jules rolled her eyes. "Whatever, Owen. Hurry up already with that drink. It's the only thing keeping me sane right now."

Owen shook his head.

"No can do, Jules. I have orders from management not to serve you anymore beverages."

Jules scanned Owen's face for a hint of his boyish grin. But the look in his eyes told Jules he was dead serious. Her own eyes widened in surprise.

"You've got to be kidding," she said. "I am a paying customer. Why can't I order a drink from the bar?"

"Management reserves the right to refuse beverages to any patron if they have reason to believe that said patron is either below the legal drinking age or impaired to the extent that to do so would cause harm to the patron in question or other guests of the establishment," Owen said in one breath.

"You don't even serve alcohol! I'd have a better chance of getting drunk off the tap water."

Owen shrugged, and began wiping down the bar. "Sorry, Jules. I'm just following orders."

"From who? You know what, forget that. Let me talk to your manager, 'cause this is—"

"Hey, is everything okay?"

Jules glanced over at a tall, dark guy who had come up beside her at the bar. He wore a look of concern on his handsome features, but Jules was too upset to notice.

"*Someone* told the bartender to cut me off," Jules said, glaring at Owen.

"Well, maybe they thought you were—" The guy stopped short when Jules turned her fiery eyes on him.

"Never mind," he said quickly. "What were you drinking?"

Jules folded her arms and shot a nasty look at Owen, who was trying his best to avoid her by acting busy.

"Just cranberry juice."

Without hesitation, the nameless stranger turned to Owen. "One just cranberry juice, please?"

Owen opened his mouth to protest, but one raised eyebrow from the guy seemed to shut him up fast.

"One cranberry juice coming up," he said, reaching under the bar for a clean glass and pouring the drink.

A few moments later Jules stole a peek at her intervener out of the corner of her eye as she sipped on her drink. After handing her the glass, he had given her a small smile, and then had gone back to leaning against the bar with not so much as a second look in her direction. They had finally introduced Truuth, and Jules could hear him warming up the audience as he prepared to start his set. But even though she was excited to see him go on, she couldn't help but glance over at the attractive man who had stopped her from making a fool of herself.

"So I feel like I have to talk to you now," Jules finally said.

He laughed, and Jules couldn't help but notice the dimple in his left cheek.

"You don't have to do anything." His eyes were still on the stage.

Jules rolled her eyes and sighed. "Yeah, but I'll feel guilty if I don't. Hi, I'm Jules," she said, turning toward him.

He grasped her outstretched hand, finally turning his gaze toward her. "I'm Germaine."

Jules breathed in sharply. His eyes were beautiful. They were an intoxicating shade of hazel with tiny golden flecks that seemed to glow like the dim chandelier lights of the lounge. She had to blink several times just to stop herself from staring.

"Uh . . . nice to meet you." She swallowed hard. "Th-thanks again for . . ." She motioned to her drink.

"No problem," he said, smiling. "Are you sure that's only cranberry juice though?" he asked teasingly. " 'Cause you seem to be stuttering a bit."

Jules silently thanked God for making her too dark to blush.

"I assure you, it is nothing but cranberry juice," she said when she recovered. "I don't usually let strangers buy me drinks; it tends to turn them into stalkers."

Germaine chuckled. "I assure you, Jules, I have no intention of stalking you."

"And yet you're still here," Jules said sweetly.

"I am. But if I remember correctly, you were the one who started this conversation."

"Only because I felt obligated."

"Well, I can't be responsible for your conscience, now can I," said Germaine. "But if it gets me a conversation with a beautiful woman, then I can't complain either."

Jules looked back at the stage, trying in vain to hide the smile that was curling her lips.

Okay. This brother was good.

She glanced back at him, admiring his angular profile, cool, mocha chocolate skin, and six foot something frame.

. . . and he's not too bad on the eyes either.

The crowd, which was pretty large for a Thursday night, was already on its feet and rocking to Truuth's up-tempo, hip-hop sounding groove. Even the guys from the media, who were always too cool to act like they liked something, were out of their seats. Jules couldn't help but grin in excitement. No matter how many times she watched Truuth perform at a show, she still got goose bumps when she saw how well he could move his audience. It made all the hard work she put into his career more than worth it.

"He's pretty good," Germaine commented.

"His name is Truuth," Jules replied. "And he's more than pretty good. He's amazing."

"Sounds like you have a little crush."

Jules glanced over at Germaine, who still had his eyes on the stage.

"Only the professional kind. He's my client."

Now it was his turn to look at her. He was about to say something when Tanya appeared.

"Some guy from *Urbanology* is looking for you. He said he talked to you this week?"

Even though she was speaking to Jules, Tanya's eyes kept shifting across to Germaine. Jules could already see the wheels in her friend's head spinning.

"Thanks, Tanya."

Jules glanced back at Germaine. He winked at her before turning back to his drink at the bar.

"Who's the eye candy?" Tanya hissed as Jules half dragged her friend across the room toward the table where Baron was sitting.

"That's Germaine."

"Interesting," Tanya said, glancing back at him. "Looks like he was feeling you."

Jules glanced back at Germaine, who was chatting with Owen at the bar, and admitted to herself that this was one time she didn't mind.

It was 12:45 a.m. before Jules got the chance to sit down. When she finally sank into the corner booth near the back of the lounge, she immediately slipped off her heels and curled her legs up under her.

She was beat. After arranging and monitoring Truuth's interview with Baron, shuffling him around to the other reporters in the house, and taking requests for digital photos and follow-ups, she was completely drained. Not to mention starving, and craving a cold beverage like nobody's business. She glanced longingly over at the bar, but knew that her feet would never carry her that far.

"What's with you? You look barely alive," 'Dre said, dropping into the chair across from Jules.

"You have no idea. I would give anything for something cold right now," Jules said, smiling sweetly up at 'Dre.

"Well, there'll be time for that later."

Jules tried her best not to roll her eyes. 'Dre was the CEO for Triad Entertainment, the small start-up company that managed Truuth along with a host of other emerging urban gospel music artists. He was sharp as a tack when it came to running the business and working with artists and record labels. But his one-track mind was sometimes too much for Jules to handle.

"I saw that *Urbanology* guy talking to Truuth. Good work on that. I might have to hook you up with some of our other artists."

"Not for what you pay me," Jules said only half-jokingly.

The stipend that Triad paid her was nothing in comparison to the value of the work she did for Truuth. In fact, if it wasn't for her day job, at Toronto Grace Hospital, she would have had more than her aching feet to worry about.

But the money didn't bother her. At the end of the day, all she cared about was using her skills to support an artist who was doing something for God. And if one person came to know Christ because he or she read Truuth's story in the paper, or heard him sing in some obscure music café on a Thursday night, then it would be worth it for her.

"Come on, Jules," 'Dre cajoled. "You know it's all about the vision."

"Maybe. But that vision of yours better quit booking Truuth for events in the middle of the week. Unlike some people, I gotta get up for work in the morning," Jules said pointedly.

"I hear you," 'Dre said, smirking.

"And next time, could you give me more than a couple days notice on the gigs you set up for Truuth?" Jules continued. "I know you're the boss and all, but it's hard for me to do my job when I don't even know what's going on. I've never even heard of this place before, not to mention I don't even know who's in charge around here. For all I know we're going to get sued for taking photos without a release form."

'Dre laughed. "Don't worry. No one's getting sued," he replied. "We've got personal connections with the guy who runs the place. It was a last-minute, easy setup; that's why we didn't bother you with it."

"Now that's my girl! Yo, Jules, I can't believe you hooked me up with Baron Levy," Truuth said, appearing out of nowhere. Whereas the media attention had worn Jules out, it seemed to have completely energized Truuth.

"It wasn't me; it was all you," Jules said, smiling.

Every time she looked at Truuth, she felt inexplicable pride swell inside her. Most people would have broken, or become bitter if they had grown up with a mother who was a drug addict and who died without giving them as much as a prayer. But not Truuth. Not only had he risen above it, he had used his experience to reach others who were still where he used to be. He used his music to show them that God could be their way out of no way, just like He had been for Truuth.

"You gotta meet somebody," Truuth said beckoning to a figure nearby. "G, you already know 'Dre; this is my publicist, Jules; Jules, this is my cousin Germaine."

For the second time that night Jules caught herself staring.

"We already met," Germaine said casually, his eyes lingering on Jules for a split second.

Jules shivered despite the warmth of the club.

"Yeah, we met," she mumbled, tearing her eyes away from his.

"I've been looking all over for you guys," Tanya said, appearing out of nowhere. She stopped suddenly, looked up at Germaine, then at Jules.

"Tanya, this is Truuth's cousin, Germaine; Germaine, this is the boss lady, Tanya," Jules introduced.

"A pleasure to meet you," Tanya said brightly, before turning back to 'Dre and Truuth. It was obvious from her briskness that she was in full business mode.

"There's this guy who's doing a gospel thing later this year. I think he might be interested in booking Truuth. Maybe we can even get him to squeeze some of the other artists into the roster."

Not one to miss a business opportunity, 'Dre was out of his seat and nudging Tanya across the room before she had even finished speaking.

"Catch up with you later, cuz," Truuth said, trailing behind them.

"Aren't you gonna do the mad dash with them?" Germaine asked, raising one eyebrow questioningly.

"Nah. They can handle it, that is if they don't scare the poor guy off with their enthusiasm first."

Germaine chuckled lightly before occupying the seat 'Dre had just vacated.

"I thought you weren't gonna stalk me," Jules said.

"It's not stalking if you enjoy it."

Before she could think of a witty response, the bartender came over and placed a glass of cranberry juice in front of Jules and what looked like a root beer before Germaine.

"Thanks, Owen," Germaine said, nodding slightly to the bartender as he left.

"Since when are you and the bartender on a first-name basis?" she asked.

"Since I hired him."

"You hired him?" Jules said. "So I guess you're going to tell me next that you own the place?"

Germaine smiled easily, his eyes never leaving Jules's.

"You're the owner? But wait, that means . . ." Jules's

eyes widened as Germaine casually took a sip from his root beer and watched her put the pieces together.

"You told Owen to cut me off!"

Germaine shrugged unapologetically. "Guilty as charged."

"Why would you do that?"

"How else could I get you to let me buy you a drink?"

Jules opened and closed her mouth several times as she searched for a response. She was sure that she probably should be mad at him. But she could only shake her head and smile. Guess she didn't have to look far for that something new after all.

"Okay, so you got a few moves," Jules said, refusing to give in so quickly. "Is that supposed to impress me?"

"I never said it should."

"Good, because it doesn't."

"I picked up on that," Germaine said easily. "Tell me something though," he said, cocking his head to the side and looking at her curiously. "What would it take to impress you?"

His eyes were hypnotizing her again, and Jules felt her stomach begin to do somersaults.

"Well, if I had to tell you, then it wouldn't be that impressive anymore, now would it."

"You do have a point there." The corner of his mouth turned up in a smile. "You're something else, Jules. A guy's gotta bring his 'A' game when it comes to you."

"Oh, you were bringing game? I couldn't tell."

"Ouch," Germaine groaned, leaning back and grabbing his chest. "You're killing me."

"Nah, you're fine. Most guys wouldn't hold out for as long as you have."

"Yes, well, I'm not most guys," he said. "I like a good challenge. You, however, are one tough cookie."

"You gotta be in a city like this," Jules said, taking a sip from her juice. "Toronto doesn't pull punches."

"You got that right," he said. Jules didn't miss the serious look that crossed his face for a quick moment. She wondered what he had been through that made him agree so strongly.

"Thanks for this, by the way," she said, raising her glass.

"No problem. You looked like you needed it," he said, his focus returning to her.

"I did."

"Did you want something to eat as well?"

Jules couldn't help but smile. "You don't have to—"

Before she could protest, he had signaled Owen to the table and had her order some food. Within moments Owen returned with a large basket of sweet potato fries. Jules narrowed her eyes suspiciously.

"How did this get here so quickly? You got some tricks up your sleeve, don't you, Germaine," Jules said, squinting at him suspiciously before popping a fry into her mouth.

"And you're making me use all of them," Germaine said.

She laughed lightly and pushed the basket of fries toward him.

"So, I'm pretty good at summing up people," Jules began, "and I definitely wouldn't peg you as a night-club owner."

Germaine shrugged. "It's not really your average nightclub," he said. "Plus, it's something to do in the evenings after the store closes."

"What store?" Jules asked in confusion.

"This store," Germaine said, looking at her strangely. "Sound Lounge is a record store from ten to seven.

Then on Sundays, Mondays, and Thursdays, we close up downstairs and use the second floor as a lounge."

Jules looked around and for the first time noticed the stairs at the back that probably led down to the darkened ground level. She had come up via the side stairs outside and hadn't even thought twice about what might be downstairs.

"Up here used to be part of the store," Germaine continued, "but we just moved everything downstairs and capitalized on this space."

"Wow. I never noticed that," Jules said, still looking around. "I thought the posters and LPs on the wall were just part of the décor, but they're actually part of the store. That's pretty crazy."

"Yeah, well, with music moving to the Internet, the record store thing is pretty much on its way out," Germaine said. "I figured if we could add some entertainment, feature a few artists a couple nights a week, and charge a small cover, then we could really boost the business. So far it's been working." He chuckled. "Your bartender friend actually manages the store during the day when I can't."

Jules cocked her head to the side and looked at Germaine, a small smile spreading across her face.

"Okay, you got me," she said. "I'm impressed."

"Imagine that," he said, popping another fry into his mouth. "And I wasn't even running game this time."

Jules threw back her head and laughed.

Chapter 2

"**Y**our boy was on fire tonight," Tanya said, as she pulled her black Lexus GS Hybrid out of the Toronto Grace Hospital parking lot, where she had picked up Maxine right after leaving the Sound Lounge with Jules. Jules and Maxine almost never passed up an opportunity to carpool in Tanya's luxury vehicle. Unlike that of the rest of them, Tanya's standard of living was more reflective of her trust fund than her income from running Triad with 'Dre.

Tanya had moved from Ottawa to Toronto to attend college several years earlier. Jules had met her at a campus fellowship meeting where Tanya had been trying to rent out her five-bedroom house to students. Even though Jules had not needed housing, she and Tanya had become fast friends. By the time Tanya graduated with her honors degree in business, she was so well integrated into Triad and its network of people that she decided not to leave.

"Don't even talk," Maxine said with a groan. "I am so bummed I missed it."

"It's not your fault. You were on call," Tanya said.

Maxine was a registered nurse at the same hospital where Jules worked. She had been planning to be at the Sound Lounge with the rest of them, but just as they were getting ready to leave, she got a page that she had to go in to work.

"I know, but I hate to think of all those heifers all up on Truuth."

"Girl, please, Truuth is fine, but he ain't that fine," Tanya said, rolling her eyes. Maxine sometimes forgot that not everyone saw Truuth through the same rose-colored glasses that she did.

"You know you just jealous, girl."

"Whatever. You should have seen his cousin though. Now he's something else."

"Who, Germaine? Yeah, the Sound Lounge is his place. That's how Truuth got the hook up to perform tonight," Maxine said. "Did you get to meet him?"

"Just for a minute. Our friend Jules spent all night chatting him up though," Tanya said teasingly.

"Is that true?" Maxine said, turning to look at Jules in the backseat. "How come you never said anything about that? Come to think of it, you've been mighty quiet back there. What's up with you?"

"Nothing," Jules said, glaring at Tanya through the rearview mirror.

"So how come you never told me you had a little thing for Truuth's cousin?"

"Because I don't have a thing for Truuth's cousin," Jules said.

"Oh really," Tanya said grinning. "Is that why you're back there all sulky 'cause he didn't ask for your number?"

Maxine burst out in laughter. "Oh, so *that's* why she's so quiet!"

"Whatever, Tanya," Jules said. "For your information I am not sulking. Can't a girl just be quiet sometimes?"

"Come on, Jules. You're gonna tell me that you're not even a little cheesed that he didn't ask for the digits?"

"No, I'm not. All we did was hang out. Can't a grown man and a grown woman hang out without people making something out of it?"

"Aww, sweetie, don't worry. I'll get Truuth to put in a good word for you," Maxine said, turning back to the front.

"No, thank you, Maxine. I'm good," Jules said.

"I can't believe it," Tanya said, chuckling. "Jules, who is too cool for every guy she meets, finally met a guy who beat her at her own game."

"It's not about being cool; it's about being cautious," Jules said dryly. "You've seen the crazies that I've had to deal with. Cheaters . . ."

"Baby daddies," Maxine added.

"Stalkers," Tanya chimed in.

"Baby daddies who were stalkers . . ."

"Okay, okay, I think we all get the point," Jules said, cutting them off before they started bringing up stories like they usually did when they talked about Jules's sitcom-worthy dating life.

"Well, Germaine's not like that, I can promise you," Maxine said. "I met him a couple times. He's good people."

"Yeah, Jules, give him a chance," Tanya said. "You might as well trust Maxine's guy-radar since yours seems to be on the fritz."

"You know, Tanya, you got a lot of talk for a girl who can't even tell her business partner she has a crush on him," Jules said, leaning toward Tanya in the driver's seat.

Tanya's pale skin immediately began to turn a deep shade of pink.

" 'Dre knows that I care about him," Tanya said quietly.

"I think you do a little more than just *care* about him," Jules said.

"She does have a point there," Maxine said.

"Whose side are you on?" Tanya asked, glaring at Maxine.

"Well, it's true," Maxine said. "You sing the guy's praises all day long. You bend over backward to please him. You drive two and a half hours in snow to pick him up from the airport—"

"Okay . . ."

"Not to mention all those times she came to my apartment depressed because 'Dre was on a date with some girl," Jules added.

"Oh, she does that to you, too!"

"Max, I have a pint of Rocky Road in my freezer just for her—"

"Okay! Okay!" Tanya exclaimed. "So I have a thing for 'Dre. Is that a crime? He's a smart, ambitious, good-looking, Christian guy. What girl wouldn't like him?"

"There's nothing wrong with having feelings for him, sweetie," Maxine said. "But those feelings aren't worth much if he doesn't know about them. And you know 'Dre don't see a blessed thing unless it's got 'Triad' printed on it. You gotta say the words, girl."

"And I would say them if they would make a difference. But they wouldn't, 'cause you both know that 'Dre doesn't do white girls."

She was right. They had all heard him say it on several occasions. And as the single white female in their tight-knit Triad family, that meant that Tanya was automatically out of the race for 'Dre's heart. It didn't matter that they had all been friends for more than five years, or that Tanya had been the one to cofinance Triad with 'Dre when it was nothing more than a dream. Even though 'Dre probably loved Tanya just as much as he did Maxine and Jules, there was a part of his love that she didn't qualify for because she had the wrong pigmentation.

Jules leaned back as the heaviness of that thought cast a gloom on the atmosphere in the car. She couldn't understand how that type of thinking still managed to pervade even the best of people. It seemed like the more things changed, the more they stayed the same.

Chapter 3

Rhonda Bowen

"Jules, the caterers just called—they want to know when we will be coming in to do the tasting."

Jules rubbed her temples and looked up at the clock hanging on the wall in front of her desk. It was only 1 p.m., but she felt as if she had already done a whole Monday's worth of work. Even though the gig at the Sound Lounge was the Thursday before, she had barely been able to recover from it over the weekend. Between the follow-up from the event and the planning for the next few weeks, she had been keeping very busy. It didn't help either that she kept getting distracted by thoughts of tall, attractive lounge owners.

Despite the tiredness, Jules still loved her day job. The excitement of planning hospital events, working with media, and communicating with staff and community members on behalf of the hospital gave her a thrill. She was sure public relations was what she had been made to do.

As far back as she could remember, she had always been organizing something. Whether it was youth emphasis day at her church, or her high school prom,

Jules knew that event coordination was in her blood. In the beginning, her family had been pretty skeptical when she had decided to study public relations in college. But so far it hadn't been as bad as they had imagined. And even though it had been almost four years since she started, she still got a rush every time she saw a story she had pitched to the media on the front page of a newspaper, or in the evening newscast.

There were times, however, when being a public relations officer for the hospital seemed to demand more from her than she had to give. Times like this week.

The hospital's volunteer awards banquet, which was coming up within the next two weeks, had her spinning in circles. There were speakers to be confirmed, gifts to be bought, seating plans to be approved, and not enough time to do it. If Jules had had the help of Penny, the public relations director, then she would have been fine. But Jules's boss had been in and out of labor relations meetings all week due to the growing unrest between the hospital's nurses and senior management. No one had said the words "industrial action" yet, but given the unpredictable nature of the nurses' union, Jules was already a bit worried.

The sound of Michelle's long, French-manicured nails drumming impatiently against the door frame broke Jules out of her thoughts. Jules looked up at the communications secretary and realized Michelle was under just as much pressure as she was. In fact, there were about four hundred guests who Michelle had to contact to confirm their attendance at the event. Jules knew because she had given the list to her earlier that morning, along with a number of other tasks.

"Tell them we will come by at two o'clock on Thursday," Jules said, updating her weekly schedule as she spoke. Sliding the tasting in had just turned her nine-hour day into a ten-hour one. But she had no choice. There was no way she would risk a repeat of last year's long-service awards dinner, where the food was so bad that most of it got left on the buffet table.

No sooner had Michelle disappeared than she heard her phone ring.

"Public Relations, Jules speaking."

"I was hoping I would get you directly."

Jules's heart skipped a beat.

"And who am I speaking with?" she asked cautiously.

"Oh, I think you know."

"I think I do too," Jules said smoothly. "But just so I don't make a fool of myself, I think you better tell me."

Jules heard Germaine chuckle, and a feeling of warmth spread through her.

"It's Germaine, Jules."

"Well, isn't that something," she said, leaning back in her chair, unable to stop the smile that curled her lips. "Never thought I'd hear from you again."

"Yeah, Truuth mentioned that you might be a bit salty."

Jules rolled her eyes, annoyed that all her friends thought they knew her so well.

"I'm just surprised to hear from you, that's all."

"Does that mean you're glad I called?"

"Now that's an entirely different question, Mr. Williams."

He laughed again, and Jules admitted to herself that she was more than a little glad that he had looked her up.

"Okay, so here's another question for you. Do you think you could stand having another meal with me?"

"I think I could survive it."

"So how about lunch?"

"When? Today?" she asked. She looked down at her gray slacks and royal blue, empire waist, button-down blouse. She knew she looked okay, but she wished she had known she might be seeing Germaine when she had gotten dressed that morning.

"Sure. I'm in your area, and I could pick you up in half an hour."

"I don't know," Jules said with mock caution. "I only met you once, and you want me to get in a car with you? Who knows where you might take me?"

"Hmm, Truuth was right," Germaine murmured to himself. "Okay, how about I bring you lunch, and we can have it there? That way it will be a little harder for me to kidnap you."

"That sounds fine," Jules said, rolling her eyes even though he couldn't see her.

"Good. Is Chinese okay with you?"

"That would be great actually."

"Okay, I'll see you at one thirty."

Half an hour later Jules spotted Germaine at a window table near the back of the hospital's first floor café area. When he finally saw her as she neared the table, he stood and pulled out a chair for her.

"You look nice," he said, as she sat down across from him.

"Thank you," Jules replied, not missing the way his eyes sparkled as he looked at her.

"So before you ask, Truuth gave me your number. He said Maxine said it was okay."

"I wasn't going to ask."

"But you were wondering."

"I was actually wondering why you didn't ask me for it yourself," Jules said pointedly. She knew she was being a bit forward, but she was too old for games.

"I wanted to be sure that I would still be interested after a day or two," he said. He was smiling, but his eyes told her that he was serious.

"So, what's the verdict?" she asked.

"Well, I'm sitting here with you four days later, so I think you can guess."

Jules smiled and took a sip of the cranberry juice he placed in front of her.

"You have a good memory," Jules said.

"Well, with you, I figure I need to be on my toes," he said, handing her napkins and a fork.

"Geez, you make me sound like an army commander," Jules said.

Germaine chuckled. "You know that's not what I meant."

"Well?"

"Come on, Jules, you know you love playing hardball," he said, looking at her knowingly. "Nothing gets past you."

"Sure," Jules said, as she speared a piece of kung pao chicken with her fork. "This from the guy who gets me food and my favorite drink before I ask for them."

Germaine grinned but said nothing.

"It's like you're always two steps ahead of me. I just met you; you're not supposed to be this good," she teased.

"Well, you can learn a lot if you just keep your eyes open," he said, watching her carefully. She let herself stare at him for a moment, loving the way she got lost in his warm hazel eyes.

There was something about him that intrigued her. She couldn't quite put her finger on it, but she knew there was more to him than he was letting on, more than the easy smile and casualness. And she wanted to know all of it.

Jules took a long sip from her drink.

"Truuth's been doing really well," she said. "It's hard being a Christian in the music business, especially here. But he's really held on to his beliefs. You must be proud of him."

"I am," Germaine said. "I understand what he's going through. I know for me it can get tricky running the Sound Lounge, and making sure it's something I can feel right doing. But I feel like it's something God's called me to, you know?"

Jules raised her eyebrow in surprise. She did not know what kind of answer she had been expecting from him, but that certainly wasn't it. He had just doubled his points in her book.

"People always ask, how I can serve God on one hand and run a nightclub on the other," Germaine continued. "But I don't really think the two are separate. Coming up, there weren't many after-hours spots where grown folk could just go and chill, hear some good music, and not worry about being shot at," he explained. "So I figured, why not make it happen?"

Jules nodded and smiled. "You love it, don't you," she said.

He grinned sheepishly. "Yeah, I do. I put a lot into that place; it's like my kid, you know. Everyone has that one thing they're meant to do. For me, the Sound Lounge is it. Isn't that how you feel about what you do?"

Jules shrugged and took another sip from her drink. "I'm not sure."

She knew she loved her job and enjoyed coming to work most days. But she wasn't sure about it being her calling.

At one time she had thought that by working in a hospital that was helping thousands of people every year she could fill that need—the need for a calling to have a life that was relevant. But although she felt good about the work she did, she knew it was the paycheck she felt really good about—particularly the security of knowing said paycheck would arrive on schedule every two weeks regardless of what happened.

"Put it this way," Germaine said. "What would you do with your time if money wasn't an issue?"

Jules thought about it for a moment. "I would do what I do for Truuth, full-time. I'd love to work with artists that have a ministry, and help them give that ministry a voice."

"Then you should do that," Germaine said simply. "If it's what God is calling you to do, then it's the only thing that will ever make you happy."

"Well," Jules said with a mischievous grin. "I'm sure there are other things that could make me happy as well."

Germaine coughed as he choked on a sip of his drink, and Jules couldn't help but laugh a little.

"I meant career-wise," Germaine said with a laugh when he recovered.

As she chatted with him about the Lounge, and about his business, Jules realized how little thought she had put into God's unique plan for her life. She had been walking along this path that she figured was the right way to go, but how could she be sure? She definitely wasn't as sure about everything as Germaine was, but she knew she wanted to be.

Germaine glanced down at his watch, prompting Jules to look up at the clock behind him. She was surprised to see that almost an hour had passed since she sat down.

"So, Jules," Germaine began, a small smile playing on his lips. "I'm gonna be real with you. I like you, I think the feeling is mutual, and I want to see where this goes. But you gotta give me a sign that I'm not wasting my time here."

Jules took another sip from her drink, her eyes still locked on his. She glanced up at the clock again. She had five minutes—the exact amount of time it would take her to get back upstairs.

As he watched her expectantly, she took her business card from her purse and wrote something on the back.

"Thanks for lunch, Germaine," she said as she stood to leave.

Then she placed the card with her phone number on the table in front of him and leaned close to his ear.

"Next time maybe you can give me more than an hour's notice."

"Hello?"

"Hi, Jules. It's me."

"Oh, hi, Mom."

"Don't 'oh, hi, Mom' me. When were you gonna call me?"

Jules sighed heavily, and tucked the phone in between her head and her shoulder, in anticipation of the ear chewing she knew she was going to get from her mother.

It was about 6:30 p.m. She had just gotten home and

was about to cut up some vegetables to go in her stew, when her mother called.

"Mom, I saw you not too long ago," Jules said, in what she knew was going to be a futile defense.

"Child, your not too long ago is actually two weeks ago. You don't think you could give your momma a call since then so I can know that you're alive?"

Jules didn't bother to answer. It wouldn't make a difference anyway, because Momma Jackson would still say whatever she was planning to say. Instead, Jules pulled another carrot from the washed pile in her stainless steel sink and began dicing it on the thick wooden chopping board.

She missed her real mother, the one who existed before her father abandoned them and moved to New York. That was the point when sweet, tender Momma Jackson had turned into some sort of superwoman, working longer hours, buying a bigger house, and moving Jules and her brother out of Scarborough, a community in Toronto's east end, into Whitby, a suburb so far from Toronto you needed a long-distance plan to call into it. It was almost as if Douglas Jackson's departure had motivated Momma Jackson to succeed. Less than five years after he left, she moved from being an underwriter to the senior manager at the insurance company where she worked.

Despite her work schedule, however, Jules's mother had never been anything less than committed to Jules and her brother Davis. She always knew every teacher's name, and remembered when every semester's report card was due. And even though Jules and Davis had been teenagers when their father left, Momma Jackson still kept them in check every time they slipped up or acted a fool. To Jules it seemed like her mother still felt the need to have her hand in every part of her children's lives. Even when it wasn't necessary.

"I suppose you too busy for your little old momma since you grown and all, with that big job of yours sucking up all your time."

"No, Momma, nothing like that," Jules said, rolling her eyes. Now wasn't that the pot calling the kettle black. It was after six, but Jules was almost sure her mother was calling from the office.

"Then how come you haven't been up here for dinner since last month? I can't understand what it is you love about Scarborough so much."

Jules knew her mother hated Scarborough with a passion. When Jules had moved back into the city her mother had worked hard for them to leave, Momma Jackson had nearly had a stroke. She didn't care that it was closer to work, or that it was cheaper to live there than in high-income Whitby. All she heard was that her daughter was moving back into poverty's playground.

"Momma, you know you ain't got time for me to be under you every minute. You and Aunty Sharon are always gone to Buffalo to shop, or you're holding some Women's Ministries thing at the house," Jules said, vigorously scraping the carrots in with the rest of the vegetables stewing slowly on the top of the stove.

"What you trying to say child? That I abandoned you? That I ain't got time for my own daughter? After I worked so hard to make sure you and your brother had everything you ever needed, you want to turn around and say something like that?" Momma Jackson complained. Jules wet a paper towel under the faucet and placed it against her forehead. "You always making excuses not to spend time with your mother," she continued. "If it wasn't for your brother I would feel like I didn't have no children at all."

Jules closed her eyes and wet the paper towel again. This was why she never called her mother, and avoided visiting her, because it always led to a comparison between what Davis did and what Jules didn't do. And no matter how many hoops Jules jumped through, or how many times she canceled her plans to be with her mother, or how many days she took off from work to drive Momma Jackson across the border to the States, Davis would always come out on top.

"As much as he ain't got no money, he calls me every week, and he's always down here to visit me," Momma Jackson continued. "He live in a whole different country, and he still visit me more often than you do, Jules."

Now that was a blatant lie. But Jules could never tell her mother that. She also couldn't tell her mother that all those trips Davis made to visit her were actually trips to visit Keisha, his longtime girlfriend who still lived in Toronto, even though he was all the way up in Michigan. And all those long distance calls that Davis made to Mom were actually free, due to the unlimited international calling plan he got when he moved, so that he could talk to Keisha all the time. But no, Jules would never say any of that. Because, apart from the fact that it would completely destroy her mother, it would also start another of their infamous quarrels— one which would inevitably end with Momma Jackson not speaking to Jules for weeks.

Sighing heavily, Jules moved back over to the stove and began stirring the pot of thick vegetable stew. She pushed the spoon around so hard that tiny brown droplets of sauce splashed over the sides. It was in moments like these that she felt her father's absence most.

Davis may have been her mother's favorite, but Jules had always been Daddy's little girl. When she used to get into arguments with her mother, her dad would be the one to tuck her into his arm and make everything better. Unlike Momma, he was reasonable and patient, and he understood Jules without her having to say a word. No matter what, she could always count on him to support her.

But that was then. Now, he was no father to her at all. She could count on one hand the number of times each year she heard from him. And enough disappointment as a teenager had taught her that trying to reach out to him was a waste of her time. He did what he could in making sure she and Davis could afford college and have the material things they needed. But that was as far as his support extended. And that was fine with Jules most of the time. But every now and then, especially when her mother was on a roll, she would wonder what it would be like if he was still around.

"Your brother's coming down next month, and I want all of us to have dinner together. Do you think you can clear your calendar for us, Miss Busybody?" her mother asked.

"I'll do my best, Momma," Jules said.

"Good, I'd love to see you," she said. "You know I love you, sugar."

"I love you too, Momma."

"I'll talk to you later, honey."

Jules hung up the phone before turning off the stove and tossing the wooden spoon into the empty sink. No longer in the mood to finish the stew, she stretched out on the sofa as a feeling of tiredness washed over her. In only a few minutes, the elation of the day had transformed itself into the turmoil of the evening.

The tension in the back of her neck began to turn into a headache.

Lord, why does it have to be so hard with my mother. I honor her like you ask. I respect her, and I give her as much as I can, but it's never enough. What more can I do?

Jules closed her eyes and willed her headache and her conversation with her mother to go away.

Chapter 4

"So, are you going to tell me where we're going?"
"Nope."

"This is what I get after two weeks with you?" Jules teased. "Secret dates where I don't know what's going to happen?"

"Don't you mean two amazing weeks with me?" Germaine countered mischievously.

Amazing was one word. Jules could also think of a couple others, like intriguing, addictive, and thrilling. She was having a hard time denying how much fun she'd been having with Germaine since their semi-date almost two weeks ago at the hospital. She'd had lunch with him on several occasions, invited him along to Truuth's events, argued with him over the best old hits, let him school her on new artists, and exceeded her text message plan chatting with him throughout the day.

"Fishing for compliments, Germaine?"

He laughed. "No, just encouraging you not to hold back. The truth will set you free."

"Nice deflection," she said. "You still haven't told me where we're going."

Jules narrowed her eyes at Germaine from the passenger side of his Honda Civic Coupe, but he just changed gears and threw her another mischievous grin.

"You're enjoying this aren't you," she said, trying to sound annoyed.

"More than you know," he said, chuckling.

"At least give me a clue."

"Okay," Germaine said, thinking for a moment. "There will be food."

"Ouch!" Germaine laughed as Jules swatted him with her silver clutch purse.

"Fine," she said, turning toward her window to watch the other cars whizzing past on the highway. She sighed loudly and shifted in her seat. After a few moments she sighed again and propped her hand against her chin. On the third sigh Germaine glanced over at her and smirked.

"You can sigh all you want, Jules, I'm not telling you," Germaine said. "It's supposed to be a surprise."

"I should probably tell you then that I don't like surprises."

"Everybody likes surprises."

"Well, I'm not everybody," Jules said. "The last surprise I got was a short circuit in my kitchen that left me with a refrigerator and freezer full of spoilt food."

Germaine laughed. "Well, I can promise you, it won't be that kind of surprise. You'll like this one."

"How can you be so sure?"

"I just know," he said. "Besides, have you ever had anything less than a good time when you're with me?"

"No," Jules admitted. "But it's early days yet."

A few minutes later as they pulled into a small parking lot in the West End neighborhood of the city, Jules was still a bit skeptical. They were in an older part of town, and there didn't seem to be much around but a few fifties-style bars and a couple mom-and-pop shops. The establishment they had stopped in front of was the last in a long cluster of well-worn two-story brick buildings that housed narrow stores, theme bars, and novelty shops.

As she got out of the car, Germaine took her hand and laced his fingers through hers.

"Trust me, you'll have a good time," he said, softly kissing the back of her knuckles. Jules felt a warmth spread through her when she saw the tenderness in Germaine's eyes as he looked at her. Involuntarily she relaxed and let him lead her up a side stairway.

Before she even got inside Leroy's, she could hear the low bass of sixties music reverberating through the air. As she stepped into the oldies club, she felt like she was stepping forty years into the past. Everything from the muted shades of brown and burgundy furniture, to the hazy orange lights, reflected the obvious vintage theme.

On the tiny stage, the house band was working over their version of an Aretha Franklin song, while a dark, slim woman with thick, curly hair belted out the lyrics as if she was the Queen of Soul herself.

Jules stood at the back of the club speechless. She had lived in Toronto for most of her life, but she had never been anywhere like this. She hadn't even known that spots like this existed. But here she was, standing in a retro club tucked away in a corner of Toronto's West End.

"So what do you think?" Germaine murmured close to her ear. She turned to see him watching her nervously. For the first time since she had met him he seemed a bit unsure of himself. "From the way you talk about music, and the songs I saw in your iPod, I figured you might like this place, but I wasn't sure. . . ."

"I love it," Jules said, squeezing his hand. Her eyes shone brightly with excitement, and she looked like she could barely stand still.

A slow smile crept onto Germaine's face, and he squeezed her hand before leading her to a small table at the side of the room.

Jules couldn't take her eyes off the stage. They had started playing "Midnight Train to Georgia," and, even though the soloist didn't have any backup singers, she was rocking the house.

"How did you even find this place?" she asked, tearing her eyes away to look at Germaine.

"See that guy over there?"

"Who? The drummer?"

"Yeah. I used to go to school with him. He introduced me to this place about a year ago, and I've been coming here ever since."

Jules raised an eyebrow at him. "Oh, so this is where you carry all your lady friends," she said teasingly.

Germaine laughed and shook his head. "No. You're actually the first woman I've ever brought here."

"Oh, really," Jules said. "How come?"

Germaine shrugged. "I don't know many people who would appreciate a place like this."

Jules opened her mouth and then closed it. She couldn't think of a single smart comment. Not even one.

"Wow. Speechless twice in one evening," Germaine said. "I'm on a roll tonight."

"Yeah, well, don't get too used to it," Jules replied, trying to hide her smile. "It doesn't happen that often."

Germaine chuckled and signaled the waitress. When

she had taken their order and brought their drinks, he
turned his attention back to Jules.

"So how come a young thing like you is so into sixties music, especially since you were born long after
that era?" Germaine asked.

Jules smiled and swirled her root beer.

"When I was little, both my mom and dad worked.
So after school me and my brother used to stay home
by ourselves. We never had cable or anything, so most
of the time we would spend the afternoons listening to
the radio. They used to play sixties music every day between three and five o'clock, and that's how I got to
know all those songs."

She laughed as she remembered something else.

"I used to buy those little sixty-minute audio cas-
settes and tape my favorite songs off the radio. By the
time I was fifteen, I had shoe boxes full of mixed tapes
I'd made." She smiled to herself. "Those were good
times."

"Your brother, he's younger than you."

"Yeah, how did you know?" Jules asked in surprise.

"When you talk about him, you get this protective
vibe," Germaine said, his eyes still watching her. "You
two are close?"

"Oh, yeah," Jules said laughing. "Our parents used
to say we would gang up on them all the time."

She looked down at her drink, which she was stirring thoughtfully. "He's away in the States in law
school," she said, looking up at Germaine. "I'm so
proud of him. So glad he didn't get caught up in the
gangs and the drugs, like so many black guys here do.
I think that would have broken my heart."

Just then the waitress arrived with their order.

"So tell me about your family," Jules said a few moments later, after they had blessed the food and started eating. "Brothers? Sisters?"

"One sister," Germaine answered. "Her name is Soroya, and she's the most beautiful ten-year-old in the entire world. She's got a mouth on her, though," he said with a raise of an eyebrow. "Kinda reminds me of you."

"Funny," Jules said with a wry smile. "What about your parents?"

"My mom is a teacher; she teaches second grade." He paused. "My dad died when I was fifteen."

Jules didn't miss the dark look that flittered over his eyes for a brief moment.

"I'm sorry," Jules said, reaching across the table to touch his hand. No one that close to her had ever died. She didn't know what to say.

"He was a cop," Germaine said, shrugging. "He died on the job."

"That must have been hard for you," Jules said, watching him sympathetically. It was clear that his father's death still affected him, even though it had happened so many years ago.

"That's life," he replied, picking up his fork again. "Not much you can do about it. You accept that God lets everything happen for a reason, and you move on."

Jules nodded and took a sip of her drink.

"So you get to see your sister often?" she asked, changing the subject.

"Not as often as I would like to," Germaine said, brightening at the mention of his sister. "Mom has her in every activity under the sun. Swimming, dance, piano lessons. Two weeks ago she started singing lessons. Since then she's been trying to get Mom to let her wear an Afro so she can be Jill Scott."

Jules let out a laugh. "Jill Scott, huh. That must be a trip."

"It is," Germaine said, shaking his head. "Mom blames me of course. She says ever since I let 'Roya borrow *Who is Jill Scott?,* she's been trying to be the next queen of neo-soul."

"Whoa, hold up," Jules said, putting down her fork. "You think Jill Scott is the queen of neo-soul?"

Germaine raised an eyebrow at her. "Of course she is. Who else would be?"

"Uh, Miss Erykah Badu?"

"No way!"

"Yes way! She's a legend," Jules protested. "Jill Scott is a newbie by comparison. Erykah was doing neo-soul before they even came up with a term for it."

"Exactly," Germaine said, opening his hands as if it was the most obvious thing in the world. "She was singing some other pop-blues-jazz business. Jill Scott defined neo-soul. Everybody knows that."

"Are you sure?" Jules said dryly. " 'Cause the people who ate up Erykah's six albums—three of which went platinum I might add—seem to think differently."

Germaine grinned smugly. "She's still a bit short of Jill's seven albums, though. And let's not forget Ms. Scott has three Grammys."

"Okay, first of all, *Collaborations* does not count as an album," Jules said, gesturing with her fork. "And it's all about quality over quantity. Don't let me even start on how many more Grammys Erykah won over Jill." She shook her head. "I might have to come over and school Ms. Soroya on the music tip. I'll help her put in some dreads too."

Germaine laughed. "Oh, yeah, Mom would love that."

His laughter was contagious, and Jules couldn't help but chuckle as well. The vision of a ten-year-old girl wearing an Erykah Badu–style turban to school made her laugh even harder.

"I think we're going to have to agree to disagree for the sake of Soroya's hair," Jules said when she had stopped laughing.

"Okay," Germaine said. "But you know what you're getting for your birthday, right?"

"What?"

"The Jill Scott catalogue, complete with all seven albums, including *Collaborations,*" Germaine teased.

Jules bit her lip. "I already have it."

She laughed at the surprised expression on Germaine's face.

"What? I didn't say I didn't like her; I just said she wasn't the queen," Jules said mischievously.

Germaine shook his head and pushed away his almost empty plate. "Jules, I think you're too much for me to handle."

"Nah, you're doing fine," Jules said, leaning back in her seat. "In fact you really surprised me tonight. I thought you would go all high roller on me and take me to some fancy downtown restaurant. But this . . ." she said, motioning to the stage and the food. "This I didn't expect."

"This is what I'm about," he said. "I want you to know who I am from the start so you know what you're getting into."

"I get that," she said. "But why did you have to go and be all awesome? I was prepared to not like you, and you totally ruined it for me."

"That's too bad," he teased. " 'Cause this is only part one of my plan for completely winning you over."

Jules sighed in mock defeat. "I guess you win this round, Mr. Williams. But this isn't over. I won't go down without a fight."

"I wouldn't expect any less."

He opened his hand to her, and Jules let him lead her to the small dance floor that had been created in front of the stage.

Miss Thing on stage was now singing a slower Roberta Flack song, and the floor was crowded with couples swaying to the music. Jules and Germaine had to squeeze past a few of them to find a space.

Germaine's hand rested comfortably on the small of her back, reminding Jules that this was one of the few times she had been this close to him. Though they'd been hanging out a lot lately, they had kept it pretty causal. But the warmth radiating from his body, and the scent of him swirling around her, was making her mind think of things. Things she hadn't been motivated to think of in a long time.

"So you and Truuth are cousins, huh," she said, trying to distract herself from her own thoughts.

"Mm-hmm," Germaine murmured.

"So how come I've never seen you two together before the other day? I think I would have remembered that."

"I was living in Vancouver for a couple years."

"Vancouver? Who moves from Toronto to Vancouver? Usually it's the other way around," Jules said.

Germaine was looking at her strangely. It was probably because she was babbling. But she couldn't help it. The more her mouth was moving, the less her mind did.

"I suppose the weather there is better," Jules continued. "But I don't know if that would be motivation

enough. You'd have to leave your friends, and everything you know. It would be like starting o—"

"Jules," Germaine said softly.

"Yeah?"

"I need you to stop talking now."

"Why?"

"Because I'm going to kiss you."

For the third time that night Jules was speechless.
But that was okay, because the next thing she felt was
Germaine's full lips on hers. Her mind went numb
while her hands, on reflex, reached up to slide around
his neck. She couldn't remember ever being kissed like
that before. It was sweet, it was gentle, and it was over
way too soon.

"Wow," Jules murmured softly. The golden flecks in
his eyes had become an intense shade of bronze, and
no matter how she tried, she couldn't seem to look
away.

"Yeah, I know what you mean," he murmured back,
his words tickling her lips.

He raised his eyebrow questioningly, and she nodded. And in no time at all, she was speechless again.

The strong smell of disinfectant and cleaner wafted
into Jules's nostrils as she walked down the hallway of
the Pearson Wing at Toronto Grace Hospital. It was the
oldest part of the hospital, and was named after Canadian Prime Minister Lester B. Pearson, who was said to
have stayed there once during a nasty spell of pneumo-
nia. The story was that he was so appreciative of the
care he received that he made a huge donation to the hospital, which was used to do renovations. When the
structural improvements on this wing were complete,

they renamed it the Lester B. Pearson Wing, and thus it
had been ever since. A large, framed black-and-white
photo monument was mounted on the wall in the lobby
entrance of the hospital to remind everyone of the
area's history.

That was part of what Jules loved about the hospital—the rich history. Knowing that she got to be a part
of that, and knowing that she worked for an organization that was making a difference in the lives of so
many, was what made coming to work worthwhile for
her. And it was the thought of this that brought a smile
to Jules's lips as her heels clicked against the hard ce-
ramic tiles that covered the hallway. That and the memory of her date with Germaine.

Even though it was more than a week since the
event, she still got a light, heady feeling when she
thought about what it was like being with him. Besides, even though they had chatted over the phone almost every day since, their busy schedules hadn't left
any time for a second meeting. So the memory of the
first date was all she had—and what a memory it was.

"Get a grip, Jules," she muttered to herself, as she
caught a glimpse of her silly grin in the reflection of a
glass door. But though she tried, she couldn't keep the
smile off her face.

"Well, someone's in a good mood," Derek said from
behind the counter in the print shop.

Jules smiled wider but ignored his comment. Derek
ran the hospital print shop, but as far as Jules was concerned that was just a part-time job. His full-time gig
was finding out everything that was going on with
everyone in the hospital and passing that information
around. It wasn't news until Derek heard it, and if
Derek said it, you knew it was true.

"Hey, Derek, are my newsletters ready yet?" Jules asked, referring to the monthly executive newsletter that the public relations department put out for the hospital's major stakeholders, and which Jules had sent down to be printed the day before.

"Yes, Miss Sunshine, they're ready," Derek said dryly, just a bit cheesed that Jules wouldn't share the juicy contents of her life. "But let me just finish printing this job, and then I'll get them to you."

Jules nodded and slid onto the bench against the wall, just as a tall, slim woman walked into the small print shop. She was pale, with her straight brown hair pulled back severely into a bun at the nape of her neck. There wasn't a single crinkle in her black business suit, and her black low-heeled pumps were so shiny that Jules was sure she saw her reflection in them. Like everything else about this woman, her face was straight, not showing an ounce of emotion.

"Are my forms ready?" she asked Derek in a clipped tone.

"Uh, yes, ma'am," Derek said, scrambling to retrieve a pile of papers from the back of the shop.

Jules raised an eyebrow in surprise. She had never seen Derek look so flustered. Usually when people came into the print shop, they had to wait on Derek to do things when he was good and ready. He might not be a doctor, but he was chief in this little part of the hospital, and he made sure everyone knew it. But this time it was different. Clearly, this unfamiliar woman was the one in charge today.

The woman watched undisturbed as Derek scuffled to get her order. During the two minutes of painful silence that ensued, she did not glance at Jules even once.

"Here you go, ma'am," Derek said, once he had put her package together.

"Thank you."

Moments later, she was gone, in the same brisk manner in which she had come.

Derek seemed to breathe a small sigh of relief as the sound of her clicking heels faded away.

"Who's that?" Jules asked, a bit bewildered at the strange exchange that had taken place.

"That's the efficiency expert," Derek said soberly. "And, girl, she scares the daylights out of me."

Jules nodded. Efficient seemed to be the right word to describe the woman who had just left.

"What's she doing here?"

Derek opened up his eyes at Jules in surprise. "Girl, you don't know? She's part of the hospital restructuring team."

Jules shook her head. "No way. I know the restructuring team, and I know I've never seen her before."

"She's new," Derek said in a stage whisper, as he leaned forward on the counter separating them. "They just brought her in early this week."

Jules was confused. Yes, she knew that Toronto Grace had been going through some tough times. After the changes to the province's health budget and an inspection into regional hospitals a few months before, almost every hospital in the region had faced hefty restructuring. Everything from hospital budgets to staff hours and emergency wait times had gotten addressed. Jules still cringed at the memory of the hours she, Penny, and Michelle had spent crafting key messages and communicating the changes to staff and patients. Up until now she had thought the worst of it was over.

"Why would they bring in someone new now?"

Jules asked, puzzled. "I thought the whole thing was almost over?"

"Tell that to all those HR people who got fired yesterday," Derek said dryly. Jules's eyes widened.

"What!"

"Yes, girl, they pretty much cleaned out HR yesterday afternoon—from the top too. Gave them girls pink slips and everything. About eight of them got let go. And I hear that's just the beginning," Derek said quietly, eyes darting around suspiciously to see if he had been overheard.

Jules felt a cold chill run through her. During the initial restructuring, the hospital had been forced to let some nurses and administrative staff go in order to get back on budget. That had been a tense time for everyone, especially Jules. She knew from the experiences of her older colleagues in the field that whenever an organization faced budget cuts, the public relations department was usually the one that got scaled down first. She had thought she had dodged a bullet, but apparently she had spoken too soon.

"I have to go," Jules said, standing and taking her stack of newsletters from Derek.

"You okay, girl?" Derek asked with concern. "You don't look too good."

Jules waved him away, but even as she walked back down the hallway toward her office, a sick feeling began to rise in the pit of her stomach.

Was her job in danger?

Chapter 5

The news of the changes at the hospital stayed on Jules's mind for the rest of the week and woke her up early on the weekend. It was only 8:30 a.m. when she stepped into Scarborough Memorial Church. Service wasn't set to start for another hour, but sometimes Jules liked to get there early so she could sit in the quiet, vacant church. In those moments she felt so close to God that she could feel His physical presence in the pew beside her. It filled her with a sense of peace and assurance she could hardly explain.

That morning the church was deathly quiet as she walked up the center aisle. In a few hours, every empty row would be filled with men, women, and children dressed in their Saturday best. The wooden rafters would shake from the vibrations of the band, with young George Raymond banging out chords on the old piano like he was the next Ray Charles. Every corner of the room would buzz with the sound of hands clapping, feet tapping, and members singing good old gospel hymns at the top of their lungs.

Yes, in a few hours you wouldn't be able to hear a tree fall outside the front door.

But right at that moment, there was no one but Jules, and God, and the beautiful rays of sunlight stealing through the stained glass window high up on the wall behind the pulpit.

Jules slipped into a row near the center of the church and sat quietly for a moment. As she closed her eyes, slowly but surely she felt that deep familiar peace fill her being.

It was a while since she had been here this early. Over the past couple weeks she had been waking up late most Sabbaths, not getting to church until well after 10 a.m. As a result she had missed this peaceful quiet time that used to center her for the week ahead.

As she sat there in the quiet church, she thought of all the things that had been weighing her down lately. First there was her job. She had always thought if she worked hard enough that she would be fine. It was one of the myths you learned living with a black mother— you grew up thinking that you could achieve anything solely by hard work. Too bad life wasn't like that. The gossip Derek had shared with her, plus the rumors going around about more staff cuts, had made her seriously wonder how secure her future at the hospital really was. She had thought about mentioning all this to Germaine or the girls, but somehow that would make it a bit too real. It would mean that she was admitting there was a possibility she could lose her job.

She loved her job and couldn't imagine doing anything else.

But sometimes she wondered if she loved it too

much. If the Lord asked her to give it up, could she do it? What if he took it away from her?

And then there was her mom. The more Jules thought about her, the more frustrated she became. If she was honest with herself, she knew part of the reason she had moved away from home was to put enough distance between herself and her mother to keep her sane. It felt like the more she tried to please Momma Jackson, the less Momma Jackson was satisfied.

"What does she want from me?" Jules asked, her frustration echoing softly across the empty church.

She sighed. It wasn't supposed to be this way. A daughter wasn't supposed to dread talking to her mother, or feel anxious at the thought of having to see her. Even though it made her feel guilty, she sometimes wished she had a mother like Maxine's, who acted like her best friend, or a mother like Tanya's, who seemed to adore her.

But what kind of daughter says bad things about a mother who has taken care of her all her life? Who supported her when her father jumped ship? No one would understand. Maybe she was being selfish. But either way, the more she thought about it the more confused she felt.

Jules was so caught up in her own thoughts that she didn't see Pastor Thomas walk up the side aisle into her pew.

"Well, good morning, Jules. I haven't seen you here this early in a long time."

"I haven't been here this early in a long time. Good morning to you too, Pastor Thomas."

Jules loved Pastor Thomas. In fact he was part of the reason she loved Scarborough Memorial and why she found it so hard to part with the church after her mother had moved them away. There was something about this tall, stocky man, with thick, graying hair, deep chocolate skin, and a warm smile, that made her feel right at home. As far back as she could remember he had been her pastor. And when her real dad left, when she was fourteen, he became like a surrogate father to her, and his wife, Sister Thomas, like a second mother.

Though he and his wife never had children, they always treated the youth at Scarborough Memorial as if each one was their own. Every young person in church knew that if he or she had a problem, he or she could talk to Pastor or Sister Thomas and be sure to receive help without judgment. This made them both very approachable. In Jules's case they were often more approachable than her own parents.

"What are you doing here this early?" she asked, as he sat down in the pew beside her.

"Well, sometimes I like to come in early before the service and sit in my office a bit. Gives me time to think about my message and hear something special God might want me to say."

Jules nodded.

"What about you?"

She shrugged. "Sort of the same thing I guess. Sometimes this feels like the only place I can really talk to God and feel Him listening."

Pastor Thomas nodded in silent understanding.

"A lot of things on your mind?"

Like you wouldn't believe. "Yeah," Jules said.

"Hmm."

Jules knew he wouldn't press her to say any more than she felt comfortable sharing, and that was fine with her. Some things needed to stay just between her and God. But there were some things she did want to ask about.

"Pastor, how do you know God's will for your life?"

"Well, a lot of that is in His word," Pastor Thomas began. "And the more you walk with Him, the more He speaks to your heart and shows you the direction to go."

Jules wasn't quite satisfied.

"But how do you know?" she persisted. "What if it doesn't feel right?"

Pastor Thomas chuckled. "Well, Jules, I think that's the case for most of us at first."

Jules looked up at Pastor Thomas in confusion.

"Just look at some of the people in the Bible. Jonah, Moses, even some of the disciples. They all were hesitant about following God's direction in their lives. Some of them didn't even like what God was asking them to do and tried to escape it.

"But going outside of God's will never works for anyone. We only end up with heartache and pain. But when we follow Him we are assured of a successful ending."

"I don't know," Jules said, thinking about her situation with her mother. "Sometimes you try to do everything you know to be right but things still seem to be going wrong."

"No one said it would be easy," Pastor Thomas continued, placing a reassuring hand on Jules's shoulder. "But that's where faith comes in, Jules. We have to trust Him though we can't see. Trust that He knows what's best for us.

"And when you have doubts, you take them all to Him," Pastor Thomas said.

Taking her hand into his, Pastor Thomas looked at

Jules with kind eyes that reminded her of what she thought a true father's eyes should look like.

"If you really want to follow God's will, Jules, He will lead you right to where He wants you to be," Pastor Thomas said earnestly. "And you can guarantee that, wherever He leads you, something beautiful will be waiting."

Something beautiful.

Jules liked the sound of that. She could use something beautiful in her life. She thought of Germaine.

Maybe she was closer to it than she thought.

Now if only God would do something about her mother.

"Okay, girl, spill it. I want all the details."

"I don't know what you're talking about," Jules said, trying to ignore the inquiring looks Maxine and Tanya were shooting her.

She knew she would have to explain exactly what was going on with her and Germaine eventually, but she was trying to delay the inevitable for as long as possible. In fact she had spent all morning dodging them at church. But as soon as the service was over, they had accosted her.

At least they had the decency to wait until Germaine left before they started the interrogation. Jules was still a bit surprised that he had even shown up. When she had invited him over the phone the night before, he had mentioned he might be busy. She knew he was pretty involved at his own church, and so she hadn't expected to see him. But when he slipped into the pew beside her at eleven o'clock, she hadn't been able to stop the smile that hijacked her face.

"We're talking about you and Mr. Hotness getting all chummy. Did you think we didn't see the two of you sitting together during the service?" Maxine asked.

"And I know you don't think we don't know about all the dates you guys have been on—even though you didn't tell us about it," Tanya said in a voice that hinted at feelings of betrayal.

"Geez, you guys wanna talk a little louder? I don't think everyone out here heard you," Jules hissed, looking around the emptying churchyard to see if indeed someone might have been eavesdropping.

"Girl, please, ain't nobody listening to you. All these people thinking 'bout now is their bellies," Maxine said.

"And stop trying to change the subject," Tanya added, as both she and Maxine followed Jules to the far side of the parking lot where Jules's car was parked.

Heavy gusts of wind coming up from nearby Lake Ontario whipped at their legs and made walking challenging, but they were so caught up in Jules's drama they barely noticed.

"All right," Jules said, placing her hands on her hips as she stood in front of her car door. "I know you heifers ain't gonna ease up. But can we at least wait until we get to my place?"

Jules's place was a one-bedroom unit on the sixth floor of a Scarborough apartment building. It looked a bit rough on the outside, but inside it was all cream walls and earth-toned furniture. On the walls were several Herbie Rose prints depicting scenes from Caribbean life. They were a tribute to Jules's own West Indian heritage, and they made her apartment feel a bit more like her grandmother's house in Jamaica, where she used to spend summers as a little girl.

As soon as Maxine stepped inside, she sank into Jules's cream-and-beige-patterned sofa and wrapped her arms around one of the chocolate-colored throw cushions. Instead of following suit, Tanya headed into the kitchen and began helping Jules take out the dishes that held their lunch.

"Okay. Let's have it," Maxine ordered.

"What do you want me to say?"

"How about starting with the first date," Tanya suggested.

"Wait, is that the lunch date or the night date?" Maxine asked, confused.

"No, that's the night date. Lunch wasn't really a date," Tanya clarified.

"You guys don't need me," Jules said with a half laugh. "You seem to already have all the details."

"Nah, we just have the facts. You have the details," Tanya said.

Jules looked back and forth between her two friends who were staring at her expectantly.

"Okay," Jules said, sighing as she wiped her wet hands on a dishcloth and leaned back against the kitchen counter. "It was . . . nice."

"Nice," Maxine repeated, wrinkling her nose disdainfully.

"Yes, it was nice," Jules said. She knew they wouldn't understand. "Come on. You know that every guy I've gone out with has always tried to impress me. Take me to some fancy restaurant and flash the Gold Card so I can see that he's about something. But with Germaine, it's different. He's not trying to be flashy, he's just being himself. It's . . . refreshing."

Jules told them about the night at Leroy's, describing how perfect the music, the food, and the entertainment had been. Though she tried to act casual, she couldn't help the smile that lit up her face at the memory, and Maxine and Tanya couldn't help but notice.

"He makes me think about things, you know," Jules said, trying to explain how she felt when she was with him. "Like where I am in my life, and if I'm where God really wants me to be. He makes me want to be more, you know?"

"Girl, this man got you turned inside out," Maxine said, with one eyebrow raised. "No wonder you can't get that silly look off your face."

"Whatever," Jules said, rolling her eyes. But she knew Maxine was right. She couldn't remember the last time she had felt this excited about someone.

Maxine and Tanya looked at each other and then at Jules, small smiles creeping onto their lips.

"I think this one's a keeper, Jules" Maxine said, raising one eyebrow knowingly. "Try not to mess it up."

"Yeah, Jules. I'm really happy for you," Tanya said sincerely.

Neither Maxine nor Jules missed the hint of sadness in Tanya's voice, and they watched wordlessly as Tanya busied herself taking out cutlery and setting the table.

Jules knew Tanya was hurting over 'Dre. Only this past week he had shown up at the office with what Maxine called his "flavor of the week." She was another of the many undiscovered artists who seemed so fond of 'Dre. Her name was Sunshine. They had all cringed every time someone had reason to say it.

"Okay, I've had enough of this," Maxine said. Jules and Tanya looked at the tiny woman curiously as she got up from the couch and put her hands on her hips. This usually meant Maxine was ready to start something, and that usually meant they all needed to watch out.

"We can't sit back anymore and watch 'Dre mess his life up with these chicken-heads when there is a woman who is perfect for him right in front of his face."

"Who?" Tanya asked in confusion.

"You, you silly girl," Maxine said. She looked from Jules to Tanya, a mischievous sparkle in her eyes. "We're gonna set up 'Dre and Tanya."

"What!" Tanya exclaimed with an even mixture of fear and shock. "No!"

"Yes!" Maxine insisted. "And if this is going to work we're gonna need your cooperation, so don't start fighting me now."

"Maxine!" Tanya exclaimed.

"Tanya," Maxine said, imitating her friend's tone. "I love you, but, girl, you're either going to get with 'Dre or get over 'Dre. The two of you have been friends for more than five years, and if I have to go through one more year of you pining after him, I'm gonna kill one or both of you." Maxine took Tanya's face between her hands. "You are a kind, brilliant, beautiful woman, with a good head on your shoulders, and more booty than I've ever seen on a white girl."

Jules laughed out loud.

"Maxine is right, Tanya," Jules said. "And trust me when I tell you, you've been better to 'Dre than a lot of those other girls have been."

"I appreciate what you guys are saying, but I still think this is a bad idea," Tanya protested.

But it was too late. Maxine had already made up her mind. As she paced the living room thoughtfully, Jules could already see the wheels turning in her friend's head.

"All we have to do is get him to see that Tanya is perfect for him," she murmured. "A couple orchestrated 'moments,' and a few planted suggestions here and there should do the trick."

"You know, that might just work," Jules said.

"Jules! I can't believe you're encouraging her," Tanya exclaimed.

"We should get Truuth to help," Jules said, ignoring Tanya. "But what about Sunbeam; don't you think she will be a problem?"

"Her name is Sunshine," Tanya corrected.

"No, she's not an issue," Maxine said dismissively. "Those wannabes always find a way to sabotage themselves. Remember Rochelle?"

"Oh, yeah," Jules said, laughing as she remembered the last girl 'Dre had been dating. Jules didn't know all the details because 'Dre refused to talk about it. But what she did know was that that homegirl had somehow managed to find her way into 'Dre's bed, buck naked. Needless to say things had not gone as she had planned. When would these women learn that not every man was motivated solely by his lower region?

"Maxine, Jules, you can't do this," Tanya said in weak desperation.

"It's already been done, sweetie," Maxine said. "I know you two are good for each other, and it's time you both stopped dancing around the issue."

"Come on, Tanya, it won't be that bad," Jules said, throwing an arm around her distraught friend's shoulder. "Worst case scenario, you'll find out how he really feels about you, and you'll get some closure."

"He won't even know what's happening," Maxine added.

"How can you be sure of that?" Tanya groaned.

"Girl, please, it's 'Dre," Jules said.

Tanya sighed heavily, and Jules instantly knew she and Maxine had won.

"All right," Tanya conceded.

"Yes!" Maxine exclaimed.

Out of the corner of her eye, Jules saw Tanya shake her head as she watched her friends dance around the kitchen.

Tanya had no idea what she was getting herself into.

Chapter 6

"**S**orry for being late, guys," Jules said, as she stepped through the door of the office that was home to Triad Entertainment. "My car wouldn't start, and I had to call Germaine to come pick me up."

As if on cue, Germaine stepped in behind her and closed the door quickly to keep out the cold air.

"It's raining like crazy out there," he said, shrugging out of his jacket and hanging it up near the door.

"I know. I hope this is not how it's going to look for the rest of the summer," Tanya said.

"Well, with Toronto you can never really tell," Germaine replied.

It was the end of June, but they had already had heat waves, a cold snap, and torrential rain. Predicting what would come next was impossible, which wasn't great considering the summer was Triad's busy season. All they could do was hope for the best, but plan for the worst.

"So have you guys been waiting long?" Jules asked, looking back and forth between 'Dre and Tanya, who were the only ones sitting in the main room. She raised an eyebrow questioningly at Tanya.

"Not too long," Tanya said, giving Jules a look that said "don't start."

Jules rolled her eyes and took a seat on the couch beside Tanya. She didn't care what 'Dre said about not dating white girls—Tanya was different. And Jules was sure that if Tanya played her cards right she could have 'Dre in the palm of her hand.

She and Maxine agreed that Tanya should start dropping a few hints of her own when she was around 'Dre, just to get the ball rolling. Tanya, however, refused to get on board.

"Okay, so I guess now that everyone's here, we can get started," 'Dre said, looking up from his laptop. Once everyone was settled, and Tanya had said a prayer to start the meeting, 'Dre put the main item for discussion on the table.

"So you guys know we want to put out Truuth's debut album early this fall. We already have been doing a few appearances around town, but we need a major publicity campaign to really push this.

"Jules, I know you and Maxine have been working on a media plan for the album release," 'Dre said, looking across at Jules. "Please don't tell me I am going to have to sell a kidney to pay for it."

"No, 'Dre," Jules said, laughing. "That won't be necessary. What we're thinking of doing is using mainstream media as well as viral marketing to promote Truuth's album. You're gonna have to shell out some dollars for advertising space for the media part, but the viral marketing shouldn't cost us much. And of course we're gonna use the Sound Lounge as our launching point for Truuth's merchandise—hence the reason Germaine is here."

"Do you really think the Sound Lounge is big enough to be an effective launch point for Truuth?" 'Dre asked. "No offense, Germaine."

"None taken," Germaine said, with a quiet look of amusement.

"Actually, 'Dre," Tanya began. "Since Sam the Record Man closed a couple years ago, the Sound Lounge has been one of the more popular record stores in the city. You know as well as I do that there aren't that many left anyway, and those that do exist are not as hot as they used to be."

"And keep in mind that the package we are looking at includes in-store promotion as well as after-hours promotion through the Sound Lounge's nighttime entertainment," Jules added.

"Plus, thanks to Jules, we get the girlfriend rate," Tanya said, grinning.

"Hey, it's not that cheap," Jules said dryly.

"Come on, Jules, you know it's a good deal," Germaine said from the love seat where he was sitting. "If you pitched that package to HMV or one of those other record stores, you'd be paying a lot of something for a little bit of nothing."

"He's right," Jules said, refusing to look at Germaine, who she knew was smirking at her.

"Though most of the promotion will go through the Sound Lounge, the album and some promotional material are still going to be at HMV and other small retailers," Tanya said, trying to appease 'Dre.

The rest of them were usually pretty realistic about what could be done with Triad's small budget. However, it was always Tanya who had to reel in some of 'Dre's larger than life ideas. But even though their projects rarely went as large scale as 'Dre wanted, his vision for the business always helped make them work harder.

"All right, we'll go with it for now," 'Dre conceded. "Any figures for me so far?"

"Better," said Jules, well prepared for 'Dre's usual skepticism. "I have the entire media plan, including our expected budget," she said, passing a slim folder to 'Dre. "Let me just warn you, from now on, we're basically going to be pushing Truuth and his music all across the city," she said. "Big venues, small venues, churches, charity functions, everywhere they need a voice to sing, he's gonna be there for the next couple months while the album is coming out. People have to know his name and his voice if they are gonna buy his music."

'Dre nodded as he flipped through the plan. "Okay, looks good. We can start with this."

Tanya and Jules looked at each other. They knew what that meant—'Dre would be making changes along the way based on the bright ideas he came up with in the middle of the night.

Jules couldn't count the number of times 'Dre had called an emergency meeting at eight o'clock on a Saturday evening because of a new vision he got for their project during the service that day. It usually meant they would have to spend hours revamping whatever plans they had, and when Jules eventually got fed up and left, as she always did, Tanya was the one who had to bring 'Dre back in focus. There would be no working with 'Dre for Jules or Maxine, if it wasn't for the middle ground that was Tanya.

"So how long before the album is actually ready?" Germaine asked.

'Dre looked thoughtful for a moment. "Technically, it's already done, but Easy and Truuth are still doing some final editing on some tracks, and they're thinking of maybe adding a bonus track. Everything should be wrapped up for sure in about two weeks."

"So can I get some more definite information about the album? Like, how many tracks, the next single, and who you all collaborated with for it?" Jules asked. "I know for some reason you all were trying to keep everything hush-hush, but it's kinda hard for me to attract fresh media coverage and put together a decent press kit without those tidbits."

"You're right," 'Dre admitted, popping up from his chair. "Let me get Easy, and he can get us all up-to-date on what's happening."

Once 'Dre had disappeared from the room, Jules turned to Tanya.

"Have you talked to him?" she whispered to her friend.

"No, of course not," Tanya whispered back. She glanced nervously over at Germaine who was skimming the newspaper.

"Don't worry, I already told him everything," Jules whispered, reading Tanya's mind.

"You what!" Tanya hissed. "So what, now you're telling everybody?"

"Not everyone, but he might be able to help," Jules said. "We're going to need all the help we can get, especially since you refuse to play ball."

"Honestly, Jules, what do you expect me to say?" Tanya whispered. "Hey, 'Dre, I've had a crush on you for years. Let's go out and ruin our perfect friendship?"

"Don't be silly," Jules chided. "You can leave out the ruin-our-friendship part."

Tanya groaned in frustration, just as 'Dre and Easy walked into the room.

"Easy!" Jules exclaimed, beaming brightly at her friend. "Haven't seen you in a while."

Of their small Triad team, Easy was the only one who didn't go to church with them, and since he was often working in the studio with Truuth or some of the other Triad artists, Jules didn't see him that often. She always went out of her way, however, to make time for him. Outside of Maxine and Tanya, he was one of her closest friends.

"Hey, what's up, baby girl," Easy said casually, as he gave Jules a quick peck on the cheek, and rested on the arm of the chair beside her.

He nodded to Tanya, and then for the first time seemed to notice Germaine, who was sitting on the other side of the room watching them carefully. The light expression that had rested on his face all evening had been replaced by a look of unease that Jules couldn't quite read.

"Easy, this is Germaine, Truuth's cousin; Germaine this is Easy, Truuth's producer," Jules said, looking back and forth between the two of them as she made the introductions.

If Germaine looked guarded, Easy looked downright hostile as he appraised Germaine. She had the distinct feeling that this was not the first time they had met.

The two men stared each other down for some time before 'Dre broke the silence.

"Yeah, Easy, we all wanted some more information about the album," 'Dre said, clearly unaware of any tension in the room. "You know, so Jules can have something for her promotional stuff."

Usually Jules would have been annoyed at 'Dre's clear misunderstanding of the PR work she did for Tru-uth, but she was too busy watching the ongoing exchange between Easy and Germaine. She glanced back at Tanya to see if she knew what was going on, but the girl just shrugged, showing that she was just as confused.

Easy stuck a toothpick in the corner of his mouth, and kept his eyes fixed on Germaine for a moment longer before answering.

"Yeah. It's got fifteen tracks, including the two singles and one bonus track. We're thinking of leaking another single in the next two weeks to generate some buzz before the album drops, but I can meet with Jules and give her the information later."

From the way Easy was looking at Germaine, it was clear that what he really meant was, he would not be discussing anymore album information in front of him.

From across the room, Jules could see the tightness in Germaine's jaw. Despite his obvious displeasure, he remained completely calm, barely moving a muscle. His demeanor reminded Jules of the quiet before a storm. In fact, as she watched him watch Easy, she realized that beneath his refined exterior was something hard and dangerous that was carefully being kept in check.

With Easy and Germaine not talking, and Jules too distracted to ask any relevant questions, the meeting soon came to an end. As soon as Tanya said the "amen" for the closing prayer, Easy disappeared to the studio, and Germaine went outside to the car.

"What was that about?" Jules asked, as she watched both men hastily exit the room.

"They're both your boys," Tanya said. "You tell me."

"Well, they might be my boys, but neither of them ever tell me anything," Jules said.

She gathered her purse and coat and headed for the door.

"Honey, I'm gonna go before Germaine leaves me," Jules said. "Looks like he's in a mood."

"Okay, love," Tanya said, giving Jules a quick hug. "I'll call you later."

"Talk to him," Jules threw over her shoulder as Tanya closed the door. She hoped her friend was listening.

"Okay, so are you gonna tell me what that was about?" Jules asked fifteen minutes later.

They were halfway back to Jules's apartment, and Germaine still hadn't said a word about the earlier exchange between him and Easy, although he was much quieter than usual. What's more, he had turned on the car radio, and was all but ignoring Jules.

"What are you talking about?" he asked, his eyes fixed on the road.

"Um, you and Easy, and whatever it is that's going on with you two."

Jules waited, but still no answer. She realized that she was going to have to pull it out of him.

"Where do you know him from?" she asked.

Germaine shrugged. "I've seen him around."

"Around where? I know Easy. He hangs out in some questionable places," Jules said with a mix of skepticism and suspicion.

"We're in the same business, Jules. We're around a lot of the same labels and distributors at industry events," he said, as he exited the highway.

Jules narrowed her eyes at him.

"So what's your problem with him then?"

"I don't have a problem with him, Jules," Germaine said. But the tightness in his jaw told a different story.

"So why were you guys looking at each other like that? I thought I might have to jump between the two of you at any minute."

"I don't know, Jules, why don't you ask him? You two look pretty close."

Jules didn't miss the suggestion in his tone, or the vein that was jumping at his temple. She felt her eyebrows shoot up in surprise. She half turned in her seat to glare at him. "Is there something specific you want to ask me, Germaine?" She didn't like what he was implying.

Germaine sighed heavily. "Baby, it's been a long day. I really don't want to fight with you."

The tiredness in his voice hit a chord in Jules, and just as quickly as it came, her anger melted away.

She looked at him for a moment before sighing herself and falling back in her seat. She couldn't shake the niggling feeling that something was off with him. She couldn't recall him ever clamming up like this about anything before. He was always less of a talker than she was, and that was okay most of the time. But at that moment it felt like he was intentionally shutting her out, and he wouldn't even tell her why.

Lord, don't I have enough people in my life who have problems communicating? Mom, Dad, and now Germaine? I don't know if I can deal with this. Tell me if I'm wasting my time.

Just as she was about to drift deeper into her own thoughts, she felt Germaine take her hand and thread his fingers through hers. He pressed the back of her hand against his lips the same way he had the night at Leroy's.

"Look," he began quietly. "I know you want me to be more . . ."

"Open?" Jules asked, supplying the word he was obviously searching for.

"Yes," Germaine answered. "But that's hard for me. I'm used to doing things by myself. I don't usually have to answer to anyone, you know?"

"Babe, I don't want you to feel like you have to answer to me. I just want you to let me in sometimes. You can trust me," she said gently.

"I know," he said. "It's just . . . there's a lot of things. . . . It's going to take some time for me."

He pulled up to the front of her building and shut off the engine. Still holding her hand, he turned to look at her.

"Just bear with me, okay?"

Jules met his eyes and felt her resolve breaking. She didn't know if it was the dimness of the evening, or the quiet urgency in his voice, but something was playing tricks with her emotions.

"Okay," she conceded with a sigh. She would cut him a break now, but it wasn't over. There was something going on with Germaine, and she needed to find out what it was.

Chapter 7

"What you doing with that dude?"

Jules looked up from her laptop at Easy. She had come into the office to do some work on the campaign because she felt she would be able to focus more. She didn't particularly enjoy working on Sundays, but after last Tuesday's meeting she realized that she had a lot of work to do. With Truuth's album launch coming up in the not-too-distant future, in less than three months, she needed to keep on top of things.

She hadn't even known that Easy had been working in the soundproof studio downstairs until he appeared in front of her, in the mini-conference room.

"What dude?"

"You know who I'm talking about, baby girl."

"Germaine? What's wrong with him?"

"What's right with him?" Easy asked. "I don't want you messing with no corny brothas."

Jules knew Easy was a little rough around the edges, which was why she let him get away with a lot of things—like the way he was talking to her. Growing up in a tough community where everyone knew your mother had abandoned you was no picnic. Even though his grandmother had done her best to take care of him, Easy had spent most of his teen years defending himself from the chides of others. And when he couldn't manage that on his own, he had gotten mixed up with local gangs, from which he had barely escaped alive. Needless to say, the softer side of his personality had been sacrificed during the experience. But even now when he seemed a bit too aggressive for Jules's liking, she knew it was only because he cared about her.

From the instant Jules and Easy had first met, they had just clicked. In fact, if he hadn't been so raw and she hadn't been what he called a "good girl," they might have gotten together. But now as she watched his mouth curl in scorn at the mention of Germaine, she began to wonder if his overprotectiveness was not just a cover for some other feeling.

"What's your deal with Germaine? He's a nice guy."

"He ain't right," Easy said, shaking his head.

"Why?"

Jules watched Easy clench and unclench his jaw. She could tell he wanted to say something but was holding back. She looked at him and tried to meet his eyes, but he wouldn't let her. She remembered her concerns from a couple days earlier and decided that it was a good time to find out from Easy what was really going on.

"What do you know about him?" Jules asked.

Easy shrugged. "Some things I've seen make me wonder about him."

"Wonder how?" Jules asked. "Did you see him with another woman? Does he have kids? Was he on *America's Most Wanted*?"

Her tone was light, but she was only half joking.

With the brothers she had encountered, anything was possible. Easy chuckled a little and shook his head.

"Talk to me, Easy," she said softly, her eyes searching his face. Instead he took her hands in his and looked down at them.

"Just be careful, baby girl," he said quietly, finally meeting her eyes. "I don't want you to get hurt."

Nervousness flitted through her chest, and Jules shifted uncomfortably in her chair as she realized how serious he was. She considered pressing him further about what he meant, but she suspected she wouldn't get anything out of him.

"Well, how is that gonna happen if you're breathing down my neck all the time," Jules said, in mock annoyance.

After a moment, Easy cracked a small smile.

"All right, baby girl, I hear you. I know it's your life; you ain't gotta say the words."

Jules laughed. "I know it's only 'cause you love me," she said, pulling him down into the chair beside her and hugging him. "So where have you been anyway? I've barely seen you around these past couple months."

"Been keeping it on the down low with my Grams. She's been sweatin' me about staying off the streets."

Easy lived with his grandmother in Regent Park—one of the less stellar parts of the city. Jules couldn't understand why he still lived there even though he could very well afford to be somewhere else. She thought sometimes, though, that he felt responsible for the younger guys he grew up with who still lived there. He probably thought leaving Regent Park would be like abandoning them.

"You know, you ought to move out of that mess," Jules said in a slightly scolding tone.

"Geez, now you starting to sound like her," Easy said. "Every day she be on that same trip, talking 'bout I'm gonna get myself killed on them streets."

Jules could understand his grandmother's concern. In the last month alone there had been three separate gang related shoot-outs in the area that had left several people in the hospital and two people dead.

"You know she's right though, Easy. Every day I read something worse about that area in the news. I wish both of you would get on up out of there."

"That's the thing, baby girl. She don't wanna go nowhere—she just wants me to go. She says she's too old to be moving into some new neighborhood. So I was like, why you think you gonna be safe here if I'm not? She says God will take care of her."

"I thought you didn't buy into all that God stuff," Jules said, using a phrase Easy had repeated to her many times before when she tried to get him to come to church with her.

"I still don't know about none of that," Easy said. "What I do know though is that one of them nights that she was extra heavy on me about staying off the road, was the same night them boys got shot at on the corner."

"Well, you know your grandmamma is crazy close to her Lord. I wouldn't be surprised if He's been talking to her directly."

Easy rolled Jules's pen between his palms and stared pensively into the distance. She could tell that there was something bothering him—and it was more than his usual anger about his mother leaving. In fact, of late it seemed like Easy had more than his normal share of demons tormenting him.

He looked down at his hands and shook his head sadly.

"Them boys ain't got nobody else but me, Jules," he said, referring to the few young men he kept an eye on in the neighborhood.

"Everybody else done walked out on them. I know what that feels like. I couldn't do that to them."

"But if you're lying dead in a gutter, you're not much use to them there either, now are you?" Jules said. "You can't take care of you, Easy. You need to let go and let God take care of you completely."

Easy chuckled. "You don't quit, do you, baby girl?"

He stood up and kissed Jules on the forehead before heading for the door.

"Don't worry 'bout me. I'll be fine. You just remember what I said 'bout that dude."

"Easy . . ."

"All I'm saying is be careful," Easy threw back, before disappearing through the door.

As Jules sat staring at the doorway through which Easy had just left, she silently wished that Easy would worry about his own self even half as much as he worried about her.

It was about 1 p.m. when Jules stepped through the doors of the Sound Lounge. She scanned the place quickly in search of Germaine. Instead she saw a heavy crowd characteristic of fifty percent Fridays—the one Friday in the month when the Sound Lounge sold all of their CDs at 50 percent off. It was a great marketing strategy, and an excellent way to clear stock before the new releases hit the shelves the following Tuesday.

Undeterred by the crowd, Jules weaved her way to

the checkout counter, where she found a skinny cocoa-colored teenager working the register.

"Hey, Tina, is Germaine here?"

"Yeah, Jules," Tina said, not taking her eyes off the CDs she was cashing out. "I think he's in the back."

"Thanks."

Shuffling through the thinning crowd toward the back, Jules couldn't stop the tingle that ran up her spine. She was glad that Germaine was here. She had actually taken a chance, showing up without calling first. But she had wanted to surprise him and take *him* out to lunch for a change.

The sound of muffled voices drifted toward her as she continued down the narrow corridor and followed the bend to the back where Germaine's office was located. As she got closer, she noticed that the door was slightly ajar, and that there were two other men inside the office with Germaine. Their backs were to her, so she couldn't see who they were, but from the expression on Germaine's face, Jules could tell he wasn't too happy to see them.

Jules slowed her steps as she wondered whether she should interrupt and let him know she was there, or just wait until he was done. She personally hated when people marched into her office unannounced. But when it came to Germaine, she didn't consider herself "people," and in any case, his door was open. Maybe she should let him know that she was there.

Before she had a chance to make a move, Germaine spotted her hesitating in the hallway. Jules watched as a mixture of shock and unease framed Germaine's features. Before she could say a word, or his visitors could see her, he swiftly stepped outside the office, pulling the door securely closed behind him.

"What are you doing here, Jules?" he asked in a tone that betrayed his discomfort and annoyance.

Jules stepped back and looked at Germaine in confusion. He had never spoken to her like that. Or looked at her like that. In fact, everything about Germaine's behavior right then was foreign to her.

"I . . . I thought I would surprise you by taking you out to lunch," Jules stammered, still recovering from his coldness.

"Now's not a good time. I'm kinda in the middle of something," he said. Jules didn't miss the slight edge in his voice, or the way his eyes kept darting back and forth between her and the closed door. It was almost as if he expected it to burst open any minute.

"I can see that," Jules said, unable to hide her own annoyance. "I'll just wait out front until you're done."

Germaine shook his head.

"Today's not a good day, Jules."

His hand was on the handle of door, and his fingers were tapping the knob in a quick uneven rhythm.

Jules narrowed her eyes as she watched him carefully. There was an ominous feeling stirring inside her gut that she could not ignore. Something was off about Germaine. Everything from his twitching arm, to the way he kept glancing back toward the room, to the way his eyes didn't quite meet hers, told her that something was up. And that something had to do with the two men who were standing in his office.

Only a couple moments passed as she stood there watching him, but the nervous air Germaine was exuding made it seem like hours.

"What's going on, Germaine?" Jules finally asked.

There was that vein in his temple again.

"Look, Jules, I can't talk about this right now. But

you probably should go. I'll catch up with you later, okay?"

"But Germaine—"

"Jules, I don't want you here now," Germaine snapped. "Just go, okay?"

Jules opened and closed her mouth several times, but nothing came out. She was dumbfounded at Germaine's behavior.

Her eyes searched his for some recognition of the man that she knew. Instead the detached eyes of a stranger stared back at her.

After a few uncomfortable moments, Germaine seemed to accept Jules's silence as consent. With one last glance, he cracked open his office door, slipped inside, and closed it with a quiet but firm thud.

Jules stood in the empty hallway staring at the door for almost a full minute before it registered to her that he had walked out on her. Slowly her shock evaporated, giving way to feelings of irritation. Turning sharply on her heel, she made her way swiftly back out of the store the way she had entered.

Jules spent the rest of the day in a foul mood. Back at the office she snapped at Michelle twice and slammed the door so hard once that she heard the walls rattle. It was good thing her boss, Penny, was not in the office, as Jules surely would have had some explaining to do.

It didn't help that her in-box kept getting flooded by e-mail complaints from nurses. Their main issue seemed to be the security at the hospital, or lack thereof. By the time Jules had received her eighty-sixth e-mail, she decided to find out exactly what was going on.

"Ward Five nursing station."

"Hello, can I speak to Nurse Simpson, please?"

"One moment, please."

Jules watched two more e-mails come into her in-box as she waited for Maxine to come on the line.

"Nurse Simpson speaking."

"Maxine, it's me."

"Hey, Jules, what's up?"

"What's with all these nurses spamming my in-box with e-mail complaints? Did I just become the hospital president and no one told me about it?" Jules asked, unable to keep the annoyance from her voice. She had just received an alert that her in-box was approaching the storage limit.

"Uh, no problem, Jules. You can borrow my car. Just meet me in the parking lot in five minutes, and I'll bring you the keys," Maxine said.

"You can't talk, huh," Jules said, understanding Maxine's code. Something was definitely going on.

"Yeah, I'm on the first level. I'll meet you there in five minutes."

"Okay."

Jules hung up the phone and waited the five minutes it took Maxine to find a secluded spot and call Jules back from her cell.

"Okay, so what's the deal, Max?" Jules asked when she picked up her phone.

"Some of the nurses in the union have organized an e-mail campaign to complain about the cuts in security. We're all supposed to e-mail the public relations director about it today between noon and five o'clock," Maxine said.

"But why the public relations director? Why not the hospital president?"

"Because everyone knows the president won't make a move without that mouthpiece giving the okay," Maxine said dryly. "And she hasn't even come down to the wards since her first couple of weeks. The e-mail thing was the only way we could think of to reach her."

Jules sighed. She had mentioned to Penny before that it was important for her to walk around the hospital and get to know the staff. That's how you learned who had the real power in the hospital. It was also the only way she could keep abreast of what was going on and get a handle on things before they got out of control—as was happening now.

But every time Jules mentioned it, Penny would bat her heavily lined eyelids and say, "That's what I have you here for, Jules." And then Jules would leave, before an unchristian side of her said some things to Penny that would probably get Jules fired.

Jules sighed. "I had no idea the nurses were so upset about things."

"Yup," Maxine said. "And the union reps are really stirring things up. I hear this is just the beginning."

Jules groaned. Suddenly something occurred to her.

"Wait, if the plan was to e-mail the public relations director, why am I getting all these e-mails?" Jules asked.

But even before Maxine said it, Jules already knew the answer.

"I guess your boss forwarded them all to you."

Jules narrowed her eyes, even more upset than she had been when she first got into the office. After hanging up with Maxine she had even more time to think about it, and the more she did, the angrier she became.

Penny knew what was going on between the nurses and the hospital administration, so she was the best person to handle it. Jules would have been more than willing to help if Penny had asked for her input. But Penny had actively excluded Jules from the process, telling her that she had everything under control. That fact alone had amazed Jules. How could the head of public relations handle an issue if she wasn't even willing to communicate the issue with her own department team?

Jules sighed and picked up the phone to try to call Penny. This was turning out to be a really bad day.

By the time Jules got home she had gone from being angry to livid. After finally tracking down Penny at about 4:30, she had to sit on the phone for half an hour working out a strategy to address the nurses' protest, based on the limited information Penny was willing to share with her. Then she had spent the next hour and a half preparing a statement from the hospital to the nurses to be placed on the intranet, and drafting a letter from the president to the union reps inviting them to a meeting to discuss their grievances in the coming week.

During those hours Jules couldn't help but muse that if Penny had let her in on the issue from the beginning, then they would already have had a meeting with nursing representatives, and things would never have come to this. But Penny, in her all-knowing wisdom, had not told her a thing.

To add to all of this her earlier conversation with Germaine continued to run on a loop in the back of her mind.

Fortunately for her the next day was church, so she

had the chance to work out all her frustration on the preparation of Saturday's lunch.

She was just about to put the chicken in the oven with the cornbread when the knock on the door came. She didn't have to look through the peephole to know who it was. A couple hours after she had gotten back to work Germaine had started hitting up her cell phone.

Tossing her oven mitt on the counter, Jules went to the door.

"What?" Jules asked sharply after looking through the keyhole and confirming that it was indeed Germaine. She didn't move a hand to lift the safety latch from its place, as she had no intention of letting him in.

"Jules, we need to talk," Germaine said, his voice sounding muffled through the door.

"Oh, so now you wanna talk," Jules said. "Sorry, it's not really a good time. I'm kinda in the middle of something."

She heard Germaine groan.

"Okay. I know you're mad. But can we please have this conversation inside your apartment? I'm sure you don't want your neighbors listening in on your business."

Jules sucked her teeth loudly, annoyed that he knew her so well. Reluctantly she removed the safety latch and unlocked the door.

"I've been trying to call you all afternoon," he said, coming inside and closing the door. Jules was already in the kitchen placing the tray of chicken pieces in the oven and readjusting the temperature.

"Yeah, I noticed," she said without turning around or stopping. "Thanks to you, there's no more space left on my voice mail."

"Jules, I'm sorry."

"Whatever," Jules said, letting the oven door swing shut as she continued to move around the kitchen, her back still turned to him.

"Babe, it was a really bad day, and I was trying to work some things out—"

"I don't care," she said, finally turning to face him. "You don't get to talk to me like that."

As she watched him leaning against the entrance to her kitchen, looking like a lost little boy, her anger slowly began to evaporate. She could tell that he was really sorry. But even though she wanted nothing more than to put her arms around him and forgive him, a part of her was holding back.

"Germaine, you can't take out your bad days on me like that," Jules said softly but firmly. "I was trying to do something nice for you, because you're always doing nice things for me, and you made me feel like dirt."

Germaine nodded silently in agreement.

"You're right. I shouldn't have taken it out on you. Baby, I'm sorry," he said pulling her close to him and burying his face in her neck.

All the remaining anger drained away from Jules as she wrapped her arms around his tall, lean frame.

"Apology accepted," she said, sighing. She hated that she could not stay angry at him.

"So who were those guys in your office anyway?" she asked, once the embrace was over.

"Just some guys we do business with," Germaine said dismissively. His hands were still resting loosely around her waist, but his eyes were doing the wandering thing she had seen earlier. The ominous feeling that had disappeared moments before was slowly making a comeback.

"Well, you didn't look too happy to see them," Jules said, trying to keep the suspicion out of her voice. "What kind of business do you have with them?"

"Jules," he began, almost apologetically, "I can't talk about it."

Jules's body grew stiff, and she tried to pull away from him, but he held her firmly in place.

"Jules, you can't get upset every time I don't tell you what you want to know," Germaine said in frustration. "There are just some things that I can't tell you yet."

Jules took a deep breath and decided to try a different approach.

"Look, Germaine, you don't owe me any explanations," Jules said firmly. "But your store is in business with my company, and I don't want it or Truuth being put at risk because of anything that's happening at the Sound Lounge."

Jules knew she was playing dirty by drawing the business card, and from the look in Germaine's eyes, he knew it too. But neither of them could deny that it was a legitimate concern.

"I understand that, and, Jules, you should already know I would never do anything to jeopardize that. Come on, Truuth is my family; I would never put him in any kind of danger.

"And as for you," he continued, looking directly into her eyes. "I know I don't have to tell you everything, but I want to. But I . . . I just need some more time. Please try to understand."

Jules looked at him long and hard. She saw the way his eyes pleaded with hers, and she knew that he meant what he said. But inside she wondered if his non-answers could continue to be enough for her.

"Okay," she answered quietly.

Germaine wrapped his arms around her again.

"Thank you," he whispered against her hair.

Jules returned the embrace and tried to push the whole thing to the back of her mind. But even as she did, she still couldn't shake the nagging thought that things were not as simple as they appeared to be.

Chapter 8

"I think Germaine is hiding something from me."

"What?" Tanya and Maxine asked in unison, as they stopped in the middle of Scarborough Town Centre to stare at her.

It was a Wednesday evening after work, and Jules had met Maxine and Tanya at the mall so Tanya and Maxine could do some shopping. Jules was on a budget this month, so the only thing she would be buying any time soon was groceries.

"I don't know," Jules said thoughtfully. "I just get this feeling that there's something going on he's not telling me about."

"Okay, where is this coming from?" Tanya asked, in confusion.

"Last week he went totally schizo on me when I showed up at the store unannounced."

"Girl, please," Maxine said, rolling her eyes and beginning to walk again. "Even I know better than to show up at Truuth's place unannounced. There ain't nothing a black man hate more than feeling like someone done snuck up on him."

"But it wasn't just that," Jules continued. "He had some guys in his office, and they looked . . . shady."

"They looked shady," Maxine deadpanned. "Well, since you put it that way, I guess we should call the police right now."

Jules rolled her eyes, ignoring her friend's sarcasm.

"What did he say when you asked him about it?" Tanya asked, tossing her long blond hair and switching her Coach shopping bag to her other arm. With all that she had spent, Jules imagined it must have been pretty heavy.

Jules couldn't imagine spending the way Tanya spent, even if she could afford to. There was something about dropping one thousand dollars on a handbag that didn't seem right to her. But Tanya had grown up with money, and so she was used to it. In fact, Jules was sure that if Tanya had to carry one of Jules's stylish, but less expensive purses, she would break out in hives.

"He just said they were guys he worked with and that it had been a bad day. He was having some problems at work, and it was nothing," Jules said, narrowing her eyes. "Then when I tried to find out more, he clammed up on me, talking about 'it's a business thing' and he can't talk about it. What does that mean?"

"It means that it's a business thing, and he can't talk about it," Maxine said.

Jules still wasn't convinced.

"Okay, well, answer me this," she said, turning to Tanya. "You're the business major. How is he keeping the Sound Lounge afloat? No way are record sales alone bringing in enough money to pay staff, and overheads, and run the night programs. They barely charge decent cover at the door."

Tanya laughed. "I don't know, Jules. Look at Triad. How are we managing to say afloat, paying for artist promotion, travel, staff, production, and everything else? It's the by-faith business model they don't teach you in school. I suspect the Sound Lounge is running on the same principle."

"Come on, do you really think Germaine is the kind of guy who would do something shady?" Maxine asked.

"I don't know. The whole thing just seems a bit strange," Jules insisted. "Maybe all this is a sign."

Tanya and Maxine glanced at each other.

"A sign of what?" Tanya asked cautiously.

"Maybe God's trying to tell me something about this guy."

"Pay up," Maxine said, outstretching her hand to Tanya.

Tanya grimaced and pulled a fifty dollar bill out of her purse and handed it to Maxine. Jules looked back and forth between the two of them in confusion.

"What's going on?"

"Maxine and I had a pool going on how long it would take you to sabotage this one," Tanya explained, looking sadly at her purse. "She said two months. I said five. I had faith in you, Jules. Couldn't you have held out a little longer?"

"Hold up," Jules said, placing her hand on her hip. "So both of you expected that Germaine and I wouldn't work out?"

"No, Jules," Maxine said, as if she was talking to one of her pediatric patients. "Both of us expected you to mess it up at some point or another. Sweetie, it's what you do."

"What?"

"Come on, Jules," Tanya said. "Every time you start dating a guy, you'll go out with him for a while and everything will be fine, wonderful even."

"But then one day out of the blue, you'll find something that's wrong with him," Maxine continued.

"Usually it's something small that you don't approve of," Tanya added.

"But no matter what it is, you'll pick at it and dwell on it until it becomes this big issue."

"And then you'll break up with him, and it will be over."

"Like I said," Maxine concluded. "It's what you do."

Jules stared open mouthed at her friends, who were ordering frozen yogurt from Yogen Fruz, as if they had not just psychoanalyzed her entire relationship history.

"You want anything, sweetie?" Maxine asked, glancing back at a dumbfounded Jules. "Yeah, you look like you could use a smoothie," she said, answering her own question. "Can I get a banana-strawberry smoothie, please?"

A few moments later, when they had found a table in the food court, Jules regained her ability to speak.

"Do I really do that? Do I really create issues out of nothing?" she asked in despair.

Maxine and Tanya nodded, looking at her sympathetically.

"Why do you think you've never had a boyfriend for more that eight months?" Maxine asked.

"You're always looking for flaws," Tanya said, licking a glob of yogurt from her spoon.

"Oh, no. I'm becoming my mother," Jules groaned, dropping her head on the table.

"It's okay, honey. Now that you know, you can do something about it," Maxine said.

"I guess," Jules said, as she stirred her smoothie with her straw. How had she not seen this before? How could she not have recognized her own destructive pattern of behavior? Jules took a sip from her smoothie thoughtfully. "I guess I just never wanted to settle, you know?"

"Yeah, but there's settling, and then there's accepting someone for who he is and giving him time to grow into the person he is going to be," Maxine said.

Jules took another sip as she thought about Maxine's words. One side of her brain knew Maxine was right. The other side still wasn't convinced.

"I don't know, Maxine. How do I know the difference between when there is a real issue and when I am just being psycho. What if God is trying to give me a heads up on a brother, but I mistake it for my own paranoia?"

"That's the other thing you do," Tanya said, sitting up suddenly.

"What?" Jules asked, now more confused than ever.

"You use God as an excuse to chicken out of things you're afraid of," Tanya said. "At the first sign of trouble you play the 'maybe it's a sign' card and pull out."

"I do not!"

"You do," Tanya and Maxine said in unison.

"You're right. I do," Jules said, as she slumped down in her chair. "It's just that . . . you guys know that I have such a bad history with guys. Remember Omar?"

Yes, they all remembered Omar, the guy Jules had dated for six months before she learned that he had not one, but two baby mammas that he was not supporting. In fact, if one of them hadn't cornered Jules in a Loblaws supermarket parking lot one Sunday afternoon, she might have never found out about it at all. Omar certainly had no intention of telling her.

Jules shuddered. Just the memory of the whole situation made her skin crawl. She had vowed never to let anything like that happen to her again.

Tanya was hunched over the table laughing as Maxine recounted the parking lot incident.

"Oh, Jules, where do you find these guys?" Tanya asked.

"In church, T," Jules said, her eyes wide.

"Look, I can definitely see where you are coming from with your perfection issues," Maxine said. "But don't use God as a crutch for your cowardice. Your relationship with God ain't always peachy, and He's the almighty. Why do you think your relationships would be perfect when you're dealing with simple, old, flesh and blood men?

"God wants to guide you in your relationships, but you can't keep running off every man He sends to you."

"Yeah, girl," Tanya said, rubbing Jules's arm encouragingly. "If you're not sure about Germaine, then maybe you should talk to the Big Man. Pray about it. And trust me, He'll give you an answer so clear, you won't have any doubt it's from Him."

Later that night, as Jules prepared for bed, Tanya's words came floating back into her mind. She slipped to her knees by her bedside and poured her heart out.

"Lord, You know I depend on You for everything, and right now I really need a word from You. I really care about this man, but I'm not sure about him. There are a lot of things about him that I don't know—a lot of things he won't share. You know I want to trust him, but I don't want to make the same mistakes I have made before. Show me what to do, and direct me according to Your will. Speak to my heart as only You can, and fill me with Your peace. I ask all this in the name of Jesus. Amen."

As Jules climbed into bed, she felt a quiet peace flow through her. No matter what happened, she knew that God would work all things out for her good. He had promised that in His word, and Jules believed it. After all, He had never failed her yet.

Chapter 9

As the day when she was to see her mother came closer, Jules grew more and more anxious. She had been so preoccupied with the Germaine mystery that she had almost forgotten about the promise she had made to her mother a few weeks earlier to have dinner with her when Davis came to town. But when Momma Jackson called two weeks in advance and told her to clear her schedule for Sunday, July 18, Jules knew there was no way she could back out.

Since then it had been like counting down to a dentist appointment. In fact the more she thought about it, the more she dreaded it. At least the last time she had seen her mother, she'd had her aunt, Maxine, and seventeen members of the Kendalwood Women's Ministry Department there acting as a buffer. It had been the Women's Ministry brunch, one of several similar events that Momma Jackson insisted on holding at her house and guilting Jules into attending.

At those types of events Jules could manage her mother. As long as she continuously mingled with the guests, and didn't stay in one spot too long, she could usually avoid her mother's death ray. However, at smaller family gatherings, it was more difficult.

She remembered painfully this year's New Year's breakfast, which she had passed with her mother, Davis, Keisha, and her Aunt Sharon. Momma Jackson had spent the whole morning lecturing Jules on how she worked too hard—so hard that she couldn't make time to start a family of her own. At that moment she had paused to commend Keisha for finding a prize like her Davis. Then Momma Jackson had launched off into her soliloquy about how God never meant for women to be alone. And, in one of the rare occasions when she mentioned Papa Jackson, she cautioned Jules to be careful that she was not becoming like her father, who was too busy and too independent to be married to anyone.

Jules cringed at the memory. Only Momma Jackson could say the word "independent" like it was some fatal disease.

Before she knew what she was doing, she was on the phone calling Davis.

"You're coming, right?" Jules asked over the poor connection. Even though they were technically on the same land mass, Davis sounded a million miles away.

"Of course I'm coming," he said, laughing. "I'll be there on Thursday evening; quit worrying."

"Momma said you were coming on Friday."

"Yeah, I was, but I changed my mind and decided to come a day earlier."

"And you didn't tell Momma?" Jules asked, surprised.

"Nah, I want to spend some time with Keisha, and I know once I get to the house me and Key' won't have a moment alone."

Jules smirked. "Well, well, is that the precious son lying to his mother?"

"I'm not lying," Davis said. "I'm just leaving out some information, that's all."

"Yeah, well, don't let me hear nothing about you and Keisha shacking up in some hotel somewhere for the night," Jules warned. "You know Keisha's big mouth sister will find out and let me know."

Davis laughed. "No way, sis. I'm staying at a friend's. Keisha's crazy momma would kill me if I tried anything like that."

Jules laughed. It was true. Even though Keisha's family had pretty much adopted Davis, they were still by the book Christians, and they would tolerate no fooling around between Davis and their daughter. Davis still joked that though he and Keisha had been together for years, he wouldn't even risk kissing her in front of them, much more trying anything else. Jules could understand. With Momma Jackson, it was pretty much the same.

"Speaking of Keisha's big mouth sister," Davis said. "I hear you've been bouncing all around town with some guy. How come you didn't tell your little brother you found a dude who could put up with you?" Davis asked cheekily.

Jules rolled her eyes. She had known it wouldn't be long before someone leaked her relationship with Germaine to her family.

"It wasn't a big deal, we just started going out a little while ago," she said, giving Davis the Cliff Notes version of the Germaine-Jules story.

"Well, it sounds like you guys got pretty serious in that little while," Davis said. "And I know you didn't tell Momma, because she would have called up the whole world by now."

Jules groaned. "Of course I didn't tell Momma. I like this guy, remember?"

"Well, it's gonna be pretty hard to keep him a secret when you bring him to family dinner this weekend. Who are you going to introduce him as? Your really good friend that you're not dating?" Davis asked. Jules didn't have to see him to know he was smirking.

"I'm not going to introduce him at all," Jules said simply. "He's not coming."

"Come on, Jules, what's the big deal?"

"The big deal is that our mother will embarrass me to death and have him running for the hills."

"If he can put up with you, then he can handle Momma," Davis said.

"Davis, please," Jules said. "Ghandi couldn't handle Momma."

Davis laughed. "Okay, but Momma is going to be really mad when she finds out you've been dating this guy for months and didn't tell her—and that's assuming that she doesn't already know, because you know she knows everything."

Jules sighed. She had thought of that possibility. But that was a chance she was willing to take. She needed to sort out her own issues with her mother before she could bring someone else into the picture. Especially someone who she was really starting to care about.

"Look at it this way," Davis reasoned. "It will be an opportunity for you to see how cool this guy is under pressure. Besides, with him around, Momma will probably be on her best behavior."

Jules snorted. She highly doubted that.

"If nothing else, bring him so I can meet him," Davis cajoled.

"I don't know about that, Davis."

"Just think about it."

Fifteen minutes later when Jules hung up from talking to her brother she began to seriously consider the possibility of inviting Germaine to dinner on Sunday. Was it too soon? She didn't want him to read more into the request than there was. But at the same time, Davis was on to something: maybe having Germaine around would tone her mother down a bit.

Or maybe it would amp her up.

She had better not take that chance. No, Germaine definitely wouldn't be going to this one.

But on Sunday morning, with the stress of the evening's event taking a toll on her, Jules felt herself caving in.

"Hello?" Germaine mumbled, clearly still half asleep. It was 6 a.m., and she knew he was probably wondering who could be calling him at that hour on a Sunday morning.

"It's me, Jules."

"Hey, baby, what's up?" he asked, only slightly more alert.

"I need you," Jules said, working hard to keep calm despite the feeling of panic building in her gut.

"Huh?"

"Can you come with me? Later? To my mom's?" Jules asked. "She wants me to come for dinner. And I know it's last minute, and I really wasn't going to ask you, because I thought it was too soon for you to meet her, but I can't do my mom by myself. I mean I won't be completely by myself, my brother will be there, but he really doesn't count 'cause she likes him—"

"Jules, it's okay," Germaine said, stopping her in the midst of her ramble. Jules's poorly disguised anxiety had fully awoken him.

"Okay? Does that mean yes? You'll come?"

"Yes, I'll be there."

"Okay. You can pick me up at five," she said, hanging up the phone before he had a chance to protest.

Eleven hours later Germaine was knocking on Jules's apartment door. On the second knock, the door flew open and a restless Jules stood before him.

She looked absolutely gorgeous in wedges and a loose-fitting, yellow halter dress. However, it didn't take much for Germaine to realize that she was more than a little uncomfortable.

"Hey, you okay?" he asked, as he stepped inside.

"Yeah, sure, I'm fine." Jules tried to force a smile. He saw right through it.

"Come here," he murmured as he pulled her into an embrace. Jules wrapped her arms around him and buried her face in his shoulder.

"It's going to be fine," he said, rubbing her back soothingly. Jules sighed. If he knew what she did, he wouldn't be so sure.

"Let's go," Jules said.

"So there are some things you need to know," Jules continued once they were in the car and on the way to Whitby. "Here are the rules—"

Germaine laughed. "There are rules?"

Jules looked at him as if he had grown a second head. Was he serious?

"Of course there are rules," Jules said incredulously. "And you plan to come out of this evening alive, then you better follow them."

Germaine shook his head.

"Okay, so here goes. My mother will ask you a million questions. Attempt to answer all of them. If you don't, she'll think you're rude. Some of them will be very personal; don't be alarmed or offended. It's just her way. She will ask you what you do. At no point can you call the Lounge a nightclub, or a disco. No matter how you try to spin it, she will think you're working for the devil—"

"So what am I supposed to call it?" Germaine asked with a laugh as he switched lanes and got off the highway.

Jules bit her lip thoughtfully.

"Say it's a record store with a café, where you have small events sometimes."

"Café . . . Wow. I never heard it described like that before," Germaine said dryly. "What if she starts asking more questions about the type of events and artists we have there? What if she asks about the bar or if there's dancing—"

"No!" Jules exclaimed, her eyes wide open. "No talk of bars, or dancing. You know what, maybe you shouldn't talk about the Lounge at all. If she asks, you sell CDs, end of story."

Germaine let out a whistle. "Was your mother that strict growing up?"

"No, actually, she wasn't," Jules said. "That developed after my father left. I guess she felt that she had to be both mother and father to me and Davis to keep us in check. And somehow even though me and Davis are both grown, she still tries to micromanage our lives."

He turned the car down the street where Jules grew up.

"Is that why you avoid her?" he asked, glancing away from the road to look at her.

"I don't avoid her," Jules corrected. "I just prefer to have her in manageable doses, which is what happens when there are enough people around to dilute her intensity."

"Does Davis feel the same way?"

Jules laughed. "Oh, no. Davis is the golden child. He can do no wrong."

Germaine parked the car where Jules indicated and shut off the engine. He leaned across and kissed her gently.

"Everything's going to be fine," he reassured her.

"Thanks," Jules said, kissing him back before opening the car door. "By the way, you can't do that either."

Jules took a deep breath and looked up nervously at the two-story home she had grown up in as she waited for Germaine to lock the car. She had to admit, despite the interesting relationship she had with her mother, she had a lot of good memories of the past. She looked down at her watch and bit her lip.

"We're late," she murmured anxiously as she and Germaine walked up the curving stone pathway that led to the front door of Momma Jackson's blue and white, split level house.

"Baby, it's just five minutes after six," Germaine said, laughing lightly. "I'm sure you're mom won't even notice."

"You don't know my mom," Jules said, knocking firmly on the front door. "She'll notice."

The door swung open to reveal a tall, dark, built young man, who looked slightly younger than Jules, but bore a striking resemblance to her.

"Hey, Davis," Jules said, reaching up to hug her younger brother.

"Hey, Jewel," he replied, as he returned the embrace. Jules smiled at her brother's nickname for her. He had started calling her that when he was three and couldn't properly pronounce her name. It had stuck ever since.

"You're late," he said, raising his eyebrow at her knowingly.

"See, I told you," Jules said, looking back at Germaine accusingly. Instead of responding to her, Germaine stretched out a hand to introduce himself.

"Hi, I'm—"

"Germaine, the boyfriend," Davis said, shaking Germaine's hand. "Jules told me you weren't coming."

"Yes, well, you know Jules," Germaine said smirking. "She tends to change her mind a lot."

"Don't I know it," Davis said, laughing. "She didn't call you this morning, did she?"

It was Germaine's turn to laugh.

"I don't think I should answer that," he said chuckling, as he glanced over at Jules who was glaring at them both with her hands on her hips.

"Davis! Boy, I know I taught you better than to hold conversations with guests on my doorstep," a strong voice said from somewhere inside the house. "You think I want them nosy neighbors up in my business?"

"No, ma'am. I'll be right there," Davis said, his eyebrows arched in amusement. "You sure you want to come in? This is your last chance to back out," Davis teased.

Jules grabbed a hold of Germaine's wrist in case he gave the idea any consideration.

"He's not going anywhere," she said, pulling him inside.

They followed Davis into the main dining room where Keisha was helping bring dishes from the kitchen to the elegantly spread dining table.

"Jules!" Keisha exclaimed, taking off her oven mitts and hugging Jules tightly. "I'm so glad you're here!"

Jules knew that what Keisha meant was: *I'm so glad I don't have to be alone with Momma Jackson anymore.*

Momma Jackson loved Keisha to death, but sometimes it was too much love for Keisha to handle.

"Jules, sugar, is that you?" Momma Jackson called. Jules could hear her footsteps as she made her way toward the dining room.

"Baby girl, you late, as usual. Didn't I tell you six—" Momma Jackson stopped short when she saw her unexpected guest.

"Well, Jules, you didn't tell me you were bringing company. If you had I would have been on my best behavior," she said, laughing but not sounding the least bit ashamed to be caught being herself. "And who might you be?" she asked, smiling at Germaine.

"I'm Germaine," he said, flashing a wide smile as he reached out to take Momma Jackson's hand. "It's so good to finally meet you."

"The pleasure is all mine," Momma Jackson said, in a manner that Jules could only describe as an attempt at demureness. Davis snorted, and Jules rolled her eyes. Momma Jackson had never been demure a day in her life.

"Please don't mind my children," Momma Jackson said, throwing a warning glance at Davis and Jules. "Despite my best efforts they still have trouble acting right around company."

Germaine laughed. "Well, I don't think your efforts

have totally been in vain. Jules has been very well be-
haved on all the occasions we've been out," Germaine
said with a hint of mischief that only Jules caught. It
was her turn to give him a warning look.

"And how many times has that been?" Momma
Jackson asked, tilting her head to the side curiously.

"Momma, I know you must have spent all day on
dinner. Let me help you get the rest of it on the table
before it gets cold," Jules said, in an effort to divert her
mother's attention.

Jules's mother looked as if she might continue questioning Germaine, but seemed to think better of it.

"All right, sugar," Momma Jackson said, waving a
finger at Germaine teasingly. "Thanks to your girl here,
you're off the hook . . . for now."

Jules didn't miss the relief that crossed Germaine's
face as she steered Momma Jackson toward the
kitchen. From behind her she heard Davis try to lighten
the mood.

"Come on, man, let me give you a tour of the place,"
he said, clapping Germaine on the back and leading
him down the hall. Keisha tried to look busy fixing the
table settings, even though there was nothing to be
fixed. Jules knew she was just avoiding going back into
the kitchen. That meant Jules was on her own.

"Why didn't you tell me you were bringing that man
over here with you?" Momma Jackson asked once they
were back in the kitchen. "Better yet, why didn't you
tell me you had a man?"

"Because it wasn't that serious at the time," Jules
said, moving past her mother to her aunt, who was
dishing out steaming hot rice and peas into a large
porcelain bowl.

"Hey, Aunty Sharon," Jules said, wrapping her arms around the short woman's ample waist.

She loved her Aunt Sharon. Even though she looked unnervingly like Momma Jackson, she was the exact opposite of her younger sister. Where Momma Jackson was sharp and straightforward, Aunt Sharon was gentle and appeasing.

She had never been married; however, she had two children, both older than Jules, who lived in New York. Her youngest child had moved out not too long after Davis had gone to college, and since both she and Momma Jackson had no husbands, they figured they would keep each other company. Aunty Sharon had been living with Momma Jackson ever since.

"Hi, sugar. How you doing?" Aunt Sharon asked, kissing Jules on the cheek.

"I'm good. How are you?"

"Blessed and highly favored child, blessed and highly favored."

"Don't think you going to get away by sweet talking your aunt, Miss Jules. I want to hear about this boy of yours," Momma Jackson interrupted. "Tell me about him."

Jules sighed heavily.

"There's not much to tell."

"There's always something to tell," Momma Jackson said, as she sliced up the cornbread that was to go on the table with the rest of the dinner. "Where does he go to church? I know you didn't bring no heathen up in my house."

"He goes to Apple Creek," Jules said, shaking her head at her mother. She could never understand why Momma Jackson needed to use twenty words to ask a question that only required ten.

"So where did you meet him?"

Instead of answering her mother's question, Jules carried the bowl of rice and peas out of the kitchen to the table.

"Dinner's ready!" she called out quickly before her mother could follow her with another round of questioning.

Within moments the six of them were congregated in the dining area. Momma Jackson had spread a thick, beautiful wine-colored cloth over the table, with cream-colored napkins and plates. Her heavy silverware, which she had gotten as a wedding present, sparkled just as much as the six gleaming wine goblets positioned around the table. Momma Jackson always set her entire table, regardless of how many people she knew would be coming. She did it for the same reason she always cooked too much food. According to her, you never knew who might drop by and you should always be prepared. Nonetheless, Davis always teased Jules that Momma Jackson set the extra place in hope that Jules would bring home some guy to fill it. In this case, Momma Jackson's hope had been fulfilled.

The table dressings were remarkable on their own, but they dulled in comparison to the spread of food. Momma Jackson and Aunt Sharon had outdone themselves, with rice and peas, steamed vegetables, roasted chicken, curried mutton, potato salad, macaroni and cheese, coleslaw, sliced tomatoes, fried plantain, and cornbread. And Jules was almost sure that she had glimpsed cheesecake and a tray of fresh fruits in the fridge when she had been in the kitchen earlier.

"Wow, Momma, you went all out," Davis said, clearly impressed with the spread. Living away from home, he rarely got to experience food like this. And even though he knew how to cook, being spoiled by all the women in his life had made him less inclined to do so.

"Well, you know how your momma do," Momma Jackson said with a wide smile. "Sugar, you come sit over here by me," she said motioning to Germaine.

When everyone was settled around the table, she motioned for them to hold hands.

"Okay, let's say grace," Momma Jackson said. "Germaine, since you're new here, you can do the honors."

Davis and Jules looked at each other in surprise. Momma Jackson never let anyone but herself say the grace over their family dinners. She must really like Germaine.

"Let us pray," Germaine said, bowing his head. "Dear heavenly Father, thank You so much for this meal that You have provided for us. Thank You for blessing us with good food to eat even though there are those who are not as fortunate. Help us not to take this for granted, and to be grateful for this gift. Please bless the hands that prepared it, and even more so bless this time that we will spend with each other. All these things we ask in Your Son's name, amen."

"Amen," they all chorused in agreement.

"Well, then," Momma Jackson said, clearly satisfied with Germaine's blessing on the food. "Let's eat."

A quiet hum of gently clanking dishes and easy conversation surrounded the table as they ate. Germaine easily held Momma Jackson's attention, and she seemed to be delighted with most of what he was saying. Jules narrowed her eyes curiously at him. She wasn't surprised at how easily he fit into his mother's upper middle-class environment. From the beginning she had figured he was one of those guys who could go from street to suave in a second. She was surprised, however, at how easily he seemed to charm her mother. Momma Jackson was no pushover.

"So tell me, Germaine, how did you meet my Jules?"

Jules's head snapped up, and she looked worriedly across at Germaine. There was no way he could tell her mother that he met her at a club. Momma Jackson was one of those old-fashioned Christians who believed God's children shouldn't be anywhere where people might be dancing to music. So it wouldn't matter that Jules had been at the Sound Lounge for business, or that it wasn't your typical club. To Momma Jackson it was still the devil's playground.

Despite her best efforts Jules couldn't seem to catch Germaine's eye. She needn't have worried though, for Germaine had clearly sized up Momma Jackson and determined what would and wouldn't fly with her.

"Well, she's actually friends with my cousin, but I really met her several months ago when her company was doing some business with my store," Germaine said.

"Oh, is that so," Momma Jackson said, looking pleased and interested all at the same time. "Tell me about this store of yours."

Jules relaxed as she realized that Germaine didn't need any coaching from her. In fact, so far the evening had been going better than expected. They had made it all the way to the end of the main course without even a minor confrontation between Jules and her mother. Jules shot up a small prayer of thanks to God for that small mercy.

It seemed, however, that the minute she opened her eyes, everything began to fall apart.

It all started with the cheesecake.

"Now, sugar, I know you are not taking a slice of

that cheesecake," Momma Jackson said loudly. "That's going to go straight to your thighs, and you know you have a weight problem."

All eyes at the table turned to stare at Jules, and she prayed that the ground beneath her chair would open and swallow her up. If there was a better way for Momma Jackson to completely humiliate her, she didn't know what it was.

Jules couldn't understand where her mother came up with this stuff. It wasn't like Jules had ever been one of those girls who complained about her weight. She had been happy with her size eight figure for the past ten years she'd had it.

But just like always, Jules would never confront her mother. To do so would be to prolong the argument, which would somehow end up being more embarrassing for Jules than for Momma Jackson.

"I think I'll be fine, Mother," Jules said, stabbing at her slice of cheesecake with her fork. She did not have the nerve to look up at Germaine and see what she knew would be a look of pity. Maybe it was a bad idea for her to have invited him here after all.

"Oh, no," said Momma Jackson. "She's calling me 'mother.' That means she's mad at me. I can't ever get anything right with you, can I, Jules," Momma Jackson said, shaking her head. "I try to look out for you because I care, because I don't want you to end up fat like me, but you act like I'm trying to hurt you."

Jules chewed slowly and continued to cut her cheesecake into small bite-size pieces with her fork. Maybe if she stayed quiet, and acted like the outburst wasn't happening, it would go away. But the less Jules spoke, the more annoyed her mother seemed to get.

"You know, Jules, you're the only one in this family

who treats me like I'm stupid," Momma Jackson said. "Davis always takes my advice. He knows his momma is only looking out for him because she loves him. But you, you act like I'm the enemy."

From the corner of her eye Jules could see that Davis had assumed his normal position for when their mother started her tirades. His head was so deep in his plate that in a few moments his nose would be able to tell them how good the cheesecake really was. Jules knew that nothing short of divine intervention would get him to say a word in her defense.

In fact none of them ever stood up to Momma Jackson for her. Keisha somehow melted into the background, and Aunt Sharon, for all her kindness, believed that she was not family enough to get between her sister and her niece when they got started. So she just sat at the other end of the table, silently spooning cantaloupe slices onto her plate like nothing was happening.

When Jules finally gained the courage to look up at Germaine, she found his eyes watching her carefully. But there was no pity there, just curiosity. Jules was almost sure she knew what he was thinking: *Was all that Momma Jackson was saying true? And if not, why doesn't Jules stand up to her mother?*

Jules laughed inwardly. If only he knew.

"It's just like when I talk to you about work," Momma Jackson continued.

Jules resisted the urge to laugh at the predictability of her mother. She had wondered when they would get to that topic. No matter how the argument started, it somehow always managed to end up being about how Jules worked too hard.

"You kill yourself working all hours at that job of yours. So much that you can't even take some time off to spend with your momma," she complained. "And for what? I don't see you getting any richer. You still paying rent for that shoe-box apartment in Scarborough. If you had just stayed here then maybe you could have saved up enough to put down a mortgage on a house of your own by now. But no, you had to move, had to have it your way. I don't know which was more important to you, being closer to that job of yours or getting away from me."

Jules closed out her mother's voice and began to do that thing she did whenever her mother's words started hitting too close to her heart. She started making lists. Lists of things she needed to do, grocery lists, work activity lists, anything to take her focus away from her mother. Today it was a "things to do when I get home" list.

1. Check my bank account balance . . .
2. Pay my credit card bill online . . .
3. Sort the laundry so I can wash tomorrow . . .
4. Get out my clothes for work tomorrow . . .

She was so far away that she almost missed Germaine's comment to her mother.

"You know, Mrs. Jackson, Jules has actually been helping my cousin Truuth promote his gospel album," Germaine slipped in casually when Momma Jackson stopped to take a breath.

Jules and everyone else at the table turned to look at him as if he was crazy. He was the only one who had dared to interrupt Momma Jackson. They all assumed it was because he didn't know better. They expected her to turn on him at any minute. But the shock of being disrupted seemed to pacify Momma Jackson for a moment.

"Oh?" she managed to squeak out.

"Oh, yeah," Germaine said casually, piling grapes and kiwi slices onto his plate like nothing unusual was happening. "She's been really supportive, helping him book performances getting his music out to places where it can really reach people who need it. Like last week he sang at the YMCA's youth empowerment concert in Scarborough, and got the chance to talk to a lot of the kids there. None of that would have happened without Jules."

"I didn't know you were at the concert, Jules," Keisha said suddenly. "I was there!" Keisha looked across at Germaine. "Truuth is your cousin? Wow, he's really good. I heard him a couple times at church, but I didn't know he was one of the artists Jules was working with."

"You been doing all of that, Jewel?" Davis asked, surprised. "I'm really proud of you."

"Yeah, Mrs. Jackson, she works that hard 'cause she really cares about letting people know that there's Someone out there who can change their lives," Germaine said. His eyes shifted to Jules and stayed there. "You should really be proud of her."

Jules's eyes met his, and she felt something stir in her chest.

"So that's what you're busy doing," Momma Jackson finally said, tilting her head and looking at Jules carefully. Jules tore her eyes away from Germaine to meet her mother's gaze. She braced herself for whatever might come next.

"Well, I guess I can't be mad at you for being on God's business, now can I," she said with a half smile. "Good for you, sugar, good for you," she said, patting Jules's hand.

And just like that, it was over.

"Davis, when were you gonna tell me about that internship of yours . . . ?"

As the conversation shifted around her, Jules shot Germaine a grateful look. He nodded slightly and smiled in understanding.

Okay.

Maybe bringing him here wasn't such a bad idea after all.

Chapter 10

"You get an A$^+$ for this evening's performance," Jules said, stretching her legs, which were resting across Germaine's lap. After escaping Momma Jackson's unscathed, they had ended up back at her apartment on the couch, with the TV, and two bowls of Very Berry Strawberry ice cream.

"Well, I do have a way with mothers," Germaine said, chuckling as Jules stole a spoonful of ice cream from his bowl.

"So I see," she said, after swallowing. "Seems like you've had a lot of practice over your twenty-eight years."

"I'm not even gonna go there with you tonight," Germaine said. He moved his bowl away before Jules could swipe another scoop.

"Okay," she conceded, dropping her spoon into her own empty bowl.

"It was just nice to have someone stand up for me for a change," she said, shivering slightly.

Germaine put down his ice cream and wrapped the

blanket, resting on the back of the couch, around her shoulders.

"You know I'm always here for you," he said, rubbing her calves gently. "But if it bothers you so much, why don't you talk to her about it?"

Jules sighed heavily. "Because my mother and I have a strange relationship. Every time I try to talk to her about the things she says to me, she somehow makes herself out to be the victim. You saw how she was tonight. I can never win with her."

"Have you ever tried to talk to her when she's not mad?"

"What do you mean?"

"Well," Germaine began, "if you're trying to talk to her about how you feel in the middle of an argument, then she probably won't hear you. But if you try reaching her when she's in a good mood, then it just might make a difference."

"Hmm," Jules murmured. "I never thought of that."

Germaine watched her quietly as she mulled over the concept in her mind.

"I think I'm gonna try that," Jules said. "That's if I can ever catch her in a good mood." She sighed. "I just wish I could have a normal relationship with my mother, like everyone else."

Germaine chuckled. "Baby, no one has a normal relationship with his or his parents. I don't think there is such a thing."

"Really?" Jules said. "The way you talk about your mom, you guys seem pretty cool. I wouldn't mind having a relationship like that."

"Don't be too sure."

Even though he said the words casually, Jules didn't miss the grimace that quickly crossed his face.

"Why not?" Jules asked, her curiosity now piqued.

But instead of answering, Germaine continued rubbing Jules's feet silently.

"Come on, babe," she said, scooting closer to him. "You've seen my mother in all her glory. I can't think of anything worse than that." Jules looked at him questioningly. She could see him wrestle with the thoughts in his head, and she hoped that for once he would share them, instead of keeping everything hidden. As if hearing her, he began to speak.

"Remember I told you I used to live in Vancouver?" he asked quietly. He had leaned back in the couch but he was gazing absently at some spot on the carpet in front of them.

"Uh-huh."

"I actually moved there when I was about sixteen," he said. "Dad had been . . . gone . . . for about a year. And my mom had started seeing this other dude. It wasn't serious. Or at least I thought it wasn't, until she told me that she was gonna marry him."

Jules raised her eyebrows in surprise but said nothing.

"Obviously I was mad as hell. My dad's body wasn't even cold yet, and she was selling his house and moving me and her into some stranger's place to live. I didn't even know this dude. It was like one morning I woke up and he was there all the time.

"Anyway. We weren't there a couple months before it became clear that one of us would have to go. It would either be me or him. My mom decided it would be me."

Jules's heart grew heavy with sorrow as she saw the

barely hidden sadness on Germaine's face. She couldn't imagine what it would be like to have her mother pick someone else over her or Davis. Momma Jackson had always had a lot of things going on in her life, but Jules knew that when it came down to the crunch, Momma Jackson would have given everything up in an instant to make sure Jules and Davis were taken care of.

Jules grabbed both his hands as he continued.

"She sent me to this boarding school in Vancouver, and that's where I finished high school. From there I went straight to UBC, did business, and that's where I was living and working afterward."

Jules looked at Germaine bewildered. "What about summers? Christmas? Thanksgiving?" she asked.

He shrugged. "I worked. Or stayed on campus," he said. "After I graduated from UBC, I got my own place, and Vancouver became home for me."

He grimaced. "I never even really knew my little sister until about two years ago. When she was born, my mom wanted me to come visit and see her. But I couldn't. Wouldn't."

"I'm sorry, Germaine," Jules said quietly. She wanted to wrap her arms around him. But with him so deeply involved in his own memories, it felt like an intrusion. So she opted for squeezing his hand instead.

"She used to write me. All the time."

"Your sister?"

He nodded.

"She'd never met me. But here was this little seven-year-old girl, writing to me about her science project, and her pet frog, and Anwar, the boy next door who would chase her around with worms," he said, chuckling.

Jules smiled, glad that there were a few happy memories among so many bad ones. But almost as soon as it came, his smile was gone, and the tension was back again.

"I missed out on so much of her life," he said, shaking his head.

"Is that why you came back?" Jules asked.

"Partly," Germaine said, sucking in a deep breath and shaking off the negative recollections.

"What was the other part?"

Germaine looked at Jules, thoughtful. "I think God was telling me it was time."

Jules raised an eyebrow. "So you still had your faith all that time?" She blew out a breath loudly. "I don't know if I could be that strong. I would like to think I would be, but I'm not so sure."

He shrugged. "God was the only one who hadn't turned His back on me. Even when my mom was off doing her own thing, He was there, taking care of me. There was no one else to trust but Him."

Jules cocked her head to one side and looked at Germaine curiously. Every time she thought she had him figured out, he threw another curveball at her. She thought of all the concerns she had had about him and the Sound Lounge before. They all seemed silly now as she sat there listening to him talk about his faith.

"What?" he asked as he caught her watching him.

Jules shook her head and smiled. "Nothing. So you and your mom are okay now?" she asked.

Germaine shrugged. "I guess. I think she's sorry about the way she handled things. But I've moved past that. She'll always be my mom, and I'll always love her. But she knows I'll never set foot in her husband's house."

"You still don't get along with him?"

Germaine's face grew dark, and Jules knew instantly that there was more to the story than what he was telling.

"Let's just say it's probably better for everyone that we keep our distance."

Jules shivered slightly, as she watched a hard look pass over his face. It was the same look she had seen him give Easy that evening at Triad. But almost as soon as it came, it was gone, and he was grinning at her.

"Like I said, no one has a normal relationship with his or her parents," he said. "But if it's any consolation, your mom probably loves me."

"Oh, yeah," Jules said, wrinkling her nose. "You've got some sort of spell over her. I think Davis has a little crush too."

Germaine laughed. "He's a cool kid. I'm supposed to help him juice up his engine before he heads back to school this week."

"What? You're already making playdates with my brother? I hope this isn't going to cut into my boyfriend time," Jules said with mock displeasure.

"Absolutely not," he said, leaning down to kiss her once. And then again. It wasn't long before Jules forgot what she was supposed to be upset about.

"Okay, I think it's time for me to go," Germaine said, pulling away from her a few minutes later.

"What! Why?" Jules moaned.

"Because," Germaine said, standing up and grinning slyly, "I want to keep being the good boy your momma thinks I am."

Jules felt her face flush, and she stood up to walk him to the door.

"Drive home safely," she said, helping him into his jacket, her hands lingering on the lapels.

"And you make sure you talk to your mom—soon."

"I will," she promised. "Thanks again for coming with me. I don't know what I'd do without you."

"Well, lucky for you, that's not something you have to worry about." He pulled her close for a quick kiss before leaving.

Jules closed the door behind him and leaned against it. She sure hoped he meant what he said, because she was really getting used to having him around.

Chapter 11

It was 5:25 a.m. when Jules pulled her car into the back alley of the Dollar Bay convenience store. The dark, early morning August sky made it seem much earlier than it was, and she shivered as a draft of cold air slivered in through her cracked car window. From the driver's seat, she gazed around at the decrepit twenty-two-story community housing buildings that sandwiched the narrow street. She hated this part of town; hated that she had to come here; hated that anyone had to live here. She wouldn't wish this roach-infested hell on her worst enemy.

After taking a deep breath, she opened her car door and got out. Instantly the putrid smell of days-old food, burning rubber, and stale garbage invaded her nostrils. It was the smell of poverty. Real poverty.

Locking her doors securely, she pulled her jacket closer around her and hurried down a shadowy alley-way, wondering all the time why Truuth needed to have his photo shoot here, in a place where everything seemed to be covered in thin layer of grime.

It was a redundant question. She already knew why.

This was where he came from. This was where he had lived, among the crackheads, drug dealers, and forgotten of society. In this place where dreams came to die, God's vision for Truuth's life had survived. That's why he needed to come back here. So his album covers, the posters, and the magazine spreads could all show the truth. Yes, this was where he came from, but it was not who he was.

As Jules hurried past it all, she wondered to herself if she could have survived this. Her problems with her own mother seemed insignificant compared to what Truuth must have gone through. It was not that she did not understand what it was to struggle. After her dad left, taking care of Jules and Davis had been a strain on Momma Jackson that Jules had been very aware of. Nonetheless, Jules knew the worst of that experience did not compare to some of the things Truuth had faced on a daily basis. If it wasn't for God, who knows how he might have turned out.

"Hey, it's about time you got here," 'Dre said when Jules rounded the corner to where Ryan Lee Chung and his photography crew were already setting up. With his sweatshirt hood pulled over his head and dark glasses covering most of his face, 'Dre looked barely awake.

"Boy, you need to check yourself," Jules answered. "It's five-thirty in the morning. The only person I get up this early for is Jesus."

"Hey! Don't be mad at me. This was Truuth's idea," 'Dre said, as Jules followed him over to the back of his van, which hosted a large metal thermos and an array of hot beverage mixes.

Over the top of the back seat Jules could see the

back of a baseball cap, and Tanya's long blond locks sticking out underneath.

"Hey, T," Jules called to her friend slouching in the front passenger seat. Tanya muttered something unintelligible and pulled her baseball cap further down over her eyes. Jules shook her head. That girl was some kind of committed. Jules wasn't sure, however, if that devotion was to the company or to 'Dre. Either way it was impressive. Even Maxine had refused to get up this early, and she was all about supporting her man.

"Where's the man of the hour?" Jules asked 'Dre, as he filled her mug with hot chocolate.

"He's in the van over there with the stylist and makeup artist," 'Dre replied, gesturing to a white van parked a few feet behind them."

"Stylist, makeup artist, and a four-man photography crew." Jules whistled. "I don't even want to know how much this is costing."

'Dre made a huffing sound and shook his head. "Trust me, you don't."

Jules leaned against the van and watched as the crew finished setting up and started taking pictures of Truuth.

"So you think this will work for both of you?" Ryan asked Jules teasingly, nodding toward the first set up: a crumbling brick wall, surrounded by scatterings of broken glass that probably came from beer bottles someone had left there weeks before.

Jules wrinkled her nose at the scene. She had already spoken to Ryan about what she wanted, after Truuth had spoken to her about what he wanted, and somehow they had managed to come to some vague agreement of what the shoot would end up looking like. Or so they thought anyway. As far as Jules was concerned, it was more of a trial and error process than anything else.

"We'll see, Ryan," Jules said with a fair amount of apprehension. "You just do your magic and make it work."

Ryan laughed and began taking more shots.

Just as planned, they were in time to catch the first rays of sunlight. And even though she was doubtful about how it would turn out, Jules had to admit that the light and scenery came together beautifully to create spectacular images. Somehow, Ryan managed to make even broken-down apartment buildings look amazing.

The time passed quickly as Truuth changed outfits and switched backdrops for different shots. By the time Ryan called for the last set, it was 9:30 a.m. and a steady stream of foot and vehicle traffic was flowing through the streets and alleys around them.

As the warm summer sunshine heated up the pavement and the air above it, Jules and Tanya ditched their jackets and lounged lazily on the hood of 'Dre's van to watch Truuth take his final shots. As she gazed around, Jules began to wonder once more what life was like in this place.

She watched a slim black woman in a faded pantsuit try her best to control two little boys, neither of whom could be more than eight years old. From where she was Jules could tell that it wasn't easy, for one boy wanted to run ahead of her, while the other stuck his feet in one spot and refused to move.

Across the street, a hunched-over old woman pushed a battered grocery cart slowly down the sidewalk. Even though it was still early, she looked tired and worn, like the night had not been a good one for her. With great effort she trudged along, barely raising her eyes above the cart she was pushing. It was too painful for Jules to watch, and she turned away.

Jules couldn't help but wonder where God was for these people. Deep in her heart, she knew that even though their situations looked dire, the Lord was still there taking care of them, and if they asked, He would supply all their needs. But at the same time, she could understand why people like Easy, who had to see this suffering everyday, had a hard time believing that there was a God who cared.

As her gaze shifted, her eyes fell on a black SUV that had pulled up to the curb a few meters down the road. The doors opened, and two men stepped out, one from either side. Jules squinted against the sunlight to catch a better look at their faces. Even from a distance, something about them looked vaguely familiar. She watched the taller one walk across the sidewalk, and up the steps of one of the better looking apartment build-ings. The other lit a cigarette, leaned back against the stationary vehicle, and watched his companion enter the complex.

Jules racked her brain trying to figure out where she had seen them before. She stared so hard at the brother with the cigarette that she swore he must have felt her eyes on him. But she couldn't help it. Something about him, from his slightly crooked cornrows, to the large ring on his pinkie finger struck a chord in her memory. She just didn't know why.

From the corner of her eye, Jules saw a silver Toyota 4Runner pull up across the street and a tall male in baggy jeans and a Sean Jean sweatshirt step out.

"Never thought I'd see you here," Jules said, slightly turning her head as Easy approached them.

"I was passing, and I saw 'Dre's car," Easy said.

"Oh, yeah, I forgot you lived near here," Tanya said from her position fully stretched out on the hood of the van. Jules knew that underneath her shades, her eyes were closed. She shook her head. Only Tanya could use Truuth's photo shoot as an opportunity to get a tan.

A movement in the distance caught Jules's eye, and she found herself again watching the familiar man as he put out the cigarette he was smoking. It was clear that he was getting a bit impatient, as he had started walking back and forth in front of the van, all the while with his eyes fixed on the apartment building. Jules leaned forward and squinted to see if there was anything going on near the building's entrance, but a hedge of grass blocked her view.

"What you looking at, baby girl?" Easy asked curiously, as he watched Jules crane her neck to get a better view.

"Huh?"

"Why you so interested in the dude down there?" Easy asked. Jules was so preoccupied that she missed the slight edge that had crept into his voice.

"I've seen that guy before," she said absently.

"That guy?" Easy asked, nodding toward where the man was still pacing. "Are you sure?"

"Positive," Jules said. "I know I've seen him before, but I can't remember where."

Just then the first man emerged from the building with a duffel bag, which he promptly threw in the back of the vehicle.

"Him as well," Jules added.

"Baby girl, are you sure those guys were the ones you saw?" Easy asked again.

"Yes, Easy," Jules said, slightly annoyed that he kept asking her the same question over and over. "Don't you think I would remember who I saw? Why do you keep asking me?"

" 'Cause those cats are pushers."

Jules's head snapped around. Easy's eyes had gone dark, and there was a grave expression on his face. Out of nowhere a nervous jittery feeling began to build in the pit of Jules's stomach.

"You're kidding, right?"

"Look at me, Jules. Do I look like I'm kidding?"

Jules looked up at Easy for a moment, then back at the scene. The men were getting into the car. Only moments later they made a U-turn and were headed down the road. Jules wished that the dismal feeling building inside her had left with them.

Even though the sun was beating down, all of a sudden Jules felt cold and uneasy. Something was coming. She didn't know what it was, but she had a feeling she was going to regret knowing what Easy had just told her. Sliding off the hood of 'Dre's van, she slipped on her jacket and went to find 'Dre. She didn't want to be here anymore. She just wanted to go home and lie down. Maybe if she slept for a little while her sudden paranoia would go away.

She found 'Dre standing with Ryan, looking at digital prints of Truuth's photos on Ryan's laptop.

"Hey, Jules, I was just about to call you over here," 'Dre said, making room for her in front of the laptop. "You want to take a look at these shots?"

"Maybe later," Jules said. "I'm gonna go, okay? I'll talk to you guys later."

"Jules, you okay? You don't look too good," Ryan said with an air of concern.

"I'll be fine," Jules said, already walking away. "I'll catch up with you later."

She was halfway to her car before Easy caught up with her. She had hoped to make it home without having to talk to anyone else, but apparently that was not going to happen.

"Baby girl, we need to talk."

"Not now, okay, Easy," Jules said, sticking her keys into the car door. She noticed some fliers sticking to her windshield, and she impatiently plucked them up and tossed them on the sidewalk.

"Yes, now."

Jules ignored him, yanked her car door open, and tossed her purse on the front passenger seat.

"Jules."

She stopped short when she heard the edge in Easy's voice. She realized then that he wasn't playing, and that she wasn't going anywhere until he had finished talking to her. She slowly turned around to face him.

"Where did you see those brothas before?" he asked her in a tone that warned her not to lie to him.

"I don't know," Jules said, trying to fight the images that were flashing in her mind.

"You saw them with your boy, didn't you," Easy said.

Jules leaned against her car as she felt her whole body weaken.

She nodded. "They were with him, in his office at the store."

"That's what I thought," Easy said flatly. "I saw him with them too. I figured that it was nothing the first time, but then I saw him get into that vehicle with them. . . ." He shook his head. "Why didn't you come talk to me, Jules?"

"I don't know . . . I didn't think . . ." She struggled with words as she tried to give a reasonable answer. But she couldn't even explain to herself what had made her put away her own concerns and trust Germaine so completely.

"I tried to tell you he wasn't right, baby girl. . . ."

Jules felt herself slide down the side of the car and crouch down on the ground. She wanted to cover her ears and block out everything Easy was saying. But every time she closed her eyes, all she saw were the two men standing in Germaine's office.

Suddenly the truth hit her like a ton of bricks.

She was involved with a drug dealer. Her boyfriend was a drug dealer.

It sounded so ridiculous in her head that she figured it couldn't be true. But somewhere in the back of her mind she knew it was.

But how? She knew him. How could she have been involved with him for so many months and not known? How was this possible?

Images of every moment she had spent with Germaine seemed to flash through her mind in quick succession as she tried to pick out anything suspicious she might have missed before. The truth seemed to float into place like pieces of a puzzle she had never been able to put together. The confrontation at the store; the way he tried to distance her from the Sound Lounge and his business; the reason he didn't like Easy. Easy had been the only one who could have revealed his secret.

A drug dealer. How could she have been so wrong about him?

How could she have been so foolish? She had never trusted another guy so completely so quickly.

But he hadn't been some random guy. 'Dre and Maxine knew him. They had vouched for him. He was Truuth's family—and Truuth was like family to her. He had come to church with her. She had let him into her world, introduced him to her friends, and trusted him with her business. Invited him into her home—invited him into her mother's home!

"Oh, Lord," Jules groaned. She felt like she was going to be sick.

"Its okay, baby girl, I'm gonna get you home," Jules heard Easy say somewhere in the distance.

"No," she murmured. She took several deep breaths before standing up. Slowly, but steadily she reopened her car door and slid inside.

"Baby girl, let me drive you home. I can get 'Dre to bring my car—"

"I'm fine, Easy," Jules said with more calm than she felt. He looked at her doubtfully, but knew she wasn't going to let him take care of her.

"Okay," he said. "But let me handle it. I don't want you going anywhere near that nig—"

"No, Easy," Jules said, shaking her head stubbornly.

"Jules, don't fight me on this one," Easy warned. But Jules wouldn't back down. She got herself into this; she would get her own self out.

"No, Easy, I'll deal with it," she said, as she turned the engine. "This is my life."

She watched Easy brooding on the side of the road. He kept closing and opening his fists, and she knew he was itching to handle Germaine in a way that wouldn't involve many words. But she refused to let him.

"Promise me you'll stay out of it," Jules said, squinting up at him through the bright midday sun.

Easy shook his head and clenched his jaw stubbornly, refusing to meet Jules's eyes.

"Easy, give me your word you'll stay out of it," Jules insisted. He stared at her hard before answering.

"All right. I'll stay out of it. But if anything happens to you . . ."

Jules didn't hear the rest. She had already sped off down the road, leaving nothing but dust and a frustrated Easy standing in her wake.

Jules checked her blind spot quickly, then slipped into the far left lane of the 401. After hearing the truth about Germaine at the morning's photo shoot, she'd had every intention of going home, slipping under the covers, and crying herself into a sorrow-induced slumber. But at some point after the McCowan Road exit but before Ajax, her despair had transformed into burning anger.

How could he do this to me? How could he look into my eyes and lie to me every day for months? How could he put me and my friends and my family in so much danger?

Realizing that she would have no peace until she got answers to her questions, Jules took the next exit off the highway, turned around, and headed back to the city.

Twenty minutes later Jules pulled right up to the front of the Sound Lounge and parked. As she slammed the car door shut, she noticed the one-hour parking sign. She wasn't worried. She wouldn't be there that long.

Storming past the front counter, she burst into Germaine's office, swinging the door shut behind her. It slammed so hard that the walls shook, and several papers on Germaine's desk blew out of place.

He looked up at her in surprise. When he caught sight of her expression, however, Jules was almost sure she saw a look of fear flash through his eyes.

He should be afraid. Very afraid.

"I'm gonna ask you one question, and I want you to think long and hard before you try to lie to me," Jules said quietly. "Are you pushing drugs?"

Even though it was supposed to be a question, it sounded more like an accusation coming from Jules. She watched as a million different expressions seemed to slip across Germaine's face, as the reality of being caught dawned on him. She wished that even one of those expressions had suggested her assumptions were wrong. But sadly that was not the case. Germaine seemed a lot of things, but confused was not one of them.

"Well? Are you gonna answer me?" Jules asked angrily, her voice going up an octave.

"Do I really need to? You've already made all your assumptions about me," Germaine said. His voice, like his face, was emotionless and impossible to read.

"Negro, please, don't even try to play the victim here," she said angrily. "I didn't assume nothing. I am standing here asking you to tell me the truth. Like I've been asking you all these months."

"Who are you kidding, Jules? You didn't come here to ask me anything. You came down here to accuse me. You already decided I was wrong long before you even stepped through that door."

"I can't believe you're trying to turn this on me," Jules said, shaking her head in anger and disbelief.

"But it is about you. It's about you not trusting me."

"When have I ever not trusted you?" Jules screeched.

"When I told you the guys you saw in my office were just people I was working with," Germaine said. "Before the words were fully out of my mouth you were already asking Maxine and your friends about me. And let's not forget how salty you got when I wouldn't lay out every inch of my business to you."

"Now who's the one exaggerating," Jules said dryly. "All I asked was what kind of business you had with those guys . . ."

"And I told you I couldn't talk about it. But now you're throwing around these unfounded accusations about my being involved in something illegal."

"Unfounded?" Jules echoed in disbelief. "Are you serious? Germaine, you've been consorting with drug dealers!"

"Oh, so that's what you think I'm doing? Who told you that? Your friend Easy?" he asked, scowling.

"He didn't have to tell me anything. I saw you with my own eyes."

"Jules, you don't know what you saw," he shot back. He was finally beginning to get upset.

"You know what's funny about this whole thing," Jules said, her eyes narrowing. "Even now, you still haven't denied anything. You still haven't said, 'Jules I'm not involved with that mess.' "

"Why bother?" he asked, tossing down his pen onto the desk. "It wouldn't make a difference to you anyway."

"How would you know? You didn't even try!"

Germaine closed his eyes and took a deep breath. His jaw was clenched tightly.

"Jules, I am not pushing drugs. I am not selling drugs, and I definitely am not involved with any drug dealers."

"Liar," Jules said, in a low, shaky voice. The hot tears that she had been holding back began to run freely down her cheeks. "I saw the two brothas in your office, Germaine. I saw them talking to you, that day you went off on me about coming here," she said shakily. Her whole body trembled as she stood in the middle of Germaine's office. "I saw them again today, at Regent Park. I know who they are. I know what they do."

She watched all the anger drain from him in a single moment.

"Jules, it's not what you think," Germaine said, getting up from his chair and moving toward her. His voice and his eyes pleaded with her to believe him. But she couldn't. Not anymore.

She shook her head. "How could you look me in the eye and lie to me like that?" she asked, her voice barely above a whisper, her eyes looking at him accusingly.

"Jules, when have I ever lied to you?" Germaine asked. "Since the day we met, I have always told you the truth. I may not have told you everything you wanted to know, but I never lied to you."

Jules sniffled but said nothing. She had thought he had been honest with her. But as far as Jules was concerned, omission was still deception. And this time the evidence was overwhelming. There was no way he could sweet-talk his way out of this one.

Germaine raked his hand through his hair in frustration. "Geez, Jules, why is it so hard for you to trust me?"

"I did trust you!" she exclaimed in frustration. "I trusted you with my friends. I went into business with you. I let you into my whole life. And what do you do?

You put me, and my family, and everything I know in danger!

"How could you do that to me?"

Jules knew she was losing it. Her eyes were swollen, her face was wet, and her throat was raw from crying and shouting at Germaine at the same time. Not to mention, she was exhausted.

She looked at Germaine and tried to catch a glimpse of the man she knew, the man who had become such a vital part of her. He was more than just some new guy she had a crush on. He was a friend, a confidant, and someone she had felt safe with. She looked desperately for the man she had grown to admire so much. But he was gone. In fact he had never existed. The Germaine she knew was just a fabrication of the stranger who stood before her.

The sadness of that thought seemed to suck all the energy out of her, and she knew then that it was time to leave. She turned to go, but Germaine grabbed her wrist before she had a chance. She flinched and pulled her hand away.

"Jules, can we at least talk about this?"

"There's nothing to talk about," she snapped, a bit of her strength returning. "I don't do drug dealers."

"Jules, this is a mistake."

"You're right. It was all a mistake," she said as she opened the door. "We're done."

As the door swung shut behind her, she felt another door close—the door to her heart.

Chapter 12

"**I** want to move Truuth's launch to a new location."
Four pairs of eyes looked at Jules as if she had lost her mind.

Jules, 'Dre, Tanya, Maxine, Truuth, and Easy were all meeting in Triad's conference room to discuss the plans for Truuth's album launch when Jules dropped the bomb. Now, with the request hanging in the air, almost all of them were looking at her as if she was crazy.

Two days had passed since Jules's confrontation with Germaine, and while she was ready to move on from him, there were some unfortunate ties that still bound them together.

"Jules, the launch is in six weeks. Half the promotional material has already been printed. We've been telling everybody about it; we can't switch venues now," 'Dre said.

"All of that is minor. The posters and fliers have been printed but they haven't gone out yet. We can get some stickers done and cover the Sound Lounge with the name of the new venue."

"That's not even the point," 'Dre said. "We've been working on this thing for months. Why did you just decide you need to change the venue now?"

Jules remained calm and emotionless. She was prepared for this question and every other question 'Dre could throw at her. It didn't matter how many objections he had. They were moving the launch away from Germaine's place.

"I think the current venue may pose a risk to the image of our company and the safety of our audience," Jules said curtly.

"So what, you didn't know this before? How come all of a sudden the Sound Lounge is a risk?" 'Dre asked. His eyes bore into her harshly from across the conference room table. "When I expressed doubts about the venue the first time it came up, you were the one who told me it was the best we could do. What's up with the sudden one hundred eighty?"

Jules gritted her teeth to stop the words she longed to say. She had decided before the meeting that she would not disclose her suspicions about Germaine, partly because she had nothing solid to back her up, but mainly out of respect for the fact that even though Germaine might be criminal, he was still Truuth's family.

"Look, 'Dre, you trusted me to do all of this for you and so far it's been working out okay," Jules said. "I don't think Ger—the Sound Lounge is the best place for the launch. I've already found a new location that won't cost us any more than we were willing to pay before. Can't you just trust my judgment on this?"

Jules kept her eyes focused on 'Dre, hoping he would believe her bluff. Truthfully, she only had a couple ideas of new venues for the launch. There was nothing sure yet.

"This is because you and Germaine split, isn't it," Truuth said coldly. It was the first time he had spoken since the start of the meeting, and all eyes in the room turned to look at him. But his eyes were fixed on Jules.

This she hadn't anticipated.

"This has nothing to do with me and Germaine," Jules said, unable to hide the irritation in her own voice. "I can't believe you think I would allow my personal life to interfere with my work."

"You didn't seem to have a problem mixing business and personal when you were giving him the contract for the event, though," Truuth shot back.

"Forget you, Truuth," Jules said. "How dare you point fingers at me when you were the first one to bring your personal life all up into the business?"

"Hey!" Maxine protested.

Jules didn't even flinch. Maxine was her girl, but she was also the only one in the room who didn't need to be there. But Truuth always had to have her in the meetings and when you ran a business with family and friends, that was the kind of thing that happened. Most of the time Jules didn't care, but if Truuth was gonna call her out on her relationships, Jules was going to go ahead and return the favor.

"Okay, you know what, everyone needs to just calm down," Tanya said, jumping in.

". . . Okay, man, I'll see you in a bit," 'Dre said. Jules looked up and noticed that 'Dre was on his cell phone.

"What are you doing?" she asked, annoyed. He was the one always complaining about cell phones on during office meetings and now he was making a call from his?

"I just called Germaine," 'Dre said. "He's not far away. He should be here in five minutes."

"What!" Jules exclaimed. "Why'd you do that?"

"Jules, I respect your opinion on the venue, but if I'm going to do a major reshuffling this late in the game, I'm gonna have to go on more than just opinion. I want to hear his side."

"So what, I'm not credible enough?"

"Considering the circumstances," 'Dre said, glancing at Truuth, "it can't hurt to do a couple checks."

Jules felt her blood pressure rising and her heart beating faster. Her ears were ringing, and though she was trying to appear calm, she was having trouble breathing. She had not seen this coming at all.

"Don't take it personally, Jules," 'Dre said. "It's just business."

Jules leaned back in her chair and closed her eyes. The room was completely silent, and she felt everyone's eyes on her. It would be so easy for her to just tell them everything she knew. But for some reason she couldn't.

After what seemed like forever, Jules heard the front door open and shuffling in the hallway. A few moments later, 'Dre returned to the room with Germaine in tow. Jules kept her eyes closed and concentrated on her breathing in order to keep herself calm.

"What's going on?" she heard Germaine ask.

"Jules seems to have some concerns about the Sound Lounge," 'Dre said. "She wants to move Truuth's launch to a new venue."

"What!"

Jules's eyes snapped open when she heard the surprise in Germaine's voice. He couldn't really expect that she would still be doing business with him after what she knew. There was no way he thought she would bring her artist into his drug den.

"Jules, are you out of your mind?" Germaine asked. "Triad is booked at the Sound Lounge for two whole weeks. How am I supposed to find new acts to fill those nights on such short notice?"

"You seem to know a lot of people," Jules said. "I'm sure you can come up with something."

"Jules, this is crazy."

"No. Crazy would be us having Truuth's launch at your lounge," Jules said knowingly. The look she gave him made sure he knew exactly what she was talking about.

For the first time Germaine seemed to notice everyone else in the room watching them carefully.

"Jules, can I have a word with you, please?" Germaine asked. His voice was much calmer, but his eyes still flashed at her angrily.

"Whatever you have to say to me you can say in front of everyone here," Jules said, narrowing her eyes at him. She folded her arms stubbornly and looked at him expectantly.

Germaine gritted his teeth and looked up at the ceiling in frustration.

"You know what, maybe it's time for a short break," Tanya said suddenly, popping up out of her chair and dragging Maxine with her toward the exit. Following her cue, 'Dre, Truuth, and a reluctant Easy left the room.

As soon as the door closed, Germaine began.

"You know, Jules, I knew you were upset the other day. But I figured once you got home and thought about it, you'd see how ridiculous your accusations were. But I never for a second thought you would take your craziness this far."

"This far!" Jules exclaimed, leaning forward in her chair. "Negro, you're lucky I didn't call the police on your coke-peddling behind."

Germaine laughed humorlessly. "What's stopping you? Go ahead and call them. Make a report on how you saw me talking with two men in my office and that you think I should be arrested. You tell them that and see which one of us ends up being locked up."

"Don't worry—that option isn't completely off the table yet," Jules threatened. "It's only because Truuth is your cousin that I haven't said anything. I'm just thinking of him."

"You're thinking of him. Have you thought about anyone else at all?" Germaine asked. "If you want nothing to do with me, that's fine. But this is my livelihood that you're talking about, Jules. My business. And since you obviously don't give a flip about me, how about you think of the people who work for me. How this affects them."

"I feel for them," Jules said. "Guess they didn't know they were signing on to work for an Escobar."

"Unbelievable. This is unbelievable," Germaine said, more to himself than to Jules as he paced the room.

Jules watched him without sympathy. She would not allow her friends to get mixed up in whatever was going on with Germaine at the Sound Lounge. She could never live with herself if someone she knew got hurt because of it.

"Jules," Germaine said tiredly. "I don't know how else to say it to you. I am not involved in drugs. I'm not a drug dealer. Never have been. Never will be."

"So what were those men doing in your office?" Jules asked. Deep in her heart she desperately wanted to be wrong. She wanted it all to be a misunderstanding. But unfortunately that was not how it was going to work out.

"They, had a . . . meeting with me," Germaine said vaguely.

"A meeting with you," Jules said, narrowing her eyes. "Did you know that they were drug dealers?"

Germaine looked uncomfortable. He looked down at the ground, then at the wall on the other side of the room—everywhere except at Jules.

"I'll take that as a yes," Jules said. "So you were having a meeting with known drug dealers in your business office, at the Sound Lounge, and I'm supposed to believe you're not involved with them."

"They just came to see me," Germaine said unconvincingly.

"Really," Jules said. "And how would you explain being in a car with them? Were they just giving you a ride home?"

Jules saw Germaine's jaw tighten, but he said nothing and refused to meet Jules's eyes.

"See? You got nothing to say, but you want me to trust you," Jules spat. She ran her fingers through her hair in frustration. "How could you get involved in something like this, Germaine? Wasn't your dad a cop?" Jules asked. "He would roll over in his grave if he could see you now."

At the mention of his father, Germaine's eyes grew

cold and hard. Something warned Jules not to take that train of thought any further.

She looked down at the conference table and sighed heavily. "You're not at all the person I thought you were."

"Yeah," Germaine agreed coldly. "I guess both of us were wrong about each other."

Germaine's words stung Jules, but she brushed them off and pretended that she didn't care.

He took one last look at her then turned to leave.

"Your deposit check will be in the mail tomorrow," he said, as he walked through the door. "You win, Jules."

As she watched him leave, she let out a breath she hadn't known she'd been holding. Without warning, her eyes began to fill with tears, and she ducked down to try to wipe them away before any of the others came back into the room.

If she had won, why did she feel like such a loser?

When Jules woke up Saturday morning, it was already 7:30. She was definitely going to be late for church. Truth be told, she wasn't even sure she wanted to go to church. The way things had been going the past couple weeks, she didn't feel like there was much she could get from the experience. She definitely wasn't interested in going to Scarborough Memorial since that was where Maxine, Tanya, 'Dre, and Truuth were likely to be. Ever since the whole incident with Germaine and the launch, there had been plenty of tension at the office, mostly between Jules and everyone else. She didn't want to have to deal with that at church as well, the one place she should be able to have some peace.

And then there was the possibility of running into Germaine.

Since they had started dating, he had become somewhat of a regular around Scarborough Memorial, with all the mature women adopting him like he was a stray in need of care. At first Jules thought it was sweet. Now, she knew it would annoy her to see them fawn over him—especially knowing what she knew about him.

All in all there were more than enough reasons to stay away from Scarborough Memorial that morning. But in her heart of hearts she knew there was no reason for her not to be in church on the day of the Lord. Which is why an hour later Jules found herself on the highway heading north toward the Toronto East Church.

As Jules walked up the sidewalk toward the large brick and wood building, she remembered why she liked this church so much. Nestled in the middle of Toronto's East York district, Toronto East was truly a community church. It was surrounded on every side by small bungalow style homes, most of which dated back almost seventy years. The church itself was pretty old, and the aging bricks and worn wooden roof showed it. But whenever Jules was inside, she felt the same warm feeling she got when she was at Scarborough Memorial. Most of the members were first and second generation immigrants from the West Indies, and when they were all amongst each other, it was as if they had never left the Caribbean.

This morning church was packed. As Jules slipped through the crowded foyer into the sanctuary she glanced at the program a smiling usher had handed her and realized the reason for the commotion. It was Music Day. Jules nodded to herself, thankful that the huge congregation would give her a chance to hide away in the back somewhere and remain unnoticed. She wasn't in much of a mood to talk to anyone this particular morning.

Though Jules had determined to be sulky and miserable, the beautiful music soon broke her resolve. As the visiting Apple Creek Youth Choir sang Sounds of Blackness's "God Cares," she felt the words tug at the strings of her heart. The truth was she had begun to doubt how much God really cared about her. It seemed like every time she turned around something else was going wrong. First her relationship with her mother, then the thing with Germaine, and now the blow-up at Triad.

Plus, for some reason unknown to her, she was really missing her dad. She hadn't been to see him in years, but in the last couple months she had gone as far as to consider making a trip to New York, where she knew he was living.

She had never felt so alone in her whole life, and a part of her wondered if God had taken a vacation from her life.

But as the words of the song seeped their way into her heart, she knew that she was not alone.

> *God cares all about you*
> *And He'll be there to see you through . . ."*

Jules felt warm tears roll down her cheeks. She had heard this song a million times before, but today it had special meaning for her. God really did care about her. That's why he'd led her to this church this morning, so she could hear those words.

"Thank you," she whispered, with closed eyes. "I really needed that."

When the service ended a few hours later, Jules filed out of church behind the other members, with a smile on her face and a lightness in her heart. Somehow she had received the assurance that she would be okay. No matter how dismal things seemed, God would work it out for her good, even if she couldn't possibly see how.

As she stepped into the foyer, a flash of bright orange caught her eye.

"Easy?"

Easy turned around at the sound of his name, and smiled when he caught sight of Jules.

"Baby girl, what are you doing here?"

"Me! What are you doing here?" Jules asked, unable to hide her surprise or her delight at seeing Easy in church.

"My Grams's choir was singing here this morning, and she asked me to drop her off."

Jules put her hand on her hip and looked at him knowingly. "That still doesn't explain why you're here now."

Easy shrugged and gave a slight smile. "I decided to stick around for a bit."

Jules grinned and tucked her arm into his. "I'm glad you did."

"Yeah, well, don't get too excited, it didn't mean anything," Easy said. But Jules could see a small smile at the corner of his mouth, and she knew that he had enjoyed the service more than he would let on.

"So how you been, baby girl?"

"So-so," Jules said, resisting the urge to slip back into her earlier funk. God had been too good for her to be anything but thankful.

"I know you've been having a hard time at Triad," Easy said. "Sorry about that."

Jules waved his apology away as they walked down the front steps together. "It hurts that Max and Tanya have pretty much stopped talking to me since this whole thing, but it is what it is," she said. "Besides, God is going to work it all out."

Easy looked at her quizzically. "How can you be so sure about that?"

"I just know," Jules said. "I was really down about everything, but being here this morning just reminded me how much He cares about me."

Easy grunted but said nothing more. Jules whispered a quick prayer in her heart and then took a deep breath.

"He cares about you too, Easy," she said. She braced herself. This was the part of the conversation where Easy usually brushed off the topic, not wanting to talk about anything related to him and God. But to Jules's surprise, this time he didn't.

"How do you know that?" he asked.

"Because I've seen it with my own eyes," Jules said confidently. "Look at the way He's taken care of you. Protected you from harm in that community you live in. Look at how he's blessed you with a grandmother who could love and take care of you even when your mother and father were gone."

Easy's brow furrowed as he listened to Jules. He wasn't objecting to anything she was saying, but she could tell that he wasn't convinced.

"If He cared so much, why would He make them leave in the first place? Isn't a good God supposed to prevent that from happening?"

Jules sighed. "God won't force us to do anything,

Easy. At the end of the day our choices are our own. I don't know why your mom left; that's a choice she made. But God made sure that someone was there for you even when she wasn't.

"Sometimes, things happen that we don't understand. But the Bible says all things work together for the good of them that love the Lord. And so we have to believe that God is doing what's best for us."

Easy pondered on Jules's words for a moment before smirking.

"So you think something good will come out of you hooking up with a drug dealer?" he challenged.

Jules smiled. "Stranger things have happened."

Easy chuckled. "You really believe all this stuff, don't you," he said, glancing at Jules.

She nodded. "I do. No one cares about you like He does, Easy. No one."

They both stood on the sidewalk, contemplating that concept, when Easy's grandmother came up.

"Jules! It's nice to see you."

"It's great to see you too, Sis Crawford," Jules said, as the tiny woman's arms enveloped her. "And it was even better seeing Easy here this morning."

"Ain't it, chile," Sis Crawford agreed. "I tell you, prayer still works."

Jules sighed as she thought about Sis Crawford's words. Yes, prayer still worked. It had to. Because with all that was going on in her life now, it was the only thing she could count on.

Chapter 13

Prayer was the only thing that kept Jules sane over the next few weeks, especially since Penny seemed to work extra hard to get under Jules's skin.

"Jules! Get in here."

Jules sighed, pushed back her chair, and made her way to Penny's office. It was the week of Truuth's launch, and the last thing she needed was drama at work, but it seemed like that was exactly what she was going to get.

"Thou wilt keep him in perfect peace whose mind is stayed on Thee," Jules whispered to herself. It was all she could do to summon God's tranquility when she had to deal with Penny.

In the year that the woman had been Jules's boss, Penny had been nothing but a couple tantrums short of a nightmare. Both Jules and Michelle disliked the loud, pushy woman, but they were able to tolerate her because she only worked from their office two days of the week. The other three days she worked with the hospital's executive team or worked out of her office at

Toronto General Hospital, the other major hospital in the Toronto Central Hospital Network.

With the hospital restructuring and the associated tension between the executive team, the staff, and the hospital's community consultation board, Penny had been out more often in various meetings trying to pacify what was slowly brewing into a stormy issue. While that meant more time spent outside of the office, it also meant that the hours when she was there, she was more snappy and sadistic than usual. Jules knew that her summons to the office would likely be another of Penny's torture sessions.

"Yes, Penny?" Jules asked, trying to force a small smile as she appeared at her boss's office entrance. From where she was, she could see Michelle looking annoyed from her position near Penny's desk.

"What's happening with the community newsletter? It should have gone out two days ago." she asked, her large green eyes boring into Jules.

"It's completed. It's just waiting for final approval."

"From who?" Penny asked, sounding slightly annoyed.

Jules grimaced. "From you."

"So where is it? Why didn't you get it to me?" Penny asked, as if it was the most obvious thing in the world.

Though wilt keep him in perfect peace.

"I gave it to you last week, Penny. And I sent you an e-mail reminding you about it three days ago," Jules said.

In fact she had sent Penny multiple e-mails, and had even spoken to her directly about the newsletter at the end of the previous week. But Penny had kept putting it off, and now that it was late, she had conveniently forgotten that Jules had spoken to her about it. This was classic Penny.

Penny sighed as if she was talking to a child. "Well, Jules, if you gave it to me, where is it?"

"It's right there on your desk," Michelle said, pointing to the two-page newsletter sitting on Penny's large, maple wood desk, in the same corner that Penny had tossed it when Jules had given it to her the week before. "Right where it's been all week."

Inwardly Jules sent up a quick prayer for Michelle, hoping that Penny didn't pick up on the woman's tart tone. Jules could tell that Michelle was annoyed with Penny, but she worried that the young woman's sharp tongue would be her undoing. In fact, the tiny Asian woman was famous for letting her dry remarks slip when Penny started with her antics.

Jules was sure that Penny would have loved to fire the girl, but even she knew that the office would probably fall apart if she did. Though younger than both Jules and Penny, Michelle had been at the hospital longer than both. As a result she was the only one in the department who knew the exact who, what, when, where, and how of the work they did. She also was the only one who knew exactly who to go to in order to get certain things done. Jules knew that she personally couldn't do her job without Michelle. She was sure Penny knew the same thing went for her, but it seemed like Penny sometimes forgot.

Penny glared at Michelle before snatching the newsletter from the corner where it lay, and quickly signing the approval slip at the bottom and handing it over to Jules. The signature wasn't really necessary, but previous incidents had taught Jules that when it came to Penny and her convenient memory, it was often best to get everything in writing.

"Let's try to get that out as soon as possible," Penny said briskly, as if she had done them all a huge favor.

Jules resisted the urge to roll her eyes. Michelle didn't.

"Anyway, that's not what I called you both in here for," Penny said. "Jules, I need you to attend this evening's community consultation board meeting."

Jules's mouth fell open, and she looked at her boss as if she had lost her mind. She had grown accustomed to Penny's passing off her responsibilities on her, but this was ridiculous.

"With all due respect, Penny, isn't that meeting your responsibility?" Jules asked, fighting to keep the annoyance out of her voice. How dare this woman pass off a community consultation board meeting on her, and at such short notice?

It wasn't that Jules had a problem with the consultations. They were a vital part of maintaining the link between the community and the hospital. Jules had been to a couple of the community meetings out of curiosity. But public consultation was not a part of her portfolio at the hospital. Penny was *the* public relations director, and was thus required by the hospital's constitution to sit on the consultation board. That had been the whole reason they hired Penny, because of her supposed familiarity with the process.

"It is, but I have an engagement this evening that I absolutely have to attend, and I cannot make it. Someone from the department has to be there," Penny said.

"What kind of engagement?" Jules asked, an eyebrow raised.

Penny blinked rapidly, seemingly surprised that Jules would question her.

"Excuse me?"

"She said what kind of engagement," Michelle repeated, leaning closer to Penny's ear. A look of perverse pleasure sat on her face as she watched Penny squirm.

"An engagement," Penny huffed, obviously flustered. "One with a very important political figure who has a lot of influence on this hospital."

"How come you never mentioned it before?" Jules asked, folding her arms. "Seems kind of sudden."

"I am the boss here," Penny snapped, her face getting red. "I don't have to tell you everything."

Jules shrugged. "Whatever. I can't make it this evening. I'm busy."

Her "busy" involved washing her hair and downloading photos of Triad's last event from her digital camera to her laptop. But Penny didn't need to know that.

"Are you telling me no?" Penny asked, bewildered.

"I'm telling you I can't make it," Jules said, turning to leave the office.

"That's too bad," Penny said to Jules's back. "I always admired your commitment to this hospital. But it looks like you don't really care at all. It will certainly be something to think about at the end of the month while I'm filling out the performance reports for our team."

Jules froze. Had Penny really said what Jules thought she said? She turned around to look her boss in the eye.

"Are you threatening me, Penny?"

This was a dangerous conversation, and even Michelle had an uncertain look in her eyes. But Jules was tired of Penny's drama.

"No," Penny said, with a look of mock sincerity. "Of course not. I just don't want you to feel at the end of the month like you could have done more but you didn't.

Come on, Jules, you love working with the community, and it's not like I'm skipping this to stay home. I'll be working too. Can't you just take this on this one time? It will only be for a few hours."

Jules sighed knowing that since Penny had laid down the law, she really had no choice. She would have to fill in.

She dreaded the thought of having to lead out at one of the community board meetings. They were filled with angry residents who were tired of the hospital's giving them sorry excuses for why they still had to wait hours for care, or why they couldn't get the tests they wanted done when they wanted them. They didn't care that funding to hospitals had been cut, or that the hospital wards and labs were understaffed. They just wanted it fixed. And they were rarely reasonable people.

"Fine," Jules said in defeat.

"Excellent," Penny said. "It's at the John Innes Community Centre at seven. Don't be late."

Jules clenched her jaw and trudged her way back to her office. This was shaping up to be a very bad day.

She had barely sent the freshly approved newsletter down to the print shop for copying when she heard the main office door open and close, signaling Penny's exit. Only moments later, Michelle was in Jules's office scowling.

"I can't believe you let her weasel you into that meeting," Michelle said, obviously more upset about the whole thing than Jules had the energy to be. "Do you know what the engagement she has this evening is?" Michelle continued, tossing her jet black hair away from her creamy white skin.

Jules shook her head, knowing that Michelle was going to tell her anyway.

"Harry Douglas's anniversary party. The invitation came in the mail two weeks ago, and she made me RSVP for her last week."

Jules's stomach fell, and she almost wished Michelle hadn't told her what she did. Penny was missing the community consultation meeting to go to a lower level member of Parliament's shindig? Didn't she realize that the hospital was in the middle of a restructuring that would involve the whole community? Didn't she realize that making sure the community was updated on the changes, and making sure they were a part of it, was more important than getting drunk with some politicians?

What's more, Penny had known all week that she would be opting out of the meeting, but she waited until the day of the event to ask Jules to take her place?

Jules shook her head. The woman was unbelievable.

"Jules, I don't know what that woman did to get this job, but she certainly didn't earn it," Michelle said, shaking her head.

Jules sighed. Generally she tried not to encourage Michelle's gossip about Penny, but she couldn't help but agree with her this time.

"Did she at least leave a copy of the progress report developed from the last consultation meeting?"

"Yeah, let me get it for you."

A few minutes later Michelle returned with a slim red binder that she placed on Jules's desk.

She shook her head as she stood at the door watching Jules flip through the document.

"I don't know how you do it, Jules. If it was me, I'd just let it all spin out of control and watch her take the blame for it."

Jules heard Michelle but said nothing. She knew

Penny well enough to know that if she ever tried that, Penny would find a way to pin the blame for the fallout on Jules. Furthermore, the public relations department as a whole would get a beating because of it. And with all the instability in the hospital, Jules didn't need anyone finding fault with her department or her. That was the way people lost their jobs, and she wasn't ready to lose hers yet.

With her other job on the skids, that was the last thing she needed.

It was 3 a.m. Sunday morning when Jules finally stopped moving. She had been on her feet for the past eight hours making sure that everything at Truuth's launch concert went as planned.

After cancelling the event at the Sound Lounge, she'd had to find a new location that would hold the crowd they expected at a price they could afford. She was almost at the point of hysterics when it occurred to her that they didn't even need to have the launch inside. It was the end of summer. No one would mind an outside venue. In fact many people would probably prefer it.

So she had called up a friend of a friend who worked with the city and managed to book Albert Campbell Square, at the Scarborough Civic Centre, a little open-air spot in the East End, for less than should be legal. With the money she saved she was able to pay for sound, lighting, and enough seating to make the empty space come to life.

The toughest part had been getting 'Dre and Truuth to go along with the new venue. If 'Dre had been skeptical about the Sound Lounge, he had been downright against the park idea. But somehow she had managed to convince him it would fly. And earlier in the evening when she overheard some friend of Truuth's telling him the venue was off the hook, she knew that the effort had been well worth it.

That was not to say that everything had gone entirely as planned.

It never did. That was the one thing Jules had learned about coordinating events. No matter how well you planned things, something always came up that you never anticipated. That was where the good event planners got separated from the great ones. If you were a good coordinator, you would find a way to fix the problem and get things back on track. If you were a great coordinator, you would know how to turn the problem into an opportunity and make it look like you had planned it that way.

That was what Jules had to do about halfway through the concert, when the amps controlling the sound for the band blew out in the middle of Truuth's performance. She would never forget the look on Truuth's face as he realized he was singing a cappella. He had completely panicked. The hundreds of fans gathered near the front of the stage continued to cheer, unaware of what was going on, while the band members began to look at each other in confusion.

"Jules, the sound is out," 'Dre had yelled into her earpiece.

"Yeah, I noticed," she had replied, trying to think fast. Truuth had finished his song, but wasn't sure where to go next.

"Can you fix it?" Jules asked 'Dre.

"Yeah. But I'll need about fifteen minutes, and we don't have that kind of time."

'Dre was right. After just five minutes of silence, the performance would begin to lose some of its momentum. In ten minutes fans would start to complain, and in eleven minutes they would start to walk out. Even if they got the sound back up by then, there would be no way to bring the crowd's energy back to the original levels. Furthermore, every journalist with a blog, podcast, or column would already be on their way home, writing a rotten review of the event. The album, and Truuth's image, would take a major hit.

"Okay, put me though to Truuth's earpiece," Jules said.

Moments later the sound of the crowd seemed suddenly to amplify, and Jules knew she had Truuth on the other end.

"Truuth, can you hear me?"

"Yeah," he muttered. He had walked back to the band for a moment, and his back was to the crowd. "The band is out, Jules, what should I do?"

Jules could hear the anxiety in his voice, and all of a sudden he sounded a lot less tough than he usually seemed.

"Don't panic, Truuth. Everything's gonna be fine. I'm gonna talk you through this, okay?" Jules said reassuringly. "Just do exactly what I tell you."

Under Jules's direction, Truuth managed to revive the crowd and get them singing one of his songs. Jules couldn't help the excitement that built up inside her as she heard hundreds of voices chant Truuth's single, a cappella style, under the open sky. With all his initial nervousness gone, Truuth was right there jumping up and down onstage, feeding the crowd's energy and acting like every bit of the entertainer Jules knew he was.

"Thank you, Jesus," Jules murmured. If she had

doubted that God had blessed this ministry before, she was sure now. Only God could make a technical failure look like they all had planned it.

A few minutes later, long before the fifteen minutes 'Dre had predicted, the amps came back on. Jules let out the breath she had been holding and said a small prayer that the show would continue without incident.

Now that everything was over, Jules could actually look back at the whole incident and smile. This was definitely one for the books.

As the euphoria wore off, the tiredness began to set in, leading Jules to sink into a chair in the last row and stretch her feet out on the seat in front of her. From where she sat she could see Truuth, Maxine, 'Dre, and his flavor of the month, Petra, milling around at the front. They were probably celebrating how well everything had gone, but since none of them were really talking to her, Jules thought she would just chill out by herself. In a few minutes she would be on her way home anyway; she just needed a minute to rest her eyes.

"Is that seat beside you taken?"

Jules opened her eyes and saw Tanya standing over her.

"Only if you mind sitting with Judas," Jules said wryly.

Tanya sighed and sat down beside her friend. "Come on, Jules, nobody thinks you betrayed them."

Jules didn't bother to answer. Tanya was always trying to be the peacemaker in the group. If she thought she couldn't create harmony among everyone she would be heartbroken. So Jules just let her think what she wanted.

"You did a really good job tonight," Tanya said.

"Thanks," Jules said, smiling. Even though she

knew things had gone well, it was nice to hear someone say she appreciated her part in it.

"Couldn't have done it without you guys, though,"
Jules said. "Truuth really killed it."

"Yeah," Tanya said. "Let's just hope all those chicks
who were lining up at the front actually buy his album
instead of downloading the bootleg off the Internet."

Jules laughed.

"So how have you been?" Tanya asked. Even though
the question was casual, Jules could see the concern in
Tanya's eyes.

Jules sighed. "I've been better."

"You know I'm here for you."

Jules shook her head. "No, you're not. Truuth's there
for Germaine, and Maxine is there for Truuth, and 'Dre
is there for the best interest of Triad and so are you.
Me, I'm just . . . there."

"It's not like that, Jules."

"It is," Jules said calmly. "But that's okay. Everybody's gotta do what they gotta do, right?"

"I know you feel like nobody's with you on this,
Jules, but you got to understand that you basically
turned Germaine into the bad guy and gave us no reason for it. It was like when you broke up with Germaine we all were supposed to break up with him too."

Germaine.

Jules was sure she had seen him at some point during the evening, but with the dusky lights and the
throng of patrons, it was hard to tell. In any case, it had
only been for a moment, and before she had time to
take a second look, someone was screaming into her
ear about something else.

Thankfully she had been too busy to think about
him. But now that Tanya had brought him up . . .

Jules gritted her teeth, and began to gather her things to leave. She didn't have the energy to go through this again.

"Whatever, Tanya," Jules said, standing. "I gotta go."

Without looking back Jules took up her purse and her supply bag and headed to her car. She dropped the larger bag into the trunk and was about to leave when she remembered she had left a box of CDs and promotional materials under the stage.

Sighing heavily, she closed the trunk and headed back toward the stage area. She noticed that everyone had left, so she walked straight up the center aisle between the rows of chairs, circled around the side of the stage, past the lighting equipment, and into the large "backstage" area the staging crew had created with curtains and ropes.

Getting on her hands and knees, she crawled under the stage and pulled out the crate of promotional materials from the area where she had stashed them a couple hours before. When she stood up again, she found Tanya, and a rather sulky Maxine standing behind her.

She sighed to herself.

Here we go again.

"I don't like this, guys," Tanya said worriedly. "We've been friends for too long for us to be holding grudges over silliness like this."

"Tanya, I'm not holding a grudge with anyone. . . ."

"Except Germaine," Maxine mumbled under her breath.

Jules's eyes flashed. "What's that gotta do with you?"

"A whole lot, seeing that he should be here now, celebrating with Truuth, but instead he's avoiding us. All because you've been treating him like some kinda criminal."

"Maybe he is a criminal," Jules shot back, glaring at Maxine. Both Tanya and Maxine looked at her in disbelief.

"Do you even hear yourself?" Maxine asked, her eyes narrowing. "That's my family you're talking about."

"Whatever, Maxine, he ain't your family yet."

"Jules, that's a pretty serious accusation," Tanya said.

Jules pursed her lips, and when she eventually spoke, the words came out firmly but quietly.

"I saw him messing with some drug dealers," she said. "They were in his office more than once, and then Easy saw him get into a car with them."

Maxine looked at her long and hard. "How do you even know they were drug dealers?" There was less hostility in her voice, but she didn't sound totally convinced.

"I didn't," Jules said. "I just saw them with him. And then I saw them again at Regent Park on the day of Truuth's shoot, and Easy told me who they were.

"That's why Easy never liked him," Jules said, turning to Tanya. "It was because he suspected it before I did. Of course, when I asked Germaine about it, he denied everything."

"Wow," Tanya murmured in shock. "I can't believe this."

"Yeah," Jules said, leaning back against the edge of the stage. "Neither could I. That's why I wanted to move the event. I didn't want Truuth or Triad mixed up in anything like that. Especially not because of me."

"Geez, Jules, why didn't you just tell us all this from the get-go?" Tanya asked. "We would have understood."

"I don't think so," Jules said dryly. "Truuth would never believe me. Furthermore he would be upset that I could even suggest something like that. And then he would have insisted on having the launch there just to prove that he was right."

She looked over at Maxine who, though silent, still looked more than a little annoyed at Jules.

"See, even now I'm telling you everything, and Maxine still isn't buying it."

"Well, what do you want me to say, Jules? Geez thanks for making my boyfriend and his family sound like hoodlums?" Maxine snapped.

"Maxine, I never said . . ."

"No, but you implied it," she said, cutting Jules off. "And so what if it's true? Okay, so maybe Germaine got mixed up in some bad stuff. Is that how you deal with it? He's only human."

Now it was Tanya and Jules's turn to look at Maxine as if she was crazy.

"Everybody makes mistakes, Jules," she continued.

"That was one hell of a mistake, Maxine," Jules said. But Maxine didn't seem to agree. In fact she seemed much more upset about the whole thing than Jules thought she had a right to be.

"So what? I didn't know you were perfect," she said. "Did you even ask him what happened or did you just throw accusations at him?"

Jules was silent. She knew she hadn't asked him what happened. She had been too angry to think that way. But why should she feel guilty about that? Anyone in her situation would have done exactly what she had—even self-righteous Maxine.

"Nobody grows up and decides to be a dealer, Jules," Maxine continued. "Nobody wants to be a disappointment to everyone around them. It's just that things happen sometimes. And you don't mean for them to happen, but they do. And you can't take them back. So you end up in this place you never wanted to be, and you don't know what to do about it. . . ."

Somewhere in the middle of the tirade, Maxine began to cry, and Jules and Tanya realized they were no longer talking about Germaine.

"Maxine, what's going on?" Jules asked with concern as she watched her friend try in vain to dry the tears that were pouring down her cheeks.

"Maxine, talk to us," Tanya said in her motherly tone, her arms already around the tiny girl.

Between sniffles, Maxine managed to warble out an answer. "I'm pregnant."

"What?"

Jules's mouth fell open, and Tanya's arms fell from around Maxine in shock. Maxine wrapped her arms around herself and nodded tearfully, her eyes fixed on the ground in front of her.

"When did you find out?" Jules asked, after she got over the initial shock.

"A . . . couple . . . days . . . ago," Maxine said, sniffling after almost every word.

"Have you told Truuth yet? . . . I mean, it is Truuth's . . . right?" Jules asked.

Despite her tears, Maxine still managed to shoot Jules a nasty look.

"I was just making sure!" Jules said. "It has been a weird couple of weeks."

"Of course it's Truuth's," she said shakily. "But I haven't told him yet. With everything that's happened with the launch and the whole Germaine thing . . . I was scared."

"Oh, Max," Jules said, walking over to her friend and wrapping her in a hug. "I'm sorry."

Maxine sniffled and buried her head in Jules's shoulder. Jules looked over at Tanya, who was standing frozen a couple inches away. She hadn't moved since Maxine had said the *p* word.

Maxine looked across at Tanya. When she noticed her stiffness, she suddenly pulled away from Jules. "See, that's why I never wanted to tell any of you," she said angrily. "I knew you would be like this."

"Be like how?" Jules asked, annoyed that she was being blamed for Tanya's standoffish attitude.

"Judgmental," Maxine snapped. "Acting like you better than me."

"Nobody thinks that, Maxine."

"I'm not judging you, Max," Tanya began. "It's just that I never knew you and Truuth were . . ."

Even though she didn't say the words, Jules could hear the disappointment in Tanya's voice.

"It was just one time," Maxine said guiltily, looking down at the ground. "We never planned it or anything, it just happened."

"You don't have to explain anything—" Jules began.

"I know," Maxine said, cutting her off. "But I want to. I don't want you to think I'm some kind of hypocrite-Christian. I knew it was wrong, and we shouldn't have done it. We both did. And we promised it would never happen again until we were married," Maxine said. "But I guess it only takes one time."

Jules pursed her lips in agreement. She knew a lot of girls who had ended up in Maxine's situation because of just one time.

Maxine swallowed hard, and sniffled. "When I missed my period last week, I took one of those two-minute tests, and it came back positive."

Even though she had stopped crying, Maxine still

looked a bit shaky, and Jules put a hand on her shoulder comfortingly.

Tanya shook her head. "I warned you this would happen, Maxine. All that time you and Truuth spend locked up together at his place. Truuth may be a Christian, but he's a man just like any other man. You turn him on, it's gonna be real hard to turn him off. The way you all act, like you already married, it was bound to happen sooner or later. . . ."

"Tanya."

Tanya looked up and caught Jules's eyes.

"I'm sorry, it's just that . . ." She sighed. "This never had to happen, that's all."

"We all know that, including Maxine."

Jules turned toward Maxine, who was shaking quietly, her eyes never leaving the floor.

"You have to tell Truuth," Jules said gently but firmly. Maxine nodded and Jules wrapped her arms around her once more. Moments later Tanya was hugging her too.

When they finally let go of each other, Maxine turned to look at Jules.

"I still meant what I said, Jules," she said, looking at her friend sternly. "I'm not saying I even believe you, but if Germaine really is involved in some kind of mess, there might be more to it than you think."

"How can you be thinking about that fool at a time like this?" Jules asked, slightly annoyed that they were back to this topic.

"Because we're family," she said. "All of us. Whether you like it or not. And it's what a family does."

Jules frowned but said nothing.

"You know I'm right, Jules," she said. "And family

don't turn their backs on each other. What would you do if it was Davis?"

"I don't know," Jules said sulkily.

"Yes, you do," Maxine said. "You would pray for him, and then you would get all up in his business and find a way to help, like you do with everyone else."

"She's right," Tanya said. "Maybe we should do that now."

Even though Jules didn't feel much like it, she didn't resist as Maxine and Tanya grabbed her hands.

"Dear Lord," Tanya began. "We want to thank You that we can come to You with anything we need. There is no situation that You can't fix. Nothing is too hard for You. At this time we want to raise up our sister and brother to you.

"Please be with Maxine in this time, and show her what to do. She has fallen, Lord, but You know she still loves You and wants to walk in Your will. Help her, we pray.

"We also raise up before you Germaine. Lord, You know what's going on with him even if we don't. I pray You take control of his situation. Keep him safe, and if he is involved in something shady Lord, provide a way out for him, as you have promised to do with all your children. Dear Lord, also show us how to love him as you desire us to love each other. Thank You for hearing and answering our prayers, in Jesus's name. Amen."

Jules mumbled her amen at the end of the prayer.

Okay, Lord, I gave it to you. You can't say I didn't try.

Chapter 14

All week Maxine's words seemed to spin around in Jules's mind. She knew that Maxine had a point, but a part of her revolted at the thought of showing any kind of compassion toward Germaine.

Jules hated drug dealers. It wasn't because she thought they were dangerous. She had known a couple of them growing up. They would hang around the school perimeter or behind the public library in the evenings after school, trying to get kids interested in whatever they were pushing. The small-time ones were pretty harmless if you stayed away from them. They were only there to make a sale, and if you weren't buying, they weren't really interested. Those she could ignore. But the big-time ones—the ones who only showed up outside bars or in nightclubs, and who were always dressed to perfection—those were the ones she couldn't tolerate.

They weren't easy to spot, but once you'd seen one of them, you'd seen them all. It was always their excessive jewelry that gave them away, or the way their eyes followed you for a long time before they approached.

Those were the dealers to the dealers. Those were the ones you kept your distance from.

Usually Jules wouldn't care, as long as nobody she knew got involved with them. But every time she saw a brother who looked like a dealer, she would remember Vanessa O'Connor.

Vanessa O'Connor was a girl from her high school who got mixed up with Jomo Bishop, a big-time crack dealer in the Scarborough area. She knew Jomo was a drug dealer. Everyone knew Jomo was a drug dealer, even the police. But they could never catch him with an ounce of crack, or find one of his small-time distributors stupid enough to sell him out. And so he had free reign to drive around the community in his black Jaguar, attracting young teens to his trade.

Vanessa was one of those that got attracted. It was understandable. She was poor. She lived with her unemployed mother and four brothers and sisters—all of whom had different fathers—in a squalid two-bedroom apartment. The school system wasn't doing much for her, so when Jomo noticed her, she jumped at the chance for something better.

But everyone knows being a drug dealer's chick is just an orientation program to being a drug dealer's employee. It wasn't long before Jules heard from friends that Vanessa was selling crack on the other side of Scarborough. And as was often the case, it seemed that she had sampled the merchandise and gotten hooked herself. Now she was her own supplier and buyer.

Last time Jules saw Vanessa, she was lying on a gurney in the emergency room at Toronto Grace. Jules almost didn't recognize her. Her skin was pale and worn, and littered with scars, probably from where Jomo beat her when she didn't have his money. It had been hard for Jules to look at. She had wanted to talk to the broken girl, but she had been unconscious. When she came back the next day, Vanessa had already checked out. That was over a year ago.

As Jules stood contemplating the Sound Lounge from across the street, she wondered which category Germaine fell into. Was he a Jomo, or was he a Vanessa?

The other part of her—the part that didn't revolt against him—desperately wanted Maxine to be right. She wanted it all to be just a misunderstanding. Or even a bad situation. Maybe he got caught up with some bad friends when he first came back to Toronto. Or maybe someone was threatening him, or the store. That she could understand. If that was the case, she could deal with it. But what if it wasn't?

Jules shook her head and brushed that train of thought out of her mind. She wouldn't think about that now.

Checking the traffic carefully, she crossed the street and made her way to the store. She had left work and taken the subway downtown, so she had made it a little before closing time. She waved to Tina, who barely nodded at her from where she had her face buried in a novel, and slipped around to the back.

She heard the voices as soon as she stepped into the passageway. They weren't loud, but were audible enough for Jules to figure out that there were at least two other persons in the office with Germaine. She got to the slightly ajar door and glanced in. As she had begun to suspect, Germaine's visitors were the same ones she had encountered in the office some months before. Unwilling to risk a repeat of that encounter, she turned and began to leave, but something she heard made her stop in her tracks.

"We like how you work, keeping our business quiet around these parts. Plus, you ain't greedy like Victor was," a voice said from the office.

Jules couldn't see from where she stood, but she was sure Germaine must have nodded because the voice kept talking.

"So we wanna bump this up a bit," he continued. "Our clients have been getting a bit antsy, you know?"

"More than usual?" Germaine asked, his voice thinly veiling his sarcasm.

"Heh heh, yeah," the voice said, laughing. "And you know it pays to keep them satisfied. So anyway, we're gonna be bringing in a little more of our favorite music, you feel me?"

The second person had begun speaking. He sounded impatient, and didn't seem to be having as much fun as his partner.

"Is that gonna be a problem?" Number Two asked. "If this is gonna bring more eyes around these parts, then it's a no-go."

"Nah, it's cool," Jules heard Germaine say.

"Good."

"So you liking our little arrangement now, eh?" Number One asked.

"Ain't nobody complainin'."

Jules cringed at the way the words seemed to roll easily off Germaine's lips.

"Good," said Number One. "You keeping bringing in this powder, and we'll keep you rolling in the paper."

So that's what he was doing. Shipping drugs for them.

Jules shook her head. She couldn't believe the kind of guy she had gotten mixed up with. What was she thinking coming over here like this? She couldn't help Germaine. This was way over her head. If those guys found out she knew what was going on, there was no telling what they might do to her.

With those thoughts pounding in her mind, Jules turned and prepared to slip out of the hallway, out of the store, and out of Germaine's life, for good.

But as she did, she tripped on a loose floorboard. She caught her footing, but no doubt everyone in Germaine's office had heard her. Before she could take two steps, the office door swung open, and a hand roughly grabbed her and pulled her in.

"Who's this?"

That was Number One. He wasn't laughing anymore, and Jules could feel his fingers gripping her arm so tightly she thought her veins would pop through. He was so close she could feel his hot angry breath on her neck.

Her heart began to pound in her chest as all the blood seemed to rush to her head.

As the three of them stared at Germaine, Jules watched a look of panic flash through his eyes. But it was gone before she knew it, and replaced with a look of supreme calm.

"Fellas, relax. This is my girl, Renee," Germaine said calmly, the lie slipping easily off his lips. "She ain't nobody."

Out of the corner of her eye, Jules saw Number One turn to look at Number Two, while keeping his grip on Jules's arm, which was burning from where he held it in a vice. She was beginning to lose feeling in her fingers.

Number Two said nothing but kept his eyes glued to Germaine, as if trying to figure out if he was lying.

"I said you ain't gotta worry about her," Germaine repeated testily. His eyes had hardened, and he was looking purposefully at Number Two.

After what seemed like forever, Number Two broke into a wide smile.

"Why didn't you just say so, man."

He nodded at Number One, who in turn released his grip on Jules's arm. Jules felt all sorts of relief flood through her as she stumbled over to Germaine.

"Baby, haven't I told you to call before you come see me," Germaine said, casually slipping an arm possessively around Jules's waist and pulling her close to him. If someone had told her yesterday that Germaine's side would feel like the safest place on earth, she would have laughed them to scorn. What a difference a day makes.

With his guests still watching in thinly disguised suspicion, Germaine placed a lingering kiss on her temple.

"Be easy," he murmured against her skin, in a voice only she could hear. She nodded slightly against his shoulder and avoided looking at the others in the room.

"I'm not trying to be up in your business," Number Two said, nodding toward Jules. "But I don't like strangers crashing my party, you feel me?"

"I got you," Germaine assured them, without the slightest trace of unease. "Have I ever done you wrong?"

"Nah," Number Two said, chuckling. "You sure haven't."

Out of the corner of her eye, Jules glimpsed something shiny and metal sticking out of the waist of Number Two. Her body began to shake involuntarily, and she felt Germaine's grip tighten around her waist. Her chest was so tight she could barely breathe.

"Good," Germaine said. "We cool then?"

"Yeah," Number Two said with a slight nod, as he slipped on his shades. "We'll be in touch."

Number One leered at Jules, a slow, greasy smile sliding across his face.

Jules shuddered as she watched him and his boss leave the office. As soon as the door closed, she felt Germaine's body tense, and his arm drop from around her. Her body was still trembling, and she felt weak all over.

"You okay?" Germaine asked quietly. Jules shook her head violently.

She heard him sigh heavily, before helping her into the chair by his desk. Moments later he was on the phone talking to someone, his voice so low, Jules could barely hear bits of what he was saying. Even if she could have heard more, she was too dazed from what had just happened to focus on anything.

She heard keys jingling and the desk drawer opening, and looked up just in time to see Germaine pull a small gray handgun from a locked metal box in his bottom drawer. Jules's eyes grew wide, and she stumbled as she tried to rise out of the chair in an effort to get away from him.

"Hey, easy," Germaine said, shoving the gun into the back of his waistband under his shirt, and stretching out a hand as a sign for her to calm down. Jules watched him watch her carefully, as if she was a skittish animal.

With his eyes never leaving her, he moved quickly back to the phone.

"Tina, I'm gonna be out for a while. Keep an eye on things till I get back, okay?"

Seconds later he was pulling Jules out of the office, down the passageway, and to his car outside the back entrance.

"No," Jules said, trying to resist his efforts to get her into the car. She pushed at him hard and tried to pull her arm out of his grasp. Even though he was taller and much stronger, she still struggled for freedom. She wanted to get away from this place, from him, as fast as she could.

"Jules, get in the car," Germaine said firmly.

"No!"

"Jules," Germaine said, grabbing both her shoulders and forcing her to look into his eyes.

She stopped struggling, and for some reason unknown to her, got into the car.

As the car sped east on the highway, Jules curled herself into the corner, as far away from Germaine as she could get without falling through the window.

A few minutes later Germaine pulled up in front of Jules's building and parked.

As soon as she stepped inside he locked all three locks on her front door. Then he turned to Jules, and all the restraint he had held thus far seemed to evaporate.

"What the hell were you thinking?" he asked, his eyes shooting fire at her.

Jules stepped back, floored by his intensity, and felt her calves hit the sofa. Involuntarily, she sat hard into the cushions, her wide eyes still glued to him.

"What were you doing eavesdropping outside my

office? Trying to get yourself killed? Do you know what those guys could do to you?"

He rubbed his hand nervously across his face and began to pace the room. Jules caught a glance at the bulge in the back of his waist and suddenly remembered what was there.

"So I was right all along," she said hoarsely as she found her voice. "You were working with those drug dealers."

"Yes."

He had stopped pacing and was standing in front of her.

"So you lied to me."

This time he didn't answer. But Jules could see his jaw tense as her statement hung in the air.

"Why, Germaine?" she asked in confusion. "Why would you do something like this?"

He rubbed his hands over his face tiredly.

"It's complicated."

"So un-complicate it for me."

"I can't."

"Try."

Germaine sat down in the seat across from Jules and rubbed his hand over his face again. He was tired. She could see it. The exhaustion was oozing out of him. How had she not noticed this before? He was always tired, even when he had been with her. Maybe the burden of lying to everyone around him had taken its toll on him. Jules wondered if he even knew who he was anymore.

He opened his mouth to say something, but his cell phone rang. He looked at the screen briefly before stepping into the kitchen to answer it. Jules strained to hear what he was saying but dared not move from the couch. She would rather not be caught eavesdropping again.

Moments later he reappeared. He looked less agitated than before, but still wasn't completely at ease.

"What's going on, Germaine?" she asked before he could say another word.

"Jules, I can't—"

"Fine. Then I'm calling the police," Jules said, whipping out her own cell phone from her back pocket. She wouldn't really do it. But he couldn't know that, and she was hoping her bluff would work.

"Jules, don't," Germaine said nervously as he watched her. She ignored him and began depressing numbers on the keypad.

"Jules . . ."

She placed the phone to her ear.

"Jules!"

Grabbing the phone from her, Germaine snapped it shut.

Jules folded her arms across her chest defiantly and stared at him expectantly. Seeing that he was beaten, Germaine sighed heavily.

"Okay," he said tiredly, sinking into the armchair across from her and resting his elbows on his knees.

He took another deep breath and then began. "You were right. I am working with those guys," he admitted. "But I am not a drug dealer," he added quickly.

"Then why—"

Germaine put up a hand to stop her.

"All I do is let them ship their stuff from Montreal to Toronto with my supplies."

Jules looked at him in confusion. "I don't understand."

"All the music for the store gets shipped from the

US through Montreal. They ship their drugs with my packages 'cause we almost never get searched. In any case, they have someone at that end who will look the other way. When it gets here, they pick it up, and pay me for the service."

"How often is that?"

"Every week."

"For how long?"

"Since I bought the store."

Jules sat back hard.

"How . . . how did this happen?"

"It just did," Germaine said, grimacing.

Jules opened and closed her mouth several times. She didn't know what to say. She had known all along that he was involved with this thing in some way, but hearing him admit the whole truth made it so much more real.

As she watched him struggle with himself, she didn't know whether to despise him or feel sorry for him. Maybe she was feeling a little bit of both.

"Don't you think of all the people who are getting hurt because of what you are doing?" Jules asked. "How can you do this?"

Jules saw the guilt wash over him. Without his even saying a word, she knew he had thought about it many times.

"You have to stop this, Germaine."

"I know. I will."

"When? You've had the store for almost a year!"

He shook his head

"It's not that easy, Jules. I just need . . . time."

"Time? Time for what?" Jules asked angrily. "Time for more people to get hooked? Time to get caught or have drug dealers shoot up the store? Time to get Truuth or someone else you care about killed? Will it be time enough then?"

"Jules, it's not like that," Germaine said, looking up at her for the first time.

Something about the look in his eyes seemed to sedate Jules's anger for a moment. He really was tortured and remorseful about what he was doing. But obviously not remorseful enough, because he kept letting it happen.

Jules shook her head and stared at him for a moment longer.

"You are so not who I thought you were," she said quietly.

"You're wrong. I am," he said, moving to kneel in front of her. "You know me, Jules. The real me. This . . . thing . . . this is not who I am. You know that."

Jules shook her head and scooted away from him. She didn't even want him touching her. "The man I thought I knew would never do anything like this," she said quietly. "The man I knew cared about the lives of others. He had principles. He had God."

"I am that person, Jules," Germaine said honestly. "I just got into some bad stuff for a while."

He turned her cell phone over and over in his hands for a quiet moment.

"Things aren't always what they seem, Jules."

He sighed, and handed the phone back to her. "I have to go."

"Where?"

"Back to work."

He got up and began walking toward the door, then suddenly stopped and turned back toward her.

"Jules, you can't tell anyone about this," Germaine said seriously. "I mean no one."

"No," Jules said, shaking her head. "I can't lie to my friends. I didn't say anything before because I wasn't sure. But now . . ."

Germaine sighed. "Jules, I told you. It will be over soon."

Jules shook her head. "If something happened to Truuth, or Maxine . . ."

Or you.

"I couldn't live with myself."

Germaine rubbed his hand over his jaw and paced the living room for a moment.

"All right," he said after a moment. "Give me a couple weeks."

"What?"

"Two weeks to clear this up," Germaine said, sighing. "By then it will be over."

Jules narrowed her eyes at him.

"How are you gonna do that?"

"I just will."

"In two weeks?"

"Yes," Germaine affirmed. "I promise you it will all be over by then."

Jules cocked her head to the side and peered at him to see if he was bluffing. But he was dead serious.

"Why should I believe you?" Jules asked. "How do I know you won't bounce before then?"

"Where would I go?" Germaine asked. "Everything important to me is right here."

Jules felt her face flush.

"I don't know, Germaine."

"Before, back at the store, when I told you to get in the car, you trusted me. Why?"

Jules shrugged. "I don't know."

Germaine looked at her knowingly. "Yes, you do.

All I need is a week and a half, Jules, two weeks max. Promise me you won't say anything until then."

Jules watched him watch her. There was that feeling again, that inexplicable feeling that she should trust him, even though it didn't make sense.

"Promise, Jules."

A lot could happen in two weeks.

"Jules . . ."

"Okay," she said finally.

He gave her one last look before slipping through her front door.

"Two weeks."

Chapter 15

"I got here as fast as I could. What's going on?"

It was near four o'clock in the morning, and Jules
was following her boss into the elevator, and down to
the ground floor of Toronto Grace. After her talk with
Germaine, Jules had barely been able to fall asleep.
Somewhere around midnight she had managed to
catch a break. However, less than three hours later
Penny had called saying there had been some kind of
emergency that required Jules to be at the hospital immediately. Jules's stomach tightened nervously as she
wondered what exactly the crisis was.

"There was an incident in the ER," Penny said. From
the tension in Penny's voice, and the way she said the
word "incident" Jules knew that something major had
happened.

"I'm not sure of the details, but we're meeting with
the head nurse on duty, and she should be able to fill
us in."

Moments later Jules and Penny were crowded into a
small windowless meeting room on the hospital's
ground floor with the head of emergency, the chief of

medical staff, the chief nursing executive, and a nurse Jules wasn't familiar with.

"Thank you, everyone, for getting here so fast," Penny said. "The president is on his way, but we need to get started because already the media is lining up at the hospital entrance. Susan, you want to tell us what happened?" Penny asked, directing her question toward the unfamiliar nurse.

The middle-aged nurse glanced around nervously at the several pairs of eyes watching her, and began to fiddle with the edges of her uniform.

"A man came into the ER a little bit after 2 a.m with stab wounds to his abdomen," she began. "We were just dealing with a gunshot wound, so we put him aside to wait, while one of the orderlies got a gurney for him."

She sighed heavily before she continued, and Jules could tell that she was still shaken up from whatever had happened.

"Before the gurney came, another man came into the ER and started waving a knife and attacked the first guy. Everyone went into a panic. I never saw what happened. All I know is the first guy ended up using one of the nurses as a shield against his attacker, and she was stabbed."

"Oh, Lord," murmured Dr. Carlos Grant, the chief of staff.

"That's not all," said Susan. "One of the male orderlies eventually tackled the man with the knife and managed to get it away from him, but he got stabbed in the arm in the process. The attacker ran out of the ER after that. We don't know where he went."

"What about the patient with the knife wound?"

"He lost a lot of blood on the ER floor. We were

going to prep him for surgery, but we ran tests and found high levels of cocaine in his blood and urine, and traces in his hair."

"So he was a user."

Jules's heart began to beat faster.

"Yeah. And he had too much cocaine in his system for us to operate."

Jules felt a cold chill run through her, and she had to force herself to focus.

"Were any other patients hurt?"

"No, but they were very shaken up," Susan said, visibly upset. "So were the nurses."

"I knew this would happen," said Kerry White, the chief nursing executive. "There's not enough security in that ER. And we've said it over and over. I guess somebody has to almost die before something happens."

"I understand, Kerry, but you know the hospital can't afford the extra security," said Dr. Grant.

"That's not good enough," said Dr. Wang. "Our emergency staff is at serious risk, especially at this time of morning."

Dr. David Wang took off his glasses and rubbed his eyes. For the past four years he had been head of Emergency, and Jules had never seen him angry. But this time he was really upset, and he was well within his right.

Slowly but surely all sense of order began to break down, as the three hospital executives in the room began to talk over each other. Jules looked over at Penny, who looked about as helpless as Jules felt.

"Penny, do something," Jules hissed in her boss's ear. "If you don't calm this down, things are going to get real ugly, real fast."

She nodded. "You're right."

Penny clapped her hands loudly. "Okay, everyone, you all have some valid points. But now is not the time to argue them. Right now, we need to make sure that our staff and patients are okay, and that means stemming the panic and getting things back in order as soon as possible."

When everyone seemed to agree, Penny continued. "David and Kerry, can you talk to the nurses and emergency staff and try to get things back on pace? If we look like we have things under control, it will put the patients at ease and make all our jobs a lot easier."

"What am I supposed to tell them?" David Wang asked. "How can I send them back to the same unsafe environment and tell them to be calm when nothing has changed?"

"You can tell them that both you and Kerry will be meeting with the hospital executive team tomorrow, including the president, to try to come to some kind of agreement about what needs to be done."

Seemingly pacified by that response, both David and Kerry moved toward the exit.

"Ask them not to talk to the media," Jules whispered to Penny.

"And can you ask your staff not to give any comment to the media, but to direct all inquires to Public Relations?"

"Sure."

Moments later only Jules, Penny, and Dr. Grant were left in the room.

"So what now?" Dr. Grant asked.

"Now, you make a statement to CTV News, 680, radio news and all the other media out there waiting to talk to someone about this," said Penny.

Dr. Grant looked back at her with panic. These doctors could perform the most complicated procedures on the delicate organs of a living human being, but for them, talking to the media was the equivalent of being thrown into the lion's den.

"Don't worry, Dr. Grant," Jules assured the slightly bald man. "We did all of this in that media training program you had last month. You'll be fine."

Jules turned back to Penny, who was already talking to the president on her BlackBerry.

"I'm gonna go prepare our press statement while you prep him," Jules said.

Penny nodded and covered the mouthpiece briefly. "Meet me down at the east entrance in twenty minutes. We'll do everything there."

Jules nodded and headed back down the corridors toward the elevator. In that brief moment alone, the thoughts she had tried to ignore came flooding back to her.

Was the man lying in a hospital bed downstairs someone who was strung out on the drugs Germaine had brought in? How many more people were out there like that?

She sighed as she pressed the button for the elevator. Two weeks was looking like a long time.

Chapter 16

With the way her week had been going, Jules should have known that Sunday would be a disaster. Despite the long talk they'd had the night of the launch, Maxine and Tanya still were giving her the cold shoulder. The nurses at work were threatening to go on strike, and she had spent all week fielding reporters' inquiries and running the office while Penny was locked away in labor relations meetings. Plus the whole Germaine thing was sitting on her mind like a ton of bricks, making it hard to concentrate on anything.

If that wasn't enough, on Friday she'd lost the keys to her apartment and had had to have all the locks changed. It seemed that even her car was mad at her because she kept hearing a funny sound every time she made a right turn. She should have known that Sunday dinner at her mother's was going to be no better.

But she never anticipated that it would be this bad.

It started with a simple question, just as all arguments with her mother did.

"Where's that handsome man of yours? I thought you were bringing him with you today."

Jules sighed. She had known that she would have to give an answer to that question sooner or later. Better it came now before dinner was served so they could handle the issue and move on to pretending they enjoyed each other's company.

"We broke up, Mom," Jules said firmly, not pausing while she laid out silverware on the table. She wished to God that Davis was there. But he was back at school in the States.

Lucky bastard.

"What you mean you broke up?" Momma Jackson asked, more than a little upset. She had stopped in the middle of the dining room and was glaring at her daughter as if Jules were twelve again and had brought home a bad report card.

"We were together; now we're not," Jules said dryly, still not facing her mother.

"Little girl, don't you play smart with me," Momma Jackson said sharply.

Jules cringed. She hated when her mother called her "little girl." It was just another reminder that Momma Jackson didn't respect the fact that she was a grown woman.

"I know what it means to be broken up," Momma Jackson continued tightly. "What I want to know is what did you do to make that boy break up with you? It was your working, wasn't it? You couldn't find any time for him, just like you never find any time for me."

Jules couldn't hold her tongue any longer.

"First of all, Momma, I am not a little girl; I am a grown woman. I make my own decisions," Jules said sharply, glaring at her mother from across the room. "Secondly, why are you so sure he was the one who broke up with me?"

"Because I know you ain't dumb enough to let go of a good Christian man who has something going on, and who's interested in you," Momma Jackson said matter-of-factly.

"Well, guess what, Momma, I am the one who broke up with him. And it had nothing to do with my work. Why does everything I do wrong have to be about that?"

"Because it usually is," Momma Jackson said. "You worship that job, like it's the only thing you got going on in your life."

"Maybe because everything else drives me half-crazy," Jules said, tossing down the rest of the silverware on the table and heading back into the kitchen, away from her mother.

Why oh why was Aunt Sharon not back from visiting her friend yet?

"Jules, you drive your own self crazy," Momma Jackson said, following her daughter into the kitchen. "You put that hospital before everything else in your life, and then you blame me 'cause I'm the only one who tells you the truth about it. I ain't gonna pet and pamper you like your daddy did, or like them friends of yours. You need to get your act right and stop alienating everyone in your life before you end up alone. The first time in your life I seen you get serious about someone, and then you run him off, for some silly reason I'm sure."

Jules turned on the faucet in the kitchen sink to rinse the dishes. She was so mad she barely noticed the hot water burning her hands. She felt like screaming. She had expected Truuth and Maxine and everyone at Triad to take Germaine's side. But now her mother too?

"That's why you're twenty-six and alone," Momma

Jackson continued. "When I was your age, I was already married."

"Yeah, and look how well that turned out for you."

The words flew out of Jules's mouth before she even had a chance to think about them. She saw the shock on her mother's face, but she couldn't stop herself. She was tired of people blaming her; tired of everyone making her feel like the wrong one for ditching a guy who was no good. She was tired of her mother using every situation in her life as an opportunity to beat her down. But most of all she was tired of trying to be the dignified one in this mess when all she wanted to do was wallow.

"You know, Momma, maybe that's the curse of Jackson family women. None of us can't ever keep a man. Not you, not Aunty Sharon, not me," Jules shot.

She didn't mean any of it. But she could see it hurting her mother, and she figured that, maybe for once, her mother would know how Jules had felt those many times before.

"Maybe that's our fate in life, to be old, dried up, bitter, and alone. Maybe that's how we're all destined to be."

Out of nowhere, Jules felt Momma Jackson's palm connect sharply with her cheek. The shock of the slap left her speechless.

"I don't care how grown you think you are, Jules Elizabeth Jackson; I am still your mother, and you do not speak to me like that," Momma Jackson said in a low, deadly voice. "Ain't no child gonna come up under my roof and disrespect me like I'm her plaything. Now you take your things, and you leave this house. And you don't come back until you know how to act like somebody grew you right."

Jules had never seen her mother so angry or hurt before. But she was too angry and hurt herself to care. Taking up her purse, she walked down the hallway and through the front door.

It was a good thing they hadn't gotten to the dinner part. She had completely lost her appetite.

Chapter 17

On Monday morning Jules woke up to a headache
so bad, she could barely see straight. It took all
that she had to get dressed and stumble into work.
When she did, she immediately wished that she had
stayed home.

"Jules, where have you been!" Michelle exclaimed,
pulling Jules into her office and closing the door behind them. Their open-concept office meant that private conversations held in the main area were not really
private, and from the way Michelle's eyes were darting
furiously around, it was clear that she did not want to
be heard.

Jules sank gingerly into her chair and winced as the
shrillness in Michelle's voice caused her head to pound
even harder.

"Didn't you see the paper this morning?" Michelle
asked in a shrieky, high-pitched voice that made Jules
cringe.

"Michelle, with the headache I have, I barely saw
the road on my way in," Jules answered, closing her

eyes beneath her oversized sunglasses and rubbing her temples gently. She definitely should have stayed home.

She was so groggy that she didn't notice Michelle had left the room until the skinny woman returned and plopped a copy of the *Toronto Star* on Jules's desk. Jules's eyes opened wide, and she snatched off her shades to make sure she was seeing right.

"TCHN paralyzed as nurses walk off the job?" Jules murmured in disbelief as she read the headline. "When did this happen?"

"About 3 a.m. this morning when the morning nurses were due to start their first shift," Michelle said. Suddenly Jules realized why the floor had seemed so empty on her way up. No doubt there were media lurking around the front entrance, but since Jules had driven through the underground parking lot and come up the back, she had not seen them.

"Oh, Lord," Jules whispered, now fully alert. "Has Penny seen this?"

"Girl, where have you been?" Michelle exclaimed. "Penny's fired."

Jules's heart began to hammer in her chest, and she could feel the blood rushing through her veins.

"They fired her this morning before she even got in. Had security come in and clean out her office and everything. I tried to get her on her BlackBerry, but it was disconnected. Her company e-mail is shut off, and she's not even answering her house phone."

"Oh, Jesus," Jules murmured, leaning her elbows against her desk and dropping her face into her hands. She wasn't using the Lord's name in vain. She really did need him. She could barely breathe.

"Jules, what are we going to do about this?" Michelle asked, pointing to the newspaper in panic. "It's all over the news on the radio and television. The phone has been ringing all morning, and all I could do is forward the calls to you. You know I don't know how to talk to the media."

Jules could hear the urgency in Michelle's voice and already knew what she was thinking. If they didn't do something, this was likely to escalate into a region-wide issue with Toronto Grace Hospital at the center. The bad press would ruin the community's perception of the hospital, cut the flow of donations to the hospital's foundation, and taint the name of the Toronto Central Hospital Network for a long time. And chances were, both she and Michelle would end up the same way Penny had—unemployed.

Jules closed her eyes.

Lord, if there was ever a time I needed You, it's now.

Taking a deep breath she looked up at Michelle.

"It's okay, Michelle. It will be all right," she said with more confidence than she felt. Michelle looked at her as if she was crazy, but Jules stood her ground.

"We'll get through this, but we have to work together and stay calm, okay?"

Michelle still looked on the verge of hysteria, but she nodded.

"Okay, now, there's a Crises Plan binder in the cabinet. Can you get it for me? I'm gonna call Kerry White and see if she can tell me what exactly is going on with the nurses."

As Michelle disappeared to find the binder, a million questions floated through Jules's mind.

Why hadn't Penny called her as soon as she knew that something had happened? She had been in meetings with the nurses' union all week. How could she not have known that they were about to go on strike? And if she did know, how could she not have said anything to the rest of them?

Jules tried calling Kerry on every number she had for her, but was unable to reach the chief nursing executive. Every call she made went to voice mail. She wasn't surprised. The head of the union had probably told Kerry not to talk to anyone from the TCHN executive team.

Jules tapped her pen against the desk in thought for a moment before picking up the phone again and dialing a familiar number. The phone rang twice before someone answered.

"Maxine? It's me, Jules."

"Geez, Jules, you know I ain't even supposed to be talking to you," Maxine hissed in a stage whisper. "If any of the other nurses catches me, I won't hear the end of it."

"Yeah, I know, but you're the only person I could call. I can't get through to anyone else. What's going on?"

"What do you mean what's going on? The nurses are on strike. We're tired of being disrespected and forced to work in unsafe conditions," Maxine said.

Jules snorted. "Is that what's on the script they gave you to read?"

"Jules, I am this close to hanging up the phone."

"No, no wait," Jules said quickly. "I'm sorry. It's just that I'm a bit stressed here. I didn't find out about all this until this morning."

"How's that? That boss of yours was at all the meetings last week."

"Yeah, well, she got canned, so it's just me and Michelle."

"They fired her? Ho-lee," Maxine murmured in surprise. "What are you gonna do?"

"I'm gonna try to fix this, which is why I need you to tell me what's going on."

"It's bad, Jules. After that stabbing a couple weeks ago, ya'll were supposed to meet with the nurses and come up with a plan, but the meeting never happened. It wasn't until the union leader started talking strike that everyone was ready to talk to us."

"What's the real problem, Max?"

"We don't feel safe, Jules. We have to deal with all types of people, and there's not enough security in the hospital, especially in the ER. Do you know how many patients I get who have weapons on them when they come in? They're not supposed to get past security with all of that stuff, but it's happening all the time. Something's gotta change before anybody goes back to work."

Jules sighed. She knew Maxine was right. In the past couple of months the number of guards on the hospital campus had dropped almost by half. What's more, guards were working longer shifts, meaning they were less efficient in their duties.

Just last week she had caught Charlie, the security guard at the east entrance, dozing off at his post. Jules had been annoyed at first. But he soon told her that he was coming off two back-to-back eight-hour shifts. Furthermore, the guard who was to relieve him hadn't shown up, so he had to stay until the security company could send out a replacement. If that kind of thing was a regular occurrence, Jules could understand why so many things were getting past security.

"I know it's bad, Maxine, but have you guys thought about the patients? Who's going to take care of them?

Especially the ones in ICU? You know there's no way the doctors can handle that alone."

Jules waited for Maxine to respond, but got nothing but silence on the other end. She narrowed her eyes. There was something Maxine wasn't telling her.

"Max," Jules said suspiciously, "what are you not telling me?"

"Nothing," Max said quietly.

"Maxine!"

"All right, all right. We have a skeleton team of nurses who are keeping things going on the floor," she said. "We might be dissatisfied, but we're not barbaric. We care about our patients, you know."

"Yeah, I know," Jules said, slightly relieved to find that patients were still being cared for.

"Jules, you can't let this get out to the media, or no one will take the strike seriously."

"I know, Max. We're not allowing the media into the building, so it should be okay for now. But I need you to do me one last favor," Jules said thoughtfully. "I think I have a plan."

An hour later Jules got the inevitable call up to the boardroom. She sighed and picked up the file she had been working on.

Here goes nothing.

"Ms. Jackson, please have a seat," Dr. Henry Conrad, president and CEO of the hospital, said, as Jules entered the room. Under the watchful eyes of the twelve other board members and executives, Jules took at seat at the large mahogany table, as Michelle, whom she had dragged along, found a seat by the wall behind her.

"Now, I'm not going to beat around the bush with this, Ms. Jackson. As you know, Ms. Freeman has been released from her duties at the hospital. I have no qualms about telling you that it was because we found that her level of commitment to the hospital, as well as her performance, had fallen below the level we thought to be acceptable."

Jules nodded slightly and tried to keep her eyes focused on the president even though her heart was hammering in her chest, and the heat of everyone's eyes on her was making her sweat.

"We also have reason to believe that Ms. Freeman was using hospital funds in a somewhat questionable manner."

Jules froze. Penny had been messing with the hospital's money? This was a lot more serious than she had imagined. She blinked rapidly and tried to force herself to listen to the president's voice, despite the fact that a million questions were already running through her mind.

"Sir, you have to know that I would never misappropriate the funds of the hospital in any way," Jules said hurriedly. "I am and have always been completely committed to the success of this hospital. And I'll say the same for Ms. Chang. We did know that certain duties were not being handled well, but neither of us knew that there were issues in regards to department finances."

Dr. Conrad nodded patiently as he listened to Jules. She watched him tap his pen thoughtfully against his palm for a moment before responding.

"We do suspect that Ms. Freeman was working in isolation, but I am going to be frank. Usually under such circumstances, we would see fit to replace the entire department.

"However, you have been with the hospital for a while, and I was pleased with the way you handled the community consultations a few weeks ago. In addition, as you know, we are in the midst of a small crisis, and now would not be the best time to be entirely without a public relations team.

"That being said, what do you propose that we do about the current situation?"

"I am glad you asked, sir," Jules said. "Before I came here this morning I had a chance to speak with the chief nursing executive about the matter. She informed me that steps have been taken to care for the hospital's most critical patients despite the strike, and I was able to gain assurance from her that patient safety will not be heavily compromised."

Dr. Conrad nodded but continued looking at Jules, expecting more.

"I know we want to get this issue resolved as quickly as possible, so I arranged a private meeting between the chief nursing executive, the head of the nurses' union, the head of Emergency, and the hospital chief of staff. We're hoping you can be a part of this meeting as well, Dr. Conrad, so that this can be settled outside of the papers."

Before anyone could cut in or Jules could lose her composure, she continued outlining the plan in place for dealing with the strike. Even when she had to field questions and concerns from the board members, she still managed to hold her own.

Inwardly she gave a sigh of relief. Maybe things would work out after all.

"I must say, Ms. Jackson, I am very impressed with

the level of effort you put into this recovery strategy," Dr. Conrad said.

Jules nodded, and tried not to smile despite the pride welling up inside her.

"However, you are a bit . . . inexperienced in dealing with this type of thing, and the board feels that maybe we need an outside party to navigate this issue."

Jules blinked several times, not sure she understood exactly what he was saying.

"We have decided to hire an external public relations agency to deal with this matter."

Jules cleared her throat nervously. "With all due respect, Dr. Conrad, the plan I laid out was very thorough. You yourself said it sounds like the right direction to go. We can do this without—"

"I'm sorry, Ms. Jackson, I think I was unclear. We have already brought in an external team to handle the issue. They will be here momentarily to begin work."

Jules looked at Dr. Conrad dumbly, unable to find the words to speak. It seemed like not even her best efforts had been enough.

"It's not that we don't agree with your strategy, but we would feel more confident having a team of experts handling the issue. You can hand over your plan to them when they get here. I am sure that the execution will be just as you anticipated."

Jules sighed. The way things had been going, she shouldn't have expected anything less.

"How long will Ms. Chang and I be working with this team?" Jules asked, trying to keep the defeated feeling she felt from spilling over into her voice.

There was an odd silence, and Jules couldn't help but notice the look exchanged between the Dr. Conrad and Thomas Donnelly, the VP of operations. A feeling of panic began to spread through her stomach as Donnelly cleared his throat nervously.

"Ms. Jackson, in light of the fact that your department is currently under investigation, we will be asking that you take a leave of absence."

"What?" Jules croaked. She heard Michelle gasp behind her.

"Just for three weeks until this issue has been sorted out. We are asking that you turn everything over to the agency and have your desk cleared out by the end of business today."

Jules's mouth fell open.

Clean out her desk? That didn't sound like a leave of absence. That sounded like she was being fired! This was ridiculous! Penny's indiscretions weren't her fault. Why did she have to take the blame? Besides, there was no way she could just turn everything over to an agency. How would they run the department without her? Without Michelle?

But as she looked around at the faces at the table, she knew that the president's proposal was not up for discussion. It had been decided long before she had even entered the room.

The one thing she had feared the most was happening at the worst time ever. She was losing her job. The career she had worked so hard for had come crashing down on her in just one day. And it wasn't even her fault.

Chapter 18

It was the ringing of the phone that woke Jules up on Tuesday. Even though it was already midday, she couldn't seem to motivate herself to get out of bed.

She pulled her pillow over her head and willed the answering machine to pick it up. Eventually it did, but a minute later the phone started ringing again.

The third time it happened Jules realized that whoever it was knew she was at home.

She groaned and rolled across the bed until she was near enough to reach the phone.

"Hello?"

"Jules, what's going on?"

It was Davis.

"I've been trying to reach you since yesterday, and I've been getting nothing but voice mail. I called your office this morning, but they said you're no longer there. What's that about?"

Jules sighed and sat up in bed, wincing at the bright sunlight that was streaming through the window. She tried to think of a way to explain what had happened at work to her brother without it seeming as bad as it was.

But for some reason she couldn't muster up the energy to do it.

"I got fired yesterday."

"What?"

"Well, not really," Jules corrected groggily. "I was forced to take a leave of absence."

"For how long?" Davis asked, alarmed.

"Three weeks, maybe more."

"What?" Davis asked, clearly confused. "Why?"

Jules calmly explained everything that had happened at work, from Penny's passing off her duties to Jules, to the article on the front page, to the accusations of fraud against her department, to Penny's being fired. When she was done Davis was speechless.

"So they're investigating you for fraud?"

"I don't know," Jules grumbled. "They won't say anything specific. They haven't asked for access to any of my private accounting information, so I think I might be in the clear on that part of things."

"I can't believe you didn't tell me about all of this before," Davis murmured. "It's really bad, isn't it."

"Yup. I'm pretty much toast," Jules said nonchalantly. "Stick a fork in me, baby brother; I'm done."

"Is that why you and Mom got in an argument—wait, but if all that happened yesterday, you didn't lose your job till after your argument with Mom," Davis said, more to himself than to Jules.

Jules cringed. "I didn't lose my job—it's just . . ."

Who was she kidding? She knew there would probably be no job at the hospital for her to go back to at the end of the three weeks.

Jules sighed. "No, my argument with Momma wasn't about that. How did you even know about that anyway?"

"I called her yesterday," he said. "I was asking her

something about Sunday dinner with you, and she said something about not having a daughter, so I figured you two had gone at it again."

Jules rolled her eyes. So her mother had disowned her. Why was she not surprised? With the way Jules had spoken to her, Jules knew she probably deserved it.

"Yeah, we did. Did she tell you why?"

"No. She wouldn't talk about it. That's why I'm calling you," Davis said. "This one sounded really serious. What happened?"

Jules replayed the argument to Davis, including all the gory details. Davis let out a low whistle.

"That was pretty cold, Jules," he said. "How could you say that to her? You know how sensitive she is about Dad."

"I know," Jules whined, falling back into the pillows and pulling her sheet over her head. "I was just so angry about everything, and she just kept getting on my nerves."

"She's still our mother, Jules," Davis said. "You know you were way over the line."

"Yeah, I know," Jules said. "She'll probably never speak to me again."

"Not unless you apologize, anyway."

"Maybe not even then," Jules said.

She had had a lot of arguments with her mother. But maybe this was the one that had truly ruined their relationship forever. It was funny how you try to get far away from someone, but the moment you realize that you may never have them around again, they are all you can think about.

Davis sighed. "So what happened with you and Germaine anyway?"

"What are you, the Jackson family police?"

"You know I can just call him if you won't tell me," Davis said.

"You wouldn't," Jules said, with a hint of uncertainty.

"Yeah, you know I wouldn't," Davis conceded sheepishly. "So just tell me what it is."

Jules bit her lip as she thought about just how much she should tell Davis.

They almost always told each other everything. The one time Davis had almost cheated on Keisha, he had told Jules, even before he had talked to Keisha about it. And when Jules had been planning to move out, Davis had been the one to look at apartments with her, even before she had summoned the courage to tell their mother. She knew whatever she said would be safe with him. But at the same time, this was big, and she had promised Germaine that she wouldn't say anything.

"We just both had some stuff we couldn't see past, that's all," Jules said vaguely.

She hated lying to her brother, and she hated Germaine for making her do it.

Davis was silent on the other end of the phone for a long time, and Jules began to wonder if he was still there.

"What are you not telling me, Jules?"

She had forgotten how well Davis knew her.

Jules sighed as she remembered her promise.

But Davis wouldn't tell anyone.

Before she could stop herself, the whole story came flooding out. Everything from her first encounter with Germaine's business partners at his office, to the day of Truuth's photo shoot, to the incident two weeks before. It was such a relief to be able to talk to someone about everything that had been going on. It was like a weight being lifted off her shoulders.

"Jules, are you crazy?" Davis asked. Jules held the receiver a slight distance from her ear as his voice barrelled through to her across the line. "Why the hell are you covering for this guy? Do you want to get caught up in this mess too?"

"I'm not covering for anyone, Davis," Jules said. "This is really none of my business. I'm not with him anymore, so I'm not linked to this in any way. In any case, he said it would soon be over."

"And you believe him?" Davis asked.

Jules knew there was no explanation for it, but for some reason she did.

"Yes, I believe him."

"What if something happens to you? What if one of those guys comes after you?"

"They won't," Jules said. "They think I'm nobody."

"Maybe. But you're a nobody who knows what they do."

Jules had thought about that. But she had assured herself it would be okay. Besides, what was she supposed to do? Go to the police? No way. She didn't trust them. Chances were they would run up on the store, and Germaine or someone else would get shot in the process. She didn't want to risk that.

"He said it will be over soon," Jules said.

"I can't believe you, Jules," Davis said. She could see him shaking his head in disappointment. "You're smarter than this. But even if you're not, I am," he said. "I have a friend in the force. I'm gonna give him a call, and see if he can give me some advice on this."

Jules sat up in bed suddenly, her heart beating faster.

"Davis, no. I told you this in confidence because you're my brother and I knew I could trust you."

"Jules, this ain't no kid stuff," Davis said. "You can't expect me to sit on this. In fact, you knew I wouldn't. That's why you told me, because you're too scared to do something yourself."

"I promised him, Davis."

"I can't believe this," Davis muttered. "You still have feelings for him, don't you?"

Jules didn't answer. She didn't have to.

"Jules, this is insane."

"He said it would all be over by the end of this week."

"And what if something happens before then?" Davis asked. "What if one of those guys jumps you in the street? You've seen their faces; you're a liability now."

"Davis, I said no," Jules said quietly. "I gave my word."

Davis sighed in frustration. "Jules, this is not up for discussion. If something happened to you, I could never live with myself, knowing that I could have stopped it. One of us is going to make that call. If you don't, I will."

Jules bit her lip, knowing that she had no choice. The best she could do was to talk to Davis's friend herself. It was the only bit of control over this situation she had left.

"Give me your friend's number," Jules said quietly after a long moment. "I'll call."

Even though her heart was already beating faster at the thought, Jules knew that she would have to be the one to take care of this. She grabbed the notepad from her bedside table and scribbled down the number as Davis rattled it off to her.

"Promise me you'll call him today, Jules."

"I'll call him."

"Today, Jules," Davis insisted. "I'm calling him first thing in the morning tomorrow, and if you haven't told him by then, I will."

"I promise I'll call him today," Jules said, though she didn't see the value of it. From the looks of things, her promises didn't seem to be worth that much anyway.

Chapter 19

"Remind me why I'm doing this again?" Jules asked, emptying another box of CDs and tapes on top of the huge pile that had already accumulated on the floor of Triad's basement.

"Because you're trying to get me to forget about that crazy stunt you pulled with Truuth's launch a few weeks ago," 'Dre said as he opened another dusty box to reveal more CDs.

"Excuse me? That 'stunt' is what helped your artist sell over fifty thousand albums in the first three weeks," Jules said. "You should be helping me clean out my basement."

'Dre smirked. "You don't have one."

"Technicality," Jules shot back. She stuck out her tongue at 'Dre and ended up sputtering disgustedly as dust particles fell on her mouth.

'Dre laughed, and Jules swatted at him.

The truth was, Jules was glad 'Dre had asked her to help him out. It was just what she needed to distract her from the pathetic mess that had become her life.

She hadn't told anyone, other than Davis, about her

leave of absence. Maxine had found out because of the memo that had gone out to the hospital about departmental changes, but Jules had sworn her friend to secrecy and so far Maxine hadn't said anything to anyone. Jules knew her friends would be sympathetic, but she really didn't feel like being pitied. So she spent most of the hours when she would have been at work, holed up in her apartment. When 'Dre called, it took all that Jules had to act unenthused. It had only been a few days, but she was already going stir crazy being off work. She was glad for the opportunity to get away from her home, even if it meant cleaning out Triad's filthy basement. But there was no way she would let 'Dre know that.

"You know, you owe me big time for this," Jules said, laughing. "Nobody else would help you do this, not even Tanya."

"You know Tanya has asthma, Jules," 'Dre said. "If she came anywhere down here, we'd have to hook her up to a ventilator for a week."

"Yeah, down here is pretty much a dust bin," Jules said, looking around at Triad's forgotten second basement.

It was initially supposed to be a storage space, but now it looked more like a garbage space that had become the permanent resting place for demo tapes and dead tracks. All the discarded music that Triad had accumulated in the last few years was scattered before them. It probably would have remained down there for another three years if 'Dre hadn't decided to turn the space into a much needed second studio. Jules had suggested that the artists who would be using the new studio be the ones to clean it out, but somehow she and 'Dre had ended up stuck with the task.

"So are we tossing all of these or what?" Jules asked, looking around at the piles of music.

"I don't know," 'Dre said. "There are a lot of memories in here."

He riffled through the pile on the floor and pulled out a CD that looked so old, it was probably one of the first compact discs ever made.

"This was my first demo, from when I wanted to be a gospel singer," 'Dre said, as he held up the disc.

Jules laughed. "You've got to be kidding. You wanted to be a gospel singer?"

"Yeah," 'Dre said. "And I was good too."

Jules grabbed the disc from his hand and slipped it into the CD player they had brought downstairs with them. "I have to hear this for myself."

Only moments later, 'Dre's scratchy, wobbly voice wafted through the speakers, doing a poor rendition of an old Kirk Franklin song.

Jules burst out in laughter. "Oh, no, 'Dre, please tell me you didn't send this to actual record producers."

"I did," 'Dre said, grinning. "I sent it to some execs at Integrity Records."

"Ho-lee!" Jules exclaimed, covering her face in empathetic embarrassment. "What did they say?"

"Nothing," 'Dre said, trying not to laugh. "They didn't even write me back."

Jules tried to contain her laughter. "I can imagine. What made you think you could be a singer?"

"I don't know?" 'Dre said, smiling. "I knew I loved music. I thought that being a singer was the only way to go. I didn't know anything about producing or artist development yet."

He looked thoughtful as he remembered the early

days. "It was actually Tanya who put me on to all of this."

"Really?" Jules asked. She hadn't known that.

"Oh, yeah," 'Dre said, throwing a couple cracked CDs into a half-full garbage bag. "She was the anchor that prevented the whole idea of Triad from drifting off to sea."

He smirked. "Sometimes I used to think that it was all her baby, and I was just the front man she needed to make it happen. But even with all her business smarts, she never doubted my ideas.

"If we were at an event, and I heard someone singing, and I said, I want to produce that artist, she would say, 'Okay, let's do it.' She never said, ' 'Dre, we don't have a studio,' or ' 'Dre, we don't have the money,' or ' 'Dre, we've never done this before.' She always just . . . made it happen."

Jules leaned back on her elbows and watched the pure admiration flow over 'Dre's face as he talked about Tanya. It was almost as if he had forgotten Jules was there. She smiled. Maxine was right. They were perfect for each other.

"You have a crush on her, don't you," Jules said when 'Dre had stopped talking.

"On who? Tanya? What—No," 'Dre said, looking all flustered. He began pulling random discs from the pile and tossing them into the garbage bag without looking at them.

Jules smirked. He had a crush all right. A big one.

" 'Dre, please," Jules said, rolling her eyes. "Listen to yourself. You talk about her like she's a gift from God, and you know you couldn't go two days without seeing her."

"That's 'cause she's part owner of my business,"

'Dre replied. "A business that is the sole representation of my entire financial worth. You bet I'm gonna keep an eye on her."

"That's not what I mean 'Dre, and you know it," Jules said, sitting up. "I bet half the time you and Tanya are together, you're not even talking about Triad."

'Dre shifted uncomfortably and refused to meet Jules's eye. "Maybe."

"And she's the only girl who has the passwords to your BlackBerry, right?"

"That's just in case of emergency . . ."

"And when you signed your first artist to a major recording label, who did you buy a custom-made Tudor watch, inset with white diamonds? Who, 'Dre?"

"She was a big part of making the deal happen. She deserved it," 'Dre said defensively.

Jules cocked her head to the side and looked at her friend. "You do have a little bit of a thing for her, don't you," Jules said coaxingly. 'Dre tried to keep his face neutral, but couldn't stop the smile that curved his lips.

"I knew it! I knew it!" Jules exclaimed, falling back on the ground.

"Jules, you can't say anything, please," 'Dre said seriously.

"But why? You guys would be great together," Jules said, propping her head up on one arm so she could look at 'Dre.

"Come on, Jules, have you seen Tanya? She's beautiful, and smart and funny, and she has this personality that just lights up a room. What would she want with me?"

Jules was amazed. The way 'Dre talked, you would think he was a hunchback. But 'Dre was no slouch. He was a good height at six feet, with even, caramel-toned skin, and finely chiseled features that easily went from pretty boy cute in one moment to business sharp in the next.

In addition, all that running around, setting up venues and lifting speakers, seemed to have done wonders for his physique. In fact, if Jules had been into light-skinned guys, she probably would have been interested in him herself. But he wasn't her type. And it was a good thing too, for even though he didn't know it yet, 'Dre's heart already belonged to Tanya.

"She'll want the same thing that every other girl wants with you," Jules said knowingly. "Plus, you're honest, trustworthy, and a good, God-fearing brother. And in case no one told you, those are pretty hard qualities to find."

"I hear you, Jules, but I'm not too sure about that," he said. "Just promise me you won't say anything to her about it."

Jules looked up to the ceiling. Enough with the promises.

"Okay, I promise," she said. "But you've got to promise me that if the opportunity comes, you'll go for it."

"I don't know, Jules. . . ."

"Promise! Or I'll leave you alone down here to die in this dungeon of bad music and dust."

'Dre laughed. "Okay, I promise. Now can we get back to work?"

"No, I think it's time for a pizza break. And since I'm doing all this for you, you can pay."

'Dre shook his head as he followed Jules up the stairs to the kitchen.

As soon as they got to the top of the stairs, the phone rang. While 'Dre went to get it, Jules went in search of the phone book.

"Yeah, I'm near one. . . . Okay, I'm turning it on now."

Jules shuffled back to the living room when she heard 'Dre turn on the television.

"What channel did you say?"

'Dre flipped the station to channel eight, to the nine o'clock news. The sound was down, but the images showed a raging fire taking place downtown. As Jules peered closer and recognized the location, her heart stopped.

"Oh, my God," she whispered, as she watched the Sound Lounge burn.

She took the remote from 'Dre and turned up the sound.

". . . This popular lounge near Dundas Street and Parliament Street downtown was the scene of a violent confrontation between drug dealers and the police. Despite the damage, no one was hurt. However, the police did arrest several men on charges related to drug trafficking. The arrests were part of an ongoing investigation by the police to crack down on major drug dealers in this area of the city. . . ."

Jules's blood ran cold through her veins, and she reached for the couch to steady herself.

"Jules, that was Truuth," 'Dre said, returning to the room, with his and Jules's jackets in hand. "We've got to go."

"Where are we going?"

"To the police station."

Jules tapped her fingers on the armrest, as 'Dre weaved his way through the evening traffic to the police station on Dundas Street.

"You okay?" he asked, glancing at her.

"I'm fine," Jules said, with more edge than she intended.

She didn't want to admit to herself that Truuth wasn't the only person she was worried about. She kept replaying her conversation with Davis's friend, Detective Hansen, in her mind. She had told him everything Germaine had told her, and he had said he would have some officers look into it. He was supposed to give her a call in a couple days to let her know if their digging had turned up anything useful. He hadn't called, and she had hoped that had meant he hadn't found anything. So much for that.

A few moments later they pulled into the station yard. They found Maxine leaning against Truuth's car, waiting for them

"What happened, Max? Where's Truuth?" 'Dre asked.

"He's inside," Maxine said. "He said I should wait out here—didn't want me in there, with all that was going on."

"I'm going in," 'Dre said, already moving toward the door. "Both of you wait out here."

"Hey, you can't tell me what to—"

"Jules, please, just wait out here. I'll be back in a minute."

Before she could offer any further protest, he was gone. Jules was about to ignore his orders and follow him inside when Maxine grabbed her arm.

"Hold up, there's something you should know before you charge in there."

Jules stopped and turned to look at Maxine.

Maxine looked around the parking lot before meeting Jules's eyes. "Germaine is in there."

Jules shrugged. "I figured he might be. Did they arrest him?"

Maxine nodded.

Jules sighed and joined Maxine in leaning against Truuth's car. "What happened?"

Maxine frowned. "I'm not exactly sure. Truuth called me, said something went down at the Sound Lounge, and I should come pick him up at the police station.

"When I got here he came out and told me they busted some drug dealers at the store. I'm not sure how the fire got started, but they caught them anyway. I don't know what Germaine has to do with it, but he's in there."

Maxine looked like she was about to cry. "I know I told you to talk to him, but . . . I'm sorry. You could have been in there. You could have been hurt. . . ."

"It's okay, Max," Jules said, hugging her friend as she began to cry. Jules knew Maxine was thinking that Truuth could have been hurt too, and that was what was probably upsetting her most. "The report on the news said nobody got hurt, so there's nothing to be upset about. Truuth's fine; I'm fine; we're all okay, thank God."

Maxine sniffled and wiped her eyes as she nodded in agreement. "I wish the guys would just get back so we can get out of here. I just want all of this to be over."

Jules watched Maxine wring her hands over and over and then nervously rub her stomach.

"Have you told him yet?" Jules asked.

Maxine looked up at Jules and then down at her stomach and sighed. "No."

"Maxine, you're more than a month along!"

"I know! But . . ." She sighed and looked helpless. "I haven't found the right time yet."

"Have you at least told your parents?"

Being the youngest, Maxine was the only one of them who still lived at home. And unlike most of them, she had both of her parents still around.

Instead of answering Jules, Maxine looked off in the direction of the station and said nothing, her hand still rubbing her tummy absently.

Jules sighed. "Oh, Max."

She put her arm around her friend's shoulder but said nothing more. She couldn't make Maxine do anything she didn't want to do. She would tell Truuth and her parents whenever she thought the time was right and not a moment before. And even though Jules might disagree with her timing, she would support her friend nonetheless.

It was more than half an hour later before Truuth and 'Dre came walking out the doors of the police station. Right behind them was Germaine, with what looked like a senior policeman. While Truuth and 'Dre continued toward the parking lot, Germaine remained near the doors talking to the officer.

"Boo, I was so worried about you," Maxine said, wrapping her arms around Truuth as soon as he got near enough. You would never believe she had just seen him an hour before.

"I'm fine," Truuth said. Even though he was talking to Maxine, his eyes were staring coldly at Jules. Jules braced herself.

"What's she doing here?"

Even though several weeks had passed since the blowup at the office, and since Truuth's launch, Truuth still refused to talk to Jules. It wasn't really difficult, because Jules was doing her best to avoid him as well.

"She was with me," 'Dre said. "Go easy, Truuth."

But Truuth ignored him.

"So you thought my cuz was mixed up in some drug mess, didn't you," he said accusingly. "Why he got to be dirty? Just because we from the ghetto? And we didn't grow up in some high society neighborhood like you?"

Jules narrowed her eyes and glared at him "You need to check yourself, Truuth," she said coldly. "You don't know anything about me."

"You didn't know nothing about G either, but you were ready to call him a criminal."

"Well, judging from everything that just went down, looks like I was right."

"No, you ain't right," Truuth said angrily. "You ain't never been right."

"Jules, Germaine was working with the police to bust those dealers," 'Dre said quietly from beside her. "That's why they were always at his store. It was a setup."

Jules's mouth fell open. "That's not what he told me," she said.

"Yeah, well, I guess he figured out early who he could and couldn't trust," Truuth said.

She looked from Truuth to 'Dre back to Truuth, who Maxine was trying to calm down. Then she looked up at the steps where Germaine was laughing with the officer. They shook hands. Then the officer went inside, and Germaine came down the steps toward them. Toward her.

Jules's head began to spin with all the new information. She was trying to figure out everything, but it was too much for her. As soon as she came to some sort of decision about Germaine, the ground would shift under her, and she'd find herself looking at a totally different person. Her mind couldn't take it.

"Yo, man, I had no idea. Sorry about everything, bro," 'Dre said to Germaine apologetically.

"It's no big deal," Germaine said, brushing it off. "I'm just sorry I couldn't have told you guys. I just realized today how much danger you could have been in. But I was under orders."

"We understand," 'Dre said.

Jules watched the three of them fuss over Germaine, but she didn't move. He looked tired. Really tired, but relieved.

She was sure there was something she should say, but she was too busy trying to figure out how she should feel. Should she apologize? But why? He was the one who lied to her. But he lied to protect her. How much of it was a lie?

"Anyway, we're gonna jet," Truuth said, reaching for the car door.

"It's about time," Maxine said. "This place makes my skin crawl."

"We'll catch up with you guys later," Truuth said. He shot Jules one last nasty look before getting into the car, with Maxine and Germaine in tow.

Jules was about to turn to leave when Germaine's eyes caught hers. His expression was unreadable, and that alone sent a cold chill through her. Without a word, he stepped into the car, closing the door behind him.

Jules watched the car disappear out of the parking lot. Then she turned around to look at 'Dre. "What the hell just happened?"

Chapter 20

B *am, bam, bam.*
Jules's knuckles hurt from the force she used to
knock on the door. When it finally flew open, she didn't
wait for a greeting. "So I've thought about it, and I've
decided that I have a right to be mad as hell right now."

"I was wondering how long it would take you to
show up," Germaine said. "Two days? Not bad."

"You lied to me."

Instead of answering, Germaine walked away from
the open door into the living room. Jules shoved the
door closed before following him.

She had never been in his apartment before. And if
she had been in a better mood, she would have appreciated the masculine feel of it, from the tan walls, to the
hardwood floors, to the chocolate-colored sofa. Everything was all shades of brown, with subtle hints of yellow and gold. It was all Germaine, and on another day
she would have noticed it. But today, she didn't even
see the thick area rug until she almost tripped over it in
her stilettos. She hadn't had time to change after church.

"Okay, Jules," he said when she finally rounded the

corner. He was sitting back in the armchair, one ankle resting on the opposite knee. "I know you like to talk, so let's have it."

"Don't mock me," Jules snapped from the middle of the living room. "You had me looking like an idiot."

"You wouldn't have looked like an idiot if you had done the one thing I asked you to," Germaine said. "But I'm glad to see that the way you looked is actually what's upsetting you the most. I guess I am the only one concerned about the lack of trust in our relationship."

"What relationship?" Jules asked with a cynical laugh. "You can't build a relationship on lies, and you were lying to me the whole time!"

"I never lied about how I felt."

"No, just everything else," Jules said. "But I guess because you were honest about your *feelings,* that makes it all okay."

"Now who's mocking who?"

"Don't make this about me, Germaine. You could have told me what was going on from the get-go, when I first suspected something was off. But you didn't. You kept the game going till the end. You even let me . . ."

Jules's voice caught in her throat, and she chided herself for crying even though she had promised herself she wouldn't. "You let me walk away."

She impatiently swatted away the tears that were rolling down her cheeks and looked away at the wall, unable to meet Germaine's eyes, unwilling to let him see just how much he had hurt her.

"I never wanted that to happen," Germaine said quietly, after a long moment. "I just wish you could have trusted me from the beginning when I told you I was straight."

"I wanted to trust you," Jules said. "But I was just scared, for me, for Truuth, for you."

"Truuth was never in danger. Neither were you, Jules."

"How can you be so sure of that?"

"Because I was taking care of it," he said. "I told you that I was handling it."

"Yeah. I've heard that before."

"Geez, Jules, what is it with you?" Germaine asked, raking his hand through his hair.

"I was just trying to help!"

"No, you were trying to fix, like you always do. Like you always have to."

"So what's so wrong with that?"

"Everything, Jules," he said, getting up and walking across the room. "Not everyone needs you to solve his or her problems. Can't you see that?"

"I thought you were in trouble, Germaine. What was I supposed to do?"

"Exactly what I asked you to."

Jules said, folding her arms stubbornly. "Why is it such a big deal anyway? If you were working with the police, wouldn't they already know what you were up to?"

Germaine shook his head. "Some of the guys we were trying to bust were in the force."

"Oh," Jules said, her hands falling from their folded position.

"We wanted to take down everyone, the dirty cops, the guys in Montreal, and everyone else who was working with them. Everything would have wrapped up in a couple days."

"Which is why you asked me to give you a couple weeks," Jules said, sinking into the couch.

Germaine nodded.

Jules shifted uncomfortably as she felt his eyes on her. "Did I mess things up?"

Germaine was silent, and Jules felt her stomach drop.

"No," he finally said. "But you made it a lot more complicated. There was never supposed to be any sort of confrontation, no risk of anyone getting hurt. Your friend, Detective Hansen, didn't know about the operation. He talked to the wrong people about it, and one of them tipped off the guys. They knew police were coming before they even got there. Fortunately we still got them, but a couple officers were injured."

"But the news said . . ."

"The news lied. That shouldn't surprise you."

Jules sighed. It didn't. "I guess there's the whole thing about your business being burned to the ground as well," she said quietly.

Germaine shrugged. "It's just a building, Jules. Material things can be recovered. It's the things that can't be replaced that I'm more worried about."

Jules knew where he was going with that. But she wasn't sure she was ready for that part of the conversation yet.

She gripped the edge of the sofa tightly and tried to slow her mind, which was currently working in overdrive. She watched Germaine lean against the wall across from her, his eyes still examining her in a rather unnerving way.

"Go ahead," he finally said.

"What?"

"I can see the questions forming in your mind," he said. "So go ahead and ask them."

"Why didn't you just tell me from the beginning what was going on? Wouldn't that have been easier?"

"When I met you, Jules, this was already happening," Germaine said. "I was already in the habit of keeping it to myself."

"So you had no problem lying to me?" Jules asked. "Even when it meant the end of us?"

"Yes," Germaine said firmly. "Because I knew it would be safer for you that way. Besides, look how well things turned out when I finally did tell you something."

Jules's head snapped up.

"That's not fair, Germaine. What would you have done if you were in my position?"

"I would have waited," he said without a moment's hesitation.

"It's easy to be self-righteous when you're on the other side, Germaine."

"I went out on a limb for you, Jules." He stepped toward her, his eyes burning into her. "I told my supervisors, no way will she say anything. She promised me. I trust her. But I guess that was my mistake."

Jules shook her head. "You wanted me to trust you, Germaine. But you never gave me a reason to. You don't just get trust like that, Germaine. You have to earn it."

"I guess I didn't earn yours then."

A heavy silence fell between them as the weight of Germaine's words hung in the air. Jules had known that coming here was going to be hard, but she had never thought it would hurt so much.

"I'm sorry, Germaine," Jules said. There was no more anger in her, just sadness as she looked up at him.

"I know you are, Jules," Germaine said. "But the thing that bothers me the most is that if you had it to do all over again, you'd probably do the same thing."

She felt her body tense, and she stood up to face him.

"You're right," she said. "I probably would, if you lied to me then, just like you lied to me before. I'm sorry if you were expecting some ride or die chick who would watch you get into trouble and not do anything about it. That's not me. I can't do that with people I care about."

"I never asked for all that," Germaine said, matching her even tone. "I just asked you to stand by me. But you couldn't do that either. Everything has to be Jules's way or the highway.

"You know what my life's been like, with my dad dying, and then my mom sending me away. I thought you understood that I needed you to have my back through everything. But with you I'll always be wondering if you're gonna question every move I make. I can't live like that."

"And I can't be that girl who's gonna follow you blindly."

"Well, then I guess we know where we stand."

"Yeah, I guess so," Jules said.

This was it. It was really over.

Jules dropped her head and closed her eyes. Her chest felt heavy with the thought of never being with him again. But she couldn't be that girl he wanted her to be. It just wasn't in her.

Opening her eyes, she slowly turned to retrieve her purse from the sofa where she had flung it some moments before. She could feel his eyes watching her. He was so close that the warmth of his body seemed to surround her, making it hard to breath. With just the slightest of movements, she could reach out and touch him. But she didn't. Neither did she dare look up, for fear that those golden eyes would make her cave. No, this time she had to be strong.

She turned to leave, but his voice stopped her halfway to the door.

"Remember when you asked me why I never asked for your number that first night?"

Jules nodded without turning around.

"It was because I wasn't sure if I should get you tangled up with all the craziness that was happening in my life. It was selfish even to consider it. I should have known it was impossible to keep it separate from you.

"If it's worth anything, I'm sorry."

Jules closed her eyes and willed the tears to stay under her eyelids as Germaine's words sunk in.

"Bye, Germaine," she said quietly, slipping through the front door and closing it behind her.

It wasn't until she got to the car that the tears began again in earnest.

Chapter 21

When Tanya called, Jules was curled up on her couch watching *Love and Basketball*. She had seen the movie at least a dozen times, but something about this favorite film of hers made it the perfect remedy for her current state of mind.

It had been two weeks since that day at Germaine's apartment, and even though she no longer cried at the thought of him, the emptiness still lingered in her heart, like a dull ache that wouldn't go away.

She had managed to avoid seeing him by avoiding everyone else. It wasn't so hard since the promotional activities for Truuth's album were pretty much over, and Triad was focusing their attention on launching one of their other new artists. 'Dre had asked Jules if she wanted to help with that, but she had declined, saying she was too tired from work. The truth was she was too tired from tossing and turning every night. She hadn't slept a full night since the last time she had seen Germaine.

If that wasn't bad enough, her mother still wasn't speaking to her, and she hadn't heard anything from work, even though her so called "leave of absence" was almost over. All in all, Jules felt that this was about as low as she could get.

As she listened to the phone ring, Jules considered not answering it. But when the caller ID showed that it was Tanya, she reluctantly put down the half-eaten pint of mint chocolate ice cream she had been nursing. She figured that if Tanya had been desperate enough to make a long distance call from Calgary to Toronto, then it was probably worth answering.

"Hello?"

"Jules, it's me, Tanya."

"Yeah, I know," Jules said. She hoped her tone would make Tanya realize she wasn't really in the mood to talk. She knew she should be excited about Truuth's nomination at the Covenant Awards, which he, Maxine, Tanya, and 'Dre were in Calgary attending, but she just couldn't muster the energy.

"Maxine, are you there?"

"Yeah, I'm here," Maxine said impatiently. "I don't get why you needed to talk to the both of us at the same time."

"Yeah, what's going on, Tanya?" Jules asked, her interest only slightly piqued. She settled on the side of the couch near to the phone and stretched across until she could reach the ice cream she had just abandoned.

"I told him," Tanya said, her trembling voice betraying her slight panic.

"What!" Maxine and Jules exclaimed at the same time.

"I told 'Dre," Tanya repeated, even though they both knew very well who she was talking about.

"When?"

"What exactly did you tell him?"

"I told him that I had feelings for him . . . just a while ago, actually."

"You didn't!" Maxine exclaimed.

"Oh, Tanya," Jules groaned in despair. "Why would you do that?"

"Because *you* told me to," Tanya whined.

"I told you to *talk* to him, not to scare him away!"

"You think I scared him away?" Tanya asked in panic.

"Okay, okay. Let's all just calm down," Maxine said, cutting in. "Tanya, I think you need to start from the beginning and tell us exactly what happened."

Jules heard Tanya take a deep breath across the line, and guessed that she was probably hidden away somewhere, hyperventilating.

"Well, we were inside the theater for the awards show," Tanya said in a squeaky high-pitched voice.

"And?" Maxine probed.

"And they announced the presenters for the Urban R&B Soul Song of the Year, the one Truuth was nominated for."

"Uh-huh."

"And I was looking at 'Dre, and he was really nervous, you know. 'Cause that song was really important to him. You know it was the one he and Truuth—"

". . . wrote together. Yes, we know," Maxine said, hurrying her along.

"Maxine, will you just let her finish?" Jules said, annoyed with all the interruptions.

"Well, she's taking forever, and Truuth's probably inside the theater wondering where I am," Maxine shot back.

"Ladies!" Tanya hissed. "Can we focus here?"

"Sorry," they both mumbled.

"So like I was saying, he was really nervous about the award, so I grabbed his hand, and he looked at me in this weird way . . . but not a bad way. . . . It's hard to explain . . . but at that moment it was almost as if everything was completely clear. . . . It was like I knew . . ."

". . . that you were in love with him," Jules finished.

"Yeah," Tanya said quietly. She sighed heavily. "So I told him."

"You told him?" Maxine asked in disbelief. "You just said, ''Dre, I think I have feelings for you'?"

Tanya hesitated for a moment. "Yeah."

For a moment none of them spoke, and all Jules could hear was the muffled sound of applause in the background, as the show continued on.

"So what happened after that?" Maxine asked.

"They called Truuth's name."

"What?" Jules asked in confusion.

"They called Truuth up for the award, and then he called 'Dre up on stage with him."

"Hmm, no wonder 'Dre looked so out of it when he got up there," Maxine said, more to herself than to any of them.

"Yeah," Tanya echoed.

"So he didn't say a word when you told him? Nothing at all?" Jules asked.

"Not a word," Tanya said in a small voice.

"After they collected the award, they went backstage, and I panicked and left."

"So where are you now?" Jules asked.

"In the ladies' room."

In that instant Jules pictured Tanya pacing around the bathroom in her Roberto Cavalli dress and matching Gucci shoes, looking absolutely incredible, except for her red eyes and running mascara.

"Maxine! How come you didn't see all this?" Jules exclaimed.

"They seated me and Truuth on the other side of the room. I didn't even know where 'Dre was until Truuth called him up," Maxine protested. "Tanya, where are you exactly?"

"In the ladies' room outside the east theater entrance."

"Don't move. I'll be right there."

"Jules, what am I going to do," Tanya groaned a moment after Maxine hung up from the three-way call.

"Nothing," Jules replied simply.

"Huh?"

"You told him how you feel, honey. Now the ball is in his court. You just have to wait. Give it a moment to sink in. You know 'Dre. He'll need some time with this one," Jules said.

"But it's gonna be so weird with him now."

"Yes, but at least now he knows how you feel," Jules said. "Don't you feel better just knowing that you told him? Even though you don't know how it might turn out, at least you don't have to carry that around anymore."

Tanya thought about it for a second. "Yeah, I guess you're right," she said thoughtfully. Then she sighed again. "I'm also scared to death that I'll lose one of my best friends."

"I don't think that will happen," Jules said. "Tanya, I think God brings certain people into our lives at certain times for a reason. I've known 'Dre for a while. And outside of his sister and his momma, I've never seen him respect any girl as much as he respects you. He doesn't know it, but that boy trusts you with his life, T, more than even me and Maxine.

"I don't know how things are gonna work out. But I'm pretty sure you and 'Dre are going to be a part of each other's lives for a long time."

"You know," Tanya said thoughtfully. "Before tonight I was seriously wondering if telling 'Dre how I felt was the right thing to do. This weekend especially it was really on my mind. I really had to pray hard about it.

"But when I got up this morning, I knew I had to," Tanya said. "I guess I just wasn't prepared for him to not say anything."

"Just wait, honey," Jules said comfortingly. "It will all work out."

Tanya was silent for a moment.

"Is that what you're doing with Germaine? Waiting?" Tanya asked suddenly.

Jules sighed. Even though she had come clean to Maxine and Tanya about everything that had happened with Germaine, she had still avoided talking much about it. She should have known better than to think her best friends would let it die.

"I'm not doing anything, Tanya," Jules said. "Me and Germaine are over. That's it for us."

"I can't believe you're giving up that easy," Tanya said. "I know how much you like this guy. Plus, I know he was good for you. You've never been with a guy who actually encouraged you to grow. That kinda thing is hard to find."

Tanya was right. During her time with Germaine, Jules knew that if nothing else, he had helped her look more closely at a lot of things, including her relationship with God.

"Yeah, but he doesn't trust me anymore. I don't think he wants anything to do with me."

"But what do you think God wants?"

"Huh?"

"You just told me that God brings people into our life for a reason, right?"

"Yeah," Jules said, uncertain about where this was going.

"Well, what if Germaine is that person you're supposed to be with?"

"If that's the case then my life is gonna be pretty pathetic from here on out," Jules said dryly.

"Come on, Jules, be serious," Tanya chided.

"I am!" Jules protested. "He's made up his mind that I am not it for him. And you know what, maybe he's right. Maybe we've got too many issues between the both of us."

"So what?"

"So what am I supposed to do with that?" Jules asked.

"Give it to God."

"What?"

"Give it to God. You told me to give my situation with 'Dre to God; you need to give your situation with Germaine to God," Tanya said. "You know, for a girl who is always encouraging others to have faith, you sure suck at having some yourself.

"Okay, so the situation looks messed up now, but don't give up on it. Now's the time to get on your knees about it."

"Please, Tanya, I can't pray to God about a man."

"Why not?" Tanya asked in surprise. "You pray about everything else. You pray about your career, about where you should live. I know you, Jules, you even pray when you go shopping. If you can ask Him for direction in those small things, why can't you let

Him lead you completely in the big things? I think determining who you give your heart to is pretty big."

"I don't know, Tanya. It just looks so hopeless."

"All the better," Tanya said brightly. "Hopeless situations are His specialty."

Jules sighed. "I guess I really haven't been trusting in God with this one. I've been so busy trying to fix things myself.

"Did I tell you he called me a fixer?"

"Who, Germaine?"

"Yeah."

Tanya laughed. "He sure knows you. And you had doubts that you two belong together."

"I still do."

"Well, we'll let Someone else have the last word on that," Tanya said.

"Okay, okay. Hey, wasn't I the one that was supposed to be helping you?" Jules asked, suddenly remembering why Tanya had called in the first place.

Tanya laughed. "We helped each other. That's what friends do, right?"

"Right," Jules said, smiling for the first time all day.

In the background Jules could hear Maxine calling Tanya, and she figured that they had somehow found each other.

"Okay, Max is here."

"Yeah, I can hear her big mouth," Jules said, laughing. "Don't let her stir you into a panic."

"I won't. I'll call you tomorrow when I get back."

"Okay, T. Take care."

After she hung up the phone, Jules stood up from the couch, retrieved the melting ice cream, and dumped it in the kitchen sink. She then returned to the living room and clicked off the TV. She had had enough of

Sanaa and Omar for the day. Now it was time for her to have a little faith.

Jules stared at the blue door in front of her and wondered if she was making a mistake.

After talking to Tanya, she had spent some time talking to God. It had helped her realize that feeling sorry for herself was not going to get her anywhere.

She also realized that in order for her to move forward, there were a few people she needed to make amends with. She had decided that this would be the first stop on her reconciliation tour. But now, as she stared at the large, foreboding doorway, she began to wonder if she shouldn't have left this particular meeting for last.

She sighed to herself.

Oh, well. I'm already here. Might as well get it over with.

Raising her hand she knocked firmly on the door. Since she had not called before heading over, she had no idea whether anyone was home. She quickly decided that if no one answered by the second knock, she would go. But before she could raise her hand a second time, the door swung wide open.

Jules felt her voice catch in her throat. "Hi, Momma," she managed to strangle out.

Jules held her breath as her mother stared at her silently, an unreadable expression on her face. It occurred to her that she might have to give her memorized apology speech on the front step, since she wasn't sure Momma Jackson would invite her in. Either way, she had come this far; there was no turning back now.

"I was wondering if I could talk to you," Jules began shakily. "I know I don't deserve your time after how—"

Before Jules could finish speaking, her mother pushed the door farther open and turned away from Jules to walk back into the house.

Jules knew that was as much of an invitation as she was going to get, and so she hurried inside, closed the door, and went to the living room, where she found Momma Jackson sitting neatly in one corner of her large chaise lounge. Her hands were folded, and she was looking at Jules expectantly.

Jules sat down across from her mother in the matching love seat and swallowed hard.

"First off, Momma, I want to apologize for what happened the last time we spoke," Jules began nervously. "I was very upset, but I had no right to take it out on you the way I did. It was wrong, and it was disrespectful, and I'm sorry."

She looked up at her mother, but Momma Jackson's face remained expressionless.

"I know you're probably going to be mad at me for a while, and that's fine. I just wanted to let you know how sorry I am," Jules said finally. She watched Momma Jackson for a response, but none came.

Sighing heavily, Jules stood and turned to leave. She had done the best she could. Now it was up to her mother.

"I'm sorry things didn't work out with you and your young man," Momma Jackson said quietly.

Jules turned slightly to look at her mother. She didn't know what she expected, maybe some remorse for the state of their mother-daughter relationship, or maybe just sympathy from a woman who knew what it was like to have her heart broken. But there was none of that on Momma Jackson's face. Instead there was just sincerity. Not enough to be soft, just enough to show that Momma Jackson was in fact sorry that things had not worked out for Jules.

In that moment Jules realized that this was what her relationship with her mother was going to be.

"Thanks," she said quietly, before continuing down the hallway. When she got to the door, she paused. Her hand was already on the knob, and she could almost taste the freedom of the outdoors, but at the same time, something told her that if she left her mother's house now, any possibility of a better relationship would leave with her.

Before she could lose her nerve, Jules walked swiftly back into the living room.

"I don't understand why all I did was never good enough for you," Jules said abruptly. Momma Jackson looked up at Jules in surprise.

"I really did try to be everything that you wanted me to be," Jules continued. She knew she had to say everything at once, or it would never get said. "I went to university, got my degree, got a good job, stayed in church, and never got pregnant, but it still wasn't enough. I've tried so hard to make you proud of me, to make sure you never had to hang your head in shame, to show you that you did good with me even though Daddy wasn't here, but it feels . . . it feels like no matter how hard I try, I can't win with you."

Tears streamed down Jules's cheeks as all the frustration of the past twelve years came pouring out. "Am I really that big of a disappointment to you?"

Momma Jackson looked stunned as she watched Jules break down in the living room.

"Oh, honey, never that," Momma Jackson said. She

got up from the couch and wrapped her arms around her trembling daughter.

"Sugar, I'm so proud of you . . . sometimes my heart just wants to burst," Momma Jackson said lovingly, as she pulled her daughter close to her.

"So why are you always embarrassing me around people, and saying things like I abandon you?" Jules asked between sniffles.

"I don't know," Momma Jackson said, throwing up her hands in frustration. Jules saw that her mother was getting upset, but realized that Momma Jackson was more angry with herself than with Jules.

"I guess . . . I guess I just wanted to get your attention," Momma Jackson said tiredly.

Jules looked confused. "What?"

"I just wanted you to show some emotion when it came to me, make me a part of your life."

"Momma, of course you're part of my life," Jules argued in confusion. "Whenever you need me, I'm here. Anything you need I make sure you have it."

"I know, I know, but I'm not part of your life," Momma Jackson said emphatically. "I see you with Maxine and that white girl. You tell those girls everything. You and Davis are thicker than thieves. Even your Aunt Sharon seems to know more about you than I do."

Jules opened her mouth to respond. But she couldn't, for everything her mother was saying was true. She did share a lot more with those people than she did with her mother. But it was just because she never felt like any of them were judging her. But she couldn't tell her mother that. Then again, maybe she should.

"And it was one thing when you lived here," Momma Jackson continued. "But when you moved, it was like I was out completely. You barely visit, and you stopped coming to Kendalwood Church like you used to when you lived here. I know you said you moved for work, but sometimes it feels like you moved to get away from me."

Jules could hear the hurt in her mother's voice, and for the first time, truly understood what her mother was going through. She sighed heavily and sat down on the couch.

"Okay, Momma," Jules began. "First off, I really did move for work. The nature of my job is that sometimes I have to be at the hospital at strange times of the day to take care of media stuff. It's hard for me to do that if I live three towns away. Secondly, I never liked Kendalwood. I told you that from the beginning. I know you don't get it, but Scarborough Memorial is like my home. Maxine, and Tanya, and Pastor Thomas are like my second family, and I know you're not going to like this, but I really needed—need a father figure like Pastor Thomas in my life."

Jules took a deep breath. This part was going to be the hardest for her mother, but she had to say it.

"And lastly, Momma, it's not that I don't want to tell you things about my life, but sometimes . . . I feel like you're judging me."

Jules swallowed and pulled one of the throw cushions into her lap in front of her.

"After Daddy left, it was like you started expecting so much more of me. And if I was less than what you expected, it was like I wasn't good enough. I felt like I always had to work harder to measure up."

"Oh, sugar, after your dad left, I wasn't sure how to handle you and Davis," Momma Jackson admitted, sinking into the couch beside Jules. "I didn't know if I would be able to take care of you both on my own, and I panicked."

"Is that why you started working so hard?"

Momma Jackson nodded. "I wanted to make sure that you children wouldn't feel the difference of living on a single-parent income. I didn't realize that I wasn't spending enough time with you. And by the time I did, it was too late. Davis would still cling to me, but you, you had become little Miss Independent. You never asked me for help with anything."

"Momma, that's not true."

"Jules, you bought your own prom dress, and got dressed at Maxine's house."

"Because I thought you didn't even want me to go to the prom! You never even asked me about it," Jules argued.

"That's 'cause you never said anything about it," Momma Jackson said. "You never even told me that Jacob—"

"Joshua," Jules corrected.

"Whatever. You never even told me he asked you. I had to find out from Sister Mullings who was chaperoning. Do you know how much that hurt me, Jules?"

"Momma, I was going out with Joshua for three months before we went to the prom. Three months," Jules emphasized. "You were never home even once when he picked me up. Joshua and I could have done . . . anything, and you would never have known. You were so wrapped up in work."

Momma Jackson sighed heavily.

"I guess we are both a little bit to blame," she admitted.

"Yeah."

"I just wish I could have been there for you, sugar," she said, sighing.

"I know."

They sat on the couch silently, thinking of all the things they should have done but hadn't. Jules noted that this was the first honest conversation she had had with her mother in a long time.

"So that boy's really out of the picture," Momma Jackson said.

Jules sighed. "More or less. I really messed up with him," Jules said.

Momma Jackson looked at her in bewilderment. "You messed up? I thought you said that boy was the one acting the fool?"

"No, it was me, and my issues," Jules said. She told her mother the whole story about thinking Germaine was involved with drugs, and then finding out he was actually working with the police the whole time.

"Well, ain't that a hot mess," said Momma Jackson.

Jules sighed and nodded in agreement.

"Do you know what you're gonna do?" Momma Jackson asked.

"There's nothing I can do, Momma," Jules said. "I didn't trust him, and he didn't trust me. There's too much stuff to get past."

"Oh, Jules, don't be stubborn. If you really care for this man, then you need to at least try to work it out," Momma Jackson said. "You need to bring the whole thing to the Lord as well. He'll always lead you right."

Jules sighed. "I wish I had been doing more of that before. Maybe then I wouldn't be in this mess. I was so sure I knew what was right for me. But I was wrong. I wasn't trusting God at all. I feel so ashamed to ask for help now."

"Oh, no," Momma Jackson said, sitting up suddenly. "I know I didn't raise you to think no foolishness like that."

Jules's eyes widened at her mother's intensity.

"Now you listen to me. We all make a mess of our lives sometimes—you can look at me as a prime example—but God still cares for us. He knows you messed up, and didn't trust Him enough. But He also knows that you're sorry and that you want to trust Him completely. But He can't help you until you let Him.

"Don't make the same mistake of trying to do things on your own again," Momma Jackson said softly, touching Jules's cheek. "Let go, and let God take care of it, okay?"

Jules nodded as tears moistened her eyes again.

"Thanks, Momma," she whispered, as her mother folded her in her embrace.

"Anytime, sugar, anytime."

By the time Jules got home from her mother's, it was almost eleven o'clock. She was glad she was still on her leave of absence from work, for she didn't know if she could have made it in anyway.

Stretching out in her couch, she idly hit the Play button on her answering machine.

"You have eight new messages."

Jules sat up suddenly in surprise. She had just been out for a few hours. How could she have missed eight calls since then?

"First message: Hey, Jules, this is Truuth. Gimme a call back as soon as you get this. It's important."

That was weird. She was barely on speaking terms with Truuth. Why would he call her?

The machine beeped as Jules skipped to the next message.

"Next message: Hey, Jules, this is Truuth again. Please give me a call. I need a favor from you."

Beep.

"Next Message: Me again. How come you're not picking up your phone? I've been calling your cell all evening, and I've been getting nothing. Anyway, buzz me back, okay?"

Beep.

Jules dug through her purse and pulled out her BlackBerry. Seven missed calls: six from Truuth and one from an unknown number. She flipped through the settings and realized that it had been on vibrate. No wonder she hadn't heard it ring. She was so distracted that she only caught the last part of the next message.

". . . I'm giving her your number so she can call. Maybe she will get through to you."

Giving who my number?

Jules was about to rewind the message when she heard an unfamiliar voice.

"Next Message: Um . . . Hey. This is Soroya. You don't know me, but Truuth said I could call you since he wasn't in town. He said you would know what to do. I'm at the hospital with Germaine. . . ."

Jules's heart began to hammer in her chest. She was gripping the chair cushions so hard that her knuckles were turning white. She didn't want to think about what might be wrong.

". . . There's no one else to call."

Jules heard Soroya pause as if she wasn't quite sure what to say next.

"We're at the Emergency room, at Toronto Grace—"
Beep.

The tape finished before Soroya had, but it didn't matter, for Jules was halfway to the door. She tried not to think about what could be wrong with Germaine, but already ghastly images of his ravaged, bloody body were invading her mind.

As she pulled her door closed, she whispered a prayer.

Please, Lord, let him be okay.

Chapter 22

Jules navigated quickly through the halls of the hospital she knew so well. The nurses and doctors on staff who knew her waved as she passed them by, but all Jules could manage was a tight smile to hide the anxiety building in her.

The nurses were in much higher spirits now that the hospital administration had agreed to their list of requests, leading to the end of the strike. And the two large, alert security guards Jules had passed were proof that it wasn't just empty talk, either. Jules was glad. A hospital, especially one as central as Toronto Grace, was not the kind of place you wanted to have labor unrest.

"Jules! Never thought I'd see you here so late," the on-duty nurse said cheerily when Jules arrived at Emergency.

Jules tried to force a smile. "I'm actually here to see a patient? Germaine Williams?"

The nurse scanned the computer at the station in front of her. Jules tapped her fingernails on the console as the woman took her own sweet time scrolling through the list of registered patients. She wished she could move her aside and check for herself, but she knew that would have been against hospital policy.

"Jules, I'm sorry, I'm not seeing any Germaine Williams here. Are you sure—"

"Jules?"

Jules turned at the sound of her name and found herself face to face with a slim young girl, with large hazel eyes and fine features. Her thick curly hair had been hastily pulled together in a ponytail, and her beautiful hazel eyes were red and swollen from crying. The instant Jules saw her, she knew she was Germaine's sister.

"Soroya?"

The girl nodded mutely. She continued to stare at Jules, as if not quite sure what to do next. Jules wasn't quite sure herself. She looked around the emergency room. There were a few people milling around, sitting on chairs or leaning against the wall, but no Germaine.

"Where's your brother?"

Soroya led Jules down the stark, brightly lit hospital hallway, past patients and nurses until Jules wasn't quite sure where she was going. Suddenly Soroya turned a corner and stopped abruptly, causing Jules to almost walk right into her.

"Soroya, I have been looking all over for you. Didn't I tell you to stay right—" Germaine froze when he saw Jules standing behind his sister. Jules tried to read the expression on his face.

She could tell that he was angry. Angry at someone, but she knew instinctively it wasn't her or Soroya. In fact even though he was looking directly at her, it took a while for it to register to him that she was there. His mind seemed to be completely elsewhere.

"What's going on, Germaine?" Jules asked with a calm that surprised her.

"Did you call her, Soroya?" he asked his sister, his eyes never leaving Jules.

"Yes," Soroya said defiantly. Jules looked down at the ten-year-old girl and saw the same stubbornness that she always saw in Germaine.

"Truuth said I could call her," Soroya continued. "He gave me her number."

"But what did *I* say, Soroya?" Germaine said with an air of impatience.

"You said you would take care of everything and not to call anybody else."

"So why didn't you listen to me?" Germaine asked quietly but firmly.

Right before Jules's eyes, all the stubbornness seemed to evaporate from Soroya.

"Because I was scared."

Germaine opened and closed his mouth several times but nothing came out. He rubbed a hand tiredly against the back of his neck but said nothing.

Jules sighed heavily and turned the slim girl gently toward her.

"What happened, Soroya?"

She realized that she wouldn't get an answer from Germaine.

Soroya looked down at the floor as tears began to pool in her eyes.

"My mom," she said, her voice wavering as tears began to pour down her cheeks. "He beat her."

"Who?" Jules asked softly. The young girl began to cry harder, and instinctively Jules pulled her into her arms. Soroya wrapped her skinny arms around Jules's waist and buried her tear-stained face in Jules's stomach.

"Her father," Germaine said quietly. Seeing his sister cry had taken some of the fight out of him, and he sank down into one of the sofas in the waiting area near the nurses' station.

With Soroya still clinging to her, Jules sat down beside him. Soroya instantly curled up on the remaining portion of the sofa and buried her face in Jules's lap. Jules stroked the young girl's hair absently as she watched Germaine.

"What happened?" Jules asked again quietly. Germaine sighed and leaned forward, resting his elbows on his knees.

"The usual," he said wryly. "He came home—drunk— and started an argument with her. Then he hit her."

Jules gasped involuntarily, and looked down at Soroya. The girl's sobs had subsided into quiet whimpers.

"He's done that before," Germaine continued, deadpan. "But this time, I guess she argued back, and he really gave it to her. When the ambulance got there, they said she was barely breathing."

Germaine's voice tightened, and he looked down at the ground as he spoke. She could hear the barely restrained anger in his voice.

"Her jaw is . . . busted open. Her eyes are swollen. And the doctors say he broke one of her ribs."

"Oh, Germaine," Jules said softly. "I'm so sorry."

She reached up to place a hand on his shoulder, but he flinched, and she pulled back. His reaction hurt her more than she thought it would. She looked away, and blinked back the tears that sprang to her eyes.

"Where is she now?" Jules asked quietly.

"She's in surgery. They're making sure that there's no internal bleeding, and that her broken rib doesn't puncture her lung."

"I'm sorry, Germaine."

Jules felt stupid apologizing for something she didn't do and had no control over. But she couldn't think of anything else to say.

Jules looked down at Soroya, who was lying still in her lap. The trauma of the evening's events had clearly taken a toll on the young girl, and she had fallen dead asleep. Suddenly a thought occurred to her.

"Did he . . ."

"No," Germaine said, reading her mind. "He didn't lay a finger on 'Roya. If he had . . ."

Jules saw his jaw tighten and his hands ball into fists. She wondered what Germaine would do to the man if he ever got near him. A part of her did not want to know. From the anger that she saw brewing inside him, there was no telling what Germaine was capable of.

Not caring whether or not he pulled away, she slipped her arm through his arm, and her hand into his, threading their fingers together. Instead of resisting, Germaine squeezed her hand tightly between both of his and looked away, but not before Jules saw his eyes moisten. She felt her own tears form as she watched his anger give way to pain and fear. If there was anything she could have done to take that away from him, she would have.

He didn't say anything, but only rested the back of her hand against his lips, as Jules laid her cheek against his shoulder. And there, in silence, the three of them waited, until the surgery was over.

* * *

"Mr. Williams?"

Germaine looked up at the doctor who had been operating on his mother. It had been two hours since they took his mother into surgery, and he had gotten no updates on how things were going.

Jules saw the nervousness on Germaine's face as he looked up at the doctor expectantly. She cringed as she felt his grip on her hand tighten painfully.

"Babe, my hand."

Germaine looked up at Jules suddenly, and Jules instantly wished she could sink through the floor.

He let go of her and stood up to talk to the doctor. Jules looked down at her hand, which now felt unusually cold, before burying it in her lap.

"Is she going to be okay?" Germaine asked nervously.

"We found some internal bleeding," the doctor said soberly. "We want to keep her here for observation for a couple days, just to make sure everything is okay, but she should be fine."

Jules watched as Germaine's features relaxed.

"Can I see my momma now?" Soroya asked. She had woken up as soon as the doctor had started speaking.

"Sure you can," the doctor said, smiling. "She is awake, so you can talk to her. But she will need her rest, so you can't stay too long."

Before the doctor was finished speaking, Soroya was up and halfway down the hall, with Germaine only a few steps behind her. She suddenly stopped and turned to look back at Jules, who was still sitting on the waiting room sofa, rubbing her hand.

"Aren't you coming?" Soroya asked innocently.

Jules looked at the little girl and then up at Germaine, who was avoiding her eyes. She sighed. "No, you go ahead. I'll be right here when you get back," Jules said, offering a brief smile. Soroya glanced up at Germaine and gave him a nasty look before continuing down the hallway. A few moments later, the two of them disappeared into a doorway off to the side, leaving Jules sitting alone.

Jules looked around the hospital waiting room. Posters on everything from hand washing to HIV testing hung in the waiting area. A small TV showing *Nick at Nite* was perched near the ceiling in the corner, but no one seemed to be paying attention.

As usual the waiting room was fully occupied with a diverse mix of waiting patients and accompanying family members and visitors. Jules glanced over at a frail old man with cotton-white hair who kept nodding off. A few seats beside him, a girl who looked to be about Jules's age held the hand of a younger guy with his right leg in a cast who appeared to be her boyfriend. The guy looked like he was in pain. Jules wondered how long they had been waiting. Across from them a teenage girl in tight yellow jeans and several gold bangles lay across several seats with her head in her friend's lap. The friend snapped her gum loudly and glared at Jules when she caught her staring.

Jules turned her eyes away, back to the hallway, where a constant stream of nurses, hospital staff, doctors, and patients moved back and forth. If it hadn't been for the clock on the wall nearby, Jules would have thought it was the middle of the day, for how busy it was.

Absently Jules wondered how long she should stay

there. Maybe no one expected her to stay. But then, she had promised Soroya she would be here when she got back, so she couldn't leave.

She sighed heavily, wishing things were different between her and Germaine. Maybe then, she wouldn't have to wonder so much about what she should do, or be so careful about what she said. She thought back to her earlier conversation with her mother and closed her eyes.

Lord, I don't have a clue what to do. Guide me in how to relate to Germaine, and to Soroya and this whole situation. And most important, please help Germaine's mom to be okay. You know that it's been hard for him since he lost his father, and that he feels alone sometimes. Please don't let him lose his mom too. He needs her. All this I ask in Your name. Amen.

When Jules opened her eyes, she found Germaine standing over her.

"Falling asleep?"

"Actually, I was praying," Jules said, too tired to muster up anything other than the whole truth.

"Oh, yeah?" Germaine asked, sitting down on the sofa. "For what?"

"More like for who," Jules corrected. "Your mom. Soroya. You."

"That was nice of you," Germaine said.

Jules shrugged. She wasn't quite sure how she was supposed to respond to that. She decided to be quiet and just wait for Germaine to speak. The less she said, the smaller the chance that she would slip up and say something awkward as she had before.

"I was hoping you could do something for me," Germaine said slowly.

"Anything," Jules answered before she could stop

herself. She cringed at the desperation in her own voice.

"I'm gonna stay here with my mom tonight, but I don't want Soroya staying in the hospital overnight. I'm not even sure they'll let her. Can you . . . can she stay with you for tonight? I know it would be an imposition, but we don't really have any other family. Tru-uth will be back in a couple days so—"

"It's fine, Germaine. She can stay for as long as she wants," Jules assured him.

She wasn't quite certain where in her one-bedroom apartment she was going to put Soroya, but at that point, she would have said yes if he had asked her to bring him water from the moon.

"Thanks so much, Jules," Germaine said, his beauti-ful hazel eyes staring at her gratefully. Jules drank it all in. She didn't know when, if ever, he would look at her like that again.

He got up and disappeared down the hall before reappearing with a whining Soroya.

". . . but I want to stay here with you and Momma," Soroya said in a singsong voice. Even as Soroya protested, Jules could see the little girl's eyes were al-ready half-shut. Jules knew that in no time at all Soroya would be asleep.

"But you can't," Germaine said patiently. "So you go with Jules tonight, and tomorrow she'll bring you back here, okay?"

Soroya pouted her little girl lips, but let her brother help her into her fall jacket anyway. Jules watched in admiration as Germaine's hands moved patiently, en-during Soroya's twists and turns.

"Thank you," he said again, once he was finished.

"No problem," Jules said with a small smile, as she

took Soroya's hand and led her down the hallway toward the hospital exit.

As they walked away she tried to resist the urge to look back at him. But halfway down the passage, she caved and snuck a glance behind her. She was pleasantly surprised to see him watching them make their exit. From the distance, it was hard to read the expression on his face. She suspected it would have been no easier even if she were standing right in front of him. She sighed as she led a sleepy Soroya toward the parking lot.

Oh, Germaine, what I wouldn't give to know what you're thinking.

Chapter 23

The next morning when Jules opened her eyes she found a pair of large hazel ones staring back at her.

"Thank God. I thought you were gonna sleep forever," Soroya said, one hand cocked on her hip precociously.

Jules raised one eyebrow at the girl who was standing over her.

"I know you know better than to use the Lord's name like that," Jules said.

Soroya looked instantly repentant, and Jules felt her heart soften toward the girl.

"Have you said your prayers yet?"

"No," Soroya said. "I was waiting on you to get up."

"Well, I'm up now," Jules said, sitting up in the sofa bed she had pulled out in the middle of the living room. As she looked around at the disarray of her apartment, she began to remember in full the events of the evening before.

She had gotten back to her apartment with Soroya at about 2 a.m. By that time, the poor girl had been so drained that Jules had barely managed to change her out of her street clothes into one of Jules's T-shirts and put her to sleep.

Jules had given Soroya her queen-sized bed, and then spent the next fifteen minutes trying to pull out and set up the sofa bed she had bought in case Davis, or Maxine, or some other friend needed to stay over night. By the time she had finished getting sheets and blankets, she was so tired that she fell asleep the instant her head hit the pillow. However, even though that was almost six hours ago, Jules felt like she had barely slept a wink.

Out of the corner of her eyes she saw Soroya watching her expectantly.

"All right, let's have it," Jules said, kneeling down with the girl to say morning prayers.

When they were through, Jules stood up and began to fold the bed sheets. Soroya watched her curiously for a moment, before grabbing the fitted sheet and doing the same with it.

Jules watched the girl's small dextrous hands quickly fold the sheet on her own with practiced ease. She had glanced into the bedroom a moment earlier and noticed that the bed Soroya had slept in was already made as well. It was clear that this little woman was very self-sufficient.

However, Jules wasn't fooled by Soroya's show of maturity. She knew that underneath it all she was still a tired little girl who wanted desperately to be just that— a little girl. Moments like last night in the hospital, when she had curled up in Jules's lap, were a reminder of that fact.

"Okay, that's done," Soroya said, looking up at Jules as if to say what next.

"I'm gonna make us some breakfast quick, so we

can get you back to the hospital to see your mom," Jules said, heading toward the kitchen. "I left a wash-cloth and toothbrush on the bathroom sink for you last night, so you can go wash up."

Jules could hear the girl moving around in the bath-room, as she cut up potatoes and beat eggs for ome-lettes. Something was bothering her, but she didn't know how to ask Soroya without seeming nosy or up-setting her. She decided to take a roundabout approach.

"Hey, Soroya, did you guys call anybody else when you got to the hospital, just to let them know where you were?"

Jules heard the faucet stop running for a moment.

"No."

Then the swishing from the faucet started again.

"I'm sure there are people who would be concerned about your mom's being in the hospital."

The faucet went off again. And Jules heard silence.

"You mean how come there was no one else for me to stay with," Soroya said knowingly from the kitchen entranceway.

Jules stopped slicing and looked around at the girl. She should have guessed that Soroya would be smart enough to figure out what she was really asking.

"My momma doesn't want anyone to know my dad beats her," Soroya said in answer to Jules's unasked question. "They probably wouldn't believe her any-way."

Soroya turned and left the kitchen, and after a few moments Jules heard the water running again. She sighed and turned back to the breakfast, understanding completely why Soroya acted like she was twenty in-stead of ten.

After eating quickly, Jules and Soroya left for the

hospital. All the maturity Soroya had displayed that morning seemed to disappear the closer they got to Toronto Grace. By the time they got to the hospital she had morphed into the anxious little girl from the night before.

As they approached the sliding hospital doors, she slipped her hand into Jules's and stayed close to her while they walked down the corridors toward her mother's room.

They were just in time to see Soroya's mother begin to stir awake.

"Momma!" Soroya exclaimed, forgetting about Jules and rushing to her mother's side.

She climbed gingerly onto the side of the bed as her mother wrapped her arms around her. Feeling as if she was intruding on a private moment, Jules looked away. Her eyes fell on Germaine, who was watching her from a chair pulled up to the other side of his mother's bed.

His eyes were bloodshot, and his clothes rumpled from sleeping in the chair. There was slight stubble on his jaw from not having shaved in a few days, and somehow his low cut hair managed to look unkempt. She could tell that he was tired. He tried to sit up, but even that seemed to require a huge amount of effort for him. The truth was he looked horrible. Jules couldn't tear her eyes away.

He seemed to be having a similar problem.

They were so lost in each other that neither Jules nor Germaine noticed Germaine's mother looking back and forth between the two of them curiously.

"Well, Germaine, are you gonna sit there eyeballin' this girl all morning, or are you gonna introduce her to your momma?"

Germaine looked across at his mother as if suddenly

remembering she was there. From the look that she gave him in return, Jules knew that any introduction would be merely a formality.

"Oh, uh, Mom, this is Jules; Jules, this is my mother, Joan Bailey," he said distractedly. Jules noticed that his eyes never seemed to leave her for more than a few seconds. Feeling very self-conscious, she turned to his mother.

"Hi, Mrs. Bailey," she said nervously.

She had always wanted to meet the mother of the man who seemed to have embedded himself in her heart. She would have preferred, however, that it had been under different circumstances.

Joan Bailey narrowed her eyes at Jules. "You the one that's been looking after my daughter all night?"

"Yes, ma'am, that would be me," Jules said quietly.

Joan stared at Jules a moment longer before her gaze softened.

"Thank you," she said quietly. "My daughter doesn't really take to people too quickly, so you must be okay if she let you take care of her."

Jules let out a breath she didn't know she had been holding. For some reason the approval of Germaine's mother had meant a lot to her. She didn't know why, since she was no longer with him, and probably never would be again.

"She's Truuth's friend," Soroya said, from her spot tucked away in her mother's arm. "She's all right."

Seeing her mother awake and strong seemed to boost Soroya's energy, and she was soon chatting away, until both she and her mother seemed to forget anyone else was in the room. Jules smiled and shook her head. Watching Soroya bounce between moods was enough to make anyone's head spin.

She felt Germaine's eyes on her again, and sure enough when she looked up she found him watching her from across the room. Jules shivered when she noticed that he wasn't even trying to hide the fact that he was staring.

"Did she give you any trouble?" he asked after a moment.

Jules shook her head. "Not at all. She was a dream."

Germaine raised an eyebrow skeptically, and Jules couldn't help but chuckle.

"I'm serious," Jules said. "She slept all night, and helped me out a bit this morning."

He looked relieved. Jules ached to put her arms around him and make everything else he was worrying about go away. Instead she offered him the small bag she had carried with her from the car.

"What's this?" he asked, taking peeking inside at the small glass container.

"It's breakfast," Jules said.

All of a sudden she felt nervous.

"I figured that you maybe hadn't eaten yet, and so when I made breakfast for Soroya and me, I thought I would bring you some. You don't have to have it if you don't want to. If you already ate it's okay, I just thought I would . . ."

Jules noticed the small smile playing at the corners of Germaine's lips, and she forced herself to stop babbling.

"There's a fork in the bag too," she said, taking a deep breath to calm her nerves.

Come on, Jules, it's just Germaine. Get a grip.

"Thanks, Jules, but I gotta make sure my mom gets something first," Germaine said.

"Boy, I ate breakfast this morning while you were

over there sleeping," Joan said dismissively. "Quit hovering over me, and go eat something. Get some air, both of you, and let me spend some time alone with my daughter."

Germaine was about to protest, but his mother sent him a warning look that got him out of his chair and halfway to the door without her saying another word.

"Okay, okay, I'm going," he said anxiously. Jules bit back a smile as she followed him out of the room.

They walked in silence through the hallway and out a side exit of the hospital into an open courtyard set up with elegantly chiselled stone benches and tables for hospital patients and visitors.

As they sat down at a table near the grass, Jules leaned back on her hands and breathed in deeply the crisp mid-morning air. It was the middle of October, but they were having one of those unseasonably warm fall days, characteristic of Toronto's unpredictable weather. It was a perfect day to be outside, and Jules couldn't think of anyone else she'd rather be out there with.

"I can't believe I've worked at this hospital for almost four years, and I've never sat out here," Jules said, looking around the courtyard.

"That's 'cause you're always too busy," Germaine said between bites. Jules mentally commended herself for packing a large helping.

"You sound like my mother."

"How are things between you two?" he asked, just before taking another bite out of the giant omelette Jules had brought him.

"Good," Jules said thoughtfully. "I finally got up the nerve to talk to her."

She bit her bottom lip, resisting the urge to spill her guts to him.

"Tell me about it."

She looked up at him suddenly. She should have known he would read her mind.

Before she could stop herself, she was telling him everything, from the big fight she'd had with Momma Jackson to the long talk they'd had just hours ago.

"You know, if it wasn't for your words banging around in my head, I never would have talked to her," Jules said.

"Well, I'm glad I could be of some use to you," Germaine said, smirking, as he rested his forearms on the table and looked over at her. "And by the way, thank you. With Truuth gone, I didn't expect anyone to show up last night."

"Yeah, well, you know me," Jules said. "Always trying to fix something."

Germaine smiled. "Believe it or not, I actually miss that."

Jules looked down at her jeans and began to scratch her nail against the coarse material.

"I miss you too," he added quietly.

She drew in a sharp breath and looked across to the other side of the courtyard.

A slight breeze was rustling the leaves of the crab apple trees that lined the hospital's east side. The sun was almost directly overhead, and its rays were peeking through the leaves, forming little pools of sunlight on the ground.

"Jules?"

She felt Germaine take her hand. She didn't resist when he pulled her closer or when he gently turned her face toward him.

"Look at me, Jules."

Obediently, she lifted her eyes to his. They were glowing for her. And she was falling for him. Just like she always did.

"Germaine!" Out of nowhere, long, slim coffee brown arms engulfed Germaine, knocking him slightly off balance. "I've been looking all over the hospital for you! What are you doing out here?"

"Hi to you too, Maxine," Germaine said, laughing at her enthusiasm.

Jules saw him sneak a glance over at her, but she had already slid away and started gathering her things together.

She saw the look in his eyes. She knew that look. But it didn't matter. It didn't change the fact that they both wanted things that the other wasn't prepared to give. And it couldn't put their broken relationship back together again. In fact, all it had done was remind Jules of how much she had lost.

A sudden wave of exhaustion washed over Jules. Between seeing her mother and being with Germaine, the day had left her feeling drained. She just wanted to go home and spend the weekend curled up under her soft feather duvet.

She looked across at Maxine, who was fussing over Germaine, and showering him with questions about whether or not he had eaten, or taken a shower, or gotten some sleep. Jules could tell that she was genuinely concerned for him.

Since he had come back into Truuth's life, Maxine had adopted Germaine as her family, just like she had Truuth. That was what you had to love about Maxine— even though she was a tiny thing, her heart was huge.

Jules watched the two of them like a stranger watching a family through their living room window. She heard Maxine tell Germaine that Truuth was inside with Germaine's mother and that she had gone looking for Germaine in order to give Truuth some time alone with his aunt.

Germaine tried to tell Maxine that she didn't have to fuss over him, but Jules could tell that he enjoyed being taken care of. She was glad that there was someone there taking care of him, though she wished it was her. She tried hard to push back the feelings of jealousy that were stabbing at her heart.

"You're leaving?" Germaine asked suddenly, as he saw Jules walk away.

"Yeah," Jules said, forcing a smile. "Your family is here now, so . . ."

So you don't need me anymore.

"Tell your mom and sister I said bye," Jules said, barely turning around. She didn't think she could look him in the eye without breaking.

"Thanks for being here, Jules," Maxine said.

Jules tried to fight her annoyance. Suddenly Maxine's self-assumed role of family spokesperson was getting on her nerves.

"I'll see you guys later."

With her bags and her broken heart in her hands, Jules walked briskly out of the courtyard, into the hospital, and through the corridors toward the parking lot.

This time, she didn't bother to look back.

Chapter 24

"So I've been thinking about that thing you said a while back."

"What thing?" Jules asked, her eyes half-closed. It was Saturday afternoon after church, and both she and Easy were sitting on Sis Crawford's porch, lazily watching the wind rustle the begonias in the backyard. Jules had spent the entire day with Easy, trying to forget the crazy day she'd had with Germaine and his family only a few hours before. So far it had been working.

They had just stuffed themselves with a lunch of pumpkin rice, chicken stewed in okra, potato salad, and corn bread, and now they could barely move. The cool afternoon breeze signaled that they were well into fall, but it was not chilly enough to keep them inside.

Jules yawned. She knew she should probably have been getting ready to go back to church for the evening's youth service, but the caress of sleep was too tempting to resist. She could barely will her brain to focus on what Easy was saying, much more prepare to leave.

"The God thing."

Jules opened one eye and peered over at Easy, who was still reclined in his own chair, his eyes closed as if he was asleep.

"You're gonna have to be a bit more specific," Jules said.

Over the past couple months, she and Easy had had multiple conversations about "the God thing." They would start randomly, like this one, with questions like, "Why would God bother with someone like me?" or "How can I know that God was really listening?" before escalating into a long discussion.

When Easy brought up the subject of God, there was no telling where it would go. But Jules was happy that he seemed to be bringing it up more and more often.

"You were saying something about God working things out for those that follow Him," Easy continued thoughtfully, with his eyes still closed, and his feet still resting casually on the porch railing.

"Uh-huh," Jules answered cautiously. She knew there would be a question coming soon.

"Does that mean then that God only takes care of Christians?"

Jules smirked. She knew a lot of Christians, including herself, who wondered on occasion if God was taking care of them at all.

"No, it doesn't mean that," Jules answered. "The Bible says that He makes the sun to rise on both the good and the evil, meaning that He sends His blessings on everyone. God doesn't discriminate with the good tidings."

"So what's the difference between being a Christian and not being a Christian then?"

"It's the difference between chocolate cake and mud pie."

"Huh?"

"Let me explain," she said, sitting up in her chair and turning to face her friend, who was looking at her curiously.

"Life is like making a cake," Jules began. "God gives us all the same ingredients, and He also gives us the book with instructions. Now if we choose to follow the instructions, then when we put the ingredients together, in the right proportion, and bake them at the right temperature, we get a great tasting cake."

"But if we decide not to follow the instructions and instead use our own proportions for the ingredients, or even add things to the recipe that God asks us not to, then we end up with . . ."

". . . a hot mess," Easy finished.

"Exactly," Jules said, smiling. "God is like the master pastry maker, and the Bible is like our baking cookbook. Some people don't want to follow God's plan for their lives because they think it's too hard, or it's not what they want for themselves. Most times they end up making a mess of things. Even when it might look like they're doing well on the outside, they're usually not.

"But those who choose to follow God's will for their lives, to serve Him completely, they are the ones who end up with the winning product at the end. It might take longer, and the process might be harder, but the end result is always well worth it."

Easy rubbed his chin thoughtfully as he considered Jules's analogy.

"So things are really better when you're doing it the God way, huh?"

"Yup," Jules replied, nodding. "It might not always look that way, but it is."

"How can you be sure?"

Jules sighed. Every conversation they had about God always came back to this very question. How can you be sure?

"You can't," Jules said. "You have to take it by faith. And then you test God to see if He's true."

"Test God, Jules?"

Jules laughed. "I know it sounds weird, but God Himself says we should. In the Bible where it talks about tithes, He says we should prove Him, and see if He doesn't bless us for our faithfulness.

"That's how your faith grows. You trust God, and let Him prove that He will take care of you. Believe me, it works every time."

Easy was quiet again. In fact he was silent for so long that Jules began to wonder if he had gone off to sleep.

"All right."

"All right what?" Jules asked. She had returned to her original position in Sis Crawford's deck chair and was enjoying a cool breeze that was sweeping across the porch.

"I want to do it," Easy said decidedly. "I want to let God run things for me, and see how it turns out."

Jules's heart began to beat faster, and she sat up suddenly and looked at Easy, to see if he was joking. He wasn't.

"Are you saying what I think you're saying, Easy? Are you saying you want to give your life to God?"

Easy shrugged and looked at Jules simply. "Yeah, I think so. I've been thinking about it for a while, and I

see how He's been taking care of Grams, and you and
'Dre and even Truuth. It's like you guys never worry,
even when things ain't right. I want that."

Jules was so excited she could barely stay still.

"Oh, I'm so glad, Easy," she said, almost knocking
him and his chair over as she flung her arms around
him.

"Baby girl . . . can't . . . breathe . . ."

Jules grinned and let go of Easy, leaning back against
the porch railing instead.

"You won't regret it, Easy."

He nodded slowly. "I have a feeling you might be
right."

Chapter 25

"Why do you want this?"

Jules crossed and uncrossed her legs nervously as she sat in the VP's office. It had been four weeks since her dismissal, and they had finally called her in for an evaluation to determine what would happen next with her job. But Jules felt as if she was interviewing for her position all over again. She almost wished they would fire her and get it over with. It would be better than sitting here, on the verge of a panic attack, trying to figure out the right answer to a silly interview question.

However, Jules had to admit that of late she had been asking herself that same question. Why *did* she want the job?

The money was good. But that wasn't what was motivating her. She had always wanted to work in PR and communications, and that was what kept her going. But lately working at Toronto Grace had been more stressful than enjoyable. She had once heard someone say, love what you do and you'll never work a day in your life. Well, this job had felt a lot like work lately, and she was beginning to doubt if she really loved it.

But now wasn't the time for self evaluation. Thomas Donnelly of the hospital's executive team was looking at her impatiently over the top of his horn-rimmed glasses, and Jules knew if she wanted this job, she would have to work for it.

But what if she didn't want it? Then what?

There were no other prospects in the near future, and while she would love to have the luxury of taking some time off to figure everything out, she knew her bank account and bills wouldn't allow it.

But what if this wasn't what God wanted her to be doing?

That, more than any other, was the thought that seemed to be nagging Jules more and more. What if He had a bigger plan in store for her?

"I want this job because I am good at it," Jules said decisively. "You need someone who knows this hospital—who knows the things that can't be put on paper. Someone who is familiar with the hospital's stakeholders and who has the training and experience needed to communicate with them in a way that ensures that the hospital continues to have a mutually beneficial relationship with each different group.

"I am that person."

Jules leaned forward and looked sincerely into the doubtful eyes of the aging gentleman.

"Sir, I know this hospital has been going through a lot of changes lately. With the restructuring and the recent strike, you need to have someone in your public relations department who can assure staff, board members, and patients that this hospital is, and will continue to be, a strong part of the community both now and in the many years to come.

"You can't do that with a new person who knows nothing about our culture. You need someone who your stakeholders are familiar with and who is familiar with them. You need someone who has a proven record of success. That person is me."

Jules took a deep breath and sat back. She had done her best. Now it was out of her hands.

Donnelly took off his glasses and rubbed them with a tiny piece of velvet, before putting them back on. He sighed wearily and looked up at Jules.

"I'll tell you, Ms. Jackson, just the thought of having to hire an entire new department is enough to give me a headache. I think we'll just stick with what we have for now."

Jules smiled.

"Thank you, sir. You won't be sorry."

She paused and looked at the VP carefully.

"I do have one more thing to ask however."

A few moments later, Jules walked out of the office with her job back in place and authorization to bring Michelle back in and hire a new employee. She couldn't believe her luck. She had been begging for extra staff for months, and now she finally had it. It seemed that everything with work was going exactly how she would have planned it.

So why wasn't she happier about it? And why was there this unsettling feeling in her stomach that wouldn't go away?

Swinging her purse lazily, she walked out of the elevator she had taken down to the ground floor and slid into a seat in the hospital café. After a moment she realized it was the same seat she had sat in the first time she'd had lunch with Germaine. She rubbed her eyes wearily. It seemed like she couldn't go more than a couple of hours without thinking about him.

Her thoughts drifted back to that first day. What she wouldn't give to go back to that moment and start all over again, knowing what she knew now. She would do so many things differently.

She smiled as she remembered how passionate he had been as he talked about the Sound Lounge. She wondered what it would be like to be so passionate about something. The only thing that came close was the satisfaction she got working with Truuth to promote his album. Every time an event came off well, or they got a good review, or someone sent an e-mail to the Web site saying that Truuth's music had changed him or her, Jules felt something move inside her. What she wouldn't give to feel that way all the time.

She sat up suddenly.

That was it.

That was what she should be doing. But as soon as the idea came, so did the doubts. How could she make a living off freelance artist promotion? It would be almost like being an independent consultant. There would be no steady salary, no health benefits, and no pension plan. Just a lot of budgeting, business planning, and bad debt. And of course there was that widely circulated statistic that nine out of ten new businesses failed within the first year.

Still, Jules couldn't help but notice that her fingers tingled at the thought of going it on her own. There were so many things that could go wrong. But there were so many things that could go right too.

There was so much to think about.

Sighing deeply, she closed her eyes and rested her hands and head on the table.

Lord, I don't know what to do. My mind is telling me one thing, but my heart wants to do another. I just want to do Your will for my life. Show me Your way, I pray. Amen.

"Jules? Is that you?"

Jules opened her eyes and looked up from the table.

"Sharifa!" she said, smiling. She stood up and embraced the tall, voluptuous woman.

Sharifa Johns was a publicist Jules had met while working for Truuth. She was the organizer for the annual Gospel Explosion concerts, and, when she wasn't doing that, she was representing artists like Lilly Goodman, Cassandra Sommers, and Ricky Dillard. There were even rumors floating around in the industry that she had worked with God's Property and Kiki Sheard while in the States. But Jules wasn't sure how true that was.

"What are you doing here?" Jules asked, still smiling as they sat down at Jules's table.

"Girl, wouldn't you know my son broke his arm playing basketball about six weeks ago," she said.

"Is he okay?" Jules asked, concerned.

"Oh, yeah, he's fine," Sharifa said with a flick of her wrist. "He just came in to get his cast taken off today. Of course, he doesn't want his momma hoverin' over him," Sharifa said, rolling big, almond-shaped eyes. "So I came down here to grab a coffee until he's done."

Sharifa shook her head and smirked. "Sixteen-year-old boys. Think they all grown until they get hurt, then they need they momma. But when everything is okay, they go right back to their old selves."

Jules laughed.

"So what about you, Jules, what you doing sitting out here like you a visitor? Don't you work here anymore?" Sharifa asked, half-jokingly.

If she only knew.

"Yeah. But today was a day off. I just had to come in quickly to do some stuff, though."

Sharifa raised an eyebrow.

"You coming in here on your day off?" she asked. "Girl, you worse than me."

Jules laughed. "You're probably right. I am glad I ran into you, though, 'cause I wanted to ask you something. How did you end up going into artist promotion full-time?"

Sharifa took a sip of her coffee and looked thoughtful as she seemed to consider Jules's question.

"Well, I guess things were different for me," she said. "When I just got out of school, I couldn't get a full-time gig like you. I just kept getting a lot of contract deals. Six months here, eight months there, a temporary project or two, but nothing full-time.

"In between all of that, I used to do a lot of work for friends who were putting on concerts, and I got a good feel for that.

"After about three years I got tired out bouncing around. I realized I really liked the gospel entertainment scene and that there was a void in the industry when it came to properly trained, experienced public relations reps. Plus, all my moving around had helped me develop a long list of potential clients and contacts. So, I just decided to take a risk and do my own thing."

Jules nodded as she listened. The way Sharifa explained it made it all sound so easy.

"How hard was it to get started?"

"I'm not gonna lie to you, Jules. It wasn't a smooth transition," Sharifa said. "I couldn't just think like a publicist anymore; I had to think like a businesswoman as well. I had to map out my finances, set my budgets and goals for the year. And I also had to make a lot of hard decisions.

"Sometimes it meant not taking on a client I really believed in because I knew that I would end up taking a loss instead of making a profit on them. Other times it meant sinking my own money into the venture.

"On top of all that, I had to learn how to get out there and sell my business to people. It wasn't just about my skills anymore; it was about how I could make the most out of the budget they gave me. I had to prove to them that what they were paying me to do was having a direct effect on their bottom line, and when you're talking to people who don't think like we do, you know that can be difficult."

Jules definitely understood that. Sometimes it was near impossible to convince her bosses—both at Triad and the hospital—that the money they spent managing their images would directly affect the profitability of their companies.

Sharifa looked at Jules closely. "Is this something you're thinking of doing?"

Jules nodded. "But I'm not one hundred percent sure yet, so don't spread it around."

Sharifa nodded. "I understand. It's a decision you have to make for yourself. Not every communicator is meant to have her own business. I'm not trying to hate on you; I'm just telling you how it is. You have to know for yourself if it's something you can handle."

Jules nodded. "What other sorts of things should I be considering?"

As they sat in the café in the after-lunch lull, Sharifa told Jules some of what she had learned from her own experience in the business. They discussed everything, from the best way to get started, to what to watch out for. When Sharifa's son eventually called and told his mother he was ready, almost forty-five minutes had passed.

As Sharifa stood up to leave, she pulled out her card and handed it to Jules.

"I know you already have my number, but I'm giving it to you again," Sharifa said. "Call me, and we can set up a time to talk about this some more. If you need me, girl—and I know you gonna need me—I'm here for you. We PR girls gotta stick together."

"Thanks," Jules said, smiling gratefully. "I just need to decide if I can really do this."

Sharifa cocked her head to the side and looked at Jules.

"Let me tell you something, girl," she said. "I've seen the way you juggle this job and work with Truuth. You've got it in you to do this. Plus, you have something I never had. You have that connection to Triad— and that's a wealth of new artists who are going to need representation but don't know the first place to look for it. You can use that."

Jules nodded. "I'll keep that in mind. Thanks again, Sharifa," she said, hugging the woman.

"No problem," Sharifa said, slipping her bag over her shoulder, "Just don't steal all my clients when you go big-time," Sharifa teased.

Jules laughed. "I'm not making any promises."

Chapter 26

"Strawberry or chocolate?" Tanya asked, as she dug through her open freezer.

"Chocolate!"

"Neither."

Tanya and Maxine turned to look at Jules in surprise. They had never heard her refuse ice cream.

"I've been binging on ice cream every weekend for the past couple months. It's time to have some restraint."

"Well, I'll have her share then," Maxine called to Tanya from her position on the couch.

"Hey, you ain't no guest here," Tanya said from the kitchen. "Come get it yourself."

Jules watched in amusement as Maxine pouted before dragging herself off the couch to the kitchen. It never ceased to amaze Jules how Maxine suddenly became demanding whenever she was around Jules and Tanya. Jules figured it was because both she and Tanya had spoiled her. They couldn't help it, though; at twenty-three Maxine was the youngest, and therefore the baby of the three of them.

Jules stretched out her legs and looked around Tanya's large, sunken living room. It was good to be somewhere other than her apartment. Since her last encounter with Germaine she had gone back to hiding in her apartment. Everything that had happened had helped her realize she needed to take a step back and figure out where she was going with her life. And she needed to do that without any distractions from Tanya and Maxine, or anyone else.

However, this Thursday afternoon, her best friends had had enough. Without warning they had shown up and practically dragged her out of the apartment to Tanya's house for a girls' night. Although she had protested at first, she was glad they had. Too much time alone wasn't good for anyone.

"So," Maxine began, when she and Tanya had returned to the living room. "You should probably know, a lot of stuff went down while you were MIA."

"Like you telling Truuth that you're pregnant?" Jules asked pointedly.

"Oh, yeah, that," Maxine said with a lot less enthusiasm.

Jules looked at her friend closely for what was the first time in a long time. She had lost weight; her skin also looked a bit dull, and her eyes were tired. Jules could understand why. After Maxine's parents had found out she was pregnant they had put her out. Since then she had been bunking it with Tanya. It had been a major adjustment for Maxine, and to some extent she was still coming to grips with the whole situation.

Jules had never understood how parents could cut their daughter off at a time in her life when she needed them most. But the Simpsons had. They called it tough love, and they said it was the only way Maxine could understand the true gravity of what she had gotten herself into. Jules shuddered. She was glad God didn't "love" us like that, or we'd all be in a lot of trouble.

"What did Truuth say when you told him about the baby?" Jules asked, pushing her negative thoughts about Maxine's parents out of her mind.

Maxine shrugged. "Nothing. He's been acting really weird about the whole thing, like's he's not sure how he's supposed to feel about it. Sometimes he gets excited; other times, it's like he's so ashamed about it that he . . ."

Maxine sighed heavily as she tried to search for the words to explain. Eventually she gave up.

"I dunno."

Jules looked across at Tanya, who just shrugged, indicating that she didn't know any more about the situation than Jules did.

"So . . . have you guys talked about what you're going to do?"

"Not really," Maxine said, playing with the hem of her blouse. "I don't think he's ready to talk about it yet."

"But Maxine, you have to—"

"Look, it will be fine, okay?" Maxine said impatiently. "Let's not spoil the evening with this."

"Maxine—"

"Guys," Maxine said firmly. "I don't want to talk about this anymore. Let's just skip it, okay?"

Jules and Tanya looked at each other worriedly. If Maxine was locking down on the issue, then there must be a reason. But it was clear that she wouldn't say more about it until she was good and ready.

"Okay," Jules agreed, shrugging.

"Okay," Maxine said, forcing a smile and seemingly shrugging off the conversation.

Only a few moments later, it seemed as if she had truly forgotten about it and was back to her old self. "Anyway, like I said, Jules, a lot has been going on."

"Like what?" Jules asked with mild curiosity.

Instead of answering, however, Maxine stared purposefully at Tanya. Tanya, though, buried her face in her bowl of ice cream and refused to look at either of them.

"Well, aren't you gonna tell her?" Maxine asked. When Tanya didn't respond, Maxine rolled her eyes impatiently.

"Okay, fine, I will," Maxine said, turning back to Jules. "Tanya and 'Dre went on a date."

Jules raised one eyebrow in surprise and looked over at Tanya questioningly.

"It wasn't a date," Tanya argued. "We just went out as friends. Just to talk things out."

"And?" Jules asked, trying to be casual.

While she hoped just as much as Maxine did that things would suddenly work out perfectly with Tanya and 'Dre, recent experience had taught her that it might not.

"He said he didn't know I felt that way about him, and asked me why I didn't say anything before," Tanya said after a moment. "Then he said he'd never thought of our relationship that way, and that he cared about me a lot."

She sighed again and looked down at her ice cream that was turning into mush.

"Then he said he wouldn't want to do anything that would jeopardize our friendship."

Jules bit her lip as she watched her despondent friend. Tanya was trying to act like she was okay with everything, but Jules could tell that it was breaking her heart. Even Maxine, who almost always had something to say, was unusually quiet.

"I'm sorry, T," Jules said quietly, with Maxine nodding her agreement.

Tanya nodded. "I guess that's the way it is sometimes."

"So what now?" Maxine asked quietly after a moment.

Jules saw Tanya shrug and give a small sniffle.

"Now we let it be," Jules said quietly but firmly.

Tanya raised her watery eyes to Jules curiously.

"Tanya, you already prayed about this, remember?" Jules said. "You asked God to let His will be done in this thing. So you have to let Him do His will. He has a plan for both you and 'Dre. And truthfully, it may or may not involve both of you being together, but whatever it is, it's definitely better than anything you could do for yourself."

Tanya nodded solemnly and sniffled again.

"You're right, Jules," she said. "Thanks for reminding me of that."

Jules smiled.

"Well, I'm glad you're being so positive about this, Jules, 'cause there's something else we have to tell you," Maxine announced.

"Maxine . . ." Tanya began.

"We said we would tell her, Tanya," Maxine said seriously. "Better she hear it from us than find out the hard way."

Jules looked back and forth between her two friends

apprehensively. She had a feeling that the calm she had been working on all week was about to be no more.

"What is it?" she asked cautiously.

Maxine and Tanya looked at each other nervously.

"Ladies," Jules said impatiently.

"Uh . . . Germaine is dating someone," Maxine said, watching Jules carefully.

"We don't know if he's dating her," Tanya said, trying to soften the blow. "I only saw them out together once. It was the night that I was out with 'Dre."

Jules swallowed hard and tried not to react, even though her insides were churning.

"It's okay," Jules said with more calm than she felt. "We're not together anymore, and he's a grown man. He can date whomever he wants."

Despite her assurance that she was fine, Jules saw a worried look pass between Maxine and Tanya.

"There's something else," Maxine said hesitantly. "The girl he was out with? You know her."

Jules felt her stomach begin to spin even more. Germaine on a date with some random girl—that she could deal with. But Germaine with someone she knew. That was a whole other thing.

"Who was it?" Jules managed to choke out.

Maxine looked at Tanya for support.

"It was LeTavia," Tanya said.

"LeTavia Dixon? From church?" Jules asked in disbelief. "You've got to be kidding."

Tanya shook her head solemnly. "I'm sorry, Jules."

Jules laughed humorlessly. Who would have thought history would repeat itself so perfectly.

She had been here with LeTavia before. Four years before to be exact. At that time, the guy had been Demore Scott. He had been Jules's boyfriend for almost a year. In her twenty-two-year-old innocence, she had even thought that they might have gotten married. But then rumors had started circulating that LeTavia, Jules's supposed friend, had been making a play for him whenever Jules wasn't around.

Jules had brushed the rumors aside because she knew that church people sometimes gossiped more than regular folk. But then Jules and Demore had had a major falling out, and before you could say "man-eater," LeTavia had shown up on Demore's arm. Needless to say, her friendship with LeTavia had died a swift and sudden death.

Jules grimaced as she thought of how the issue had divided their friends at Scarborough Memorial. Even though she had never confronted LeTavia about it, a lot of people had felt the need to take sides over the issue. Demore and LeTavia had not lasted very long, but some of the division that had occurred because of it had.

Jules sighed. All that fuss over one guy, who wasn't even around anymore. She wouldn't let that happen again.

"So what are you gonna do?" Maxine asked, with an air of hostility. Jules looked up at her flighty friend, who seemed to be gunning for a fight.

"Come on, Jules, you can't let her do this to you again."

Jules herself had expected to feel some sort of anger, but instead a strange calm seemed to wash over her. A verse kept repeating itself over and over in her mind, seemingly of its own accord.

"And we know that all things work together for good

to them that love God, to them who are the called according to His purpose."

Jules shrugged. "She's not doing anything to me, Maxine. LeTavia is just being LeTavia. I can't blame her for what happened with me and Germaine."

Jules stretched her legs out in front of her lazily, looked thoughtful for a moment. "You know, when everything with Germaine first blew up, I was really upset. But I've had a lot of time to think about it, and I realize that all of this could be God's way of teaching me something."

"What a way to learn a lesson," Tanya said wryly. "I hope you at least figured out what it was."

Jules shrugged. "I think the lesson was that it's not about me."

Tanya and Maxine looked at her in confusion.

"It's like what you said the other day, Tanya," Jules explained. "You know that I always try to do everything myself, try to figure out everything on my own, and when something goes wrong I try to fix it by myself. It's like, I had given my life to God, but I was still holding on to the reins.

"But it's not about me making things work. It's about God. It's not by my might or my power, but by His Spirit.

"So, even though I know you heifers were looking for a battle," Jules said with a mischievous grin and a flick of her hand, "it's not gonna happen.

"I still miss him. But it's out of my hands. I'm gonna do what I should have done a long time ago. I'm gonna let God take care of it."

"Well, look at you, acting all grown and evolved," Maxine said with an air of admiration. "I'm glad to hear you talking like that, though," she continued, breathing a sigh of relief. " 'Cause I thought we were gonna have to go old school and beat a sister down!"

"Not even," Jules said with a laugh.

"Girl, you know I'm too cute for prison!"

Chapter 27

Though she had acted strong with Maxine and Tanya,
Jules knew LeTavia and Germaine together was
the last thing she wanted to see. But not even that could
keep her away from her home church on the day of
Easy's baptism. From the moment she stepped into
Scarborough Memorial she felt that something special
in the air. It was the feeling you get when you know
something wonderful is about to happen.

It was the first time she had been back at her home
church in almost a month. In her efforts to avoid any
kind of drama, she had alternated between Toronto
East and Apple Creek, where Easy usually went with
his grandmother. But Easy had spent a lot of time talking with Pastor Thomas and had subsequently decided
that Scarborough Memorial was the place where he
wanted to make his decision to follow Christ public.

That was great for Easy, who got to be with Truuth
and the rest of the Triad family. Not so great for Jules,
who had to alternate between avoiding everyone she
knew and answering questions about where she had
been for the past couple weeks.

And then there was the whole Germaine and LeTavia thing.

Sitting together in a pew near the middle of church, they were the first two people Jules saw as she stepped into the sanctuary. She closed her eyes for a quick moment and tried to remember the text she had read that morning.

When thou passest through the waters I will be with thee . . . when thou walkest through the fire thou shalt not be burned.

Jules opened her eyes and glanced at LeTavia's red dress. It sure looked enough like fire for her.

With those words rolling around in her mind, she pulled down the brim of her cartwheel hat, which she had dug out of the back of her closet that morning, and walked smoothly down the main aisle to the front, slipping into the row behind Easy's.

"Hiding from someone?" Tanya asked.

She had slid in beside Jules only moments after Jules had sat down.

"Why would you think that?" Jules asked, feigning ignorance.

"No reason," Tanya said dryly. "Except that if I hadn't recognized my Gucci pumps on your feet, I wouldn't have been able to tell who you were."

Jules silently chided herself for not returning Tanya's shoes months ago after she had borrowed them to wear to the hospital's volunteer banquet.

"Shhh," Jules hissed, trying to quiet Tanya and change the subject at the same time. "Pastor Thomas is about to start."

"Oww!" she exclaimed quietly as she felt Tanya pinch her hard. She rubbed the sore spot on her arm and glared at Tanya as much as she could from under the wide brim of the floppy, elegant hat. But Tanya was already ignoring her.

"This morning I want to talk to you church about surrender," Pastor Thomas began. "Have you truly surrendered your life to God?"

Pastor Thomas's message seemed to hit a chord in Jules's heart. She knew that it was the type of sermon he usually gave when someone was about to give his or her heart to Christ, but that morning she felt as if he was speaking directly to her.

"Surrendering means trusting God to lead even when things don't look the way we think they should. Sometimes it may even feel like God is not there. But I tell you, friends, all of this is often a way for God to get us to look to Him.

"I know a lot of you are going through some hard times. I know because I can see it in your faces. In the tired smiles you bring with you on Sabbath morning. I know because many of you have shared these concerns with me. But I tell you that even though things look bleak, never should you think that God is not there. Sometimes God does not reveal Himself immediately because He is waiting to see if we will trust Him."

Had she really trusted God fully? Jules wasn't sure she had. Instead of trusting, she had been sulking about how much things hadn't been going her way. But what if what seemed wrong to her was right in God's eyes?

"I will tell you another thing, friends," Pastor Thomas continued. "Sometimes surrendering means walking in a path that doesn't feel right. The book of Proverbs, chapter 16, says, 'there is a way that seemeth right unto a man, but the end thereof are the ways of death.' God sees the end from the beginning, and sometimes, by leading us in a path that feels uncomfortable, He is saving us from an evil end."

The words hit Jules like a ton of bricks. What if she was supposed to lose her job, so that God could open a door to something else? And with that thought came an even more difficult one. What if she was supposed to lose Germaine?

Jules closed her eyes and sank a little lower in the pew. She didn't know if she wanted to hear that. Earlier in the week, she had thought she just might be able to let go, but seeing him this morning had made her a lot less sure. How could God make her get so attached to someone, only to have him taken away? That didn't seem right.

The thought bothered Jules so much that she didn't even notice when Pastor Thomas sat down and Sister Crawford took the mike. It was only when the small woman's strong contralto voice began to fill the church that Jules sat up and took notice.

"In the morning, when I rise. In the morning when I rise, in the morning when I rise, give me Jesus."

Jules felt the words wrap around her and seep into her soul.

She knew this song. Momma Jackson used to sing it in the kitchen on a Sunday morning as she kneaded the dough for the homemade bread she used to bake every Sunday up until the week Jules's father left. Jules remembered sitting on the steps to the back porch and listening to her mother's sweet voice. She had never grasped fully what the song meant then, but as she sat there thinking of all she was willing to give up, and all that Easy was prepared to give up for Jesus, the full meaning came to her.

She couldn't stop the tears that filled her eyes as the last few words of the song hung in the air. It was true; the only thing she needed was Jesus. He alone knew what was best for her, and if she trusted Him, in His wisdom, He would give her exactly what she needed.

A few minutes later, when Easy came out of the water, Jules found that she wasn't the only one crying. In fact there wasn't a dry eye in the house.

As Jules watched different people embrace Easy, she became overwhelmed by the warmth that the members at Scarborough Memorial showed to her newly converted friend. To many of them, he was a stranger, but still they welcomed him in and celebrated him as if he was one of their own.

"I am so proud of you," Jules said at the end of the service, as she pulled Easy into a bear hug in the church courtyard.

"Thanks, baby girl," he said, smiling. "If it wasn't for you and Grams on my back, I don't know if any of this would have happened. But I can't say I'm not grateful."

Jules beamed at him. She hadn't been sure this day would ever come, and she was so glad it had. She had always had a special place in her heart for Easy, but now he felt more like family than ever before. Now he was part of the eternal family.

"Hey, I hope you don't think you're gonna have him all to yourself," Maxine said, squeezing in beside Jules and throwing her arms around Easy. Jules laughed and made space for the throng of well-wishers who were lined up to congratulate Easy. There would be plenty of time to talk with him later.

Not wanting to linger much longer, Jules retrieved her keys from her purse and began to make her way to the exit. But before she could stop herself, she found her eyes searching the crowd.

It didn't take long for her to spot him. He was standing near the front exit to the church, and he was all alone.

Jules found herself frozen in the churchyard, watching him. A big part of her wanted to walk over and say hi. She desperately wanted to know what was going on with him. How were things going at the Lounge? Maxine had told her that he had shut down the place and was planning on moving to a new location. Had he found somewhere yet? How were his mother and Soroya doing? And of course there were her own selfish questions, like if he ever thought about her at all.

As if hearing her thoughts, he looked up and caught Jules's eye. Even though he was a good distance away and half the church population stood between them, Jules's stomach still began to churn nervously.

Somehow in the midst of her panic, she managed to muster up a small smile and a tiny wave. He smiled back, and Jules let out the breath she didn't know she had been holding. She was almost sure he was about to offer a wave, but a slim female figure cloaked in red stepped right in front of him, cutting off Jules's line of vision.

LeTavia.

Jules had almost forgotten about her.

As she watched the girl slide her hand seductively down Germaine's arm, she wondered if it was laziness, or just plain maliciousness that made LeTavia go after every man Jules happened to be involved with. And if the latter was the case, she wondered what she had ever done to the chick to make her hate her that much.

It didn't matter now anyway.

Exhaling loudly, Jules turned around and made her way to the parking lot alone.

Guess it's just You and me, Jesus.

"Yo, J!"

Jules glanced back and was surprised to see Truuth walking toward her.

"Let me holler at you for a minute."

She stopped and stood shading her eyes from the bright midday sun as she waited for him to catch up with her. She wondered what it was he could possibly want.

"I wanted to talk to you," Truuth said when he was close enough.

Even though he was standing right in front of her, his eyes were darting down to the side as if he was nervous about what he was going to say.

"What's up?" Jules asked.

"I know I been giving you a hard time, but I just wanted to say thanks for holding it down at the hospital with G and 'Roya the other day," he said quietly.

Jules shrugged. "It wasn't a big deal."

"Yeah, but I know you and him got some issues, and me an' you wasn't really cool like that, so you could've easily walked it off, you know? But you didn't, and I respect that."

Jules nodded. She could still see Germaine standing in the churchyard with LeTavia over Truuth's shoulder.

"How's his mom doing?" she asked hesitantly.

Truuth shrugged. "It's been hard for her. And G won't talk about it much. But I think she's doing a lot better. She's out of the hospital, and she's staying at his apartment with 'Roya until they can find another place to stay."

Jules nodded. She wanted to press for more, but knew it wasn't her place.

"Tell them hi for me next time you see them, okay?"

Truuth nodded solemnly. Then he cocked his head to the side and looked at Jules curiously. "You really care about them, don't you."

Jules nodded.

"You're not a bad chick, Jules Jackson," Truuth said. "Maybe I was too hard on you.

"That don't mean I forgotten about all that mess from before," he added quickly. "But if you was willing to step up like that, then you probably okay. Plus, we both believers, and you know God ain't down with that malice stuff."

Jules smiled at Truuth's roundabout way of patching things up.

"Thanks, Truuth," she said. She narrowed her eyes at him suspiciously. "Did Max put you up to this?"

"Nah, J, this was all me," he said, grinning. Jules rolled her eyes. Maxine had definitely been chewing his ear off.

"But on the real, though," he said, getting serious again. "We cool?"

"Yeah, we're okay."

He nodded his head in approval and gave Jules a quick hug.

"A'ight. I catch up with you later then, Jules."

Jules watched as he loped through the parking lot toward the church gate where Maxine was standing and pretending not to watch him.

"Hey, Truuth!"

He stopped short, and Jules walked the small distance to catch up with him.

"Tell Maxine to swing by me tonight. I wanna take her out to dinner," Jules said.

"A'ight, I'll let her know."

"And, Truuth?"

He looked back at Jules one last time.

"Tell her to make it just the two of us."

"So I notice you've been missing lately. That morning sickness got you on lockdown, don't it?"

"Like you wouldn't believe, girl," Maxine said, rubbing her tummy. She had barely started showing, but she had already adopted the pregnant woman stance. "It's more like all day sickness. It never really ends," Maxine said, rolling her eyes.

"Yeah, well, you're a nurse. You should know how to take care of that," Jules said.

Maxine shook her head. "It's different when you're on the other end."

After much persuasion Maxine had agreed to go with Jules to Mandalay, a small Southeast Asian restaurant near the corner of Markham Road and Lawrence Avenue, to catch an early dinner. Jules was glad that Maxine had come, for Jules was starting to feel guilty about how little time she had spent with Maxine lately. Jules knew that with everything going on in Maxine's life, Maxine would need her support now more than ever—even if she was too stubborn to ask for it.

"Ladies, what will you be having this evening?"

"Pan-seared salmon with pad Thai noodles," Jules said, handing her unopened menu to the waiter. She had been here enough times to know exactly what she wanted.

Maxine glanced through the menu a bit longer before ordering the same thing. It wasn't until their drinks came that Maxine turned to look at Jules seriously.

"Okay, so what's this about?" she asked.

"What do you mean?" Jules asked, trying to feign innocence.

"Why'd you make such a big production of asking me to dinner and telling me not to tell Tanya?"

"It's not a big production," Jules said defensively. "Is something wrong if I want to have dinner alone with one of my best friends?"

Maxine gave Jules a look that told her she wasn't buying it.

"Okay, fine," Jules said, dropping the act. "I wanted to talk to you about the fact that you've been missing from church lately."

After the service earlier Tanya had told Jules that Maxine had been absent from church almost every week during the past month. And the one week Tanya had convinced her to show up, she had left halfway through. It seemed that Maxine had shut down on Tanya and had refused to talk about it, so Jules figured she might as well try to break through on her own.

"I didn't know if it had something to do with you and Tanya, so I didn't want to call you at the house or ask you in front of her," Jules continued.

"Oh," Maxine said. She looked down at her drink but said nothing more.

"So? What's happening with you? Are you and Tanya having a fight or something?"

"No."

"So how come you haven't been to church, or even to the studio for the last couple of weeks. Is the morning sickness really that bad?"

"No."

"Then what?"

Maxine sighed and began stirring her drink with the straw, still not looking at Jules.

"Max . . ."

"It's because . . . It's because I don't feel comfortable, okay?"

Jules looked at Maxine in confusion.

"I'm not following you."

"I'm starting to show, Jules," Maxine said, looking purposefully down at her stomach and then back at Jules.

"So?"

"So . . . now everybody's got something to say," Maxine said, visibly upset.

"Everybody like who?" Jules asked, getting annoyed herself.

She loved Scarborough Memorial, and most of the people there were warm and supportive. But she knew that Maxine was right—there were always a few people who felt that their mess didn't stink and that that gave them the right to talk down to others. But all Jules wanted was a name—just one name, so she could tell that person where to get off.

"Never mind," Maxine said, trying to defuse the situation.

"Maxine."

Maxine heard the warning in Jules's tone and knew that if she didn't tell her, Jules would make it a point of duty to find out anyway. She sighed.

"A couple weeks ago, I was sitting up in the front at church, when Sis Henry comes over to me during the opening song and says that maybe I shouldn't be sitting there. That she has a seat for me near the middle of the church where I might feel more comfortable. I told her I was fine, but she kept insisting, so I just got mad and told her that I wasn't going anywhere and God Himself would have to move me if she wanted me out of that seat.

"When she heard that she got mad and started talking about how girls like me are the reason all the young girls in church are losing their morals. She said everyone knew that I was pregnant and that I had no shame, parading around like it was okay."

Maxine's voice had become shaky, and Jules could tell that just recalling the incident was making her upset. Jules was getting upset just hearing about it.

"Then she told me I was a disgrace to my parents."

Jules's mouth fell open in shock.

"Max, I'm so sorry."

Maxine sniffled and tried to wipe at her damp eyes with a napkin.

"That was the worst part for me, Jules," Maxine said quietly. "Everything else she said just rolled right off me, 'cause I knew it wasn't true. But that, that was too close to home, you know?"

Jules nodded and reached over and grabbed her friend's hand.

"I'm so sorry, Maxine," she said. "That woman had no right to say that to you."

How dare Sis Henry talk to Maxine like that? Who gave her the right to judge? Especially since Jules had never seen her husband in church even once. The nerve of that woman. Just thinking about it made Jules angry.

But all her anger evaporated when she looked at her friend.

Maxine had always been the mouthy one. When they were younger, Jules and Maxine would get into a lot of fights because Maxine would mouth off on some girl and Jules would have to jump into the fray when someone started swinging. But even though it had gotten Maxine into trouble plenty of times, Jules could always count on Maxine to say exactly what was on her mind. However, Jules sometimes forgot that the loudness was just a cover for Maxine's insecurity. She wasn't nearly as tough as most people thought she was. Jules knew that, and it was why she felt like she needed to protect her friend most of the time.

At that moment the waiter returned with their orders, placing the large steaming dishes in front of them. But they had both lost their appetites.

Maxine was still sniffling, and even as Jules held tightly to her hand, she couldn't think of one thing worth saying.

Dear Lord, please give me the words to assure her, and please comfort Maxine now.

Jules took a deep breath.

"Maxine, listen to me. I know you're feeling down on yourself right now, but remember that God still cares for you. It doesn't matter what anyone else says, or what mistakes you've made, He still loves you, and He'll always be there for you. And He loves this baby too.

"He wouldn't have allowed you to have this baby if there wasn't a purpose for both your lives in it. So just remember that. Just give Him everything you have, and He will make something beautiful out of it, just like He always does."

Maxine nodded and sniffled. "I hope you're right."

"You know I'm right," Jules said firmly. "And if anyone tries to tell you otherwise, you tell me, and I'll deal with it."

Maxine laughed.

"Thanks, Jules."

"Anytime, honey. You know I'm always here for you."

"Yeah, you are," Maxine said ruefully. "It's like I can't get rid of you."

They both laughed.

As they began to eat, however, Jules heard Maxine sigh again.

"I just wish my parents felt the way you do," she murmured.

"They'll come around eventually," Jules said, even though she wasn't one hundred percent sure. "I'm not gonna lie, though. I can't believe they really made you leave."

"They're not bad people, Jules," Maxine said, picking up on her friend's disdain. "They've just got their principles that they have to live by.

"My momma had done told me, from I was about twelve, that any day I got pregnant, that was it. I had to go. And for the next eleven years that was enough to scare me away from even thinking about messing with some dude."

"I guess you weren't thinking about her this time," Jules said dryly.

Maxine smirked. "Trust me, Jules, when Germaine has your back up against his kitchen wall and his business all up between your legs, you'll be thinking about a lot of things. But your momma ain't gonna be one of them."

Jules grimaced.

"So what are you going to do now?" Jules asked. "I know you, and living with Tanya isn't gonna fly for much longer."

"You got that right," Maxine said, with a touch of irritation. "Can you believe that heifer woke me up at 5:30 yesterday morning to do yoga with her white self?"

Jules laughed out loud. "You lie!"

Maxine sucked her teeth in annoyance.

"You should have heard her, talking 'bout how it will be good for the baby. I nearly hit her over the head with the bedside lamp."

Jules doubled over as she envisioned Tanya in her full-body leotard, trying to wake Maxine before the sun came up.

"You know she means well," Jules said, wiping away tears of laughter.

"Yeah, well, she needs to go mean well with someone else," Maxine said.

Maxine rubbed her palm against her forehead and closed her eyes as if exhausted.

"Jules, I gotta find me somewhere to live," she said, resting her elbows tiredly against the table. "I don't know how much more of Tanya I can take.

"I need somewhere close to work, where my roommates won't drive me crazy, and where I won't feel like I'm living off someone's pity."

Jules sighed. She figured that some day in the future she was probably going to regret her next words.

"Why don't you move in with me?"

Maxine raised one eyebrow at Jules curiously.

"Jules, you live in a one bedroom."

"Yeah, but there are some two bedrooms open in my building. It would be nothing to move across. My lease is almost up anyway."

"I don't know, Jules. We've haven't lived together since summer camp when we were fourteen," Maxine said skeptically. "And I know we're best friends and all, but just based on my experience with T, I know best friends don't always make the best roommates."

"True, but look at the up sides," Jules reasoned. "You already know me. You know my building and the area. It's close to work. It's close to church. You'd be paying your own rent, so it's not like I'd be doing you a favor.

"And at least you'd be close to a friend. You know, just in case you need someone to hold back your weave while you throw up from the morning sickness," Jules said mischievously.

Maxine stuck out her tongue at Jules, and they both laughed.

But Jules could see that her friend wasn't convinced.

"I don't know, Jules."

"Come on. What other choice do you have?"

Maxine shrugged. "Tanya's not so bad when you give her a chance."

"I guess you're right," Jules said casually as she stuck a piece of juicy salmon into her mouth. "By the way, how are you liking Tanya's Sunday morning aerobics classes?"

Maxine shot Jules a dirty look. "Get me some estimates on rent, and we'll take it from there."

Chapter 28

"I can't believe you fed Tanya that 'don't want to ruin the friendship' mess," Jules hissed at 'Dre.

It was the first weekend in November, and all of Triad Entertainment, plus 'Dre's family and a host of acquaintances were packed into 'Dre's mother's house for his thirtieth birthday party.

Most of the guests were milling around in the back-yard and on the deck, in an effort to enjoy the Indian summer Toronto had been experiencing over the last few days.

Jules was trying to enjoy the festivities, but between 'Dre avoiding Tanya, Tanya avoiding 'Dre, 'Dre avoiding Maxine and Jules, and Jules avoiding Germaine, Jules was having a hard time staying in one place for any extended period. She had finally managed to corner 'Dre sitting alone at the side of the house with a large plate of food. 'Dre grimaced when he saw her. From the look on her face, he knew he was about to get an earful.

"Geez, Jules. Go easy, it's my birthday," 'Dre pleaded.

"Yes, it is your birthday," Jules chided. "You're all of thirty years old. Don't you think it's time you quit messing with these random chicks and get serious about someone?"

"Jules, this thing with me and Tanya, is between me and Tanya. And we're . . . dealing with it," 'Dre said uncomfortably.

Jules looked at him as if he had lost his mind.

"Excuse me? I know you just didn't tell me to butt out of your business," Jules said saucily.

'Dre dropped his fork and put down his plate when he realized that there was no getting rid of Jules.

"Weren't you the one who told me you were having feelings for Tanya?" Jules asked.

'Dre nodded and rubbed his hands over his face in frustration.

"So what's the deal? The girl tells you she cares about you, and you tell her you just want to be friends? Are you trying to break her heart?"

"You don't understand, Jules," 'Dre said tightly. "Me and Tanya . . . it can't happen. No matter how much I care about her, there's no future for the two of us. And I can't just do a casual thing with her. She's too important to me."

Jules looked at 'Dre carefully. She realized that he was really stressed out about the situation. It wasn't that he didn't want to be with Tanya; it was that something else was in the way.

"What's going on 'Dre?" Jules said softly, sitting down beside him. "Talk to me."

'Dre sighed heavily. "My mother."

Jules was confused. "What does your mother have to do with this?"

"Everything," 'Dre said sadly. "She would never accept Tanya."

"Why? Because she's . . ."

'Dre nodded. "Because Tanya's white."

"I don't understand, 'Dre; you have tons of white friends," Jules said, looking around at the myriad of guests in the backyard. "A lot of them are here now."

"Yeah, but I've never dated a white girl before," 'Dre said. "Did you think that was a coincidence?"

Jules shrugged. "I guess I never thought about it. We had heard you say you don't do white girls, but I thought that was just you being you. Just like how you used to say you don't wear colored sneakers, until Nike came out with the new Freestyles."

'Dre shook his head. "It was more than that."

Jules sighed heavily and leaned back on the bench. She had always known there were some black women who didn't like the idea of interracial relationships. Even her own mother wasn't too thrilled when she found out Jules was dating a white guy during high school. In retrospect, however, she realized her mother's displeasure could have been based on the fact that said guy had several piercings at strategic points on his face.

Nonetheless, she knew that reverse racism was real within the black community. But she never guessed that Momma Clayton, a woman she had known for years, who sang louder than anyone else in the church choir, would harbor this kind of prejudice. It was almost too ridiculous to consider.

"Are you sure? About your mom?" Jules asked, not quite convinced.

"Trust me, I'm sure," 'Dre said knowingly. He sighed heavily and slumped back onto the bench in despair.

"I can't even imagine my life without Tanya, Jules," 'Dre said honestly. "I don't even want to think of her being with someone else or telling someone else her dreams and crazy ideas."

He laughed. "Can you picture Tanya going camping in the middle of winter for anyone else?"

Jules laughed. She definitely couldn't. Tanya's idea of the great outdoors was her parents' cottage in Niagara, which was fully furnished with hot water, cable television, and all the amenities of modern life. Even though Maxine and Jules had begged her, she had never gone camping with them. But last winter, when 'Dre's dad died and he needed to get away, she had made the five-hour drive with him several miles north of Toronto, to Lake Dore, in Eganville. And even though she had no electricity, no heat, and no running water, she had pitched her lopsided tent and stayed the whole weekend with 'Dre, so he wouldn't have to be out there alone.

"But just think about that, 'Dre," Jules said earnestly. "Where do you think you will ever find a girl willing to make sacrifices like that for you? Are you going to turn your back on that just because of your mother's prejudice?"

'Dre looked tormented as he thought about Jules's words.

"You say you don't want to lose her, but you keep pushing her away," Jules said. "You keep pushing, and one day she's going to be gone for good."

"I wish I knew what to do," 'Dre said. "No matter which way I go, somebody gets hurt."

Jules placed a comforting hand on his shoulder.

"No one said this thing was going to be easy. Nothing worth having ever is," she said. "But look inside your heart. Where do you feel God is leading you on this one? If He's saying to let her go, then let her go. But if not, you know what you should do."

'Dre sighed. "Yeah. I think I do."

Jules watched contentedly as 'Dre went off to find Tanya. If only she could just as easily find the logic in her own love life. She glanced around and made sure Germaine was nowhere nearby. She was serious about letting the Holy Spirit lead her, but she was making sure she wasn't anywhere where she might feel tempted to take things into her own hands.

As she scanned the yard for any sign of Maxine, she noticed Easy step off the deck into the backyard. Jules grinned to herself. Trust Easy to show up near the end of the party when most of the food was gone and everything was almost over. She was about to go over and say hi, when she noticed him heading for a far corner of the yard. Jules leaned forward and squinted to get a better view. Her eyes widened when she saw who he was talking to.

What did he want with Germaine?

Even though Jules had told Easy that Germaine had never been involved with drugs, Easy had still kept his distance from Truuth's cousin. So she was surprised to see them have what seemed like a civil conversation in 'Dre's backyard. Jules was even more surprised when she saw them shake hands.

Easy said something to Germaine, and he laughed

in response. Soon the two of them were chatting like best buds. Jules felt more than a little annoyed.

So what, they're friends now? Unbelievable.

Jules decided she had had enough. It was time to go home. Slipping into the house, she looked around for 'Dre so she could say her good-byes. There were only a few people inside, but she thought she heard 'Dre's voice, and so she followed the sound into the kitchen.

"Momma, you know you wrong," Angela, 'Dre's older sister, said, enraged. Her eyes were flashing angrily, as she stood glaring at her mother, who seemed equally upset. 'Dre was standing on the other side of the kitchen island looking more upset than Jules had seen him in a long time.

Realizing that she had walked into a family conversation, Jules began to back out of the kitchen.

"I ain't no kinda wrong. I told you I don't want to see you messin' with no white girls. I don't care if she's Lady Di reincarnated. Don't bring no white trash up here in my house to me!"

Jules's mouth fell open as Momma Clayton's words stung her ears. She had not heard such blatant racism in a long time, and certainly never from anyone she knew and respected—or used to respect anyway.

Suddenly everything 'Dre had said fell into perfect harmony for Jules. She understood completely why he was hesitating with Tanya. He never wanted her to have to deal with this kind of unkindness.

But it was too late. Because in the heat of the argument no one had noticed Tanya enter the kitchen from the back deck. She had been just in time to hear Momma Clayton's scorching words.

" 'Dre."

'Dre noticed Jules for the first time, and followed her eyes across the kitchen to where Tanya was standing. A mixture of fear and horror framed his face when he realized that she had heard everything. But it paled in comparison to the look of brokenness reflected in Tanya's features.

He rushed toward her, but she was already pushing through the door to the deck.

Jules glared at Momma Clayton, who, even after seeing Tanya's despair, didn't seem the least bit apologetic.

"Look what you did, Momma," Angela said to her mother angrily. "How could you say something like that?"

Jules didn't stick around for the answer. Exiting the kitchen, she looked around for either Tanya or 'Dre.

"What's wrong with Tanya?" Maxine asked, appearing out of nowhere. "She just rushed past me looking crazy upset."

Jules quickly explained what had happened in the kitchen to Maxine. When she'd heard it all, Maxine seemed even more enraged than Jules.

"The nerve of that woman," she muttered angrily.

"Did you see where Tanya went?" Jules asked worriedly.

"Yeah, she ran in there," Maxine said, motioning toward the downstairs guest room where all the guests had been asked to leave their coats.

"Wait," Jules said, grabbing Maxine's arm to stop her from rushing into the room. "Did 'Dre go in there with her?"

"Yeah."

"Then we should probably let him handle this,"

Jules said. "The two of them have a lot of things to work out."

As Maxine and Jules stood in the middle of the hallway wondering what to do next, Easy appeared.

"Hey, baby girl," he said, throwing one arm around her in a half embrace. "How come you didn't come holla at me?"

" 'Cause you were busy with your new best friend," Jules said. She grimaced as her own words stung her ears.

"Who, Germaine?" Easy asked, puzzled.

"Yes," Jules said grudgingly. "Who else?"

"Hey, you were the one who was on my back about him being good people," Easy said, shrugging. "We were kicking it at Truuth's place the other day, and it turns out he's not too bad. You know he used to do some production for a label out in Vancouver?"

Jules rolled her eyes. "So what, now you're his number-one fan?"

Easy chuckled. "He's really got you turned out, don't he, baby girl."

Jules threw Easy a nasty look. He shook his head and grinned in reply.

As if on cue, Germaine came strolling up to them, casually taking a swig out of the soda in his hand. He was looking at Jules curiously. Jules wished he wouldn't look at her at all.

"Okay, I'm gonna go," she said suddenly, walking toward the coat room. It was getting a bit too crowded for her.

"I thought you were gonna give them time?" Maxine called after her.

"They've had enough time," Jules threw back.

"Has she been like that all day?" Jules heard Easy ask Maxine.

"No, just since certain people got here," Maxine replied. Without looking back she could tell that Maxine was glaring at Germaine. Jules wished they would all go away and leave her alone. But if they wouldn't go away, at least she could.

As she cracked the door open, it occurred to her that maybe she should have knocked first. If she had, she might not have caught 'Dre and Tanya kissing. They jumped apart as soon as the door opened.

"Maybe knock next time, Jules," 'Dre said, annoyed.

"Sorry, guys," Jules said, grinning as she quickly grabbed her jacket off the chair. "As you were," she said cheekily. She hurriedly exited the room, but not before she caught a glimpse of Tanya blushing furiously.

Without any other farewells, Jules slipped through the front door and headed toward her car. She was so busy digging through her bag for the keys that she didn't notice Germaine leaning against the driver's side, until she was less than three feet away from him. She stopped suddenly.

"So how long are we going to do this?" Germaine asked casually.

"Do what?" Jules asked innocently, rooted to her spot.

"Avoid each other."

"I'm not . . ." Jules stopped short. There was no point in lying. But since there was also nothing else she could think of to say, she just stared at him.

"I think we have an unfinished conversation," Germaine said, watching her carefully. "Remember, the one we started at the hospital?"

"You seemed to have finished it with LeTavia," she said dryly. For the second time in less than an hour, Jules wished she could take back her words.

"Wow," Germaine said, raising an eyebrow in mild surprise.

"I'm sorry," Jules said, closing her eyes. "I shouldn't have said that."

She stood in the middle of the sidewalk fingering her keys. The truth was, she did not know what she should say. Everything she wanted to say seemed wrong. She sighed heavily.

"What do you want from me, Germaine?" she asked tiredly. She searched his eyes for any sign that he was as tired of this back-and-forth as she was.

"I meant what I said, Jules," Germaine said, taking a step toward her. "I do miss you."

Jules noted that there was considerably less emotion in the way he said it this time. Maybe she had just imagined something more the morning at the hospital. She was starting to think that she had imagined a lot of things, like how much Germaine seemed to care for her while they were together. If you cared for someone that much, how could you let it go so easily? How could you so casually move on to someone else?

Lord, I am trying, but You really got to work with a sister on this one.

"I miss talking with you. And working with you," he said, taking another step toward her. Jules resisted the urge to step back and away from him.

"Look, we're going to see each other a lot. I don't want everyone feeling like they have to pick a side when it comes to the two of us," Germaine said practically. "Can we at least be friends?"

Jules looked at him closely to see if there were any

visible signs that he had lost his mind. Who was he kidding? She couldn't be in the same room with him for more than a few minutes, and he wanted them to be friends? To work together? To hang out together? There was no way on earth that was possible.

"Okay," Jules said. "Friends it is."

Chapter 29

Yes, this "'friends" thing was definitely a bad idea.

"He wants us to have lunch," Jules said, clicking her cell phone shut and rolling her eyes.

"Who? You and him?" Tanya asked from the treadmill beside Jules's.

Jules glanced in annoyance at her friend, who didn't seem to be the least bit out of breath even though she had been in a brisk jog for at least twenty minutes. Jules, meanwhile, could barely keep up, and kept having to drop her speed. She knew it was her own fault, since she hadn't been to the gym in a full three weeks. But that knowledge didn't make it any less irritating.

"All of us . . . Me . . . you . . . 'Dre . . . Easy, the whole gang . . . after church this weekend," Jules said between breaths.

"Oh," Tanya said thoughtfully. "That's nice of him."

Instead of answering, Jules grunted and lowered the speed on her treadmill again until she was at a brisk walk. It was less than a week since Jules had agreed to the peace treaty with Germaine, and it was already backfiring on her.

"Come on, Jules, you have to admit it was a nice gesture, considering we've always invited him over to our places," Tanya said reasonably.

"Whatever," Jules said, still annoyed. "I just don't get why he has to call me. Couldn't he tell Truuth and Maxine, and let them spread the word around?"

"He could, but he knew that if he didn't invite you directly, you probably wouldn't show up," Tanya said knowingly.

Jules snorted. That "probably" was more like a "definitely."

"I don't know what you're so upset about. You were the one who agreed to be friends with him," Tanya said, smirking.

"Only because he asked," Jules said. "What was I supposed to say? Sorry, I'd rather not see you again for the rest of my life?"

"I don't know, is that what you told all your other ex-boyfriends to make them disappear?" Tanya asked, laughing.

Jules shot Tanya a dirty look. Tanya was well aware of Jules's rule about ex-boyfriends: they were neither to be seen nor heard from ever again. Germaine was the only one who seemed to have slipped under the radar.

"Who stays friends with their ex, anyway?" Jules countered, in annoyance. "He was the one who said he didn't trust me. Why would he want me around?"

"If I remember correctly, Jules, what he said was, 'I can't be with someone who doesn't trust me,' " Tanya corrected. "He didn't say he didn't trust you. He said you didn't trust him."

"Thanks, Tanya," Jules said. "I'll remember not to

share any details with you the next time a guy kicks me to the curb."

"What? You know it's true," she said, as she slowed the treadmill down so she was walking at pace with Jules.

"You also know that deep in your heart you hope he'll change his mind, which is why you've agreed to this fake friendship with him," Tanya said.

Jules bit her lip but said nothing. Tanya could think whatever she wanted, but Jules knew she didn't have to confirm or deny any of it.

"Furthermore, if he wasn't unsure about things himself, he never would have brought up the friendship thing anyway," Tanya continued.

"Should I start calling you Dr. Phil now? Or should I wait until you get your own talk show?" Jules asked.

"Whatever," Tanya said, not the least bit miffed. "Everybody knows the two of you still have feelings for each other."

"Funny how that everybody doesn't include me," Jules said, turning off the machine and grabbing her towel. "I'm done. But you're free to stay here and analyze my life on your own."

Tanya rolled her eyes and followed Jules back to the changing rooms.

"Look, honey, I'm not trying to upset you," Tanya said gently. "I just want what's best for you. I know you've been trying to hide it, but I can tell that you're hurting over this thing with Germaine. I just hate to see you like this."

"Thanks for your concern, but I'm fine," Jules said. " 'The Lord gave and the Lord hath taken away. Blessed be the name of the Lord.' "

But deep inside Jules didn't feel half as sure as she sounded. Though she was trusting God to take her through this rough patch in her life, she admitted to herself that there were days, like today, when she couldn't understand His plan. She knew that every experience He gave her was to teach her something, but she was finding it hard to find the lesson in the emptiness that filled her heart.

Jules could tell from the expression on Tanya's face that she wasn't buying Jules's optimism either, but before Tanya could respond, her cell phone rang.

"Hello? . . . Hey, sugar, what's up?"

Jules rolled her eyes, knowing from the change in Tanya's voice that it must be 'Dre on the line.

"Oh, Lord . . . Where are you? . . . Oh, God . . ."

"What's wrong?" Jules asked with concern as she watched Tanya cover her mouth, while her face went from pale to white. Tanya looked up at Jules, and the fear in her eyes turned Jules's blood to ice. Wordlessly Tanya handed Jules the phone before sinking in tears onto a bench in the changing room.

"Hello? 'Dre? What's going on?" Jules asked, unable to keep the panic out of her own voice. Already a million horrible thoughts were flashing through her mind.

"Jules, it's Easy," 'Dre said. His voice was hoarse, and he sounded strained. Jules felt her heart pound faster in her chest as an ominous feeling began to build in her stomach.

"There was . . . a shoot-out, in front of his place," 'Dre began shakily. "He was getting out of his car, and he got shot . . . three bullets to his chest. They took him to the hospital but . . ."

Jules sank to the floor, her whole body shaking.

"No, no, no . . ." she whispered, as she cradled the phone by her ear, tears streaming down her cheeks.

"They did everything they could, Jules," 'Dre said, his voice shaky on the other end of the line. "But he didn't make it."

Jules began to feel dizzy as 'Dre's words came into focus for her. This could not be happening.

Please, Lord, no . . .

"I'm sorry, Jules. Easy is gone."

Chapter 30

The day of Easy's funeral was bright and sunny. Though it was the beginning of December and bitingly cold, the weather had been unusually dry. Since the dusting of flurries they'd had a couple days before, not a drop of snow had fallen, and so the ground, though cold, was clear of ice.

As Jules stood near the burial plot, she was vaguely aware of the minister's words. Since the day she had seen Easy's body at the hospital, something had changed. A thick fog had wrapped itself around her mind, separating her from everything and everyone. Jules felt as if she was moving slower than everyone else around her. Life went on, but for Jules it seemed to be happening at some distance ahead of her.

Her eyes moved slowly across the thick crowd that had gathered at the graveside. Usually people didn't bother to go to the interment, especially on a day as cold as today. But for Easy, a lot of people seemed to have made an exception.

There were so many faces. Some Jules knew well, others were only slightly familiar, but most she had never seen before. In fact, during the days following Easy's death, Jules had met more of his friends than she had in the several years in which she had known him.

Beside her she could hear Maxine sobbing quietly. She had not stopped crying since the day at the hospital. It seemed that every time the tears would dry up a bit, a fresh bout would start. From the worry lines that had taken up permanent residence on Truuth's face, Jules could tell that he was concerned about Maxine. He shouldn't have been. He knew Maxine. Excess emotion was her thing. But Jules figured that his worrying about her was just his way of distracting himself from the fact that Easy was gone. Jules knew Truuth was used to people leaving him. But just because you were used to something, it didn't make it any easier to deal with every time it happened.

Beside Truuth, 'Dre was standing with Tanya. From the outside he looked pretty composed, but underneath his Christian Dior sunglasses, Jules knew that his eyes were red. Earlier that morning at the church, Tanya had revealed that 'Dre had broken down the night before, after his visit to Easy's grandmother. From her own interaction with him Jules knew he had shut down, just like when his father died. Word was, he hadn't been to the office since Easy died, and apart from Tanya, he pretty much wasn't talking to anyone unless it was absolutely necessary.

And then there was Tanya. Jules looked over at her fair friend, who was holding 'Dre's hand tightly. Taking care of everyone else, like she always did, seemed to be helping Tanya deal with Easy's passing. Unlike Jules she had cried a couple times, but not as excessively as Maxine. And while the rest of them were content to keep their feelings to themselves, she'd been the only one freely talking about how sad she was that Easy was gone. She had even gone as far as to see a grief therapist, and had made appointments for all Triad employees to do the same. Jules wasn't sure how many people would actually show up, but it was the thought that counted.

A sudden creaking in front of her drew Jules's attention to the one place she had been trying to avoid. The grave.

She watched as the coffin was slowly lowered down into the ground on the horizontal straps positioned across the open burial plot.

" 'Blessed are the dead who die in the Lord from now on. They will rest from their labor, for their deeds will follow them.' "

The minister's words drifted through the haze of Jules's mind. The coffin was halfway down, and Jules could barely see the top anymore. A part of her mind refused to believe that Easy was in that coffin, and that they were putting him in the ground.

Jules took a step toward the grave so she could keep her eyes on the casket. It was the last time she would see her friend. She wasn't ready to let go yet.

" 'Behold, I show you a mystery; We shall not all sleep, but we shall all be changed. In a moment, in the twinkling of an eye, at the last trump: for the trumpet shall sound, and the dead shall be raised incorruptible, and we shall be changed.' "

By the time the coffin had come to rest, Jules was standing at the very edge. As the workmen pulled the lowering bands out of the grave and began to remove the burial apparatus, particles of dirt slipped down from the sides of the plot onto the casket.

The sound of the gravel hitting the coffin seemed to lift the fog from Jules's mind and send her careening back into reality. They were burying Easy. They were burying her friend. He wasn't coming back.

" 'We commit this body to the ground; earth to earth; ashes to ashes, dust to dust.' "

All of a sudden Jules felt weak. With each flower that fell onto the coffin, it became harder and harder for her to breathe. She wasn't ready for him to be gone. She hadn't told him how much she loved him. She hadn't told him how proud she was of what he had become. He hadn't had a chance to live yet. Not fully and completely anyway. No, it was too soon. She hadn't said good-bye.

But as the men slid the heavy slab of concrete resolutely over the top of the grave, she knew it was too late.

That was enough.

Jules felt her body go limp, and a gut-wrenching scream curled its way up from the core of her being, echoing across the solemn cemetery. She would have sunk onto the cold, hard ground had it not been for two strong arms that grabbed her and pulled her close.

Jules buried her face in Germaine's chest and let her cries get swallowed up in his strong frame. She hadn't seen him enter the cemetery and certainly had not seen him come up behind her. But he had seen her, and he had known that it would be too much for her.

She collapsed against him, letting his strength support her. She was too tired to be in control.

The sobs that wracked her body made her feel weaker still, and she closed her eyes and tried to block it all out. She couldn't watch them seal off the tomb, or cover it with dirt. She couldn't even watch the people leave, which they soon did. Because their leaving meant that it was over. This was the last moment in time that would be about Easy. She would have to let him go. She couldn't do that. She wasn't ready.

A cloud of grief seemed to have seeped in, replacing the fog that had been there before. It was so heavy that Jules could feel its weight rest on her, making her bones ache, making it hard to breathe.

"It's okay. It's okay. . . ." Germaine's voice drifted softly in through the jumble of her mind, his soothing words echoing over and over, in a rhythmic pattern. Slowly but surely, it seemed to sedate Jules's tumultuous emotions, and transform her wracking sobs into gentle whimpers. Eventually she stopped crying, and began to breathe again. After what seemed like forever she opened her eyes.

Germaine loosened his grip, but kept a supporting hand on Jules as she stood back a bit and looked around. The cemetery had emptied, leaving only the two of them standing by Easy's grave. Jules finally managed to look at the spot that was to be her friend's final resting place.

The workmen had done a good job of covering the plot neatly, and someone had placed a wreath of yellow and white carnations and tulips on top. The headstone would not come until later in the week, so for now this would have to do.

Jules sighed. It was a pity Easy couldn't see the big fuss everyone had made for him. He wouldn't have believed it.

Kneeling down, she placed the single white rose she had on top of his grave. On her last birthday Easy had sent her eleven white roses. When she had asked him why eleven, he'd said because eleven was one rose short of a dozen, just like Jules was one screw short of crazy.

She smiled. She would miss those things about him. The way he insulted her in love, the way he was over-protective, the way he was always asking her questions about God out of the blue. But more than that—she would just miss him.

After a few more moments, she took a deep breath and stood up, brushing away the tears that threatened to fall again. She turned around to find Germaine handing her a handkerchief. Jules snorted.

"You have a handkerchief?"

He shrugged as she took it. "It came with the suit."

His hands were stuck in his pockets casually, but he was watching Jules carefully. As distraught as she was, she didn't miss the look of concern in his eyes.

"Oh, geez, I must look a mess," she mumbled, wiping her eyes and sliding her sunglasses off her head. But Germaine reached out and took them from her before she had a chance to put them on.

"It's okay," he said gently.

Jules stared at him for a moment, before taking back her glasses and putting them on anyway. It was bad enough that he seemed to be able to guess her every move. She didn't need his intense eyes peering into her soul as well.

"Everyone left?" she asked, as they walked toward the parking lot.

"Yeah. They went back to 'Dre's house," Germaine said.

"There goes my ride," Jules mumbled. Since her car had been in the shop again, she'd gotten a ride with Maxine that morning.

"I told Max I'd take care of it."

"Oh."

An awkward silence fell between them as they covered the rest of the distance to the parking lot. When they got to the car, Germaine opened the door, but Jules didn't get in. Instead, she hugged her small black purse to her and stared at the ground. She could feel Germaine standing silently behind her.

"You don't want to go to 'Dre's, do you," he said.

She shook her head.

"You want me to take you home?"

She nodded.

"Okay."

She slid into the front seat and buckled the seat belt, as he closed the door.

Jules didn't know whether it was the finality of Easy's funeral, or the general confusion of her life, but something about the familiar feeling of Germaine's front passenger seat put her at ease. She snuggled deeper into the velvet cushioning and stared out the window as the city whizzed by. It felt like the world whizzing past her life.

She felt her cell phone vibrating, but ignored it. It was probably Tanya, or Maxine, or even her mother. But her throat was raw from crying, and a dull ache was resting behind her eyes. She wasn't in the mood to talk to anyone.

Eventually, her phone stopped buzzing. But only moments later, she heard Germaine's go off.

"Hello? . . . Yeah, she's with me. . . . No, she's not feeling too well. . . . Okay . . . Yeah, I'll make sure she gets home okay. . . . Bye, Tanya."

As Germaine clicked the phone shut, she closed her eyes and allowed the momentum of the car to lull her mind into a dull calm.

Jules didn't remember waking to give Germaine the keys to her apartment. Neither did she recall him leading her inside, or taking off her shoes as he helped her into bed. The only thing she remembered was the feel of her soft pillow as she drifted off into a dark and restless sleep.

Chapter 31

Jules slept through most of the weekend.
Even though Easy's funeral had been on a Thursday afternoon, she didn't crawl out of bed until the following Friday evening. And even then, it was only to drink a bit of tea before crawling back under the sheets. Same thing on Saturday evening. It was not until Sunday morning that she finally got up. And even then she still felt exhausted.

As she started the kettle to make some more Peppermint Persuasion, she noticed the blinking red light on her answering machine. Sighing deeply, she pushed the Play button.

There were twelve messages, half of which were from Tanya. The others were from her mom, Davis, Maxine, and even 'Dre.

She deleted them all before taking her mug of tea and a half-eaten packet of saltine crackers onto her balcony.

It was bright, and bitingly cold, and Jules wrapped the blanket she had taken with her tighter around her shoulders.

She could see the wind rustling the large pine tree outside the building. Even in the winter it was green and full of foliage. It would be Christmas in a couple of weeks, and her neighbors in the building across the street had already put out Christmas lights and decorations. Children bundled in winter jackets and scarves ran ahead of their parents on the sidewalk below, seemingly immune to the cold winds. Jules wished that she could be like them, happy and carefree. But all she could think about was that this would be the first Christmas in five years she would spend without Easy.

Every year they had gone with Maxine, 'Dre, Tanya, and Truuth down to the waterfront to catch the fireworks. This year he would not be there. Jules didn't bother to wipe the tears that ran down her cheeks.

Jules wasn't sure how long she sat out there. It wasn't until she heard the locks on her front door open behind her that she stirred.

Feeling less alarmed than she should have been, Jules shuffled from the balcony into the living room, her blanket still wrapped tightly around her.

"Wow. You look a mess."

Jules rolled her eyes when she saw it was only Germaine, and pulled the sliding balcony doors shut, effectively cutting off the cold air from the rest of the apartment.

"I wasn't expecting company," Jules mumbled scratchily, as she plopped down on her couch, pulling her feet up under her.

"I can see that," Germaine said, wrinkling his nose. "You stink too."

Jules glared at him, decked out in his crisp red and white bomber jacket, dark blue jeans, and sparkling clean Timberlands. He looked like a Tide commercial.

"I'm sorry, did I invite you over while I was sleeping?"

"No," Germaine said, ignoring her caustic tone as he dropped into the recliner in the corner. "But word on the street is that you've been holed up in this place for the last couple days feeling sorry for yourself."

He pulled off his gloves and stuck them in his pocket as Jules watched.

"Think of me as the rescue party."

"Thanks for your concern," Jules said. "But I'm fine. You can go now."

"Not until you've had a shower, and something to eat. In that order," Germaine said. "Then we'll both go."

"I'm not going anywhere," Jules said. "And I don't need a shower."

Germaine raised an eyebrow doubtfully, and Jules looked away. Okay, maybe she did need a shower. But she certainly didn't need him telling her what to do.

She pouted and folded her arms stubbornly.

"Okay, Jules," Germaine said casually, reclining and resting his right ankle over his left knee. "We can do this the easy way or the hard way. But I should tell you, the hard way will either involve me calling your mother, or you finding yourself in your tub fully clothed. The choice is yours."

Not liking either option, Jules reluctantly pulled herself from the couch and tried to ignore the smug look on Germaine's face as she shuffled her way to the bathroom.

Half an hour later she emerged from her bedroom fully dressed in sweatpants and an oversized hoodie. Her wet hair was pulled back in a bun, and she had to admit that she felt much better than she had an hour ago.

As the hot water had beat down on her in the shower, she'd had time to think about how much of a waste the past three days had been. No amount of wallowing and hiding from the world was going to bring Easy back. Furthermore, even though Easy had written the book on brooding, he wouldn't have wanted to see her acting like this.

She found Germaine in the kitchen with his sleeves rolled up, preparing eggs, toast, and hot chocolate. When he saw Jules, he smiled in satisfaction.

"Much better."

She scowled and sat down at the dining table as he placed a plate and mug in front of her. It wasn't until the smell of the cheese and mushroom omelette wafted into Jules's nostrils that she realized how hungry she really was.

Grudgingly she dug into her food, as Germaine sipped on a mug of hot chocolate and watched her in amusement.

"Why do you have keys to my apartment?" Jules asked when she was finished eating and was watching him curiously.

"Because it was the only way I could lock up after I dropped you off on Thursday," Germaine said.

Jules said nothing, but kept staring at him, her eyes narrowed. What was he trying to pull?

"Jules, I'm not trying to trick you," he said sincerely, his expression turning serious. "I know what you're going through. I'm just here to help."

"Who said I needed help?"

Instead of answering, Germaine stood up, took her plate and mug, and headed toward the kitchen.

"We're leaving in ten minutes."

* * *

Even this close to winter, Lake Ontario still managed to be spectacular. As she watched the afternoon sun glinting off the smooth surface, Jules couldn't think of anywhere more beautiful. She didn't know what had made Germaine think to bring her to this area of the waterfront, located a couple miles east of the city, but she was glad he had. Jules felt there was nowhere else she should have been.

As she sank down onto the ground, she felt the dull ache in her heart begin to subside slightly.

"You know, the summer I turned seven, my dad taught me how to swim at this very spot," Germaine said from a few feet over.

Jules said, wrinkling her nose, "That's disgusting."

Some areas of Lake Ontario were known to be pretty questionable during the summer. In fact, people were often urged to stay out of the water until public health issued an advisory saying it was safe for swimming.

As far as Jules was concerned, the mere fact that they had to issue an advisory at all was enough to keep her out of the water for good.

"It wasn't that bad," Germaine said, laughing. "It was one of the best times I had with my dad before he died."

Jules sighed heavily.

"How do you do that? How can you think of him gone and sound . . . happy?" she asked in frustration. "Every time I think about the fact that I'll never see Easy again . . ."

Her voice wavered, as the tears that had been falling all weekend threatened to make an encore appearance.

"It takes time, Jules," Germaine said softly. "It wasn't

always like that. I was mad for a long time after my dad died. I thought it wasn't fair, and I was mad at God for taking him."

Jules bit her lip and rocked back and forth. She knew a bit about that. In fact if she was honest, she knew she had barely said a prayer since the day she got the call saying that Easy had died. She felt betrayed, like God had broken a promise to her.

"But after a while I learned to accept it," Germaine continued. "That didn't mean I stopped missing him. I just learned how to get past it."

"I don't know if I can do that," Jules said, sniffling. "Losing Easy feels like losing a part of myself. I feel like something in me is missing."

Germaine reached for Jules's hand, and squeezed it gently. "I know."

He continued to hold her hand tightly as the tiny sobs shook Jules's body. It felt like she would never stop crying.

How could Easy be gone? Just as soon as He'd started to make things right in his life, his life was over. What was the point of that? And how could God take one of her closest friends away from her without even giving her the chance to say good-bye?

"It's not the end, Jules," Germaine said. "You know that you'll be with Easy again one day. When he turned his life over to God, he made sure of that."

Jules nodded.

"He's just gone for a while. Not forever."

She knew Germaine was right. And just as always he knew just what to say to make her see things the way she ought to.

I'm sorry, Lord. I still don't understand, but help me to accept this as part of Your master plan for all our lives. Even though he's gone, thank you for putting Easy in my life.

Jules closed her eyes and breathed in the cool lake air as it blew gently across her face. It felt refreshing to her lungs, and it was just what she needed to remind her that no matter how hopeless things seemed, God was still in control.

She glanced over at Germaine, who was sitting, relaxed, with his arms resting on his knees, as if this was the most natural place for him to be. He was staring idly out to sea as if he had all the time in the world. But Jules knew that he was just waiting for her, and that he would have sat there as long as she needed him to. Because that's the kind of person he was—that's the kind of friend he was.

Too bad she wanted more than just friendship from him.

She turned her eyes back to the lake, silently chiding herself for thinking about her feelings for Germaine when she should have been mourning Easy. But she couldn't help it. What she wanted more than anything was to curl up in Germaine's arms and forget the world for a while—just until the pain went away.

But even though it hurt that she couldn't do that, she was more than grateful for his being there.

"I feel like I'm always thanking you for something," Jules said after a moment.

Germaine smiled without turning around, and Jules could see the dimple in his left cheek.

"You're welcome," he said.

"You don't have to do this, you know," Jules said, suddenly feeling restless.

"Do what?"

"Be here. Take care of me, like I'm a child. I can take care of myself."

"I know," Germaine said.

"So why are you doing it?"

"Because I want to."

"Why?" Jules asked, her heart beating a little bit faster. She knew she shouldn't, but she couldn't help but hope.

"Because that's what friends do," Germaine said, turning to look at her for the first time.

"Right," Jules said, barely hiding her disappointment. "That's what friends do."

Jules bit her bottom lip in frustration. Yes, she had agreed to this friendship thing, but she wasn't sure she could go through with it. It had been long enough, but her feelings for Germaine hadn't gone away. Didn't that mean something? And how was it even possible that she could feel so much for him, and he not feel anything for her?

God, why are you doing this to me?

It had been a long day. In fact it had been a long couple of weeks. And since Jules didn't see how things could possibly get any worse, she thought she might as well go for it. She might as well tell him how she felt. At the very least she would know once and for all that it was totally and completely over, and there was no hope for them. Life was too short to spend it on what-ifs.

"Jules?"

"Huh?" Jules mumbled in surprise, as Germaine's voice cut into her mental ramble.

"Is something wrong?"

Jules looked at him in surprise, afraid that he was reading her mind again.

"No . . . I mean, yes . . . there is something."

Jules's voice caught in her throat as she watched him watch her.

"Well?" he prodded gently. "What is it?"

She knew she had to tell him how she felt.

"I . . . think I'm gonna quit my job."

Where did that come from?

She had been thinking about it for a while. In fact, she had been talking to God about it for a long while. She had been praying about it, and struggling with the feeling that it was what God wanted her to do. But thus far she hadn't even mentioned this consideration to anyone. She could already hear everyone's reaction.

From Maxine it would be something like: "Jules, you done lost your mind? Why would you give up that good money?"

Tanya would try to be supportive, but even she would look at Jules skeptically. And Jules didn't even want to think of what her mother would say.

Although Jules had talked to Momma Jackson about how much she needed to respect Jules's decisions, Momma J was still having a bit of a problem with the concept. It wasn't that she wasn't trying. It was just that it was hard to change a twenty-six-year-old habit. So Jules knew this idea would definitely start Momma Jackson's speech about how women had to be wise, and that she couldn't be quitting her job to follow a pipe dream when she had bills to pay.

But at that moment, when Jules heard the words out loud for the first time, she suddenly knew that was exactly what God wanted her to do.

She looked across at Germaine, who was silent. His was the only reaction she hadn't been able to anticipate.

He had gone back to staring out at the water, and his brow was furrowed in concentration as if he was thinking hard about what Jules had said.

"What are you planning to do?" he asked thoughtfully.

Jules took a deep breath.

"I want to become a full-time independent publicist."

Germaine nodded, as if that was the answer he had expected. "Go on."

Jules explained how she intended to work exclusively with gospel artists to develop their public image through media exposure, event development, and community involvement.

Since her first conversation with Sharifa, she had done extensive research. She knew all the figures— how much it would cost to start a business like this, what the failure rate was, how she would need to bill her clients—every single detail had been considered.

Then she had put her plan on paper, compiled a list of potential clients who she would initially approach— mostly Triad's—and subsequently developed an initial pitch. And just in case 'Dre didn't buy into her idea, she had made a secondary list of artists and agencies outside of Triad that she could approach. There was still a big risk involved, but she could see how it could work. And even if things fell apart along the way, she had already decided it was what she needed to do.

"So you're just doing artists," Germaine said.

"Yeah, that was the plan," Jules said. The tone of Germaine's voice told her that he had something else in mind.

"Well, what about small agencies or outside events?"

"What do you mean?"

"Well, what if you get offers from other organizations to coordinate events for them?"

"Every offer would be evaluated on an individual basis to determine its viability. If I took on a project I would have to make sure that doing so would be beneficial to me and to the company that was proposing it."

Jules felt confident about her plan. She also couldn't help but notice that it felt good to think about something other than Easy's death.

"Would you contract other staff?"

"If it became necessary, yes. It wouldn't be a regular feature, however, and I would have a predetermined list of other professionals I would be willing to work with."

"What about your start-up capital?"

"I'll get a small business loan. I've already identified a couple of institutions that I can approach who have reasonable rates."

"And your collateral for a loan?"

"I've got it covered."

Germaine looked over at Jules curiously, one eyebrow raised.

"I've got it covered," Jules repeated confidently.

She knew what he was thinking, but there were a lot of things about Jules that Germaine didn't know. Like the small rental property Jules's father had bought in her name when she was fourteen and had given to her officially three years ago. It was her backup plan that no one, not even her mother and brother, knew about.

"Okay," he said with a small smile, turning back to the water.

He continued shooting questions at Jules. Many she had already considered, having spoken to Sharifa. But there were some that even Sharifa hadn't prepared her for.

"Well, what do you think?" Jules asked, fifteen minutes later when the questions finally stopped coming.

"I just have one more question," Germaine said.

Jules groaned and let her head fall back in a show of exhaustion, even though she was grateful that Germaine was making her think about her proposal so thoroughly.

"Why do you want to do this?"

That was the one question that Jules was completely prepared for.

"Because it's what God wants me to do," Jules said. "I can feel it in my bones. No decision that I have ever made in my life has felt as right as this one. I feel like my life has finally come into focus and that I am fulfilling the purpose He has for me.

"I read somewhere that, if you were meant to cure cancer or write a symphony or crack cold fusion and you don't do it, you not only hurt yourself, but you hurt the whole world, including the generations to come. It's like spiting God, who created you with this gift, this way to move the world closer to Him.

"I don't want that to be me. I know that this is what I was meant to do. So I have to do it."

Jules breathed out another deep breath. "Is that good enough for you?" she asked defiantly with a smirk.

"Jules, I always knew this was what you were supposed to do, from that first day you told me in the café at the hospital," Germaine said smoothly.

Jules's mouth fell open. "So why did you just spend twenty minutes giving me the third degree?"

He grinned. "I just wanted to make sure you knew."

Jules couldn't help but smile. But only moments later, a look of worry crossed over her face.

"I'm scared, Germaine," she said quietly. "What if this fails? What if I can't find any clients? What if I can't make any money out of this? What if I default on my loan and end up going bankrupt? Or worse, what if I ruin some artist's career?"

"Hey," Germaine said. She pulled her eyes from the ground and turned to look at him.

"It will be fine," he said softly but firmly. "I'm not saying it won't be difficult, but you will get through it. You know why? Because this is not your plan, it's God's, and God's plan can't fail, right?"

Jules smiled again. "Right."

"So quit worrying," he said, pulling her into a quick hug, as he kissed her temple reassuringly. "You'll be fine."

Okay, I definitely have to tell him.

Jules took a deep breath.

"Germaine?"

"What's up?"

His eyes glowed in the dusky afternoon light, taking her breath away. They were beautiful. He was beautiful. In fact, she didn't know if it was the way he was totally supporting her or because she was missing Easy, but everything about him from the inside out was looking beautiful at that moment.

She couldn't believe she had ever thought him capable of the evil she had accused him of. And she also couldn't believe that it had taken her losing him, for her to find out that she was completely in love with him.

She opened her mouth to tell him just that, but just like before, she couldn't make herself say the words.

What if he rejected her again? Then who would she go to? Who would she talk to when she knew no one else would understand? Even if they were never together again, at least this way she would always have him as a friend.

She couldn't tell him. The possibility of losing him was too great, and she didn't know if she could take it.

"I'm ready to go home now."

He looked at her curiously for a moment before rising from the sand and reaching a hand down to help her up. Jules accepted it, and soon found herself following him back to the car.

So much for that. It looked like this was as much love as she was going to get.

She could feel her heart breaking all over again.

Chapter 32

"I'm sorry, you said what?" Maxine asked in disbelief, as both she and Tanya looked at Jules as if she had grown another head.

Jules picked up another box and began to walk down the hallway to her new place.

It was moving day. In a lot of ways it was also moving-on day. Less than two weeks had passed since Easy's funeral, but already things were heading back to business as usual.

Jules and Maxine had finally agreed on an apartment in Jules's building and were in the process of moving in Maxine's stuff and transferring Jules's things from the old apartment. Tanya had been a bit cheesed that Maxine had chosen to move out, but eventually she got over it enough to help them make the transition.

They had started out early that Sunday morning with 'Dre, Truuth, Germaine, some guys from church, and even Davis, who was in town for the weekend. But as soon as most of the heavy furniture had been moved, the guys split, leaving the girls to finish up with the small stuff. That had left a lot of time for them to talk about everything under the sun, including what had happened with Jules and Germaine the weekend after the funeral. As she recalled the afternoon's events, Jules conveniently left out the part about her quitting her job. They were her girls, and she loved them, but she wasn't ready to tell them about that yet.

"I told him I was ready to go home," Jules said shamefully.

"Why?"

"I don't know," Jules moaned, dropping the box into the already crowded living room of the new apartment. Everywhere she looked there were boxes upon boxes that they would eventually have to unpack. Today was going to be a long day.

"Jules, why didn't you just tell him how you felt?" Tanya asked. "Aren't you the one who has been pretending not to pine over Germaine for the past couple of weeks?"

"I'm not pining over him," Jules said.

"Girl, please," Maxine said, rolling her eyes and leaning against the door frame. "With the two of you it was like a constant game of musical chairs; once one of you came into the room, the other would leave, and you were usually the one doing the leaving."

Jules pouted, but said nothing. She knew what Maxine said was the truth.

"Jules, I don't understand what the problem is," Tanya said. "Don't you love the guy?"

"Yes," Jules whined.

"So why not just tell him, so the two of you can live happily ever after and spare the rest of us from having to do the song and dance around the both of you? It's just like me and 'Dre. If we had never talked to each other about how we felt, we never would have ended up together as happy as we are."

Jules shot a look of annoyance at Tanya. Ever since she and 'Dre had finally gotten it right, she had started acting like the relationship guru. She seemed to have forgotten that it had taken years for her and 'Dre to get together, and it never would have happened without some creative maneuvering from both Jules and Maxine.

"Okay, Miss New Love, you need to stop, because you know you and 'Dre would have never gotten it together if it hadn't been for me and Jules," said Maxine, echoing Jules's thoughts.

Tanya blushed and escaped the room to get the last set of boxes.

"As for you, Jules," Maxine said, turning back to her confused friend. "You need to figure out what you want. Stop waiting for life to happen to you and do something. God opened a door for you by keeping this man in your life; now it's your turn to decide whether you're gonna walk through it, or walk away. Either way, it's time for you to make a decision."

Jules knew Maxine was right. But it was easier said than done. She still would rather have Germaine as a friend than not have him at all. And that was what she was risking by telling him how she felt.

In addition, there was also the humiliation of having someone tell you he didn't love you the same way you loved him. That was something Jules's pride could definitely live without.

"Whatever," Jules said, waving the topic away and going into the kitchen to grab a bottle of water—the only thing that was in her new fridge. "Enough about me. What's happening with you and my niece?" Jules asked, glancing at Maxine's belly, which seemed to grow a little more each time Jules saw it.

"Apryll is fine," Maxine said, taking a sip from her own water bottle. During her last ultrasound, Maxine had found out that the baby was a girl, and she had already named her. "I had a checkup earlier this week, and the doctor says everything is okay."

"What about Truuth?"

"What about him?" Maxine asked.

Jules raised an eyebrow at the sharpness in Maxine's tone. "Come on, Max. Tanya told me about the big fight you guys had at 'Dre's house after the funeral."

"Well, then Tanya needs to learn to keep her big mouth shut."

"Hey!" Tanya protested from the doorway. "Judging from the way you were carrying on that evening, so do you!"

"It's not just that, Maxine," Jules continued. "I saw how he was when he was here earlier. The two of you barely said a word to each other."

Maxine crossed her arms over her chest stubbornly and looked off through the window, refusing to meet either Jules's or Tanya's eyes.

"Maxine, we're just trying to help," Tanya said in her usual coddling tone. But Jules put up her hand to stop her. If they kept treating Maxine like a baby, she would continue acting like one, and right now she had to start thinking about her own kid.

"What's the deal, Max?" Jules asked simply.

Maxine turned even more of her back to them and still remained silent.

"You can sulk all you want, but we're not going anywhere," Jules said. She took a seat on a box by the wall and began to get comfortable. Knowing how stubborn Maxine was, they could be there for a while.

Maxine turned around to look at her two friends, all the fight gone out of her.

"We broke up," she said calmly. "That's what happened."

The room was so silent, Jules was sure she would have heard an ant crawl across the floor. It seemed that even the traffic and the wind outside had come to a stop.

"What?" Tanya whispered in disbelief. "That's impossible!"

"Maxine, you guys have been together for more than three years," Jules said, when she finally found her voice. She wasn't sure what she had expected Maxine to say, but that definitely wasn't it.

"Yeah, well, that's over now," Maxine said quietly. "And I don't want to talk about it."

Without another word she walked across the living room into the bedroom and closed the door.

Tanya and Jules looked at each other, dumbfounded, as they heard the lock click behind her.

It was after 10:30 when Jules stepped into the Sound Lounge. She had been ready since nine, but had spent an hour panicking and praying about what would happen when she got there. At 10 p.m. Maxine told Jules she was driving both her and Apryll crazy and kicked Jules out of the apartment. And so here she was.

It was the first time she had been inside the new Lounge. She had passed by a couple times and seen the workmen doing renovations. Maxine, who had been there for the relaunch, had told her the place looked great. Unlike the old venue, it was completely outside the club district, but Jules preferred it because it was closer to Scarborough, and she liked the area better. This was the first time she would actually see the inside.

A slow smile spread across Jules's face as she took in the lights, setup, and décor. Germaine had definitely been inspired.

It was a good night, and it took Jules a while to move through the crowd over to the bar. Slipping onto a stool, she made herself comfortable. She suspected that she was going to be there for a bit.

"Merry Christmas, beautiful, haven't seen you here in a while."

"Merry Christmas to you too, Owen," Jules said, trying not to laugh at the Santa hat perched on the side of her bartender-friend's head. It had been so chaotic the last couple weeks that had it not been for the decorations and lights everywhere, she would have forgotten that Christmas was only a couple days away.

"What can I get you?" he asked, serving a drink to a customer beside her. From the crowd Jules could tell that he was pretty busy.

"Just the usual," she said.

"Cool. One cranberry juice coming up," he said, already reaching for a glass from under the bar. "Do you want me to tell him you're here?"

Jules shook her head. "No, that's okay. You already have your hands full."

Owen passed her a drink, and shot her a quick smile before slipping off to the other side of the bar where the patrons were getting impatient.

Jules took a sip and turned her attention toward the

stage where a slim Filipino girl was singing her heart out to the backing of a full band. Jules thought she recognized the girl from *Canadian Idol,* but she couldn't be too sure. She wouldn't be surprised if that was the case though—on new music night at the Sound Lounge, anybody could show up.

Jules had to admit that a big part of her was proud of the way Germaine had bounced back from all that had happened. In the months since the fire, not only had he recreated the Sound Lounge at a new location, but he had also managed to establish its reputation as a hot spot for live music. If the review she had read in the *Metro Toronto* daily was anything to go by, the Sound Lounge was definitely doing better than it had been before.

The thought of that, however, seemed to stir the butterflies in Jules's stomach and make her even more nervous. Germaine was a success now. Before he had been just a guy with a struggling music store and a dream. Now he was a businessman, in every sense of the word, and she had noticed that it had made him more confident. What would he want with a girl like her? Especially one who had already disappointed him.

Taking another sip from her drink she scanned the room quickly. Even in the dusky lights it wasn't long before her eyes found him. It was always like that with him. It didn't matter how large the mob, she could always pick him out of the crowd.

She watched as he chatted casually with some guys near the stage and then moved through the crowd, working the room, making sure that his patrons were satisfied. As if feeling her gaze, he suddenly looked up and caught Jules staring at him. Her stomach flip-flopped anxiously.

"Lord, please don't let me throw up," Jules murmured.

Tearing her eyes away from him, she swallowed the rest of her drink in one gulp and turned back to the bar, where she found Owen smirking at her.

"Guess he found you," he said mischievously. He looked down at Jules's empty glass, which she had rested on the bar but which she was still gripping tightly.

"Need a refill?"

Jules nodded, not able to calm her nerves enough to work up some words. She squeezed her eyes shut and breathed in deeply, praying for help.

She opened her eyes and slowly took a sip from the new drink Owen had placed in front of her. As the cool, tangy liquid scorched a course down her throat, she felt her nerves settle a bit.

"Hey," Germaine said, coming up to the bar and giving her a quick kiss on the cheek.

"Hey," she said with a smile, as she tried to ignore the burning effect his lips had had on her skin.

"Haven't seen you here in a while."

"Yeah, well, I've been hearing a lot of hype about this little joint, so I thought I'd check it out for myself," Jules said easily.

Germaine chuckled. "So, what's the evaluation, Ms. Jackson?"

"It's all right," Jules said, trying to act nonchalant.

Germaine cocked his head to the side and looked at her knowingly.

"Okay, fine, it looks great," Jules admitted grudgingly as Germaine smirked. "But it does have a familiar air to it."

"Really," Germaine said, dodging her eyes.

"Yes, really," Jules said, shifting her head so her gaze met his. "It reminds me of this little place I once went to in the West End. I don't know if you've heard of it. It's a spot called Leroy's?"

"This place looks like Leroy's?" Germaine asked, pretending to look confused. "Whatever do you mean?"

Now it was Jules's time to give him a look.

"Okay, okay, you got me," he conceded with a grin. "But I couldn't help it. You know how much I love that place, Jules."

"Yeah, I do," Jules said, smiling. His eyes were doing that sparkly thing they did when he was excited, and she found herself getting excited too.

She didn't even realize they were staring at each other until the person sitting on a stool nearby bumped into Germaine as she got up. As Germaine turned aside to wave away the woman's apology, Jules took the opportunity to catch a breath and refocus.

"So it looks like you've been doing really well for yourself," Jules said a couple moments later. Germaine had taken the seat the woman had vacated, and they were both looking out at the stage and the crowded Lounge.

"I've been blessed," Germaine said humbly. "God just brought everything together for me. I never could have done this on my own."

She was wrong. Germaine's success hadn't changed him. He was still the same humble guy he always was. He still trusted God for everything.

"Yeah, well, you deserve it," Jules said simply, as she glanced over at him. "I know you really worked hard."

"Thanks," Germaine said, meeting her eyes. "That means a lot coming from you."

Jules felt herself falling again. She didn't know if it

was the lights from the chandeliers or the golden yellow of his crisp button-down shirt, but she was sure she
could see those little golden flecks dancing in his deep
hazel eyes. And she was almost sure they were hypnotizing her. Maybe that's why she was finding it so hard
to look away.

She took a deep breath. It was now or never.

"Germaine, there's something I wanted to say to
you—"

"Yo, G, we got a problem with the sound," a skinny
guy in a shiny red shirt and a fedora said to Germaine,
cutting Jules off mid-sentence. Jules recognized him as
one of the guys from the band.

"What's up?" Germaine asked. His body was still
facing Jules, but his eyes were on the guy, and his
voice was all business.

Jules listened as the guy explained that one of the
monitor boxes had burnt out, and they couldn't continue playing unless they had a replacement. She
glanced on stage and noticed that the band had indeed
taken a break.

"I think I have a backup somewhere in the storage
area. Give me a second, okay?"

He turned to Jules apologetically. "Jules . . ."

"It's okay. Go," she said, waving him away.

"Don't go anywhere. I'll be right back, okay?"

"Okay," she agreed with a small smile, taking another
sip from her drink.

She made a face when she realized that it was practically lukewarm.

"Owen, can I get some ice?"

*   *   *

When Germaine finally returned a few minutes later, Jules was busy laughing with Owen. He had been telling her about a couple who had come in the week before and kept sneaking off to different parts of the Lounge to get busy. In one incident, security had caught them half-naked in the storage room near the back. After that they had been kicked out. But the way Owen told the story was what made it so hilarious.

"Glad to see you found someone to entertain you," Germaine said, as he came up on Jules and Owen laughing. Even though Germaine's tone was playful, Jules could have sworn she detected a slight hint of jealousy.

"Well, someone had to, after you abandoned me," Jules said.

"Jules, I'm—"

"It's okay, Germaine, I was just teasing," she said, smiling. "I know you're working."

He said nothing, but looked at her curiously. Jules shifted uncomfortably as she watched his eyes scrutinize her. It was almost as if he was trying to read her mind, and it was unnerving.

"So there was something you wanted to tell me?" he asked, after what seemed like forever.

"Umm . . . yeah," she said, gripping the edges of the bar stool. She took a deep breath. "I just wanted to tell you that—"

"Germaine, we got an issue with some guys near the front."

This time it was Milton, the head of security for the Lounge.

"We asked them to leave, but they say they're not budging till they see someone in charge."

Germaine sighed heavily and looked at Jules.

"I'll be right here," she said, grinning.

He shot her an apologetic look, before following Milton into the crowd, toward the stage.

Jules sighed. It was going to be a long night.

By the time Germaine got back it was 12:05 a.m. Jules could feel the tiredness in her body and knew she couldn't last much longer, especially since it was a Thursday night, and she had work early the next morning. She was trying not to get fired before she quit.

"I'm so sorry," he said, taking her hands in his. He looked like a little boy who was about to get a scolding. Jules resisted the urge to reach out and pat him on the head to make him feel better.

"It's not your fault, Germaine," she said, smiling. "I understand. Really I do."

He smiled, looking a little relieved.

"Okay," he said. "But I promise no more distractions."

"That's too bad," Jules said with a half smile.

"Why?"

"Because this would be the first time you break a promise to me."

Germaine closed his eyes in defeat. "What now?"

"Jules, I'm so sorry," Owen said, interrupting. She waved him off. She had seen him come up behind Germaine and knew that there was an issue at the bar.

"Germaine, we're out of club soda."

Germaine's forehead crinkled in disbelief. "That's impossible, Owen. I put a whole case back there earlier this evening, and we never finish that in one night."

"Look around, boss; this place is packed. We're running out of everything tonight."

"Can't you just get another case from the back?"

Jules tried not to laugh as she heard the slight frustration in Germaine's voice.

"And leave all these people waiting here?" Owen said, nodding toward the growing number of men and women packed around the bar. "Yeah, that's a good idea."

Germaine groaned and turned his eyes reluctantly toward Jules, who had already slipped off the bar stool and grabbed her tiny silver clutch.

"Jules . . ."

"It's okay, Germaine," she said with a resigned smile. His eyes pleaded with her to stay, but instinctively Jules knew the rest of the night would be just like this. Besides, it was late, and she needed to get home.

Impulsively, she slipped her arms around Germaine's neck and gave him a quick embrace.

"I'm really proud of you," she said sincerely, as she hugged him. She took one last look at him before she let him go.

"Take care of yourself, Germaine."

And with that she was pushing her way through the crowd toward the exit. Some things, it seemed, were just not meant to be.

Chapter 33

After what seemed like forever, Jules finally managed to push her way out of the Sound Lounge and step into the cool, morning air. It was amazing that even at this time of the morning, the streets of Toronto were still buzzing as if it was the middle of the day.

The music from the Sound Lounge mixed with the sound of the traffic, and the buzz from a bar across the street created a comfortable hum of street sound. Ahead in the distance, she saw a group of teenagers chatting and laughing as they walked down the street, uninhibited by the cool December wind. From somewhere nearby the sweet smell of Greek pastry wafted into her nostrils.

She loved this city. And if she had to spend the rest of her life alone, there was nowhere else she would rather be.

She tried to ignore the feelings of sorrow that were tugging at her heart. She wasn't quite sure what she had expected when she came here tonight, but she knew what her heart had hoped for. And it wasn't this.

"Geez, God, if You're not going to let me be with

him, the least you could do is take these feelings away,"
she said out loud.

Feeling frustrated, and noticing people looking at
her strangely, Jules walked a bit faster toward the side
street where she had parked her car, all the time digging in her purse for her keys.

Suddenly she noticed heavy footsteps moving faster
behind her. Could it be . . . ?

"Jules, you forgot your keys on the bar."

No, it was only Milton.

"Owen saw them, and asked me if I could run them
out here to you."

"Thanks, Milton," Jules said, forcing a smile as her
heart crashed into her stomach.

"No problem, girl," he said, dropping the heavy,
metal bunch into her palm. "You just be careful next
time, okay?"

She nodded and smiled at the Latino man's slight
accent and overprotectiveness.

"I will."

She watched him walk back to the Lounge, before
briskly covering the rest of the distance to her car.

"Stupid girl," she chided herself silently. "Who did
you think it was, Germaine? Get real."

She violently flipped the bunch of keys in her hand,
in an effort to channel her frustration somewhere else.

She was so preoccupied with finding the right key
on the bunch that she didn't notice Germaine sitting on
the car hood. She stopped suddenly and dropped her
keys on the ground when she did.

He was looking at her curiously, the way he had
been all evening. And just like before, it was completely unnerving her.

After what seemed like forever, he slid off the hood

and retrieved her keys from the ground. But instead of giving them to her, he slipped them and his hands into his pockets.

She cocked her head to the side and squinted at him. "How did you . . ."

"There's a backdoor to this alley," he said, nodding to an inconspicuous metal door in the side of the building near where Jules was parked. A few yards further into the alley was Germaine's car. Somehow she hadn't noticed it when she first arrived.

"There was something you wanted to say to me," he said patiently, still watching her.

Jules opened and closed her mouth several times before she was able to say anything.

Why was she acting like this? It wasn't as if she had never been this close to him before, and it wasn't like they hadn't had a million conversations before this one. So why couldn't she find the words to say what she had to say?

"I . . . it doesn't matter," she said pulling her gaze away from his and looking down. "Forget it."

"Are you sure?" he asked.

Jules nodded, not meeting his eyes. "Yeah, I'm sure."

"That's fine, 'cause there's something I wanted to say to you anyway," he said quietly.

Jules looked up. "What?"

Germaine took a deep breath as his eyes flitted around the quiet side street.

"This friendship thing, it's not really working for us," he said.

"What?" Jules asked in a slight panic.

"I . . . I don't think I can be friends with you, Jules."

Jules couldn't breathe. She felt like she wanted to

cry. The very thing she was holding on to, she was about to lose. This was too much.

"Why?" she squeaked.

"Because . . ." He sighed heavily and looked more uncertain than Jules had seen him in a long time. "Because I'm in love with you."

Jules froze. Did she hear what she thought she heard?

"But you said . . ."

"I know what I said," Germaine replied, cutting her off as he bounced her keys around in his pocket. "But I was angry and afraid that you might get hurt because of me. Plus, you never, ever do what I expect you to."

"But you always knew I would be like that," Jules said.

"I know," he said. "But I didn't expect it to frustrate me that much."

Jules fingered the latch on her purse distractedly.

"So what changed?" she asked quietly.

Germaine smiled and took her hands in his.

"I saw how kind you were to my family even after we broke up. I saw how you never gave up on the God thing with Easy, and how you've been going out of your way to make things easier for Maxine. I guess I saw the real you, the Jules that God was trying to show me all along."

Jules's heart began to beat faster.

"And I realized that my life was way too boring without you in it.

"That's why I can't be your friend, Jules," he said, pulling her closer. "Because I want more than that. I want you. All of you."

Jules saw the sincerity in his eyes and knew that

everything he said was true. He loved her. Just like she loved him. It seemed so unreal.

He took another deep breath.

"Look, I know I took a long time to tell you all this but . . ."

"Germaine?"

"Huh?"

"Shut up," Jules said, smiling.

Then she reached up, wrapped her arms around his neck, and kissed him just like she almost had that day in the hospital. It was like they had never been apart.

"I love you too," she said, pulling back only slightly to look into his eyes. "That's what I came here to tell you."

"Then what took you so long, woman?" Germaine asked, his eyes dancing in that familiar way Jules loved.

Jules smirked. "Your bartender, and your security guard, and the guy from the—"

Before she could finish, his lips were on hers again, and his arms were holding her close. It was a good thing too, because she was so happy, she felt like she would float away. Nothing could ruin this moment.

Suddenly she pulled away.

"Wait," she said, holding up her hand in protest. "What about LeTa—"

"Nothing happened," Germaine said quickly.

"Did you—"

"Not even on the cheek."

"So why did you even—"

"It was all Truuth's idea," Germaine said, grinning.

Jules's eyebrows drew together. "I'm gonna kill that boy . . ."

"Don't," Germaine said, chuckling. "He felt bad that I was so miserable."

Jules cocked her head to the side and smiled.

"So you were miserable without me, huh."

Germaine raised an eyebrow knowingly. "Just as miserable as you were without me."

"I was not miserable!"

"Yeah," Germaine said, smirking. "I heard about your solo ice cream parties."

Jules's mouth fell open in surprise, but in moments she was grinning sheepishly.

"Okay, maybe I was this miserable," she admitted, holding her thumb and forefinger only millimeters apart.

"I think you were a little more miserable than that," Germaine said knowingly, tilting his head toward hers.

"Okay, maybe, just a little more," Jules murmured just before his lips found hers again.

And just like always, it wasn't long before she forgot what they were arguing about in the first place.

Chapter 34

"**D**early beloved, we are gathered here today, to join in holy matrimony, two souls which the Lord has sought to bring together."

As she stood at the front of Scarborough Memorial Church gripping her bouquet of yellow and white tulips, Jules's eyes began to tear up at the familiar words. There was something about weddings that made her weepy. Today was no different.

Even though she was supposed to be looking at the minister, Jules couldn't help but steal a glance at Germaine. His eyes met hers, and he gave her a slow smile, and a quick wink from down in the pews. She couldn't stop the smile that curved her own lips, anymore than she could stop the warm glow that flowed through her insides. She had to make a concerted effort to tear her eyes away.

She glanced over at Maxine, who was sniffling beside her. It seemed like everyone was a bit teary-eyed today—everyone except Tanya that is, who only had eyes for her groom. The both of them, it seemed, were in their own little world that consisted only of each other. In fact, since the moment Tanya had stepped through the rear doors of the church and made her way to the front in her beautiful Dior wedding gown, 'Dre hadn't been able to take his eyes off of her. It was no wonder—she looked absolutely stunning.

The whole wedding had come as a surprise to everyone. It seemed like 'Dre and Tanya had only been engaged a week before they announced their wedding day to be a month and a half later.

Jules had thought they were crazy to think they could pull off planning a whole wedding in so short a time, but somehow they had managed to do it. It wasn't as hard as she thought it would be since, both Tanya and 'Dre had only wanted a small ceremony with a few close friends and family.

So here she was, maid of honor to her best friend, who finally got to marry the love of her life. Jules smiled. She couldn't think of anyone who deserved it more.

" 'Charity suffereth long, and is kind; charity envieth not; charity vaunteth not itself, is not puffed up; doth not behave itself unseemly, seeketh not her own, is not easily provoked, thinketh no evil; rejoiceth not in iniquity, but rejoiceth in the truth; beareth all things, believeth all things, hopeth all things, endureth all things.' "

Endurance.

That was definitely something she had learned a lot about these past couple months. Endurance and patience and trust.

Looking back, she knew now that these were lessons that she had to learn, and learn the hard way. It was what God had let her go through to teach her to depend on Him more, both for the big and the little things. As she thought about her resignation letter, which she had handed to her boss at Toronto Grace just earlier that week, she knew that there was a lot more *depending* to do, and a lot more lessons to be learned. But she was ready for them, whatever they might be. As long as God was there with her, she'd be fine.

"By the power invested in me, I now pronounce you man and wife. You may kiss the bride."

Jules cheered with the rest of the bridal party and guests, as 'Dre pulled Tanya into his arms and kissed her soundly. It was a good thing Momma Clayton wasn't there to see her son kiss his bride. She would have probably had a heart attack.

Jules sighed and wrapped her arms around herself. This was a day to remember.

As the crowd spilled out of the church, into the parking lot, Jules stood on the front steps and looked around for Germaine. She stood on her tiptoes and tried to scan above the heads of the guests for that special head of low cropped hair, but it was nowhere to be seen. Just as she was about to get out her cell phone, she heard a voice behind her.

"Looking for someone?"

Jules spun around and found herself face to face with the man who she had been looking for all her life.

"Yeah, I am actually," she said coyly. "He's about your height, and complexion, but much cuter," she teased.

"Is that so," Germaine said slyly, stepping closer to her.

"Uh-huh," Jules said, trying to keep a straight face.

"Well, I don't see him anywhere," he said, slipping an arm around her waist. "So I guess you're stuck with me."

"Yeah, I guess I am," Jules said in mock disappointment.

Germaine chuckled, as he pulled her closer and kissed her slowly. Jules closed her eyes and relished the feeling of being loved. It was amazing how that never got old.

"Did I mention that you look gorgeous?" Germaine murmured against her ear. "I think I need to send someone a thank you card about that dress."

Jules laughed, glad that Tanya had made them pick their own dresses instead of forcing them to wear some hideous bridesmaid creations.

"You're not looking too bad yourself, Mr. Williams," Jules said, as she reached up to straighten his tie. In his slate gray suit, pink shirt, and matching tie, he was looking ridiculously fine. In fact, as far as Jules was concerned, he was the best looking man in the room— no exceptions.

"I can't believe you and Tanya pulled off this whole thing in about a month," Germaine said. "You guys are something else."

Jules shrugged. "Tanya's my girl. She would have done the same for me," she said, straightening his tie.

"I hope you're right," Germaine said. " 'Cause you might need to collect on that favor soon."

"Careful," Jules said, smirking. "You might start putting ideas in my head."

"That's the intention."

Jules's hands froze, and her eyes snapped up to meet Germaine's.

"What are you saying?"

"I'm not playing, Jules," Germaine said, his eyes dancing as they locked with hers. "I already told you I love you, and I want to be with you," he said, rubbing her arms gently. "This is it for me."

Jules could barely breathe. All of a sudden, she

couldn't hear the chatter around her, or see the wedding guests moving past them toward the parking lot. Most of the people were heading out to the reception, but Jules couldn't tell. For, at that moment, there was no one else in the world but her and Germaine.

"Are you asking me to . . . ?"

"No, not yet," Germaine said, smiling. "But that's where we're going with this. I just wanted to make sure you knew."

He watched her carefully, as she took a deep breath and tried to calm the butterflies that were doing the tango in her stomach.

"Okay," she said simply after a long moment.

"Okay?"

"Okay."

"That's it? You're not gonna hit me with a flood of questions? Ask me when, where, and how?" Germaine asked, with one eyebrow raised suspiciously.

Jules laughed and locked her arms around his neck. "No, baby. I'm just gonna wait, and trust you to keep that promise," she said, smiling.

Germaine kissed her forehead and hugged her tightly.

"Hey, lovebirds, think you can tear yourselves apart for the people who actually got married today?"

Germaine and Jules laughed, and walked hand in hand over to the limo where Tanya, 'Dre, Truuth, and Maxine were waiting for them.

Most of the guests had already made their way to the reception, and only the six of them were left standing in front of the church.

"So I think this calls for a toast," Truuth said, pulling a bottle of cider out of nowhere.

As soon as he did, 'Dre ducked into the back of the limo and emerged with six wine glasses. Jules laughed.

"I see you guys were well prepared."

"Always," 'Dre said, winking.

"Okay, so what are we toasting to?" Tanya asked, taking a glass from 'Dre and tossing her headpiece into the back of the limo.

"To you guys, of course," Jules said.

"All right then," said Truuth, raising his glass. "To the Claytons, may they have a marriage as happy as heaven, and a honeymoon as hot as hell!"

They all laughed.

"To the Claytons," they all echoed as they clinked glasses.

Jules smiled as she watched her closest friends joke and laugh with each other. She couldn't help the feeling of love that swelled her heart as she thought of how much they meant to her.

Nonetheless, she couldn't help but notice how Truuth and Maxine casually managed to keep the rest of the group between them.

Just then, she felt Germaine slip his arms around her from behind and rest his lips against her ear.

"They'll be okay," he whispered. "God will work it out."

Jules began to relax. He was right. Maxine, Truuth, and Apryll would be all right as long as they put themselves in God's hands. Hadn't she seen that for herself? Hadn't she learned that by now? All she had to do was trust Him, and He would take care of the rest.

She leaned back, into Germaine's strong frame, and felt his arms tighten around her in response. She smiled. Yes, trusting was good.

Trusting was definitely good.

Don't miss Rhonda Bowen's

Get You Good

On sale in March 2013!

Turn the page for an excerpt from *Get You Good* . . .

Chapter 1

Sydney was never big on sports.

It wasn't that she was athletically challenged. It was just that chasing a ball around a court, or watching other people do it, had never really been high on her list of favorite things.

However, as she stood at the center of the Carlu Round Room, surveying the best of the NBA that Toronto had to offer, she had to admit that professional sports definitely had a few attractive features.

"Thank you, Sydney."

Sydney grinned and folded her arms as she considered her younger sister.

"For what?"

"For Christmas in October." Lissandra bit her lip. "Look at all those presents."

Sydney turned in the direction where Lissandra was staring, just in time to catch the burst of testosterone-laced eye candy that walked through the main doors. Tall, muscular, and irresistible, in every shade of chocolate a girl could dream of sampling. She was starting to have a new appreciation for basketball.

Sydney's eyebrows shot up. "Is that . . .?"

"Yes, girl. And I would give anything to find him under our Christmas tree," Lissandra said, as her eyes devoured the newest group of NBA stars to steal the spotlight. "I love this game."

Sydney laughed. "I don't think it's the game you love."

"You laugh now," Lissandra said, pulling her compact out of her purse. "But when that hot little dress I had to force you to wear gets you a date for next weekend, you'll thank me."

Sydney folded her arms across the bodice of the dangerously short boat-necked silver dress that fit her five-foot-nine frame almost perfectly. It was a bit more risqué than what Sydney would normally wear but seemed almost prudish compared to what the other women in the room were sporting. At least it wasn't too tight. And the cut of the dress exposed her long, elegant neck, which she had been told was one of her best features.

"I'm here to work, not to pick up men," Sydney reminded her sister.

"No, we're here to deliver a spectacular cake." Lissandra checked her lipstick in the tiny mirror discreetly. "And since that cake is sitting over there, our work is done. It's playtime."

"Focus, Lissa." Sydney tried to get her sister back on task with a hand on her upper arm. "Don't forget this is an amazing opportunity to make the kind of contacts that will put us on the A-list. Once we do that, more events like this might be in our future."

"OK, fine," Lissandra huffed, dropping her compact

back into her purse. "I'll talk to some people and give out a few business cards. But if a player tries to buy me a drink, you best believe I'm gonna take it."

Sydney smirked. "I wouldn't expect otherwise."

"Good." Lissandra's mouth turned up into a naughty grin. "'Cause I see some potential business over there that has my name etched across his broad chest."

Sydney sighed. Why did she even bother? "Be good," she said, adding a serious big-sister tone to her voice.

"I will," Lissandra threw behind her. But since she didn't even bother to look back, Sydney didn't hope for much. She knew her sister, and she'd just lost her to a six-foot-six brother with dimples across the room.

Sydney eventually lost sight of her sister as the crowd thickened. She turned her attention back to their ticket into the exclusive Toronto Raptors NBA Season Opener event.

The cake.

Sydney stood back and admired her work again, loving the way the chandelier from above and the tiny lights around the edges of the table and underneath it lit up her creation. The marzipan gave the cream-colored square base of the cake a smooth, flawless finish, and the gold trim caught the light beautifully. The golden replica of an NBA championship trophy, which sat atop the base, was, however, the highlight.

She had to admit it was a sculpted work of art, and one of the best jobs she had done in years. It was also one of the most difficult. It had taken two days just to bake and decorate the thing. That didn't include the several concept meetings, the special-ordered baking molds, and multiple samples made to ensure that the cake tasted just as good as it looked. For the past month and a half, this cake job had consumed her life.

But it was well worth it. Not only for the weight it put in her pocket, but also the weight it was likely to add to her client list. Once everyone at the event saw her creation, she was sure she would finally make it onto the city's pastry-chef A-list, and Decadent would be the go-to spot for wedding and special-event cakes.

She stood near the cake for a while, sucking up the oohs and aahs of passersby, before heading to the bathroom to check that she hadn't sweated out her curls carrying up the cake from downstairs. She took in her long, dark hair, which had been curled and pinned up for the night; her slightly rounded face; and plump, pinked lips; and was satisfied. She turned to the side to get a better view of her size six frame and smiled. Even though she had protested when Lissandra presented the dress, she knew she looked good. Normally she hated any kind of shimmer, but the slight sparkle from the dress was just enough to put Sydney in the party mood it inspired. OK, so Lissandra may have been right—she was there for business—but that didn't mean she couldn't have some fun, too.

By the time she reapplied her lipstick and headed back, the room was full.

She tried to mingle and did end up chatting with a few guests, but her maternal instincts were in full gear and it wasn't long before she found her way back to the cake. She was about to check for anything amiss when she felt gentle fingers on the back of her bare neck. She swung around on reflex.

"What do you think you're doing?" she said, slapping away the hand that had violated her personal space.

"Figuring out if I'm awake or dreaming."

Sydney's eyes slid all the way up the immaculately toned body of the six-foot-three man standing in front of her, to his strong jaw, full smirking lips, and coffee brown eyes. Her jaw dropped. And not just because of how ridiculously handsome he was.

"Dub?"

"Nini."

She cringed. "Wow. That's a name I never thought I would hear again."

"And that's a half tattoo I never thought I'd see again."

Sydney slapped her hand to the back of her neck self consciously. She had almost forgotten the thing was there. It would take the one person who had witnessed her chicken out on getting it finished to remind her about it.

Hayden Windsor. Now wasn't this a blast from the past, sure to get her into some present trouble.

She tossed a hand onto her hip and pursed her lips. "I thought Toronto was too small for you."

"It is."

"Then what are you doing here?"

"Right now?" His eyes flitted across her frame in answer.

"Stop that," Sydney said, her cheeks heating up as she caught his perusal.

"Stop what?" he asked with a laugh.

"You know what," she said. She shook her head. "You are still the same."

He shrugged in an attempt at innocence that only served to draw Sydney's eyes to the muscles shifting under his slim-fitting jacket.

"I can't help it. I haven't seen you in almost ten

years. What, you gonna beat me up like you did when you were seven?"

"Maybe."

"Bully."

"Jerk."

"How about we continue this argument over dinner?" he asked.

"They just served appetizers."

The corner of his lips drew up in a scandalous grin. "Come on, you know you're still hungry."

He was right. That finger food hadn't done anything for her—especially since working on the cake had kept her from eating all day. But she wasn't about to tell him that.

Sydney smirked. "Even if I was, I don't date guys who make over one hundred thousand dollars a year."

He raised a thick eyebrow. "That's a new one."

"Yes, well," she said, "it really is for your own good. This way you won't have to wonder if I was with you for your money."

"So how about we pretend like I don't have all that money," he said, a dangerous glint in his eyes. "We could pretend some other things, too—like we weren't just friends all those years ago."

"I'm not dating you, Hayden," Sydney said, despite the shiver that ran up her spine at his words.

"So you can ask me to marry you, but you won't date me?"

"I was seven years old!"

"And at nine years old, I took that very seriously," Hayden said, his brow furrowing.

Sydney laughed. "That would explain why you went wailing to your daddy right after."

He rested a hand on his rock-solid chest. "I'm an emotional kind of guy."

"Hayden! There you are. I've been looking all over for you!"

Sydney turned to where the voice was coming from and fought her gag reflex. A busty woman with too much blond hair sidled up to Hayden, slipping her arm around his.

"This place is so packed that I can barely find anyone." The woman suddenly seemed to notice Sydney.

"Sydney!"

"Samantha."

Samantha gave Sydney a constipated smile. "So good to see you."

Sydney didn't smile back. "Wish I could say the same."

Hayden snorted. Samantha dropped the smile, but not his arm.

Sydney glared at the woman in the red-feathered dress and wondered how many peacocks had to die to cover her Dolly Parton goods.

"So I guess you two know each other?" Hayden asked, breaking the silence that he seemed to find more amusing than awkward.

"Yes," Samantha volunteered. "Sydney's little bakery, Decadent, beat out Something Sweet for the cake job for this event. She was my main competition."

"I wouldn't call it a competition," Sydney said, thinking it was more like a slaughtering.

"How do *you* know each other?" Samantha probed.

Hayden grinned. "Sydney and I go way back. Right, Syd?"

Samantha raised an eyebrow questioningly and Sydney glared at her, daring her to ask another question. Samantha opted to keep her mouth shut.

"So this is where the party is," Lissandra said, joining the small circle. Sydney caught the flash of recognition in Lissandra's eyes when she saw who exactly made up their impromptu gathering.

"Hayden? Is that you?"

"The very same," Hayden said, pulling Lissandra into a half hug. "Good to see you, Lissandra."

"Back at you," Lissandra said. "Wow, it's been ages. I probably wouldn't recognize you except Sydney used to watch your games all the—oww!"

Lissandra groaned as Sydney's elbow connected with her side.

"Did she?" Hayden turned to Sydney again, a smug look in his eyes.

"Well, it was nice to see you all again," Samantha said, trying to navigate Hayden away from the group.

"Samantha, I can't believe you're here." Lissandra's barely concealed laughter was not lost on Sydney or Samantha. "I thought you would be busy cleaning up that business at Something Sweet."

Sydney bit back a smirk as a blush crept up Samantha's neck to her cheeks. Samantha went silent again.

"What business?" Hayden looked around at the three women, who obviously knew something he didn't.

"Nothing," Samantha said quickly.

"Just that business with the health inspector," Lissandra said, enjoying Samantha's discomfort. "Nothing major. I'm sure the week that you were closed was enough to get that sorted out."

Hayden raised an eyebrow. "The health inspector shut you down?"

"We were closed temporarily," Samantha corrected.

"Just so that we could take care of a little issue. It wasn't that serious."

"Is that what the exterminator said?" Lissandra asked.

Sydney coughed loudly and Samantha's face went from red to purple.

"You know," Samantha said, anger in her eyes. "It's interesting. We have never had a problem at that location before now. It's funny how all of a sudden we needed to call an exterminator around the same time they were deciding who would get the job for tonight's event."

"Yes, life is full of coincidences," Sydney said dryly. "Like that little mix-up we had with the Art Gallery of Ontario event last month. But what can you do? The clients go where they feel confident."

"Guess that worked out for you this time around," Samantha said, glaring at Sydney and Lissandra.

"Guess so," Lissandra said smugly.

Sydney could feel Hayden eyeing her suspiciously, but she didn't dare look at him.

"Well, this was fun," Sydney said in a tone that said the exact opposite. "But I see some people I need to speak with."

Sydney excused herself from the group and made her way to the opposite side of the room toward the mayor's wife. She had only met the woman once, but Sydney had heard they had an anniversary coming up soon. It was time to get reacquainted, and get away from the one man who could make her forget what she really came here for.

* * *

By the time the hands on her watch were both sitting at eleven, Sydney was exhausted and completely out of business cards.

"Leaving already?" She was only steps from the door, and he was only steps in front of her.

"This was business, not pleasure."

Hayden's eyes sparkled with mischief. "All work and no play makes Sydney a dull girl."

This time her mouth turned up in a smile. "I think you know me better than that."

His grin widened in a way that assured her that he did. "Remind me."

She shook her head and pointed her tiny purse at him.

"I'm not doing this here with you, Dub."

He stepped closer and she felt the heat from his body surround her. "We can always go somewhere else. Like the Banjara a couple blocks away."

Sydney scowled. Him and his inside knowledge.

"If we leave now we can get there before it closes."

She folded her arms over her midsection. "I haven't changed my mind, Dub."

He grinned. "That's not what your stomach says."

Sydney glanced behind him, and he turned around to see that Samantha was only a few feet away and headed in his direction. Sydney wasn't sure what string of events had put Samantha and Hayden together that night. The woman was definitely not his type. Or at least she didn't think Samantha was.

"I think your date is coming to get you," Sydney said, her voice dripping with amusement. "Maybe *she* wants to go for Indian food."

"How about I walk you to your car?"

Without waiting for a response, he put a hand on the

small of her back and eased her out the large doors into the lobby and toward the elevator.

"What's the rush?" she teased.

"Still got that smart mouth, don't you."

"I thought that was what you liked about me," she said innocently, as he led her into the waiting elevator.

"See, that's what you always got wrong, Nini." He leaned toward her ear to whisper and she caught a whiff of his cologne. "It was never just one thing."

Sydney tried to play it off, but she couldn't help the way her breathing went shallow as her heart sped up. And she couldn't keep him from noticing it, either.

His eyes fell to her lips. "So what's it going to be, Syd? You, me, and something spicy?"

He was only inches away from her. So close that if she leaned in, she could . . .

"Hayden!"

A familiar voice in the distance triggered her good sense. Sydney stepped forward and placed her hands on his chest.

"I think you're a bit busy tonight."

She pushed him out of the elevator and hit the DOOR CLOSE button.

He grinned and shook his head as she waved at him through the gap between the closing doors.

"I'll see you soon, Nini."

For reasons she refused to think about, she hoped he kept that promise.

GREAT BOOKS, GREAT SAVINGS!

When You Visit Our Website:

www.kensingtonbooks.com

You Can Save Money Off The Retail Price
Of Any Book You Purchase!

- **All Your Favorite Kensington Authors**

- **New Releases & Timeless Classics**

- **Overnight Shipping Available**

- **eBooks Available For Many Titles**

- **All Major Credit Cards Accepted**

Visit Us Today To Start Saving!
www.kensingtonbooks.com

All Orders Are Subject To Availability.
Shipping and Handling Charges Apply.
Offers and Prices Subject To Change Without Notice.